# Breaking
## the
# Rules

❁

ALSO BY BARBARA TAYLOR BRADFORD

## Series

THE RAVENSCAR TRILOGY
**The Ravenscar Dynasty**
**The Heir**
**Being Elizabeth**

THE EMMA HARTE SAGA
**A Woman of Substance**
**Hold the Dream**
**To Be the Best**
**Emma's Secret**
**Unexpected Blessings**
**Just Rewards**

OTHERS
**Voice of the Heart**
**Act of Will**
**The Women in His Life**
**Remember**
**Angel**
**Everything to Gain**
**Dangerous to Know**
**Love in Another Town**
**Her Own Rules**
**A Secret Affair**
**Power of a Woman**
**A Sudden Change of Heart**
**Where You Belong**
**The Triumph of Katie Byrne**
**Three Weeks in Paris**

# BARBARA TAYLOR BRADFORD

# Breaking
# the
# Rules

**Doubleday Large Print
Home Library Edition**

ST. MARTIN'S PRESS
New York

This Large Print Edition, prepared especially for Doubleday Large Print Home Library, contains the complete,
unabridged text of the original Publisher's Edition.

This is a work of fiction.
All of the characters, organizations, and events
portrayed in this novel are either products of the
author's imagination or
are used fictitiously.

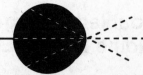

**This Large Print Book carries the
Seal of Approval of N.A.V.H.**

This book is for my husband, Bob,
who knows the many reasons why,
with my dearest and abiding love.

# Contents

# Prologue

March
2006

He was a stocky, slightly rotund man, in his thirties or thereabouts, and he leaned against the van, looking perturbed. He took a long drag on his cigarette, wondering why Bart was taking so long. To his way of thinking, Bart should have done the job and been back before now. And they should have been speeding away from the scene of the crime. He glanced at his watch; it was just a few minutes past four. They needed to be on their way. Heading back to London.

Wondering whether to go looking for Bart, he suddenly tensed, leaned forward, squinting in the sunlight coming through the trees. He listened acutely, frowning, wondering exactly *what* it was he had just heard. Scuffling? Branches breaking? Yes, that was it. And also a muffled scream? He wasn't sure there had been a scream . . . *but maybe there had.*

He hoped to God that Bart wasn't up to his old tricks. They'd be in the shit if he was. Really and truly in it. *Like dead.*

His impatience spiraled up, dragging with it sudden apprehension. Sam, for that was his name, made an instant decision. He dropped his cigarette on the dirt path, grinding it under his foot. Pulling the key out of the ignition, he shut the door of the van and hurried down the path into the woods. It grew dimmer, sky and sunlight obscured by the density of the trees which formed a dark canopy above him.

Within a couple of minutes Sam was close to the clearing; sounds became more distinct. Bart cursing and hissing and breathing heavily . . . and then a female scream cut short by Bart. And more scuffling.

Sam cursed under his breath, began to run, shouting, "Bart! Bart! For Christ's sake, stop it!"

Startled, Bart swung his head sharply, turned his body toward Sam, and in so doing left himself vulnerable.

The young woman pinned under him seized her opportunity. Bringing her right hand up, she bashed Bart hard on the side of his head with a rock with unusual force. Dropping the rock, she pushed him hard with both hands. Blood spurting, Bart fell backward.

Scrambling to her feet, pulling up her jeans, the girl ran away, sped deeper into the woods, shouting, "Gypo! Gypo! Come on, boy!"

Sam was still frozen to the spot, filled with shock at their failure. A horse whinnying, hooves thudding along the path told him the girl had escaped. They'd never catch her now.

Rousing himself, Sam ran over to Bart, who lay on his back, his eyes closed, his head and face covered in blood. Sam bent over him, found a faint pulse, heard even fainter breathing. Bart was alive. Well, for the moment. Stupid bastard he was, trying to screw her. Served him right, it did.

Getting hold of Bart under the arms, Sam dragged him along the dirt path, pausing from time to time to catch his breath. He was sweating profusely. It was unusually warm for March. When he finally got him to the van, he opened the back doors, managed to drag Bart inside. He hid him under a blanket, closed the doors, raced around to the driver's seat, then backed the van along the dirt path until he came to the incline. Making a U-turn, he headed onto the main road, began driving south. He didn't know whether Bart was now dead or not. All he knew was that he had to get away from this area as fast as possible, before the girl raised the alarm.

His body was taut, his expression grim as he pushed ahead; after a while he began to slow his speed. All he needed was a local traffic cop on his arse.

Bloody hell, this was a disaster. Sam grimaced. The boss would have their guts for garters for messing up the way they had, for failing to eliminate the girl. No, hang on, it was Bart who'd failed. Not him. But understanding the way the boss operated, he was certain they'd both end up dead as doornails.

Not if I can help it, not me, Sam muttered. But what to do with an injured Bart or Bart's body? Dump it outside a hospital in another town? Leave it by the side of the road? He didn't know. All he knew was that he had to save himself from the boss's wrath. . . .

# Part One

# FALLING IN LOVE
## August–December
## 2006

Come live with me, and be my love,
And we will some new pleasures prove
Of golden sands, and crystal brooks,
With silken lines, and silver hooks.

John Donne (1572–1631)

# One

The young woman who hurried down Fifth Avenue was unaware of the stares as she plunged determinedly through the downpour as though oblivious to it. She was, in fact, too consumed by her thoughts to notice passersby.

They noticed her. They stared, nodded approvingly, or smiled with admiration. She drew attention for a number of reasons. She was rather exotic-looking, with high cheekbones, black eyebrows beautifully arched on her broad brow above large dark eyes. Her jet-black hair was pulled back into a sleek ponytail, which fell almost to her waist. Though not beautiful in the classical sense, she was arresting and had a unique look about her.

Tall, slender, lithe, she moved with grace and had an inbred elegance. Her clothes were simple; she was wearing a sleeveless black cotton shift and ballet slippers, her only jewelry large pearl earrings and a watch. She carried a battered old black Hermès Kelly bag, well polished, which had obviously seen better days but looked just right on her arm.

The rain was coming down in torrents and she was already drenched, but she no longer bothered to look for a cab. There was no point; they were all taken. She was heading home, and much to her relief she wasn't very far now. Two blocks down, three avenues to cross and she would be at West Twenty-second Street and Ninth Avenue.

A month ago, through her only friend in New York, a young man called Dax, she had found the perfect place: a comfortable room with two good-size closets and its own bath in a brownstone on this rather lovely old street. Chelsea reminded her of

London, gave her a sense of well-being, and she felt at home here.

When she had left London, she had left behind her name; now she was known as M, and M did not mind the rain today. It was cooling on this blistering August afternoon. Earlier, around lunchtime, it had been at least a hundred and one in the shade. Leni, the young receptionist at the Blane Model Agency, had announced with a big grin, "Betcha we could fry eggs on the sidewalk today, M. How about giving it a try?"

M had laughed with her, wanting to be nice. Leni had endeavored to be helpful since the day they had met. M had gone to Blane's within days of arriving in Manhattan, two months ago now. Although the agency had not found work for her so far, they had been encouraging, and Leni's friendliness had helped. M knew she was going to make it as a model. She had to, she had no choice. Not only had she something to prove to her family but she had something to prove to herself as well, and nothing was going to stop her.

Glancing at her watch, M winced. It was

already four o'clock, nine at night in London, and she usually called her sister on Fridays around this time. Although M was in her early twenties and considered herself very capable, her elder sister worried about her being alone in New York. But then she worried about everything; that was her nature. M loved her, missed her, but making it on her own had been too compelling to ignore. So here she was trying to become another Kate Moss. She smiled inwardly at that idea. If only, she thought. Increasing her pace, she crossed Seventh Avenue, striding out toward Eighth, in a bigger hurry now.

The brownstone was on Twenty-second halfway between Ninth and Tenth, and as she drew closer, she saw somebody huddled on the top step, leaning against the front door. At once she realized it was her friend Dax. Dressed in jeans and a T-shirt, he was protecting himself with a newspaper, which he held over his head. He was as drenched as she was, and the minute she ran up the steps, she saw he was shivering, looked pale and pinched.

"Dax, what are you doing here?" she exclaimed, pulling the door key out of her bag.

"Getting decidedly wet," he shot back, grinning at her.

"So I see. Let's get you inside. You're shivering. . . . Are you sick?"

"I've got a bit of a cold," he answered, "that's all," and standing up, he followed her inside.

The two of them stood dripping water in the tiled entrance for a moment, until M took hold of his arm and led him into the small cloakroom, reminding him that Geo, from whom she rented her room, insisted her house be kept pristine. "Get undressed in here and dry yourself, Dax. There're towels in the cupboard next to the coatrack. I'll be back with something dry for you in a minute."

"Thanks," he answered, still shivering, offering her a wan smile.

M went out, took off her wet ballet shoes, and ran upstairs to her room. Within seconds she had shed her soaking dress and underwear, thrown them in the tub, rubbed herself dry, and put on cotton pants, a cotton T-shirt, and dry shoes. Taking a large terry-cloth robe out of the closet, she went downstairs, knocked on the door of the cloakroom, and when it opened put the robe over Dax's outstretched arm. "That should fit you, Dax. You'll find me in the kitchen. . . . I'm going to make us a pot of really hot tea."

"The English cure-all for everything," he muttered.

"Don't knock it," M said, hurrying into the kitchen. Once the kettle was on the stove, she pulled her cell phone out of her pants pocket and dialed her sister in London. "Hi, it's me!" she exclaimed when the phone was answered. "I'm alive and well and kicking! How are you, Birdie?"

"I'm fine, darling, very okay this week, and listen to me. You know I hate that nickname you gave me when you were little. Let's forget it, shall we?"

Hearing the laughter in her voice, M chuckled, then went on, "How's business? Has everything been going well?"

"Yes, it has, and I heard from Mummy and Dad. They send their love. So does Gran."

"How is Gran? Is she feeling better?"

"Loads, yes, and I'm sure it's because Mummy and Dad are in Australia. You know how our mother cheers everyone up, makes them instantly feel better. And

Gran's no exception, she responds immediately to her much-loved daughter."

"I'm glad to hear Gran's better. I'll give
her a call over the weekend. Any other
news?"

"Not really . . ."

The sisters talked for a few minutes longer, then said their good-byes. Putting her
cell phone on the countertop, M opened
the cupboard and took out her large brown
teapot, which she had bought when she
moved into the brownstone.

After putting six English Breakfast tea
bags into the pot, she poured the boiling
water over them. Her thoughts remained
with her sister; she was concerned about
her constantly now that she was on her
own, a widow. Tragically, her husband had
died of a heart attack two years ago, and
M was well aware she was still grieving.
But that was natural. They had been so
very much in love, joined at the hip to M's
way of thinking. Then suddenly, he was
gone . . . just like that, in the flicker of an
eyelash. He had been only thirty-three, far
too young.

At the time, her elder brother had said life
was full of surprises, seventy-five percent of

them bad. She had disagreed with him, calling him a cynic, but now she wasn't so sure that he was wrong. Life did have a way of coming up to hit you in the face. Her father's comment during this conversation had been typical. He had reminded her, and her brother, that what was meant to be would be, and that life had its own rules, rules no one could change. M sighed, stood with her hand on the teapot, thinking about her sister, missing her more than ever. They had always been close, best friends.

"Did I offend you? About the tea, I mean."

M jumped and swung around to face Dax. She exclaimed, "I didn't hear you come into the kitchen. You startled me."

**"Sorry."**

M grinned at him. "Of course you didn't upset me, Dax. I'm not so easily offended, you know." She frowned at him, added, "You still look chilled to the bone. This hot tea will help." She reached into the cupboard as she spoke, took out two mugs, poured the tea, and added milk. Carrying the mugs to the table under the window, she went on, "Come along, Dax, come and sit with me here."

Tightening the belt of the robe, shrugging into it for warmth, he sat down opposite her and put his hands around the mug. "I came looking for Geo," he volunteered after a few seconds. "But I'm glad she's not here. I realize it's you I want to talk to. . . . I feel more comfortable with you when I need to discuss my problems."

"You know I'll help if I can," M murmured, eyeing him carefully, thinking that perhaps it was Geo he wanted to talk *about.* She couldn't imagine why he said he felt more comfortable discussing his problems with her, when he had never done such a thing in the past. It's just his way of getting around his awkwardness, she decided and said, "Go on, then, Dax, tell me what's wrong."

"Everything," he answered after a moment of thought. "And because nothing is going right for me here, I'm seriously considering going to L.A."

"Do you mean permanently, or simply for a visit?" she asked.

"*Permanently.* You know I want to be an actor, not a male model, and I think the only way I'm going to make it is by moving to L.A., taking a chance out there."

M's dark eyes narrowed, and she said, very slowly, "But, Dax, you'd just be changing one city for another. You'll take your problems along with you."

"Not all of them. If I do move, I will be leaving Geo behind, and that will certainly solve one problem."

"It will? Which one?"

"My muddled love life."

"Is it muddled? Really and truly?" She sat back, took a sip of tea, and looked at Dax over the rim of her mug, waiting for a response.

"I think it is. Look, my relationship with Geo has stalled. Actually, if you want the truth, it's stagnant. I do care about her, and I thought I'd connected with the love of my life when we first got involved. But it's just not going smoothly, and I think she's lost interest in me . . . and I've got to confess my passion for her has been diluted." He sat back in the chair and took a long swallow of the tea, relieved to unburden himself.

"Perhaps that's because *you* think *she's* lost interest in *you,* and I'm certain she hasn't. . . . She's always happy when you call her, I can attest to that. I live here, remember."

"There's another problem, actually," Dax volunteered, and leaning closer across the table, he whispered, "I've fallen for some-one else. . . . Geo's been away a lot lately, and I've been on my own, and well, look, I met someone who really turns me on, and who's crazy about me."

*"Oh."* M stared at him, at a loss for words.

Dax said, "He's just great, really spe-cial."

"Oh, I see," M muttered and put down her mug.

"Don't look so upset." Dax drew closer once more as he added, "I'm a member of both churches, if you know what I mean. And I'm quite happy in her church. And also in his." He smiled suddenly, his face lighting up. "But I don't want to get too deeply involved with him, and so I think I should go to L.A. Follow my lifelong dream, so to speak, try to make it as an actor, and put my love life/sex life on hold, if you get my drift."

"Yes, I do, and I'll say it again. You will still take your problems with you wherever you live."

"No, I won't. I'll be leaving Geo and Ja-son behind. Two problems dealt with! I'll only have my career to worry about." He suddenly started to cough, jumped up, excused himself, and hurried out of the kitchen.

M stared after him, frowning. Although she had been surprised when he confided he was bisexual, she was neither troubled by the revelation nor judgmental. But she *was* worried about Dax's health. He looked genuinely ill to her. A moment later he was back, blowing his nose on a tissue.

"Sorry about that," he said, sitting down again.

"You've got a really nasty cold, you know." She stood up, went to one of the cabinets, took out a bottle of Tylenol, and gave it to him. "Take some of these, and drink your tea."

"Yes, Mom," he said, grinning at her, and took three of the pills. "Well, thank God it's stopped raining at last," he murmured, staring out the window. "So, tell me, M, should I go to L.A. or not?"

"I don't know how to answer that, not really," she responded quietly. "I suppose it might be easier out there, to get an acting job, I mean. On the other hand, I keep hearing that actors are two a penny in Hollywood, and that all of them are gorgeous and talented, male and female alike." She gave him a probing stare and finished. "Maybe you're just running away from Geo and Jason. Do you think that might be it?"

"Not at all. I'm only thinking about my future . . . in films. And you know I've been to so many auditions, looking for parts, trying to get an acting job, long before we met at the Blane Agency when you first came to New York."

"Then think about this move just a little longer. Give it a few weeks, try to find something here in New York, an acting job in television or maybe in the theater. And as for Geo, tell her it's over if it really is. She's a big girl, she'll understand, and anyway, you said she'd sort of lost interest in you. As for Jason, you have only two choices. You can stay with him. Or tell *him* good-bye as well. So that you can concentrate on your career."

Dax gaped at her for a long moment, then began to laugh hilariously, ending up coughing into his tissue. When he had settled down, he said, with a knowing grin, "If nothing else, you're certainly outspoken, tell a guy what you really think."

"Do I? And what do I think?"

"That I'm full of b.s."

"No, you're wrong. I don't think badly of you, Dax, honestly. But my sister always says I have a way of getting to the heart of the matter. And that's what I've done with you—" She broke off as the phone rang, and leaning over, she picked it up. "Hello?" After a moment listening, she went on, "That's fine, and you'll be staying there all weekend?" There was another pause as M listened again, and she silently mouthed, "It's Geo. Do you want to speak to her?"

Dax shook his head vehemently.

M said, "Okay, Geo, I'll do that, and I'll be here all weekend. I'll see you on Monday. Bye." Placing the receiver in the cradle, she explained, "Geo's at her sister's in New Jersey. For the weekend, as you've no doubt guessed."

"I'm right, you know, she *is* cooling it with me."

"And you've done the same, you've even moved on a step or two, wouldn't you say?"

He nodded, knowing she had called it correctly.

"I'm thinking of making a big soup, a healthy French soup," M announced. "Do you want to stay for supper?"

"What's a big French soup?"

"You know, with vegetables and pieces of chicken . . . one of those soups that's always on the hob in French kitchens." She smiled at him cheekily. "I'm a good cook, you know."

"I'm sure. I'd love to stay for supper. And perhaps we can talk some more."

M groaned. "Just as long as we don't talk about your problems."

"Absolutely not. Anyway, you've solved them for me, M. You got right to the heart of the matter, as apparently you always do."

# Two

He had known her for only a few weeks, but he trusted her, and his trust was implicit. Dax had never experienced this feeling with anyone before, and he had quickly come to understand that M was a very special person, one who had strolled into his life unexpectedly and had a tremendous impact on him.

It was neither romantic nor sexual. Although she *was* beautiful, she was just not his type: too tall and dark, and just a little too exotic to suit him. He had always had a predilection for blue-eyed blondes who were petite, and he did not mind at all if they weren't very bright. He preferred them to be a bit dumb, actually.

M, on the other hand, was extremely intelligent, practical, and straightforward. She fairly took his breath away with her incredible honesty. It seemed to him that M thought more like a man than a woman, got straight to the point in a flash. There were no holds barred, she just spit out what she had to say. Well, she had said that herself, that her elder sister believed she got right to the heart of the matter.

Dax knew where he stood with her, and he liked that. She didn't seem to have any agenda, except for wanting to be a model, and there was no deviousness in her. Too many people he knew played both ends against the middle and some ended up being treacherous.

Now, as he watched her preparing the soup for them, he couldn't help thinking that she moved with the lightness and grace of a dancer. Before he could stop himself, he blurted out, "You must be a dancer, M, the way you move."

M swung to face him, a smile lighting up her dark eyes. "I *am* a dancer, Dax, but not a professional one. I took a few lessons when I was little, then got more interested in sports. But I do think I have the spirit and soul of a dancer. . . . I just love it. I prefer dancing to exercising, and running ruins the hips, so I dance all the time. When I'm alone."

She turned back to the countertop, began pouring cartons of College Inn chicken broth into a large pot, adding chicken, carrots, potatoes, onions, and parsnips she had prepared, reached for the jar of herbes de Provence, threw a handful into the soup along with some bay leaves. "There, that should do it," she murmured, turning on the gas. "All I have to do now is chop a few sticks of celery," and she reached for this, began to cut off the leaves as well as the hard stem at the other end.

"There seems to be no limit to your talents," Dax said, still watching her. "It strikes me that you're a good cook; certainly you look as if you know what you're doing."

Her cheeky grin flashed. "I know how to cook a few dishes, but I don't have a huge repertoire. I can almost prepare this chicken-in-the-pot with my eyes closed, and I'm even better at it since I came to New York.

I always make it on Friday evening, and it lasts me all weekend, Dax."

"You are practical, aren't you?"

"I suppose so," she agreed and threw the celery into the pot. "Do you cook?"

"Not me, no," he said and sat back in the chair, sipping the second mug of scalding hot tea she had pressed on him a short while ago.

His light gray eyes rested on her as she cleaned the countertops, put the lid on the pot, lowered the gas, carried dirty items over to the sink. She intrigued him, and mystified him sometimes.

Leaning against the sink, the wet sponge in her hand, M said, "What does Dax stand for? It's unusual."

"Derek Alan Kenneth Small. That's what it is. *Ugh!*" He made a face and explained, "At school the kids called me Daks, because I told them to, and when I got older and went to college, I changed the spelling. I thought Dax was more . . . sophisticated." He grinned. "Are we all dumb at times?"

"I guess so. But you know, I like it. Dax, I mean. It sort of suits you, and your personality. Not to mention your blond good looks. Matinee-idol looks, I might add."

"My mother always told me I resembled Leslie Howard." Placing the mug on the table, he murmured, "If you know who he was."

"Do you think I'm an ignoramus, for heaven's sake! Of course I know who he was. He played Ashley Wilkes in *Gone With the Wind*. And guess what? Since I'm Marie Marsden, they called me M and M at school. How about that?"

Dax chuckled and then stood up. "I think my clothes must be dry by now. I'd better go and get dressed. See you in a minute."

❖

In Dax's absence, M set the table for supper, tasted the broth, added a few extra shakes of pepper, and lowered the heat under the pot. Then she went into the little entrance foyer and down the corridor which led to Geo's studio at the back of the old brownstone.

On the phone earlier, Geo had asked her to check that all the blinds were pulled down and also to make sure the air conditioner was on low. When M walked into the vaulted studio, she saw that the room was properly shaded and cool: the paintings stacked here and there against the walls were well protected from the daylight. She glanced at the thermostat; Geo had turned it to low earlier, but perhaps she had forgotten.

Moving forward, M stood in the center of the floor for a moment, thinking what a perfect studio this was. There were three windows, all of them large; a skylight had been installed at one end, where a portion of the room jutted out into the backyard. No wonder Geo loved this place so much and painted so well here. M had been captivated by Geo's paintings when she first saw them, and she admired her talent. Geo had an uncanny way of capturing light on canvas, as only a few artists could.

M thought suddenly of an extraordinary painting she knew intimately since it was a family heirloom. It was a breathtaking picture by the great J. M. W. Turner, the late eighteenth-century, early nineteenth-century artist. His forte had been capturing light on canvas, and nobody had ever excelled this master, perhaps no one ever would.

M unlocked the back door and stepped

out into the yard. There was a wrought-
iron seat, two chairs, and a small table on
the tiny flagged patio, and beyond, a mi-
nuscule lawn and some flowering shrubs.
M took a deep breath, sniffed the air. The
rain had stopped, and it had cooled off; the
stifling heat of the afternoon was fortunately
diminished. Returning to the patio, she sat
down on the wrought-iron seat thinking that
this verdant patch in the middle of Manhattan was like a miniature oasis that truly
pleased the senses.

A moment later, a rush of sadness engulfed her as she thought of her mother's
garden in England. Closing her eyes, she
saw it in her mind's eye, saw all of its wondrous glory, walked along its winding paths.
And for a few moments she was transported back to her most favorite place on
this earth, the place that was always in her
heart, would always be embedded there,
the place where she had been her happiest. *Go back home, go back straightaway,*
a small voice whispered in her head. *You've
nothing to fear.*

A second later M heard Dax's feet clattering across the terra-cotta floor of the
studio. She roused herself from her rev-

erie, brushed a hand over her eyes, blinking back tears that had momentarily blinded her.

Dax did not appear to notice anything amiss as he came to a standstill in front of her and said, "My clothes were dry, and I had a quick shower in Geo's bathroom before I got dressed. I feel much better, and my cold seems to have gone."

"I hope so," M answered, wondering whether he ought to be using Geo's shower, then decided she must clean it later. She didn't want to go into a lot of explanations about Dax's presence here this afternoon. Who knew what kind of relationship he and Geo now had?

He went on, "Geo's lucky to have this backyard, even though it's the size of a postage stamp. And the studio is awesome, isn't it?"

"Yes, it is, and *you* would be *really* awesome if you went back to the kitchen and poured us both a glass of wine. I bought a bottle of Sancerre the other day, and it's in the fridge. You can't miss my bottle, it's got a big red *M* on the label."

"At your service," he said, grinning, and went back into the brownstone.

Leaning back against the wrought-iron seat, M closed her eyes once more and pictured her room at home, full of all the things she treasured, and she mentally walked through her parents' house, opening doors, peeking inside other rooms. Inwardly she smiled; how she loved her family home. . . . One day she *would* go there again . . . in a year or two . . . when she was sure it was safe . . . when she knew for a certainty that no one could harm her. . . .

"Here I am!" Dax exclaimed, handing her the wineglass and sitting down next to her.

"Thanks," M said and touched her glass to his. "Down the hatch."

He chuckled, looked at her, and chuckled again.

"Why are you laughing?"

"It's such a masculine toast. My father always says that."

"So?" She gazed at him, her eyes narrowing. "What are you getting at?"

"Nothing really, it just struck me it's a man's toast, that's all."

Finally, M gave him the benefit of a wide smile. "I suppose I picked it up at home. . . . Like your father, mine often uses those words, too."

Dax took a long swallow of the wine and said, "I know you don't want to hear my problems, but there's just one thing I'd like to say . . . okay?"

"Shoot," she responded and sipped her wine.

"I'd like you to explain *why* you're so against my going out to L.A. I mean, what do you have against Hollywood?"

"I don't have anything against it, nor am I against you going, actually. I was just trying to point out that moving to another city doesn't solve problems. Not for anyone. Because the problems are inside the person . . . a new city won't change a thing, Dax. Anyway, I was always led to believe that Hollywood was a bit . . . well, overcrowded, especially with young talent."

"I hear you, and you're right, M. But I haven't been able to get acting work here, and I do want to be an actor. . . . I've been acting since I was a kid, you know. I thought I ought to go out to the Coast and give it a try, take my chances."

"I understand. I suppose if you don't go, you might end up regretting it."

"Does that mean I have your blessing, M?"

"Not really. Because I do think you should try again to get a job here. But I understand why you want to go to the Coast."

"Thanks for saying that. And listen, it will remove me from the scene here. . . . I think I'd like to make myself scarce, if only for a few months."

M nodded, pursed her lips together, and then said softly, "I'll miss you, Dax."

He was an observant young man, and he noticed the sadness flickering in her eyes. Reaching out, he put an arm around her, pulled her closer, and held her tightly against him. "I'll stay in touch. And you know what, I'll miss *you,* too, babe." He turned her face to his and kissed her on the cheek. "We can call each other, text all the time."

"Yes, I know," she murmured, and putting a brave face on it, she went on, "I think we'd better go in. The soup must be ready by now, and I don't want it to burn."

❖

"What do you think is wrong with us, Dax?" M asked a little later, sitting back in the chair, eyeing her friend across the kitchen table.

Frowning, he said, "What exactly do you mean?" As he spoke he put down his soupspoon, and with his head to one side, threw her a quizzical look.

"Not being able to get work. Look, you've been trying hard to find an acting job, and I'm striving to be a model, but no one seems interested in us, do they?"

"True enough, but it has more to do with the time of year than anything else, at least as far as modeling is concerned. And let's face it, you've only been in New York two months. Things are bound to pick up in the fall. As for me, I just explained why I'm seriously considering going to the West Coast. I want a change of scenery, new contacts, and I *do* think there are opportunities there."

M nodded, picked up her spoon, and finished the soup. For a moment her mind focused on her elder brother, who had often taken her under his wing and tried to guide her in many ways. He had once said that looks and talent weren't always enough, that other factors frequently came into play in a successful career. Such vital things as timing, being in the right place at the right time, and most important, having Lady Luck on one's side. Although M disagreed with her brother about certain things, she was well aware he was wise and scrupulously honest. He told it the way it was, and she trusted him.

"Penny for your thoughts," Dax said, peering at her.

After a small silence, M responded. "I haven't seen you act, but I'm assuming you can, and you're certainly good-looking, and you photograph well. But you've got to *really* want it, to be an actor, I mean. It's got to be the most *important* thing in your life, and you must have immense drive, discipline, and determination. And total dedication. There are a lot of good-looking, talented young men out there, and you've just got to want it *more,* be *better* than they are. If you're going to succeed, that is."

He leaned forward. "But that *is* the way I feel, and I *am* very dedicated and determined, M, honestly. I just need one break."

"I know that. Sometimes it's just a question of being in the right place at the right time, and of course, there's another vital element involved—"

"What's that?" he asked, cutting in.

"*Luck.* You've got to have Lady Luck on your side."

He grimaced. "So far *she* hasn't been anywhere in sight."

"Listen, go to Hollywood, Dax! Do it! Don't listen to me and other naysayers. Take a chance, go out there and make it. I'm certainly behind you. Forget what I said about it being crowded with good-looking, young talent. . . . Go and compete, and I wish you lots of luck!" She laughed. "Just don't forget me, will you? You're the only friend I have in the whole of America."

"How could I ever forget *you*? You're an original, M."

# Three

M was dozing, almost asleep, when she heard the noise. It brought her up with a start, and she tensed, straining to hear. There it was again . . . fainter now but nevertheless quite distinct, like metal falling on a hard surface.

*There was somebody in the house.* She remained very still, her mind racing. It couldn't be Geo, she was in New Jersey. And Annette Lazenby, who rented the small attic apartment above M, was in Afghanistan on one of her journalistic assignments.

But there *was* somebody in the entrance hall, somebody who had broken into the brownstone; how they had done this she wasn't sure. M knew she had locked the door of the studio which led to the garden, and later, when Dax had gone home, she had definitely double-locked the front door. But the alarm system was on the blink again, and she hadn't been able to turn it on.

Was there a window open somewhere?

She swallowed, fear rushing through her, and for a split second she was paralyzed, wondering what to do. Then taking a deep breath, endeavoring to steady herself, M threw back the sheet and slid out of bed. Quickly taking off her nightgown, she dressed in the clothes she had shed a short while before, noticing that her hands shook as she zipped up her cotton pants.

After stepping into her loafers, she found her old Louis Vuitton shoulder bag in the cupboard, took it out, dropped in her cell phone, wallet, and door key, then slung it over her head with the strap across her chest. That was the safest way to wear it, especially now. She might get into a tussle with whoever it was downstairs.

After moving closer to the bedroom door, she stood listening for a split second; the silence was deafening. Her umbrella was hanging on the hook behind the door, and she decided to take it with her. It was the only weapon available.

Taking care to be scrupulously quiet, she opened the door an inch or two, peered out. Everything was in darkness and very still. Summoning all of her courage, she went out into the corridor and crept the few short steps to the head of the staircase; slowly, she began to walk down the stairs, holding on to the banister.

M was almost at the bottom of the stairs when a strong hand grabbed hold of her arm and pulled her forward. Startled and frightened, she began to scream and struggle, endeavoring to free herself. At the same time she lifted the umbrella and started hitting the intruder over and over again.

"Stop it! Stop it!" Geo shouted, instantly letting go of her. "It's *me. Geo!* Stop hitting me, M." As she spoke, she ran across the hall and switched on the light.

Still trembling and upset, M sat down heavily on one of the stairs, gaping at the other woman. "My God, what on earth were you thinking about, Geo? Creeping into your own home in the dead of night, frightening me to death. I thought you were an intruder."

"I was a bit distraught earlier, and I rushed back home in quite an emotional state." A deep sigh escaped the other woman, and she shook her head.

M was baffled. "Why were you distraught and emotional? Is something wrong?"

"I don't know. You tell me."

M's dark brows drew together in a frown. "I don't understand . . ." Her voice trailed off, and she gave Geo a curious look.

Without saying another word, Geo stepped past M on the stairs and flew up to the first floor, rushed into M's bedroom, glanced around, and then came back downstairs, moving more slowly.

Because she was intuitive and exceedingly bright, M knew at once what was going on, and she said softly, "You thought Dax was here, didn't you? With me. That's what this is all about."

Geo nodded, looking sheepish. "My next-door neighbor, Alice Foley, called me in New Jersey. . . . She's kept an eye on the house for me for years and often calls me at my sister's. She saw Dax huddled on the steps earlier this afternoon, and then later noticed the two of you in the garden. He had his arm around you, she said, and was kissing you. I thought *you* were the other person he was seeing. Because he *is* involved with someone else."

M was silent; she just sat staring at Geo, who was standing in the middle of the hall again. After a moment, M said, "He's certainly not involved with me, and I don't know whether he's seeing anyone or not. All I know is that he and I are simply friends, pals. When I got home this afternoon, he was on the steps, soaked to the skin and looking really ill. I brought him in and told him to dry himself off. I did the same, and then I made us hot tea."

"But she saw the two of you making out in my garden," Geo protested.

"No, she did not!" M shot back swiftly, glaring at Geo, suddenly angry. "What your neighbor saw was Dax giving me a quick hug and a peck on the cheek. There is nothing between us except friendship, and frankly I rather resent you suggesting otherwise. Anyway, what kind of woman do you think I am? Sneaking around stealing other women's boyfriends is not my style. I think you should apologize."

Geo looked shamefaced, and she slowly walked across the hall, pushing back her long blond hair, shaking her head regretfully. "I'm sorry, M, really sorry. I shouldn't have accused you, shouldn't have paid attention to Alice. She is an old busybody. But I've been perturbed about Dax and our relationship. I think he's lost interest in me, and I really do care about him."

"Apology accepted, Geo. Are you in love with him? Is that what you're saying?"

"Yes, I am. And I thought he felt the same. Now I'm not so sure. Has he said anything to you? About me, or *us*?"

M shook her head, and quickly changing the subject, she asked, "Did you knock something over when you came into the house? I heard a crash, like metal hitting a hard surface."

Geo nodded and gestured toward the wrought-iron coat stand. "I walked slapbang into that, and it woke you up, right?"

"Yes, it did, and then I heard a fainter sound of something metallic hitting the floor. What was that?"

"My flashlight." Geo began to laugh. "I'm an idiot, creeping into my own house like this, walking into the coat stand, dropping a flashlight, and wondering if I was going to catch you and Dax in a hot clinch in your bed. And wondering how I would handle *that*."

M joined in her laughter and stood up. "I don't know about you, but I'd like a cup of tea, or hot milk. What do you fancy?"

"To be honest, a vodka. How about you?"

"That sounds great. . . . It'll help to calm me down."

Geo glanced at her swiftly, frowning. "I really frightened you, didn't I?"

"Yes. Absolutely. I knew someone was here in the hall. I was prepared to knock him down and get out." She patted the old Louis Vuitton bag. "I stuffed this with a few essentials, like my cell and wallet, as well as the door key, just in case I had to run."

"That was smart of you." Geo walked toward the kitchen, saying over her shoulder, "Come on, M, let's have that drink. I think you might need it more than I do. You're as white as a sheet."

Geo moved around the kitchen swiftly, taking a bottle of vodka out of the freezer, then filling a glass bowl with ice. As she arranged these items on a tray and went back to get a lime out of the refrigerator, her thoughts settled on M for a few moments. She liked her tenant, or paying guest as M preferred to call herself, and she was filled with chagrin for having even considered that M might be having a relationship with Dax.

How truly stupid she had been to think such a thing, even more stupid to have crept into her own house at such a late hour expecting to find them together. She must use much better judgment in the future; certainly she must question Alice Foley more carefully whenever she calls her in New Jersey. Her next-door neighbor meant well, but she had jumped to silly conclusions this evening.

Taking two glasses out of the glass-fronted cabinet, Geo stole a surreptitious look at M, who was sitting at the kitchen table looking forlorn.

There was no question in Geo's mind that M had been frightened to death when she crept downstairs clutching the umbrella. The girl's face remained pale, almost translucent, and apprehension lingered in those dark eyes. Poor kid, Geo thought, she's enough problems without me adding to them, scaring her when she was asleep.

Geo was a smart young woman, and at twenty-eight she had lived life to the hilt, seen enough to have insight into people. She had recognized from the start that M, full name Marie Marsden, came from a good family and had had a superior up-bringing. She had impeccable manners, a cultured, rather beautiful speaking voice, and refinement. Even though her few pos-sessions were well worn, they were of the best quality. On several occasions Geo had seen her carrying different-colored antique Kelly bags, and the old Louis Vuitton she was using tonight. They were more than likely hand-me-downs from her mother or her older sister, whom she had referred to once. Otherwise Geo knew very little about this reserved, polite young Englishwoman who had oodles of self-confidence. Not to mention looks to die for.

Georgiana Carlson, artist by profession, landlady by necessity, had never met any-one quite like M. There was something mysterious about her, and Geo couldn't help wondering, yet again, what the real story was.

Turning around, picking up the tray, Geo suggested, "Let's have our nightcap in the den. It's much cozier than sitting at the kitchen table, isn't it?"

M nodded and jumped up. "I'll go ahead and put on the lights." Hurrying across the hall and into the den, she switched on the desk lamp and made space on the coffee table for the tray, then dropped her shoulder bag on a chair.

The two young women sat down opposite each other; lifting the vodka bottle, Geo filled two glasses, put in ice, and added a chunk of lime to each glass.

"Thanks," M said and gave her a faint smile as she took the drink.

Sitting back in the chair, Geo said, "Cheers."

M repeated the toast and took a sip of the vodka, made a face. "That's strong. *Wow!*" Placing the glass on the coffee table, she stared at Geo for a long moment, finally said, apologetically, "I hope I didn't hurt you. . . . Obviously I didn't know it was *you* I was bashing so hard with the umbrella."

Geo grinned. "I deserved it, though. I behaved like an imbecile tonight." She shook her head, looking bemused. "*Men! They sure can drive us crazy, can't they?*"

M was silent. Her fear and anger had subsided, but only slightly. A hint of resentment still lingered. That Geo believed her capable of duplicity was annoying. Slowly, she said in a quiet voice, "Well, I suppose they can get a rise out of us. . . . Although I haven't had that experience, because I haven't had many boyfriends. And those I have had I haven't had to steal from another woman."

Geo caught the hint of sarcasm and realized at once that M continued to be miffed, so she answered swiftly, "Please, M, let's get over this. . . . I told you I was sorry, and I am. Tonight has taught me a lesson. I mustn't jump to conclusions, and I'll have to question Alice more diligently should she ever call again to tell me there are strange goings-on at my house." Geo took a sip of vodka and asked, "How *is* Dax? I haven't seen him for ten days."

"He's got a terrible cold, and sitting on the steps here didn't do him any good. Otherwise, he's just the same, trying to get an acting job, or a fashion shoot. Neither of us have been lucky about finding work." M peered at Geo and murmured, "He was waiting for *you,* actually. He certainly hadn't come over here to see me."

Geo nodded. "He's left several messages on my cell, but I haven't called him back yet. Unfortunately, I've had to make these sudden trips to New Jersey to help my sister. She lives with our aunt Gerry, who isn't well at the moment."

"I'm sorry. Is it something serious?"

"She has a heart condition, and we have to keep an eye on her. She's in her eighties and has no family but us."

M gave Geo a sympathetic look. "I hope she's going to be all right."

"So do I. My sister, Joanne, is very loving and caring, and she's lived with our aunt for a few years now. She moved in after she was widowed. She used to be a booking agent for fashion photography but after she lost her husband it became too much. And having something to do, someone to care for, has really helped her to cope with her grief."

"I know what you mean. My sister is a widow," M volunteered and could have bitten her tongue off. Why had she suddenly confided this to Geo? She didn't want anyone to know one thing about her. Anonymity, that was her goal. Her past was blotted out. Only the future mattered.

Geo looked at M alertly and said, "You never mentioned that. What did he die of?"

"A heart attack," M answered laconically.

"So did Joanne's husband. Dick was fifty-nine when he passed. How old was your brother-in-law?"

"Young, in his thirties," M muttered. Changing the subject, she went on quickly, "Dax isn't seeing another woman, I'm sure of it. He's very focused on his career. He's got the acting bug, you must know that."

"Yes, I do, of course. And I have a feeling he's hankering to leave New York, go out to the West Coast. What do you think?"

"It's possible, he has mentioned it, I must admit. But why don't you tackle *him* about it? That's what I would do, anyway. You and he should talk it out, clear the air between you."

"I think I'll do that tomorrow. I'll call him, go over and see him, look after him if he's still sick. He's awfully neglectful of his health, that I know. Now, what about you,

M? Is there anything I can do to help? I do know a few fashion photographers, and I could call them up, introduce you."

M sat up straighter in the chair and nodded. "That would be wonderful, Geo! How sweet of you to offer. Personal recommendations are the best."

"Consider it done," Geo responded. "I'll get in touch with two of them on Monday. I know Hank George and Frank Farantino are in town, and we'll see how they respond. It's certainly worth a try. In my opinion, you'd be very photographable."

# Four

She could not fall asleep; M lay there in the dark, listening to the house, listening to its many voices.

She had grown up in old houses. To her, they were living things . . . they breathed and sighed, and groaned or moaned, especially in winter. And they frequently rattled their ancient bones, and sometimes shifted on their poor old feet. Her grandfather had once told her that the foundation of a house was like a pair of feet, and she had never forgotten this. She smiled to herself now, remembering him, Popsi, she had called him, remembering how he had confided that it was merely the wood used in the structure of the house that was expanding and contracting, and that she mustn't be afraid of the noises. "A house is a safe harbor," he had said that day. "The one true haven."

M was well aware it was not the creaking house that was keeping her awake but her many anxieties. She had been scared out of her wits when she had heard those noises downstairs. How thoughtless Geo had been and, yes, *stupid,* to come into the house with such stealth. And all because of a man. Dax.

M turned over onto her back, staring up at the ceiling, suddenly thinking of the house where she had grown up and had lived, until very recently, with her parents. She and her siblings had been schooled to always put the alarm system on, especially at night, and that lesson was forever engraved on her mind.

She had broached the subject of the alarm system here before coming back to bed tonight. Only when she volunteered to split the cost of having it checked and properly fixed, if this was necessary, had Geo reluctantly agreed. This decision had brought

a degree of relief to M, and she was determined to make sure it was carried out.
She had no intention of leaving this job to
Geo, who once she was lost in her painting, was lost to the world, with all practical
matters obliterated from her mind.

M was a pragmatist by nature, and she
believed she had inherited her practical
mind-set from her mother, who had always
had her feet firmly planted on terra firma.
Her Mum was diligent, disciplined, a stickler for work, and shrewd to boot. M loved her
mother and father; they were extraspecial.
She knew no one else who had parents like
hers, and she missed them tremendously.
But even if she had been in London at the
moment, it would have been the same
state of affairs. They had gone to Australia
for six months, mostly to see her mother's
mother, and M knew she would have been
alone in London except for her favorite sister, which wasn't a bad thing, after all; but
all of her other siblings were abroad, living
the life, or so she supposed. And working,
of course. That was a certainty.

The Protestant work ethic had been
force-fed to them by a couple of crazy

zealots, *their parents,* who believed they were all going to be struck dead if they didn't work their bums off.

She and her siblings knew that if they didn't work they wouldn't get breakfast, lunch, supper, or whatever. "You're positively Dickensian in your attitudes!" M would yell at her parents, and they would simply laugh and give her the famous *V* for Victory sign à la Winston Churchill. And then, relenting, they would cuddle her, spoil her, and congratulate her, telling her she truly was a chip off the old block and was really earning her stripes. Then they'd take her somewhere special or buy her a unique gift.

And now here she was, in Manhattan, doing sweet nothing and getting bored. Dax *would* go to the Coast, M was convinced of that, and she must endeavor to get a job. She was not used to lolling around—that was the way she thought of it. Tomorrow she would make an effort to get a part-time job as a waitress. Or a shop assistant. No, waitress. Easier in so many ways. They were looking for somebody at the All-American Cheese Cake Cafe, not far from

West Twenty-second Street. It would be something to do, and it would give her extra money. Yes, she would go there tomorrow. Talk to the manager. He liked her. Always gave her a big smile.

M turned restlessly in her bed, suddenly focusing on her plans to become a model. Well, she would, she knew she would. After all, she *had* come here to reinvent herself.

She was seeking obscurity and anonymity, and now she laughed out loud. How truly ridiculous she was. Seeking to go unnoticed yet she would put herself on a runway. Or in front of a camera to be featured in a magazine fashion spread. A dichotomy? Surely.

On the other hand, perhaps not. She *was* a different person now, no longer the young woman she had been when she first arrived in New York in June. Anyway, reinvention was exactly *that,* taking on a new persona. And how simple it was to accomplish. A new name, first off, but one close enough to the old to be easy to respond to without hesitation. A new set of facts about one's life, also as close to reality as possible, so as not to get into a muddle.

And then reinvent . . . adding new facts to the best parts of the earlier life. This was what she had done; she had even been able to obliterate the bad things, most especially the one true Bad Thing that had happened in March. She never thought about that; it was buried deep, very deep indeed. She would never speak about it, never had. It was her big secret. Private, extremely personal, and therefore verboten. Nobody would know. Gone. It was gone. It had never happened . . . push it away. A deep sigh escaped her, and then M turned on her side, closing her eyes.

Sudden and unexpected happenings still alarmed her. Yet she had always been intrepid, even as a child. Nothing had ever fazed her when she was growing up. Her brothers said she had total courage and fortitude, and neither of them was prone to pay her compliments needlessly. She had lost her courage for a while, but it had come back in Manhattan. To her surprise, she felt extraordinarily safe in this great metropolis, was at ease in this glittering city. Furthermore, it was not hard to reinvent oneself here.

No one bothered about where you'd been

to school, what your parents did, whether or not you had an aristocratic background, or came from wealth. It was truly a classless society; that's what she liked about it. In fact, this was a society of achievement. Brains, brilliance, talent and tenacity, drive, ambition, and success. Those were the things which made the biggest impression in Manhattan, and made it the place to be as far as she was concerned. She had been content here.

As she lay contemplating the future, M suddenly thought of her rules—Be brave, be true to yourself—and realized she had broken rule three in her book: *Keep busy.* Quite unexpectedly, she understood how much time she had wasted with Dax: going to coffee shops, taking in movies, listening to him pontificate about his life, watching TV shows with him, keeping him company. Because he was lonely. And so was she, if she was truthful.

Being a member of a big family meant she had been brought up in a crowd. And she had been teased, applauded, sometimes shouted at, but always very much loved, and rarely alone.

I'm going to go out and get a job, she

promised herself now. It would fill up her spare time, and the money would be useful. She had brought enough money to New York to last her for a year, provided she was careful. She had opened a bank account and used the money very sparingly, for rent, food, and transportation, although mostly she walked everywhere. Locked in the suitcase under her bed was an envelope of traveler's checks, which her sister had forced on her before she left London. She hadn't wanted to accept them but knew only too well not to argue with Birdie, who termed the envelope "your safety net," and that's how she thought of it. They were meant to be used only in extreme emergency.

Starting tomorrow, she would find a part-time job so she could continue to haunt the modeling agencies, and she hoped Geo would keep her promise and contact those two photographers. They were old friends Geo had known through her sister.

Fingers crossed, M thought, and very shortly she fell asleep. It was an exhausted sleep, and dreamless.

# Five

M was filled with excitement and anticipation, and there was a spring in her step as she walked down West Twenty-second Street. She was on her way to see Frank Farantino, the photographer, who had told Geo to send her to his studio today.

On the one hand, she had lost a friend with the departure of Dax to Los Angeles; on the other hand, she had gained a friend in Georgiana Carlson.

After that debacle in the middle of the night a few weeks ago, Geo had tried her hardest to make amends. She had spoken to Hank George and Frank Farantino about

M, and several days ago both photographers had been back in touch with Geo, and appointments had been made.

The first was with Farantino, at his studio in the Meatpacking District, an easy walk from Geo's brownstone, especially on this beautiful September day. The sky was a soft pale blue, puffed with wispy white clouds, and it was sunny and balmy, but not too hot because of the light breeze blowing off the Hudson River to the west.

Ever since she had come to live in Manhattan, M had done a lot of walking, wanting to get to know the city. In particular, she loved West Chelsea, where she lived, was captivated by its art galleries and cafés, and those lovely tree-filled streets in the West Twenties.

But to M there was something extraspecial about the Meatpacking District. Now considered the most fashionable part of New York, it had recently been named a historic district. Over a hundred years ago it had been full of slaughterhouses and meatpacking warehouses, some two hundred and fifty. Almost all of those buildings were gone, and in their place were some of the most elegant stores, belonging to top fashion designers, as well as nightclubs, bars, cafés, restaurants, and spas. It had become a chic place for the young, the hip, and the upwardly mobile, and it was littered with celebrities day and night.

M smiled to herself at that thought. Some of her family were quite well known, and certainly she didn't need to meet strangers who were famous. Dax loved to party with them, and although she liked to hang out with him in the MePa, as it was called, she had managed to slip away when he set his sights on movie stars and the like, becoming oblivious to her.

Dax had gone to the West Coast to seek his fame and fortune, and she wished him well. Deep down she felt a gloomy, gnawing feeling; she knew enough about Hollywood to understand it was a world of pain and heartbreak, disappointment and disillusionment.

He had come to say good-bye, her friend Dax, with his blond handsomeness, quirky personality, and flashing smile. And his rather childlike innocence. He had also had dinner with Geo before flying away, and later Geo had confided that their romantic relationship was indeed over but they remained friends, and Geo seemed relieved about this.

M was well aware that Dax had gone alone to the West Coast; his entire being was now concentrated on his career. He, too, had confided in her . . . about his love life. Giving her a big hug, he had whispered, against her hair, "I took your advice to heart, M. The only thing I am going to think about is becoming a movie star. Nothing else matters."

She thought about this as she continued to walk toward the Meatpacking District for her appointment at noon. *Movie star.* If that was what Dax wanted to be, and wanted it enough, he might well get it. Certainly he had the looks, and a unique kind of charisma, a presence. But could he act? Well, that didn't really matter, did it? Some movie stars were great actors, others couldn't act their way out of a paper bag. Dax had willpower, and that would help him. But was he ruthless? She pondered that. And was he tough enough to withstand the battering, the rejections, and perhaps most important of all, the competition? She wasn't sure; she could only hope that he was, for his sake.

Someone she knew very well had once done a stint in Hollywood and had explained that one needed the stamina of a bull, the skin of a rhinoceros, the brain of Machiavelli, and the looks of a Greek god to make it in Dreamland, as he had called it. Perhaps her brother was right. . . . And so she would say a prayer for Dax. He would need lots of prayers. And luck.

Frank Farantino's studio was on the second floor of what had once been a meatpacking warehouse. The huge black wooden door, decorated with brass nailheads, had farantino painted on it in bright red, and there was a bright red arrow painted above the doorbell. ring it had been written out in brass nailheads, and she did as she was instructed.

A split second later the door was pulled open by a petite, very pretty woman with startlingly blue eyes and bright red hair cut in a short, spiky style. She was dressed entirely in red: T-shirt, tights, and cowboy boots.

"Hi!" she exclaimed, craning her neck, staring up at M. "You're the appointment, right? The friend of Geo?"

"Yes, I am."

Opening the door wider, the girl said, "Come on in then, don't stand there. What's your name again? I've forgotten it."

M laughed. "It's very simple. . . . I'm called M, as in a capital *M*."

"I see. What's it stand for? The *M*, I mean."

"Marie."

"So why don't you call yourself Marie?"

"I prefer to be called M."

"I guess a lot of girls are calling themselves by an initial these days. So it must be the 'in' thing. My brother saw it on YouTube or somewhere. Maybe it was on Facebook. Or MySpace."

"Actually, it's not something new. The Duchess of Devonshire, who lived long ago, was called G. That was *G* for Georgiana, by the way."

"Who?" The girl stared at her, a look of puzzlement flashing across her delicately boned face.

"Never mind, it's not important. And may I know your name?"

"Caresse."

"It's pretty, very unusual. I don't think I've ever heard that name before."

"I hope not, because *I* invented it. I didn't like my own name, so I came up with my . . . *invention.*"

"What was your real name before you changed it?"

"Helen. Ugh. So dull." She made a face.

*"Helen,"* M repeated softly. "The face that launched a thousand ships. A very famous name, in fact."

"What do you mean?" The redheaded pixie gave her a hard stare.

*"Helen of Troy.* . . . She was so beautiful her husband and her lover fought a terrible and ultimately tragic battle over her. . . . It was known as the battle of a thousand ships."

"When was that?"

"Twelve hundred years before the birth of Jesus."

Caresse gaped at her, slowly shaking her head. "How do *you* know that?"

"I learned it at school." Clearing her throat, M went on quickly, "Anyway, here I am to see Mr. Farantino." She glanced at her watch. "And I'm on time. It's exactly noon."

"I'll go and get him," Caresse announced and hurried away.

M watched her go, frowning. Caresse had seemed very young at first glance, but now she thought this pretty, pixielike creature was nearer to thirty than to twenty. She seemed so nice, though, and M had taken an instant liking to her.

# Six

Frank Farantino was one of the best known and most successful photographers in New York. In the world, in point of fact. And in the entrance foyer of his large studio, he stopped dead in his tracks when the tall young woman wearing a white cotton shirt and black trousers turned around to face him.

He held his breath for a split second as he took in her dark, exotic beauty, her unique looks. Thank you, Geo, thank you very much, he thought. He knew at once that his old friend had sent him a winner, and he was extremely pleased, *thrilled* if he was honest with himself, that this extraordinary girl was standing here.

A wide smile enlivened his saturnine face, and then he strode across the floor, his hand outstretched as he drew to a standstill in front of the young woman.

"Frankie Farantino," he said, shaking her hand.

"I'm very pleased to meet you, Mr. Farantino," M answered politely, as was her way, smiling back. "Thank you for seeing me today."

"My pleasure, and drop the Mr. Farantino, would you, please? The whole world calls me Frankie. And your name is . . . M?" He threw her a questioning look. "I am correct about that?"

"Yes, you are. And before you ask me, my full name is Marie Marsden. My nickname at school was M and M, and I decided it might be better to drop one *M* when I started my modeling career." She grinned.

He grinned back at her. "English, eh? Geo didn't tell me that. So, how long have you been in New York?"

"I came here in June, and I've been looking for work ever since. I'm afraid I haven't been too successful, but then I haven't been here all that long."

"How did you meet Georgiana Carlson?"

"Through a young man I know . . . he's called Dax. He's a model and an actor."

"Oh, sure, I know Dax. I've used him from time to time. Geo's boyfriend."

"That's right. And he's gone off to the West Coast to try his luck."

"He's smart. So let's go into the main studio, give it a whirl. How much modeling have you done?"

"A little. In London."

"Did you bring any pictures?"

"Yes. They're in my tote." As she spoke she picked this up and hurried after him into the studio. "As for actual modeling, I haven't done much of that . . . been on the catwalk, I mean," she admitted, looking suddenly rueful.

"Let's see the pictures." Frankie Farantino stared at her intently, immediately understanding that she was a novice looking for that first break, but this did not trouble him at all. He preferred young women who had not been trained and often tainted by other photographers. One of the things he most enjoyed as a photographer was molding a girl, actually *creating* her, giving her a special look of his own invention. Taking the batch of photographs M handed to him, he flicked through them swiftly, then glanced at her and half smiled. "They're not bad, and at least I can see you photograph well. But these just don't do you justice." He handed them to her.

"I suppose not," she murmured and swiftly put them back in the tote, deciding not to show them to anyone again, especially a photographer.

"Okay, so let's get started," Frankie said. "Go and stand on that raised platform, and turn slowly, so that I can view you from every angle."

She did as he instructed, slowly turning, and turning again when he told her to keep moving. "Slowly, *very slowly,*" he intoned.

Watching her intently, Frankie saw a lot of remarkable things simultaneously: She moved gracefully, like a dancer, and although she was rather tall, her height was balanced by a good figure and a kind of inbred elegance. Her face fascinated him . . . she reminded him of someone he could not quite place. That vague image flickered at the back of his mind, and just as he thought he was about to grasp it, it floated maddeningly away.

"Come on down," he said at last and stretched out his hand to help her off the platform. "You brought a skirt, didn't you?"

"Yes, I did, and a dress. A simple black sheath. High heels and a pair of flats."

"Good. There's a dressing room over there." He indicated a door set in one of the soaring walls. "Please change into . . . well, anything you want."

M nodded and hurried into the dressing room. She selected her flared, red cotton skirt, which went well with the pristine white shirt, added a wide black leather belt, slipped her feet into her favorite black ballerina slippers. Glancing at herself in the mirror, she decided to pull her hair back into a ponytail, added hoop earrings, and used a brighter red lipstick to define her mouth.

Frankie was loading his camera and looked up when M walked back out into the studio. Instantly he knew who she resembled. A young Audrey Hepburn. He felt excitement surge through him; he could hardly wait to capture her image on film.

Only then would he know what he *really* had.

"You look great, M!" he exclaimed. "I'd like you to stand over there, in front of that white picket fence with the backdrop of a green field."

Frankie followed her, put his camera on a side table, and explained, "Move around a little, honey. Move your arms, strike a few poses you're familiar with. Like this." He gave her a quick demonstration, picked up his camera, and stepped away from her. "It's okay, practice for a few seconds. Don't look so worried. Smile, M, give me a few dazzling smiles."

She did as he suggested and proved so adept he started to shoot immediately, constantly throwing out encouraging words. "That's great! Right on! Now turn left, move your body more. Hey, honey, you're a natural. Wow! That's great! Hold that pose. You're fabulous!"

He went on photographing her for half an hour, exclaiming encouragement and praise, pausing only to grab a different camera or reload film. Finally he stopped, sat down on a tall stool, and beckoned to her. "Stand here, M, in front of me."

"Was I all right?" she asked quietly. "Did I move the way you wanted?"

"*Absolutely.* You're great. But I need to ask you something. . . . Have you ever had bangs?"

"Do you mean a fringe?" She ran her index finger across her forehead. "That's what we call it in England . . . a fringe. And no, I haven't."

"What about short hair? Or have you always worn it long?"

"Mostly. It was short when I was much younger, when I was a little girl actually. Why? Don't you like my hair?"

"It's magnificent. Beautiful. So long and glossy, and yes, even dramatic. There's a lot you can do with long hair." Frankie pursed her lips, held his head to one side, and then, suddenly turning away from her, he shouted, "Caresse! Come on in here, would you please!"

A moment later the redheaded pixie was running into the studio. "Yes, Frankie, here I am. What do you need?"

"Where's Agnes? Is she here?"

"She said she'd arrive by two. With Luke Hendricks, remember? He's doing that shoot for the ad agency with you."

Frankie looked at the big round clock on the opposite wall. It was almost one. Turning to Caresse, he said in an urgent voice, "Find Agnes. Try her cell. Ask her if she can come in as soon as possible, and locate Marguerite Briguet, please. Tell her I want her to do a very special makeup job. Okay?"

"Right away, Frankie!" Caresse scooted off.

Leaning forward, Frankie gave M a hard, penetrating stare. "I need to give you a whole new look. It will be wonderful for you, but we might have to cut your hair."

M gasped, her dark eyes widening. She was momentarily speechless. Cut off her hair?

Frankie murmured in a gentler tone, "I promise you it will change your life. And it will be a truly *unique* look, very special to you—"

"A reinvention?" she asked finally, cutting in. "Is that what you're suggesting?"

He nodded, continuing to stare at her speculatively. "That's what I mean. Will you go for it?"

"*Absolutely.* I love reinventions, Frankie."

❈

"I really don't want to cut this hair," Agnes Manton said softly, smoothing one hand down the long black hair which was one of M's great assets. "Look at it, Frankie, it's like a . . . a mantle of shining black silk. It would be criminal to cut this off."

"Don't be so melodramatic," Frankie shot back, a brow lifting. "It is only *hair,* for God's sake. It will grow back again, Agnes."

"I don't mind," M interjected, swiveling her head to look up at the hairdresser. "And Frankie's right, you know. I *can* grow it back if I want to."

Agnes nodded but remained silent, studying the young woman carefully, liking her.

Frankie said, "I want to show you something. Just a minute." He stepped away from the dressing table in the hair and makeup room at the back of the vast studio, headed for the bookcase at the far end. Taking down a picture book, he flicked through it, quickly found the photographs he wanted, and walked back to the two women.

"Look at these, Agnes, and you'll better understand what I'm aiming for. Here." He handed her the book, indicating several pages.

When Agnes saw the title "audreystyle"

and stared at the first few pictures, she knew at once what he wanted. *A replica of Audrey Hepburn with one of her short gamine hairdos.* Nodding, Agnes said to Frankie, "I can create the look you want without cutting off all of M's hair." She flipped through the book, showed him several other photographs, explained, "Here, take a look at this one. Bangs but with the back in a tight chignon. I should try this first, don't you think? I just don't want to be hasty, cutting off all this gorgeous hair."

Frankie took the book away from her, glanced at the photograph she was talking about, and had to agree that there was truth in what Agnes was saying. With bangs and a twist at the back, Audrey looked more sophisticated and elegant, but she was still Audrey Hepburn.

M said, "Can I see the book, Frankie, please? So I know what the two of you are talking about."

He gave it to her without a word.

M exclaimed, "Oh, my goodness, Audrey Hepburn! Is that what you want to do, turn me into a new *Audrey*?"

Frankie laughed. "You got it, kid. Any objections?"

"No, not at all. I'd love it, actually."

"Okay then, let's do it."

"I don't want to do any cutting," Agnes reminded him, a warning look on her face.

"That's okay with me," Frankie answered and then said to M, "You told me you'd brought a black sheath and high heels. Correct?"

"Yes. Would you like me to go and put them on?"

"No, not for the moment. Agnes is going to copy this hairstyle here." He turned to the stylist, said in a firmer voice, "You must cut the front, though, because I want M to have bangs, and copy this upswept look, please. It's a very elegant Audrey here . . . this photo is from *Roman Holiday,* I believe."

"But—" Agnes began and stopped when she saw the adamant expression on Frankie's face. She had worked with him for years and knew when to stop arguing with him.

"Bangs okay with you, M?" he asked, took the book from her, found the picture he wanted, then handed it back to M, pointing at a page.

"Bangs are very okay with me," M responded and stared down at the book, then smiled at Agnes. "Let's do it, shall we?"

Placing a cotton cape around M's shoulders, Agnes picked up her most expensive scissors, took a deep breath, and began to create the bangs Frankie insisted on.

M sat back in the chair, watching Agnes work, saying nothing, secretly loving the idea of becoming an Audrey Hepburn look-alike. That was genuine reinvention and then some. She smiled inwardly, wondering why she hadn't thought of this herself. God knows, her brothers had often teased her about having such a marked resemblance to the famous actress.

Frankie announced, "I'll leave you to it, Agnes, and when Marguerite arrives I'll send her in immediately." Resting one hand on M's shoulder, he added, "Marguerite is another genius, and Agnes and she together *will* turn you into the woman in these pictures. You'll be the real thing, par excellence."

# Seven

Wow!" a male voice exclaimed in a soft, awed tone from the shadows at the back of the main studio. Finally walking out into the bright light, the man added, "Wow! Wow! Wow!" and stopped just a few feet away from Frankie, who was photographing M seated on a tall stool.

"Hey, Luke!" Frankie cried as he swung around and saw his friend. "She is a *wow, wow, wow,* isn't she?"

Instead of responding to Frankie, Luke looked at M and addressed her. "You certainly are spectacular, just as you were in

*Breakfast at Tiffany's,* looking exactly as you do today." He shook his head, a wide grin spreading across his handsome face. "Of course I know you couldn't possibly *be* Audrey, but you certainly could be her twin. So what's your *real* name?"

M started to answer him, but Frankie cut across her. "This is M, Luke. She's known simply as M, and she's my new discovery. I'm going to launch her modeling career, yes indeedy, and I have big plans for her. I *know* what I'm seeing through this lens. And it's something sensational."

"Congratulations, Frankie," Luke responded and then walked toward M, his hand outstretched.

As they shook hands, the two of them sized each other up.

M found herself looking into a pair of light gray eyes set in a puckish face, which appeared to be full of merriment. With his short, curly blond hair and slight build, Luke reminded her of a choirboy. But perhaps a rather devilish one.

For his part, Luke was captivated by the young woman dressed in the black sheath and wearing tons of pearls and sparkling drop earrings. A few minutes ago he had been talking to Agnes and Marguerite in the hair and makeup room, and both women had told him how Frankie had instructed them to play up M's striking resemblance to the late movie star. There was no question that they had done a truly magnificent job. This young woman was stunning, but he knew she would be even if she weren't an Audrey look-alike.

"I'm happy to meet you, Luke," M finally said.

Luke cleared his throat, suddenly realizing he was gaping at her like a dumbstruck schoolboy. "Me, too, er, what I mean is, I'm glad to meet you. You're English?"

"Yes, I am, but I'm living here now. I came over about three months ago." As she spoke, she gently extricated her hand from his tight clasp.

"If you need someone to show you around Manhattan, need anything at all, I'd be glad to help you. Just let me know." He took out a business card and handed it to her.

"Thank you," she said, smiling at him.

"Hey, hey, hey, not so fast, Luke, my boy! No poaching my talent. After all, I discovered her. And M's going to be working for me *exclusively.*"

"I was merely volunteering to be a friend."

"I know, Luke, I know." Stepping closer to the younger man, Frankie said in a lower tone, "Thanks for coming in to help with the ad agency shoot. The models are here, changing before they go into hair and makeup. We'll start shooting in about forty minutes, because I want to finish up with M."

Luke nodded. "Are we shooting in this studio? Or one of the others?"

"The big one at the back. The scenery's already set up for the first session, and I'm sure Ted is in there already, looking at the new backdrops, which came in last week. Why don't you go introduce yourself and have a few words with him? He's a nice guy, genuine, and he's been throwing a lotta work my way lately."

"Okay," Luke responded, gave a wave to M, and hurried off, fully aware that Frankie preferred to shoot without spectators. Unless it was a "civilian" like Ted Langton, or some other friendly agency guy. Even Luke himself was tolerated only when he was actually *working* as Frankie's first assistant, otherwise he was forbidden to enter just like the others.

❖

Once M and Frankie were alone, he explained, "Luke's one of my protégés, and he's already on the way to becoming a great photographer. He's got a small studio of his own and has a couple of regular clients, but I give him as much work as I can. I want to help him get ahead."

"That's nice of you, Frankie," M said, meaning it. She and her siblings had been brought up to be helpful to others; it was one of the family rules.

"I've always believed that everyone is worth helping, most especially if they have potential," Frankie now added, put down his camera, and walked over to her, studied her for a moment. "I think you should take off all the pearls, M, and the earrings for the next few shots. I'd like you to look simpler. Your hair is fine, but Marguerite needs to powder you down. I'll go and get her."

Before she could volunteer to go to hair and makeup herself, Frankie had hurried to the far end of the studio.

In his absence, M walked over to a trestle table, took off the many strings of pearls he had draped around her neck earlier, and the earrings as well. She placed them in one of the boxes which contained costume jewelry; in the others were artificial flowers, small kerchiefs and ribbons, all kinds of accessories. On the spur of the moment she took out a piece of black velvet ribbon, went over to the mirror on the wall behind the table, and tied the ribbon round her neck. Standing back, she eyed herself.

M was thrilled and excited that Frankie Farantino had seen something so special in her he had spent so much time photographing her. She realized that this might be the break she had been waiting for. Perhaps Lady Luck *was* with her today; she suddenly thought of her big brother, who always gave such credit to Lady Luck, decided he would have been proud of the way she had worked this afternoon. He had instilled one thing in her: *Be professional.*

As M walked back to the center of the studio, Frankie reappeared with Marguerite, carrying her basket filled with the tools of her trade.

"According to Frankie, you need a touch-up," the makeup artist said, smiling and peering at her face appraisingly. Marguerite took out a damp sponge, went over M's face with it, patted her dry with a tissue, dipped a brush in powder, and flicked it over her cheeks. "You're not as shiny as I expected. Now all we need is a little blush on top of the powder and you're ready. Your eyes are fine, M, they don't need anything." Marguerite finished her work, stepped back, and said, "You've weathered the hot lights very well."

"Thanks, Marguerite," M answered and went back to the middle of the floor, sat down on the stool.

Frankie, who was busy reloading film, looked across at her and exclaimed, "The ribbon looks great, honey, and that's all you need."

He photographed her for another twenty minutes, taking shots of her from different angles, praising her, telling her to hold a certain pose, until he finally had everything he wanted.

"That's it, M. At least for today. And you've been a great subject. You know what, you're good at this, honey."

"And thank you, Frankie. Actually, I've enjoyed it," she told him. Walking across to him, she now asked, "Did you mean it when you told Luke you were going to launch my modeling career?"

He was taking the film out of his camera, and he glanced up and nodded. "Yes, I did."

"I'm so pleased about that! So, what happens next?" she asked, her excitement reflected on her face.

"I have to start using you in some of my fashion shoots for the magazines. That's how we'll begin."

"And when will that be?"

"Not for a few weeks," Frankie murmured, putting the camera down on a table. "I have to go to Morocco on Monday, to do a fashion spread for *Harper's Bazaar*."

M nodded and gave him a quizzical look. "So when should I plan on being here, Frankie?"

"I'll have to let you know. You see, I'll be in Morocco for a while, honey, it's a big spread."

"And there's no way you could include me in that?" she asked, her eyes riveted on him.

He shook his head. "No, the models have all been selected. In fact, some are already on their way over there."

"I understand." She gave him a bright smile, although she was disappointed, and went on, "I'd better let the Blane Agency know about our session today, and your intentions, don't you think?"

Startled by her unexpected business-like manner, he stared at her, his eyes narrowing, then said, "But Geo told me you were registered with a number of modeling agencies. Why are you mentioning Blane's in particular?"

"Because I signed with them when I first came to New York, and I like the women working there. They seem sincere to me, and they've tried to be helpful. I should have proper representation anyway, shouldn't I?"

"Okay, you're right, and I understand. So yes, you can go ahead and tell them."

"And what about the photographs you've taken today? When can I see them? I'd love to know how I look in them."

He grinned at her. "Of course you would. Drop over next week and Caresse will have a set for you."

"Thank you." She moved back to the

small table near the stool, retrieved Luke's business card, then swinging around, she asked, "What do you plan to do with the pictures you took today?"

"What do you mean, M?" He sounded puzzled.

"Are you going to place them with a magazine? Or use them in some way? Or was this a . . . a dry run, I suppose you would call it."

"That's right, it was exactly that. I usually do a session with a new girl if I think she has potential. And you know already I feel that about you. Some of them are duds, you know, but certainly not you. I foresee a great future for you as a model, M, and I do plan to help you get to the top. When I come back from Morocco."

Frankie walked across the floor, put his arms around her, and gave her a big hug. "Thanks again, honey, and I'll see you in a few weeks."

# Eight

It seemed to M that the next few weeks passed extremely quickly. Always well organized, even when she was a child, she made herself a schedule and kept to it.

Every other morning she went to the Blane Model Agency to check in with Leni, the receptionist, and afterward visited another two agencies, International and Famous, where she was also registered. Three afternoons a week she worked as a waitress at the All-American Cheese Cake Cafe, and on Thursday she helped out as a sales assistant at Jennifer Allen's chic boutique in the Meatpacking District.

She enjoyed being busy, and working helped to deflect some of her worry about Frankie Farantino. She hoped he would keep his word to her.

According to Caresse, whom she called several times a week, he was still in Morocco, and would be going on to the South of France to finish the shoot. This was a new development in his schedule. Only after that would he be back in New York. But Caresse reassured her that Frankie *would* keep his word, as did the women she knew at Blane's. Leni, and Marla Golding, who handled bookings, had been pleased when she conveyed Frankie's interest in her. He enjoyed a good reputation, and they told her they deemed him trustworthy. Also, the two of them had been impressed by the photographs Frankie had taken of her, as she had herself.

Only Geo seemed hesitant about the "makeover," as she called it, pointing out to M that she was beautiful in her own right and did not need to become the replica of a dead movie star.

"If you don't know how gorgeous you are, go and look in the mirror," Geo had said that Thursday afternoon when M returned from the shoot at Frankie's studio. "I love your hairstyle, though, and you should definitely keep the bangs; they really suit you. They'd work with a ponytail, too, you know, as well as the twist." Then quite suddenly Geo had frowned and peered at her rather intently, shaking her head, and added in a gentle tone, obviously not wanting to give offense, "I think your eye makeup is a bit too heavy, and your eyebrows far too thick, M, if you don't mind me saying so."

M had listened attentively to Geo, and everyone else, and weighed their comments. She tended to agree with Geo about the eye makeup and later decided not to bother with it, especially when she was working at the café and the boutique. She would look ridiculous in those venues if she did an over-the-top theatrical eye job on herself.

M also kept herself busy when she wasn't working. She went shopping for groceries and her everyday needs, kept her room scrupulously neat, and looked after her clothes and shoes. She e-mailed her parents in Australia and called her sister in London, either on Friday or on Sunday, depending on her new work schedule.

And of course she waited impatiently for Frankie's return to New York. She had canceled the interview with Hank George, on the advice of Geo, who pointed out that Frankie would probably be annoyed if M went to see another photographer at this stage. After all, he had made it crystal clear that he wanted to launch her modeling career; he had even agreed that she could inform Blane's of his serious intentions. In fact, he had behaved impeccably.

"You'll just have to be patient until he gets back," Geo had murmured recently. "Everything's going to be all right, I just know it is. And when he does return, Blane's will get you a worthwhile contract with him."

M thought of Geo now as she wandered around one of the many art galleries in West Chelsea. She often did this on weekends, looking at paintings by people she had never heard of, always deciding that Geo was a much better artist. In fact, Geo was enormously talented, in M's opinion, and working extremely hard at the moment, endeavoring to finish a series of paintings of scenes in Connecticut. They were intended for an exhibition of her work, and

M was encouraging her to stick to it, cheering her on every day.

After meandering around the gallery for a short while longer, M left, and walked toward West Twenty-second Street, having decided it was time to go home.

She was enjoying the late September weather, and it struck her that today was one of those gorgeous Indian summer days which she and her mother so loved . . . sunny and warm with a light breeze and an impeccable clear blue sky without a single cloud.

"A day to be outside in the garden," her mother would say years ago on days like this and head outside, beckoning her children to follow.

M experienced an unexpected pang, a tightness in her chest when she thought of her mother, longing to be with her . . . in that glorious garden, but she couldn't go back there . . . it was too dangerous. . . .

✿

When she got home, M found Geo in the kitchen filling the kettle. "Oh, lovely! I'm just in time for tea," she exclaimed.

"That you are," Geo agreed, laughing.

"I sort of anticipated you, I suppose." Lighting the gas under the kettle, Geo went on, "Come into the studio for a moment, M, please. I've finished the painting you liked. . . . I'd love your opinion of it."

"Lead the way," M said, hurrying after Geo into the light-filled studio.

M stood in front of the large oil painting, instantly captivated. It was of a grand lake with stands of trees clustered on the rise of a hill at the far side. The canvas was brilliant with fall colors . . . russets, reds and pinks, amber, a strange purple-wine color, and varying shades of gold. And the entire painting was suffused with soft golden light, which seemed to shimmer across the surface of the water.

Stepping back, M stared at it from a distance for quite a long time. Finally turning, she said to Geo, "Don't touch it again. Leave it alone. It's finished, and it's superb. The way you've managed to capture light is brilliant. I've noticed this in some of your other paintings, and it's such a marvelous ability. Congratulations, Geo." She squeezed the other woman's arm. "All your hard work has paid off."

Geo's face was wreathed in smiles. She said softly, "Thank you. I'm so thrilled you like it. I value your judgment."

The whistling of the kettle startled them both, and swinging around, Geo hurried across the studio, heading for the kitchen.

M lingered in front of the painting, continuing to study it; she had become somewhat awed by Geo's work, understanding that her friend was an artist of enormous talent who needed a break, just as she herself did.

Sighing, M went to the kitchen, hoping that Geo's exhibition would be a stunning success.

The two women sat in the windowed area of the kitchen, sipping their mugs of tea, talking about the exhibition. And then, somewhat abruptly, Geo changed the subject. She said, "I'm glad we've become friends, M. I like you such a lot." She shook her head wonderingly, bit her lip. "When I remember how ridiculous I was, suspecting you and Dax, I feel like a real fool. I apologize again, M."

"Don't be so silly, Geo, I've forgotten it."

Geo smiled, but she was fully aware that M hadn't forgotten it. She knew she had frightened M, and badly, and she had a feeling that this fear still lingered. M had insisted that they install a new alarm system, and Geo had had no option but to go along with it, splitting the bill with M. Well, essentially M was right, wanting their security.

Aware of the growing silence, Geo now said swiftly, with a laugh, "I have to admit it was jealousy of all things, silly, stupid *jealousy. . . ."*

M nodded her understanding, then glanced away at the little back garden, lost in her thoughts. Suddenly sitting up straighter, she murmured, "In jealousy there is more self-love than love."

Geo was taken aback, and after a moment's reflection, she exclaimed, "There's a great deal of wisdom in your words, M."

"Oh, no, not my words," M responded, shaking her head. "They were written by the Duc de La Rochefoucauld in the seventeenth century. Still, I believe they're as applicable today as they were then."

"Absolutely," Geo agreed, took a sip of the hot, sweet tea, and wondered how M could remember that obscure but interesting quote. On the other hand, the young

Englishwoman sitting opposite her was filled to overflowing with knowledge about so many things. She could talk expertly about books and plays, movies and opera, and she knew a lot about art. Geo admired her for all this, and also because she was so brave, coming alone to New York, wanting to make it on her own. M's aspirations were similar to her own, and Dax shared the same kind of ambition.

"How did you learn so much about art, M? I mean, you speak so expertly—yes, that's the best word—about Renoir, Monet, Bonnard, the Impressionists and Post-Impressionists, and Turner, especially Turner. Even I don't know everything you do."

"From my sister," M responded swiftly. "She took me to a lot of art galleries even when I was a kid, and she instilled a great deal of knowledge in me. Force-fed me, I suppose you could call it. I've always said that children learn so much from exposure to the arts in general, and certainly my exposure to all the great galleries in England and France helped to create my love of paintings."

M gave Geo a big smile. "I can admire,

but I can't do it, paint I mean, and you can, Geo. You're enormously talented, and don't ever forget that. You'll see—your exhibition will be a tremendous success. And you'll be on your way."

"Oh, God, I hope so. All I can add is, from your mouth to God's ears." Leaning across the table, Geo now murmured, "Guess who called me earlier."

"Dax."

Geo looked startled. "How did you know? Oh, he probably called you, too."

"No, I haven't heard from him today, but he's the only person we have in common."

"Yes, that's true. Anyway, he's back in New York."

"Already!" M sounded surprised, and she began to shake her head in disbelief. "Sooner than even I thought."

"Yes, me, too. But he's back because he's got a job in the theater at last. Can you imagine, he went to L.A. to look for work in the movies, then ends up with a part in a play on Broadway."

"But that's wonderful! How did it happen?"

"He was introduced to Iris Ingersoll in Beverly Hills, at some party. Through an

actor he met there. Iris is a Broadway producer."

M was about to say she knew that but
swallowed the words. She realized she
had been saying too much to Geo lately,
revealing things, so she merely nodded.

"He's starting rehearsals next week.
He's got the second lead, and the thing is,
M, he's invited us to a party to sort of . . .
well, celebrate, I guess. I hope you don't
mind, but I said yes. For both of us."

M gaped at her, frowning, but remained
silent.

Geo exclaimed, "Oh, don't look so upset, M! It'll do you good to get out of this
house. All you seem to do these days is
serve cheesecake and help women try on
expensive dresses. And visit the modeling
agencies, which earns you nothing but
disappointment. Come on, say yes. Go
with me. It will be a treat for both of us."

"When is it?"

"Tonight."

"Short notice, wouldn't you say?" M
asked and raised a dark brow.

"Yes, it is, and Dax said that himself.
But he just decided to do it today. He called
it an impromptu party, and he really does

want us to come. I've nothing better to do. Do you?"

"Where's he having it?" M asked, ignoring Geo's question.

"At Iris Ingersoll's apartment. On Park Avenue. Drinks at nine and a buffet supper around ten-thirty. To cater to the theater folk, you know, who'll get there late."

"What are we supposed to wear?"

"Something festive, Dax said."

"I guess I'd better go upstairs and ransack my closet," M murmured, finally smiling at Geo.

"Oh, M, this is great! You're going to come?"

"Why not? I'd like to see Dax, congratulate him. He's wanted this for so long. It's nice to know one of us finally got a break."

"And you never know who you'll meet there," Geo announced, grinning.

Although her room was only medium in size, M had liked it from the moment she saw it. Painted a creamy-buttery color, it had a large window looking out onto West Twenty-second Street; it was airy and light-filled, and very sunny this afternoon. The dark red and gold Oriental carpet covered the entire floor and added a warm, cozy feeling, as did the dark red curtains. There was a daybed along one wall with a dark red damask cover, and piles of gold and red pillows, so that it served as a sofa; nearby, a large armchair upholstered in the same dark red fabric as the curtains faced the television set on a stand. A coffee table, a large chest of drawers, and several lamps completed the room.

Her golden rule was no clutter, and there was a paucity of personal things here, especially photographs of her family; only a few books stacked on the chest revealed something about her, and that wasn't very much.

M walked across the room and picked up her cell phone, which had been charging while she was out. She saw a missed call and knew at once that it must be from Dax. It was, and she called him back; his phone was turned off, so she left a message. After congratulating him, she said she would see him that evening and ended the call.

Wondering what to wear, she headed toward the closet and opened the double doors. She had several suitable outfits, all black except for a gray-silk trouser suit, which Birdie had given her a couple of years ago. Pulling it out, she held it up and stared at it critically, pursing her lips, then hung it back in the wardrobe, mentally discarding it.

Quite suddenly she knew without a doubt that she mustn't go to the party. It was too risky. There would be lots of theater people there, she was certain of that, and some might very well know various members of her family and recognize *her.* But not if I go as Audrey, she instantly thought, realizing that this would be the most perfect disguise of all. She smiled to herself, warming to the idea.

Hurrying into the adjoining bathroom, M stared at herself in the mirror, her head to one side, visualizing the image Agnes and Marguerite had created. She made a moue, instantly remembering how Geo had thought the look was a bit overdone. Half an Audrey, she now thought. I'll go as half an Audrey, and I'll be safe. Nobody will know who I really am, and I can simply play the role of M.

# Nine

I suddenly don't want go to the party," Geo announced, coming to a standstill on Park Avenue, turning to look at M. "Let's forget it, shall we?"

Taken aback, M stared at Geo and exclaimed, "But you were the one who was so anxious to go. Why have you changed your mind?"

"I know what these Park Avenue parties are like. It's going to be a boring evening with lots of famous people who are dull, or stupid, or full of themselves." Geo made a face, took hold of M's arm firmly, and said, "Let's go and have supper. There's a little bistro I know on Lexington. Swifty's. You'll love it, and it's my treat."

"But we can't leave Dax in the lurch," M protested. "He's expecting us, and he'll be awfully disappointed if we don't show up. We're probably the only friends he's invited. Besides, we'll look really mean if we don't go." M threw Geo a knowing look and added, "We don't want him to think we're jealous because he got a break before I did. And before you've had your show."

Geo sighed. "Yes, I suppose you're right, and if we don't like the party we can always leave after half an hour."

"Hey, Georgiana! What on earth are *you* doing lingering around here? If you're not careful, you'll be arrested for loitering with intent. Can't have that now, can we?"

At the sound of the man's cultured English voice, Geo swung around and began to laugh. "Hi!" she cried, waving to the old acquaintance hurrying toward them. "And what are *you* doing around here?"

"Probably going to the same party as you. At Iris Ingersoll's flat," he responded, coming to a stop next to them and immediately eyeing M with great curiosity.

Geo nodded, and before she could introduce the man to M, he thrust out his hand. "James Cardigan."

"Marie Marsden," M said swiftly, shaking his hand. "But everyone calls me M, Mr. Cardigan."

"Call me James."

Her cheeky grin appeared as she said, "Into the Valley of Death rode the six hundred . . ."

"Honor the charge they made! Honor the Light Brigade. Noble six hundred," he answered and continued, "I think Tennyson got it right, don't you?"

"Yes, he did. Absolutely." M paused, then asked, "Are you related to that particular Cardigan?"

He shook his head. "No, but I've always been teased about my name. Unavoidable, I suppose."

"Heavens to Betsy, what are the two of you going on about?" Geo asked, looking from one to the other in bewilderment.

James explained, "When M heard my name, she at once associated it with the Earl of Cardigan, who was in command of the light cavalry at the Battle of Balaklava in the Crimean War. In 1854. It was James

Cardigan, a general in the British army, who led the charge of the Light Brigade. M quoted a line from Lord Tennyson's famous poem about the charge, and I responded by quoting another line." He grinned. "You know what we Brits are like, Georgiana, steeped in our history."

"So it seems," Geo responded pithily. Then she hurried on, "And what did you mean when you said I might be arrested for loitering with intent?"

"Intent to solicit men," he told her and winked. "But I'm sure the police don't follow that practice here. So don't worry."

Geo did not respond, but she had the good grace to laugh. She had met James at several parties over the past year. And she liked him. Also, he usually made her laugh.

Seizing the moment, M exclaimed, "We'd better hurry, Geo. It's already nine-thirty, and we really shouldn't be much later, you know. It's awfully rude."

"Right! Let's get a move on then," James said. Situating himself between the two young women, he took one of their hands in each of his and ushered them toward the building where Iris Ingersoll lived.

"How long have you known Iris?" James asked Geo as they drew closer to the building.

"We've never met," Geo said. "But M and I know Dax, the actor she's giving the party for. It was Dax who invited us."

"I see. Well, she gives smashing parties. You're both going to have a terrific time."

"Let's hope so," Geo murmured, quickly looking at M, who remained silent.

❖

A uniformed maid ushered them into the apartment, and the three of them stood for a moment in the long entrance foyer.

M quickly took everything in and understood immediately that it was typical Park Avenue decor: the floor was composed of black-and-white marble squares, the walls covered in a silver wallpaper patterned with large branches of orange blossoms, a faceted crystal chandelier dropped from the ceiling. Traditional decorating, of high quality and *safe.*

James led the way down the hall, followed by Geo; M was at the rear as they edged slowly past the assembled guests.

As they made it through into the large living room, M's eyes swept the gathering.

She spotted Dax immediately. He was standing near the white marble fireplace and looking much better than he had when he left New York. He had obviously been enjoying the California sun and boasted a perfect tan. His blond hair was much blonder, and he had a confident air about him.

Dax saw her with Geo and waved. He instantly excused himself to the man he was talking to and maneuvered his way through the crowd, intent on reaching them.

M propelled Geo toward him and stepped aside so that the two of them could greet each other. A moment later he was kissing M's cheek and enveloping her in a bear hug. Then he held her away from him, stepped back to stare at her.

A wide smile broke across his face. "So this is the new look you told me about? The Audrey Hepburn look—"

"Only half an Audrey," M corrected him, grinning. "It's just the hairstyle, really, and slightly thicker eyebrows."

"So I see, and I approve, definitely and

absolutely approve. Let's find a corner and catch up." His gaze took in James, who was standing with them. Stretching out his hand, he said, "Hi, I'm Dax."

"James Cardigan. Pleased to meet you."

"Come on, let's go over there to the window, it seems quieter." Dax went on, "Come with us, James, the girls and I have no secrets."

They pushed through the crowd; Dax grabbed a glass of champagne from a waiter passing with a tray and handed it to Geo. James did the same, taking two flutes, one for M and the other for himself.

When they had grouped themselves in the window area, Dax lifted his own glass. "Cheers! You two are certainly a welcome sight. I've missed you both."

"So did we, miss you," Geo exclaimed, smiling warmly.

M simply nodded, then said swiftly, "Congratulations again, Dax. I think it's wonderful that you have this part. Miraculous, I'd say, since you got it on the other coast. One never knows what's going to happen in life."

Dax laughed, his eyes sparkling when he said, "You can say that again. It was like . . . well, meant to be, I guess." He then told them the story of how he had met Iris Ingersoll at a dinner party in Bel-Air, had been taken to it by the English actor Colin Burke, a new friend, and how Iris had thought he would be perfect for the play she was producing on Broadway. Second lead, no less.

M was listening, but her eyes were all over the room. Much to her relief, she saw no one who might know her family, and she relaxed. She was also growing aware that James Cardigan was as curious about everyone as she was, perhaps even more so.

It seemed to her that there was nothing and no one he missed. She had taken an instant liking to this rather attractive, wiry Englishman, slight of build and slender, with his sandy-auburn hair and hazel eyes. She decided he was in his forties and worldly wise. He had a sense of humor, and there was a naturalness, an easiness about him. It was obvious that he was successful, if his clothes were anything to go by. Although he was as informally dressed as the other men present, wearing a white, open-necked shirt and gray slacks with a dark sports jacket, she had noticed the excellent quality of the fabric and the cut of the jacket. She wondered what he did. Banker? Broker? Business executive? Real estate tycoon? Instantly she dismissed all these professions and unexpectedly thought, *No, not James. He's a cop.* Where this thought came from, she had no idea, and it so startled her, she took a quick sip of the champagne and stared at him, frowning.

At this exact moment James moved closer to her and said, "Are you in the theater also, M?"

She shook her head. "No, I'm a model. And what do you do, James?"

"I have my own company—"

"What kind of company?" she interrupted swiftly.

"It's a security and investigation company, but on an extremely high level. I can provide someone with a bodyguard or minder, pull up a detailed dossier on almost anybody in the world, find a missing person or missing valuables. You name it, we can do it. We offer a unique service and work with absolute discretion. And this is all within certain boundaries, of course."

"You *are* a cop!" she cried, staring at

him harder, her eyes twinkling. "That's exactly what I thought you were a moment ago."

"Well, well, well, did you really? I wasn't a cop exactly, something similar though. However, I do have a lot of former law enforcement officers working for me."

"Where were you not-exactly-a-cop? In London?"

He leaned into her and said, sotto voce, "I was with MI6, and operating abroad, as MI6 agents always do. Only MI5 agents can work in the U.K."

"Oh, my God! A spy! A proper Walsingham, eh?"

He burst out laughing. "Aren't you the one, M! You're certainly up on your English history."

"Especially when it comes to the men who worked for Elizabeth Tudor. Anyway, why did you get out? Did you get bored?" she probed, riddled with curiosity.

"Not at all, I like danger. But I decided it would be a good idea to make some money, so I completed the assignment I was working on and resigned. Or rather, I retired from the agency. I started my company in London five years ago, then decided I wanted to be in New York, so here I am, running this end of the operation."

Before M could respond, Dax and Geo, who had been talking quietly, came closer and Dax said, "I think I ought to go and find our hostess, to introduce you both. Stay right here. I'll be back in a minute."

Geo watched Dax rush away, turned to M, and said, "I'm thrilled he's going to be in *A Streetcar Named Desire.* I've never seen him so happy, he's like a different person. Don't you think so, M?"

"Yes, I do, but it's natural, isn't it? He's wanted to be an actor for so long, and now he has his chance. Oh, here he is, coming back with Iris."

Dax came to a standstill and said, "Iris, I would like you to meet my friends Georgiana Carlson, called Geo, and Marie Marsden, who's known as M. And this is Iris Ingersoll."

Fashionably dressed, Iris Ingersoll was a tall, imposing woman with silver hair and a rather lovely face; she looked much younger than her sixty-odd years. She shook Geo's hand and then M's. "I'm so glad you could come. Dax has told me how you both encouraged him to pursue his acting career and have been so supportive."

Turning to James, Iris gave him one of her most dazzling smiles. "And how very nice to see you, James, thanks so much for coming. You're such an asset at a party."

"It's my pleasure to be here, Iris. It always is, actually."

Iris inclined her head, then turned to Dax. She continued, "I'd like you to meet a few other people who might be important to you one day. Anyway, the more people you know in this business the better off you'll be."

Dax gave M and Geo a funny grin, raised his eyebrows, and followed Iris.

M laughed, and so did James, who then looked from M to Geo and asked, "How about freshening up your bubbly, ladies?"

"Not for me, thank you," M murmured and put her glass down.

Geo said, "I think I will, and thanks, James." She handed him the empty flute.

Once they were alone, Geo said, "I'm glad I took your advice and wore this black lace outfit, M. The women are quite dressy tonight, don't you think?"

"They are, and they're most definitely New Yorkers," M answered.

"Because they're dressed in black!" Geo grinned, eyeing M and admiring her dress once more. "Aren't you pleased you wore this? You *were* hesitant about it."

"Yes. Anyway, it *is* my favorite frock. But I don't often have the chance to wear it." M looked down at the skirt and smoothed her hand over it, smiling to herself. The dress was made of black taffeta and was cut in the simplest style, with a straight neckline that stretched from shoulder to shoulder. It had short sleeves, a plain front, and a bell-shaped skirt, which dropped just below the knee.

Geo now told her, "You know, M, I thought that skirt was a bit too long at first, but it works well on you, and it does give the dress balance." She threw M a questioning look and asked, "Where did you buy it?"

"I thought I told you my mother bought it for me. I think she found it in a little boutique in London."

"It looks as if it comes from Paris to me," Geo muttered, her head to one side, her eyes thoughtful. "Paris couture, maybe?"

M began to laugh and looked away. And caught her breath.

A man was standing in the doorway of the living room, and he was watching her. Staring hard, in fact. She stared back at him boldly and discovered she couldn't tear her eyes away. He held her gaze. Mesmerized by him, she felt a sudden weakness in her legs, wished she had a chair to sit down in or lean against.

He began to walk toward her, and his blue eyes never left her face. She knew who he was. Suddenly she was nervous and just a little bit afraid. Not of him but of herself and what she might do.

# Ten

He walked toward her.

The crowd had thinned out; the living room was half empty, and she stood waiting, watching *him* now, just as moments ago he had been watching her. Their eyes were locked on each other.

It seemed to M that no one else existed in this room. Her stomach was in knots, and her heart lurched when he finally stood in front of her.

His face was without expression, but his eyes were intense. They were a very deep blue, the color of cornflowers, and echoed the color of the shirt he was wearing. She knew at once that they saw only her.

At last he spoke. "My name is—"

"I know who you are," she cut in.

"And I know who you are," he answered, smiling at her.

Genuinely shocked by this announcement, M took a deep breath to steady herself. "You *do*?"

He reached out, took hold of her hand, and held it in his. "Yes, I do. You're the elusive woman I've been searching for all of my life."

Relief flooded her, and she felt herself relax. Normally she would have thought: Oh, what a good line *that* is, and her cynicism would have risen to the surface and brought a swift dismissive comment to her lips. But she didn't think that at all. Not now. Not with him. She believed him.

He leaned into her. "Though I must admit, I don't know your name."

"It's Marie Marsden, but everyone calls me M."

"Not M and M?" His blue eyes were suddenly twinkling mischievously.

"No." She laughed, staring into his face, a face which had been engraved on her heart since she was a little girl. "Just M is fine."

"How old are you?"

"Old enough," she shot back, an eyebrow lifting. "And that was a rather rude question to ask me."

"Yes, you would think that, especially with your upbringing," he remarked. A small amused smile lurked around his mouth.

Ignoring his comment, she said, "I know how old *you* are. . . . You're thirty-five, which actually makes you twelve years older than I. But numbers don't matter to me."

"Nor to me."

"Actually, I know a great deal about you."

"Not too *much,* I sincerely hope," he exclaimed and threw her a look of mock dismay.

"Enough."

"And why do you know so much about *me*?" he asked, a dark brow lifting quizzically.

"I saw you in *Hamlet* and got an instant crush on you. So I needed to know all about you."

"I'm so glad!" He eyed her appraisingly.

"When I was ten years old," she went on quickly, wanting to clarify; then leaning closer to him, she added, "I was dreamy-eyed about you."

"Are you still?"

"Of course not! I'm a grown woman now."

"What a pity you don't feel the same way."

"I'm older," M answered, smiling at him enigmatically.

"Are you here with anyone?"

"No. Well, that's not strictly true. I came with my friend Geo. She's over there somewhere. Oh, there she is, near the fireplace."

He followed the direction of her gaze and murmured, "The pretty blonde, right?"

M nodded.

He asked, "And why are you both here? Do you know Iris?"

"No, neither of us does. We're friends of Dax, the guest of honor."

"Oh, yes, Iris's new protégé. The story is he's a good actor. Is he?"

"I don't know. Does that matter these days?"

He heard the pithiness in her voice and laughed. "And what about you, Miss M? Are you an actress?"

"No, I'm a model."

He stood away from her slightly, looking at her steadily, not speaking.

She gazed back boldly.

They were suddenly lost for words, lost in each other. The chatter swirled around, people moved past them, and they were unaware of everything except themselves. Her hand was still in his, and he pressed it against his chest.

Finally he broke the silence when he said, very softly, "You're the woman . . . the woman I want to run away with. . . . Let's do that, shall we?"

"Now?"

"Yes, of course now. If not *now,* when? Let's find a desert island and set up camp . . ."

She noticed the amused twinkle in his eyes again, heard the laughter in his mellifluous voice. "But I can't leave Geo stranded here," she protested.

"We can't take her with us!" he exclaimed. Then he warned, "You know two's company, three's none. Let's move out into the foyer, it seems quieter there. . . . We can make our plans."

He led her across the room, and once in the foyer he leaned against a wall and drew her even closer so that her body rested against his.

M began to tremble, suddenly finding it difficult to breathe, to be in such close proximity to this man with whom she had been infatuated as a child. Over the ensuing years he had remained her ideal, and she had always measured other men against him.

He asked gently, "Are you all right?"

"I'm fine." Her voice sounded faint to her.

"I don't want to stay here. Too many folk. I want to be alone with you. Wouldn't you prefer that?"

"Yes," she whispered.

"Then it's a done deal. I'm going to take you somewhere quiet for supper. There's a little place I know."

"All right," M began, then paused. Geo, walking determinedly toward them, was accompanied by James. "Geo's coming this way with James Cardigan."

"I'll head them off, don't worry," he said in a confident tone.

For the last ten minutes or so Geo had been fascinated by the way M had been glued to Laurence Vaughan. She had noticed how the famous movie star had made a beeline for M when he arrived, and they had come together like old friends. Maybe they were exactly that, Geo thought. After all, they were both English. As she and James edged toward the foyer, weaving through the thinning crowd, Geo asked, "Do you know him, James?"

"Only from the silver screen. And by reputation," James answered. "But I've got to admit, I'm a genuine fan. He's one of the greatest actors on the English-speaking stage today. Nobody's played Hamlet better, except perhaps for Christopher Plummer. And he's a handsome son of a gun. No wonder women fall all over him."

Including M, Geo thought, and stepping forward, she smiled. "You two must be old friends, the way you've been chatting non-stop."

"We are indeed . . . very old friends," he answered, offering Geo his most engaging smile.

M jumped in swiftly and said, "Geo, James, I'd like you to meet Laurence Vaughan."

After the three of them shook hands, Larry went on in a firm voice, "I'm trying to persuade M to come to supper with me, but she's worried about leaving you to fend for yourself, Geo."

"Oh, please don't concern yourself about that, M," James answered quickly. "I'll fend for her anytime. Is that all right with you, Geo?"

"Of course it is, James."

They had taken a cab to the restaurant in the Eighties just off Lexington. In the cab he had ached to take her in his arms, hold her close, kiss her passionately. He had managed to resist this impulse, held her hand instead, just as he had been doing for the previous hour at Iris Ingersoll's apartment.

Larry had not wished to frighten her off, not that he thought she was the kind of young woman who would be easily frightened. To him she seemed self-confident, more intrepid than most. Yes, that was it— there was a *fearlessness* about her that intrigued and appealed to him.

Now, sitting opposite her at a corner table in Le Refuge, a favorite hideaway of his, Larry smiled inwardly, thinking of their earlier banter. She could certainly think on her feet, was fast on the draw, rather bold, and just a little bit cheeky. He especially liked *that* about her; it made her unlike the women he knew.

It suddenly struck him how lucky he had been to meet her tonight. He almost hadn't gone to Iris's party, had fought the idea of it all day, feeling depleted and depressed. But at the last moment he had realized he owed it to Iris to show up. And so he had shaved, showered, dressed, and gone over there, and spotted M the moment he walked in.

He had moved toward her at once, drawn to her in the most compelling way; the feeling was so intense it startled him, and he realized he had not experienced anything like it before.

Funny thing, attraction. It was always the powerful physical *pull* initially, being entranced by the way someone looked . . . the curve of a brow, the line of a cheek, the set of the mouth, the expression in the eyes, the color of the hair, the overall set of the jib . . . that's what captivated the heart.

Unfortunately, character did not always live up to great physical beauty, and a woman without character soon palled on him. He adored beautiful women; on the other hand, beauty had never been enough, did not wholly satisfy him, not in the long run. Ultimately it was . . . *boring.* That's why he had always moved on, had never married any of the women in his life.

"You're staring at me, Larry," M said, looking across the table at him, putting down the menu. He had the oddest look on his face.

His thoughts interrupted, he answered swiftly, "I'm sorry, love. I was just thinking how lucky I am you were there tonight, and that *I* found you."

"Do you really mean that?" she asked, studying him with great interest, her head to one side.

"Certainly. I wouldn't say it if I didn't mean it. You feel the same way, don't you?"

She merely nodded, her gaze focused on him. His eyes were a very deep blue in the soft light of the bistro, and most beguiling. Just as he himself was beguiling. But then he had always been that, hadn't he? Even when she was a child, she had been spellbound when she saw him on a stage or in a movie.

"I realize we haven't actually *met* before

tonight," Larry now said, "but I have this extraordinary feeling I *do* know you, M. You seem so very familiar to me."

"Perhaps that's because I'm half an Audrey."

"What on earth does that mean?" He sounded puzzled.

"Some people think I have a look of Audrey Hepburn. But I'm only half like her."

His amused smile of earlier flickered again. "Come to think of it, there is a resemblance. But it's not *that*. . . . I have a sense of *knowing you*."

"Perhaps we met in another life," she suggested, her voice teasing.

"Maybe we did." He glanced away, looking off into the distance, then focused on her again, frowning.

"Honestly, we haven't met before, Larry," she murmured.

"If we had, you wouldn't have escaped, I can assure you of that."

M shook her head, laughter mingled with happiness in her large dark eyes. "That's a rash thing to say, isn't it?"

"What do you mean?"

"I might take you seriously." She responded so quietly she was hardly audible.

"I hope you will." Larry gave her a thoughtful look, then reached for her hand resting on the table, held it in his. "I hope this is the beginning . . . of something special, M, I really mean that. I've said quite a few things to you tonight, things which may have sounded odd to you, but I promise I've never said them to any other woman. You have to trust me on that."

Continuing to hold his hand tightly in hers, she said in the same low voice, "I do trust you, and not just about the things you've said to me." A faint smile touched her mouth, and she added, "I'd trust you with my life, Laurence Vaughan, and I mean what I say."

"I'll always keep you safe and sound. *Promise.*"

Leaning across the table, M studied him for a moment; she knew he meant it. In a confiding tone she told him, "When I was ten I used to dream about you, Larry. Every night."

"Do you still?" he asked.

"No, of course not! That was long ago, when you were my dashing Hamlet. Oh, I had such a crush on you, I couldn't see straight."

"And what kinds of dreams did you have

about me?" he asked, enjoying this light-hearted mood, thinking how refreshing she was.

"Oh, you know, little-girl-with-a-crush dreams . . . *all mushy.*"

"Do you think I might one day infiltrate the big grown-up girl's dreams?"

"You never know," she answered lightly. "I hope so."

"And you can bet that I hope so, too."

Finally releasing her hand, Larry sat back and announced, "I have a feeling that everyone you meet thinks you're special."

"Oh, I don't know about that . . ." She allowed her voice to drift off, took a sip of wine, eventually muttered, "I'm just an ordinary sort of girl."

"Like hell you are!" Larry picked up the menu. "I think we ought to order, don't you? Do you know what you want, M?"

"Yes. I was thinking of having grilled sole."

"Fish, eh? You grew up on an island?"

"Yep. In the North Sea. Just like you did," she retorted and winked.

He inclined his head, amused, and motioned for the waiter, ordered grilled sole for two and a bottle of Montrachet. Once the waiter had hurried off, Larry changed the mood slightly when he asked, "How long have you been living in New York?"

"A few months. I've tried to find modeling work, but without much luck. It was Geo who arranged for me to meet the fashion photographer Frank Farantino. That worked out rather well. We did a shoot. He's the one who decided I looked like Audrey Hepburn and said it should be played up. His stylists did a makeover on me."

"You hardly needed that! Anyway, *did* he help you?"

"Frankie has gone to Morocco on a magazine fashion shoot, but once he's back he's going to launch my career," M explained.

Larry leaned back in the chair, let her continue talking. He was listening attentively, found her voice pleasant, soothing. And he was genuinely enjoying being with her. This young woman was having quite an effect on him. As the evening progressed, he realized that being with her lifted his spirits, gave him genuine happiness, a feeling that had long been absent in his life. He wondered how to keep her with him . . . permanently.

# Eleven

Laurence Vaughan stood staring out of a window in the library of his father's apartment on Beekman Place. He loved this view of the East River and Long Island City beyond, especially after dark, and tonight was no exception.

It was two o'clock in the morning, but some of the colorful lights of the city were still brightly reflected on the rippling surface of the river. It flowed on toward the Atlantic under a high-flung sky. An ink-black sky, littered with tiny pinpoints of light. A beautiful, romantic, starry night . . .

Larry sighed, thinking of the unique and

provocative young woman he had met earlier. It sometimes happened like that— meeting a special person when one least expected it. She was captivating in her dark beauty, and she *was* beautiful; there was certainly no need for her to emphasize her resemblance to a dead actress. He couldn't help wondering why the photographer had considered this so important. M was a knockout as herself; she had no need to be an imitation of someone else.

Larry ran the evening through his head, thinking of the fun it had been, so light-hearted at times. It had also been extremely emotional for him. There was no question in his mind that he had been swept away by her. Not ever in his entire and somewhat adventurous life had he been so knocked for a loop by a woman.

Over the years, many women had oc-cupied his time and his life, but none of them had captured him quite like she had. Even now, he felt taken aback at his ex-traordinary reaction to her.

*Engulfed,* he thought, that's what it is. I've been engulfed by her. And excited by her . . . by the way she makes me feel.

Larry had wanted to bring M with him to

this apartment after dinner, reluctant to let her out of his sight. Then, unexpectedly, he had changed his mind. This had occurred when they were outside Le Refuge. Once they were standing in the street facing each other, eyeball to eyeball, he had given in to the urgent need he had to hold her in his arms. As he had reached for her, she had reached for him, and they had drawn together, kissing passionately, clinging to each other. M had responded to him ardently, as aroused as he was and seemingly willing to follow his lead.

When they had finally drawn apart, a little stunned and reeling, he had been taken by surprise by the look in her eyes. It was one of undisguised apprehension. He had recoiled slightly, not only baffled but also worried. It struck him then that she was not very experienced when it came to men, even though she appeared to be a genuine sophisticate. And so, because he had serious intentions, he had taken her home instead of into his bed, dropping her off at the brownstone on West Twenty-second Street.

Detecting a sudden hint of disappointment in her as they had ridden downtown in the cab, he had put his arms around her and pulled her close to him. "Will you spend tomorrow with me?" he had asked, and she had nodded, giving him the benefit of a very big smile. "It's already tomorrow," she had murmured. "If you're referring to Sunday, that is. It's nearly one o'clock." They had both laughed, and he had instantly known that whatever had troubled her outside the restaurant, it had vanished.

And so she would come here later. At noon, he had told her. They would have brunch and perhaps go to a movie, and he would let things take their natural course. He did not want to rush her, and he had all the time in the world to court her properly.

Turning away from the window, Larry moved across the library. As he did, his eye fell on the photograph of his mother in a silver frame, sitting on a walnut chest amongst other family photographs. He stood staring at it, thinking what a beautiful woman she was, with her mass of blond hair and light eyes.

*Pandora Gallen.* One of England's greatest actresses but still his mother, and mother to his many siblings, and wife to his father.

As he often did, Larry heard her light, musical voice echoing in his head, explaining something of importance to her. "You can know a person for forty years and never know them. Yet you can also meet someone and know them in an instant. It's all about recognition, you see. Recognizing that you're the same blood type. Or, if you prefer, from the same tribe." She had smiled at him and given him a very knowing look. And he had instantly understood that at some time in her life his mother had met someone whom she had recognized immediately and wanted to be with.

As he had just done. He had told M she seemed so familiar to him he was positive they had met before. She had insisted they hadn't, and yet he *had* recognized her. She and I are very alike, he suddenly thought. We're the same breed. There was no need for her to tell him anything about herself; he already knew everything there was to know just by having spent an evening with her. She was from an upper-class family, well spoken, highly educated, and cultivated. Probably one of a brood, he decided, more than likely the youngest, both picked on and adored. It struck him that she had crossed the Pond to make it on her own steam, without the help of family.

He smiled to himself, liking this idea. Plucky, he thought, she's plucky and courageous . . . and just possibly a carbon copy of me.

❀

Larry found it hard to sleep. He tossed and turned for two hours; finally, in desperation, he got up. He went to the kitchen, poured himself a glass of milk, and then sauntered into the library. This was a comfortable, charming room, and the one he used the most.

Turning on a lamp, settling in one of the big armchairs, he took a few swallows of the milk and put the glass down on the table next to the chair. His father's chair. No, it wasn't his father's chair any longer. *It was his.* He had bought this apartment and its contents several months ago, and it was his home now, his only home, and the first he had ever owned.

"We really wanted to give you the apartment," his mother had told him a few weeks ago when she was in New York to pack up her belongings as well as his father's clothes and objects of importance.

"But we couldn't, because of the others. They would have kicked up a fuss; that's why we decided to offer it to all of you at a bargain price."

*All of us,* he thought, grimacing.

He was one of six; he had three older brothers and two older sisters. All of them were contentious, competitive, contradictory, and complex. They had fought like hell when they were growing up in the big old house in Hampstead, and sometimes they still did, but they loved one another nonetheless. Or at least some of them did; others gave lip service to that idea. He *did* love his brother Horatio and his sister Portia, but Miranda was too aloof and remote for him, by far the most snobbish woman he had ever met. His brother Edward had made his life miserable when they were kids, but now there was a truce between them. Well, sort of. As far as his brother Thomas was concerned, Larry respected and admired him, the firstborn of the Vaughan tribe, but they had never been close. The age difference had probably been a stumbling block.

None of his siblings had wanted to buy the apartment, mainly because they did not want to live in New York. Edward commuted between Los Angeles and London; Thomas had a manor house in Gloucestershire and a pied-à-terre in London; and Horatio was a Londoner born and bred, and would never dream of living anywhere else on earth. Portia felt the same, while Miranda was a country bumpkin in rural Kent when she wasn't working on set designs up in town. She owned a small studio near Eaton Square, where she stayed when she was working on a play, but mostly she preferred to muck about in the country.

There were no two ways about it; his father *had* sold him the apartment at a bargain price: exactly what he himself had paid for it twenty years ago. If it had gone on the market, the price would have been four times as much, if not more. But his father hadn't been trying to make money, he had simply wanted to be rid of the apartment he no longer used, because he was rarely on Broadway these days. Larry had believed his mother when she confided that they genuinely wanted to give him the apartment but had been wary of his siblings, their older children.

Quite right, too, he thought, shifting his

weight in the chair. The buggers would have made a hell of a stink if Dad had done that. *Jealousy.* He'd always been a target of their insane jealousy because he was the youngest; they considered him the most favored and spoiled.

"You're also the best-looking of the bunch, and the most talented," his mother had frequently reminded him, but he did not agree, felt she was endeavoring to make him feel better. And he had to give his siblings credit where it was due. They were all brilliant in their own ways, and good-looking to boot. Actors all, except for Miranda.

"The Glorious Vaughans" they had been dubbed by the press, who deemed them the first theatrical family in the land, theatrical royalty. Six brothers and sisters who won all the prizes, took all the bows on both sides of the Atlantic.

Larry saw Edward in his mind. Tall, slender, blond, and green-eyed. He was an elegant and charming man today, with a mind like a whiplash and a tongue to match, but he'd been a tantrum-throwing thug as a child. How cruel Edward had been when he was little. . . . Closing his eyes, Larry drifted with his thoughts, caught up in a memory from long ago. . . .

Laurence stood his ground, his feet firmly planted on the gravel driveway, the cheap child's sword in his right hand, his left hand on his hip. He was seven years old, and proud of his stance. His father had shown him exactly how to stand and taught him to fence properly, and so he knew he was the best.

His twelve-year-old brother, Edward, unexpectedly jumped forward, brandishing his own sword and shouting, "I'm coming in for the kill, you knave!" But Edward merely leapt around, behaving like a wild circus dog and looking silly.

Thrust and parry, thrust and parry, Larry reminded himself, picturing his father's performance as Caesar in one of his films. Taking a deep breath, he moved forward. Tin met tin in a clash of toy swords, and he immediately jumped back, hastily retreating from Edward, who was well known to be dangerous and never played by the rules.

His brother sprang closer to Larry, and suddenly he slashed out, catching Larry on his left arm. "You've cut me, Edward!" Larry cried. Much to his horror, he saw blood spurting through the cotton fabric of the fake chain-mail tunic. "You're not supposed to do that," he shrieked, backing away, dropping the sword he was holding, bringing his right hand to his arm, endeavoring to stanch the flowing blood.

"Coward! Coward!" Edward shouted, waving his sword over his head and advancing on Larry, crazily jumping from side to side and laughing wildly. "I will defeat you now, you alien dog! Not one of *us.* Not one of *us.* Changeling! Darkling! You're not one of *us.*"

Growing frightened of his brother, Larry picked up his sword, then backed away and tripped, fell down on the gravel, his sword skittering across the drive. Catching his breath, he tried to push himself to his feet.

Enjoying his triumph over the younger boy, Edward knelt down next to Larry and began to pummel him on his shoulders, chest, and face. "No mercy for the enemy. Kill the enemy!" Edward snarled, a spiteful gleam in his pale eyes.

Wrapping his arms around his head,

Larry endeavored to protect his face while still pressing one hand on the sleeve of his blood-soaked cotton tunic. He tried to get up, but Edward was much stronger than he was and held him down, gloating.

The clatter of high heels running down the front steps sent relief rushing through Larry. Their mother's voice screamed, "Get off him, Edward! Get off him at once! You're really in for it, my lad." She was suddenly looming over Edward, furious, and grabbing him by his collar, she yanked him to his feet, shouting into his gaping face, "I'll have your guts for garters, you little bugger!"

Literally throwing Edward to one side and looking totally undisturbed as he fell hard on the ground, his mother crouched next to Larry. She was appalled by the amount of blood covering his tunic. Larry's face was bruised and bloody where his brother had hit him.

"My God! I can't believe this!" Pandora exclaimed, and she put her arms under her youngest child and lifted him closer, held him for a moment against herself, hurting for him. She said, "Do you think you can get up, darling?"

He nodded.

Pandora stood, and bending over Larry, she helped him to get to his feet. Slowly they walked across the drive and up the front steps, and Pandora murmured to him lovingly as they stepped inside the house.

"Mother," Edward said from the driveway.

Pandora glanced over her shoulder. Her face was white with shock, her anger unabated. "What?"

"I didn't mean to hurt—"

"Like hell you didn't!" Pandora raged. "You're getting to be a menace. I've just about had it with you."

"But, Mother—"

"Shut up. And stay out of my way. I don't want to see your face. And I will certainly deal with you later. It would be wise of you to prepare yourself for harsh punishment."

Edward gaped at her, his face now as white as hers. He was terrified of his mother when she was angry. None of them knew what she might do when she was in the grip of a fury such as this.

Turning away from him, Pandora led Larry into the hall, hurrying him down to the kitchen. "Molly was a nurse, you know, before she became our housekeeper. She'll know exactly what to do."

"I'm all right, Mummy," Larry whispered and stumbled bravely on. . . .

Moving about restlessly as he slept in the chair, Larry swept out an arm and knocked the glass of milk off the side table. The crash awakened him. He sat up blinking, for a moment thinking it was already morning. And then, as he glanced around, he realized it was still the middle of the night. Rising, he returned to his bedroom and got into bed, shaking his head. How strange it was that such a lot of his childhood memories remained in his head and were so easily recalled. And lately remembering them had become a curious pattern.

Within minutes he was asleep, Edward's cruelty to him as a child forgotten.

# Twelve

Geo looked up as M appeared in the doorway of her studio and smiled. "Well, there you are! Good morning, Miss M. How're you today?"

"Fine, thanks, Geo, and you look pretty good yourself."

Geo inclined her head, then said, "Your actor seemed very taken with you last night. Are you going to see him again?" She grinned. "That's a stupid question, isn't it? I'm sure you are."

"I'm having lunch with him today," M answered, leaning casually against the door frame. She took a sip from the mug of tea she was holding and gave Geo a smile that filled her face with sudden radiance. "And then we're going to the movies."

"I thought he was going to swallow you whole last night," Geo remarked with a grin, her eyes dancing. "Gobble you up!"

"Like the boa constrictor and the Little Prince?" M raised a brow, laughing.

Geo also laughed, delighted by this response, and exclaimed, "I just loved that book when I was little, didn't you?"

"Of course, it was my real favorite, I think, and everyone who reads it loves it, adults as well as children. It's enchanting."

Geo, intrigued by Larry and M after having so closely observed them together, now asked with great eagerness, "So, go on then, tell me everything that happened. *Everything.*"

"There's not much to tell," M responded. "We went to dinner at a little unassuming bistro Larry likes, and then he took me home. Truly, nothing happened . . . if you mean what I think you mean."

"To his home? Is that where you went?"

"No, don't be silly! He brought me here,

to this house, to *your house.* I was back not long after one o'clock, and you were still out, weren't you?"

"I was, with James Cardigan. We had something from the buffet at Iris's, but then the apartment seemed to fill up with all sorts of people. Actors, actresses, and some other rather strange types, James thought, and so did I. Anyway, we decided to leave because it became so crowded. James didn't want the evening to end, so he took me to a bar he knows in the MePa, and we stayed there for quite a while, having drinks and talking into the wee hours. I got to know him better . . . he's really charming . . ."

"Is he married?" M wondered out loud, giving Geo a questioning look.

"He's never been married. Well, so he said." She put down her paintbrush and sighed. Rising, she walked over to the sofa near the window, lowered herself onto it, sighed again, and looked across at M, still loitering in the doorway.

"What is it, Geo?" M was aware of the long, contemplative stare her friend was giving her.

"Do you have a few minutes to spare? I want to tell you something."

"Of course. *What is it?*" M asked again, joining Geo on the sofa, puzzled by her friend's sudden change in mood.

"There's a problem I'd like to discuss with you," Geo murmured.

Staring at her intently, M said, "You look very serious all of a sudden. Is there something the matter?"

Geo did not answer for a few moments, and when she did she spoke slowly, her voice low. "I like James . . . like him a lot, and I must admit I'd forgotten how nice he is. Anyway, the point is this, I'd like to see him again. *Want* to very much. I believe I made a big mistake with him last night, though. In fact, I'm sure I did."

"What do you mean?" M leaned closer. "It can't have been all that bad, surely."

"Look, I had a lot to drink at the party, and later. More than usual, and I got far too garrulous. I told him too much about myself, and it might have put him off."

M was taken aback by this statement. Geo was not a particularly talkative person, nor was she very confiding. For a split second M was silent; then she asked, "What on earth could *you* tell him about yourself that would turn him off?" Her puzzlement was apparent. When Geo did not answer, she asked, "You haven't murdered somebody, have you?"

M said this in such a droll manner, Geo couldn't help laughing. "No, I haven't. But I have been married twice, and stupidly I told him this, and I think he was really shocked."

"I doubt that! He's not the shockable type, if I know my Englishmen. He runs that security and investigation company, so I'm positive he doesn't shock easily. Besides which, I think he might well have been a cop or something like that. He would certainly have been in some sort of law enforcement agency before in order to start that kind of company."

"I think he might have been a spy. . . . I vaguely remember someone telling me that ages ago. Still, he did look shocked, I promise you."

It struck M that Geo might have simply misunderstood James's reaction, and she said this to her friend, adding, "I'm sure it was only *surprise*. You don't look old enough to have been married *twice*."

"I'm twenty-eight, didn't I tell you that?" Geo asked and sat back on the sofa, closing her eyes for a moment and looking pained.

"Are you all right?" M asked swiftly.

"Yes, I'm okay." Opening her eyes, Geo sat up straighter and continued, "I can't imagine why I told him. I think it was because he reminded me of my first husband, Andy, who had that same wiry look as James. Oh, God, there's not much I can do about it. I told him, and that's that. Let's face it, I've probably blown it."

"I'm sure it's not a problem," M ventured and frowned as Geo closed her eyes once again, leaning back against the sofa. Her face was pale, and she trembled slightly.

After a moment, M took hold of her hand. "What is it, Georgiana? You can talk to me about private things if you want to. You know I'd never break a confidence."

Opening her eyes, Geo said, "I know you wouldn't. It's just that . . . well, I usually get a terrible ache inside when I think of the way Andy died. I was heartbroken. I almost died myself when he had that fatal accident, and our baby certainly died. . . . I had a miscarriage within days of Andy's fall."

"Oh, darling, I'm so terribly sorry, how very, very tragic. And your grief must have been enormous . . ." M's voice trailed off; she was at a loss for words. Anyway, weren't words meaningless in such a situation? Although her mother constantly said that loving words *did* help a person to cope with sorrow and grief, with most things, in fact.

"I don't think I'm overstating when I say it was overwhelming," Geo murmured. "It did take me a long time to recover. I was only eighteen . . . when Andy fell . . . and my life fell apart."

Clearing her throat, M hesitated before quietly saying, "Perhaps it would help if you told me about it, as you told James last night."

"Andy was a construction worker here in Manhattan," Geo began, "like his father and two brothers. He loved it, loved being up there, 'hitting the sky' he used to call it. Still, it was frightening at times to most of the guys. In fact, Andy often said that no one knows what fear really is unless they've dangled high in the sky with nothing between them and the ground but a narrow edge of metal and empty air. There's another thing; the men worry about getting 'the freeze.' That usually occurs when a guy has seen one of his buddies fall, which happened to Andy one day. He saw a friend slip and was never the same again.

The freeze took hold of him. Naturally, he understood that he couldn't keep going indefinitely, and he became apprehensive about hitting the sky because he might fall off a girder. If they're going to keep their jobs, the guys do have to keep on going *up,* because the building keeps going up and up and up. I begged Andy to quit, and he promised he would as soon as they reached the next floor of the skyscraper. Unfortunately, he never made it to that floor. . . . He slipped off a girder, fell and broke his neck, smashed his head on the pavement. . . . At least he died instantly."

Geo stopped speaking, sat very still, and M held her hand for a long time, not knowing how else to comfort her.

At last Geo spoke once more. "I eventually pulled myself together and kept going as best as I could. After Andy's awful accident, my mother died. She'd had a long fight with cancer, had been in pain for years. In one way it was a blessing for her, she was no longer suffering. I had gone to live with her after Andy's death and inherited this house from her, where I've been living ever since."

"I'm so sorry about Andy and the baby,

and your mother. How you coped I'll never know," M murmured, her heart going out to Georgiana.

Geo nodded. "I suppose I coped by getting married again. When I was twenty-two, and it lasted a big two months. One day Ken packed his bags and left, without even saying good-bye. We eventually got a divorce, thank God." Now Geo glanced at M and finished, in a sad, low voice, "I'm known as a person who never talks much about the past, but I certainly talked last night . . . to a man I liked, and in a way I never spoke to Dax. You go and figure that one. And I'll never hear from James again."

"I understand what you're saying, but I don't believe James Cardigan was shocked, or put off. How could he have been? And if he's the man I think he is, then I'm sure he felt tremendous sympathy for you. I certainly do."

"You're a woman, you would be sympathetic. Men sometimes aren't at all empathetic, certainly about the kinds of things I've just told you . . . death, illness, and all that. It's too much for them to handle."

"Oh, I do think you're wrong! There are any number of men who are sympathetic, compassionate, and very caring. At least I know a few."

"Introduce me to one. I'd like to meet a sympathetic man," Geo muttered.

"Actually, I believe you were with one last night. Give James a chance. I think he's worth it. And you know what? I bet you he calls today."

"We'll see, won't we?" Geo answered, but she did not sound very convinced.

Later, in her room, as she got ready to go out, M discovered that her mind remained focused on Georgiana. She had been touched and moved by the conversation they had just had, their most intimate to date. And now she realized yet again how little they knew about each other really. Yet they had become closer in the last few weeks, had quickly discovered they liked the same things: going to the theater and the movies, reading good books, especially biographies, listening to their favorite music. And art. That was the one great link between them, their love of beautiful paintings. And there was something else. Geo was endeavoring to make it on her own without cashing in on her mother's name.

A week ago, Geo had confided that her mother had been Constance Redonzo, a well-known artist in the seventies, eighties, and into the nineties. M was familiar with her work and knew that she was from the school of Marie Laurencin and Mary Cassatt, specializing in paintings of children and women in the Impressionist style. Geo had explained that soon after her mother's death, she and her sister began to understand there was a very viable market for their mother's work. Many of her fans, reading of her death, had been in touch with the gallery which represented her, suddenly wanting to buy paintings. "Joanne and I had an unexpected but wonderful windfall. We made a lot of money, and that's why I am able to paint in peace. For now," Geo had explained.

Later, Geo had shown M some of her mother's paintings, and M had been impressed, by one in particular, longing to buy it on behalf of her father. But she did not dare. Such a move would expose her. She had too much to hide, she knew that, and then she wondered if James was aware of who she was. After all, he was in the business of . . . information. She doubted it, though.

And what about Laurence Vaughan? Did he suspect she was not who she said she was? Not at all, she was positive of that. Although she did have to admit that he was patently aware she came from a certain echelon of English society. Their backgrounds were almost identical in so many ways, and he couldn't have failed to notice the telltale signs.

As she buttoned the white cotton shirt and tucked it into her navy blue trousers, M contemplated the combination of Geo and James. It seemed to her that they fit well together. She hoped he would call this morning because that would make Geo exceedingly happy.

Turning away from the mirror, M pulled on a three-quarter-length navy blue knitted coat, added her pearl earrings, snatched up a battered red Hermès Kelly, slung it over her arm, and left her room. She ran downstairs, strode down the corridor and waved to Geo, wished her well, and swiftly exited the house. She hailed a cab, excited and intent on her purpose—being with Larry.

# Thirteen

Laurence Vaughan's face was wreathed in smiles as he opened the door, greeted M, and added, "I just knew you'd be punctual, and thank God you are! I couldn't wait to see you."

She smiled back at him. "I know what you mean . . . and good morning, Larry."

Taking hold of her hand, he brought her into the front hall swiftly, drew her into his arms, and closed the door with his foot, all of these movements executed with a smooth fluidity.

He held her close, kissing her on the cheek, taking in the perfume of her—lilies of the valley, he decided—and the fresh, lemony tang of her newly washed hair. She was wearing it loose today, and it fell around her face like a sleek black veil.

A crooked smile lurked at the edges of his mouth. "You are beautiful, M, simply perfect." His eyes narrowed slightly, held a mischievous glint as he finished. "And just imagine, you're not even half an Audrey today. You're just M, and that's good enough for me."

"I'm glad you like *me*."

"You bet I do." Taking hold of her arm, he led her into the living room, walking her through to the library. "This is my favorite room," he explained and immediately took her over to the bay window. "Just look at this view, isn't it great?"

"It's fantastic. I feel as if I'm on a ship," M responded, looking up at him. She was wearing flat shoes today, which made her a couple of inches shorter than Larry, who was six feet tall. She was five-eight in her stocking feet. We're a perfect fit, she thought, most probably in every way. I hope we are.

"You really ought to see the view at night, then you'll realize how spectacular it

actually is," Larry told her. "How about staying for dinner?"

M couldn't help laughing. "We haven't
even had lunch yet. But yes, you're right, I
shouldn't miss this view at night. So of
course I'll stay for dinner. I'd love to."

"That's a big relief." He grinned at her. "I
thought you'd be fleeing after lunch, leaving me alone again."

"Aren't we going to the movies?"

"We'll do whatever you want. In the
meantime, how about a Bloody Mary?"

"Thank you, yes, that'd be nice."

"Coming up in three shakes of a lamb's
tail." He strode across the floor to a chest
which held a silver tray filled with bottles of
liquor, a jug of tomato juice, and various
other important ingredients for drinks.

She smiled to herself, remembering a
nanny she'd once had who constantly used
that old and rather curious phrase: three
shakes of a lamb's tail.

Larry busied himself with the drinks,
and M turned to look at the amazing collection of silver-framed photographs lined
up on another chest, positioned to one
side of the sofa.

Taking pride of place was an eight-by-ten of Larry's father when he had been a much younger man. How devastatingly handsome Nicholas Vaughan was, truly glorious-looking in this particular picture by Patrick Lichfield. It hit her then. Larry, as he was today at thirty-five, was the spitting image of his father in this photograph. Except for the hair. Larry's was as dark as a raven's, like hers, while his father's was a light brownish blond, almost nondescript. It's the eyes, she thought, they're exactly the same blue, the color of cornflowers, and they're powerful, mesmerizing. And both men have the same classical features, the same straight nose.

Her eyes moved on to the picture of Larry's father and mother, standing together on a stage dressed in the costumes they wore as Antony and Cleopatra. Next to this was a portrait of Pandora Gallen alone, so blond, so beautiful, Larry's exceptional mother, a talent beyond belief. And then came a collection of smaller photographs of Larry with his various siblings. My God, they were a good-looking bunch. Just like her lot were.

"Sorry the drinks took so long," Larry

said, walking across the room with two glasses. Handing one to her, he lifted his Bloody Mary. "Cheers!" he said.

"Cheers, and thanks." M took a sip and exclaimed, "Wow, oh wow, that's very strong! But great."

Larry glanced at the photographs arranged on the chest and then at her, a brow raised quizzically. "Since you know so much about me, and you did claim that, you don't need me to explain who all of these disreputable ruffians are."

"You don't have to do that, no, I can reel off their names to *you*. But I would like to know *about* them. I'm very curious about your siblings."

"Take your pick, and I'll give you the lowdown."

"This is Horatio, isn't it?" She pointed a finger at one of the men in the photograph.

"Yep. And my favorite brother. He's a good guy, a good friend, always on my side, as I'm on his. You'll like him a lot."

"Named for Hamlet's friend Horatio, correct?"

"Absolutely."

"And Portia is named for another favorite Shakespearean character of mine . . . straight out of *The Merchant of Venice.*"

"On the nose, babe. And Portia's a friendly sort. No agenda."

"And you like her, I think, more than *like,* actually. You *love* her."

"How did you guess?"

"It's the expression on your face, Larry. Your eyes are warmer, and you smiled when I mentioned her name, and your face is relaxed."

"My favorite sister. I certainly don't like the other one, Miranda. A pain in the ass, that one. Don't worry, you won't have to meet her."

M burst out laughing. "And Thomas? Tell me about *him.*"

"We're not so close. He is the eldest, but you're aware of that, if I know you. He's serious, a little bit dull but hugely talented, and we're friends, respectful of each other. But no, we're not close."

"And that leaves us with Edward."

"Unfortunately."

"Don't you like him?"

"He bloody well beat me up when we were kids, so I'm always wary of our crafty

Edward, but we're pals, at least to some extent, these days. And he's aimed to please me for years. We have a sort of truce, I guess you'd call it. Edward's okay, in small doses. But questionable."

"He's probably suffering from terrible guilt for smacking you around when you were little, don't you think?"

"Possibly. One never knows with Edward. Cagey bugger, that he is, and a past master of the art of dissimulation." He took a swallow of the Bloody Mary. "And he can be a real bastard with women."

M said, "I love this photograph of your mother and father as Antony and Cleopatra. They became legends after that play, didn't they?"

A huge smile lit up his face, and he nodded enthusiastically. "They sure as hell did! The greatest stars of the English theater, that was them in their heyday. And it's a tough part, Cleopatra. Most actresses are scared to touch it; you need quite a range to play Cleo. My mother did it to perfection. It's Shakespeare's greatest play, at least in my opinion, and still very modern: politicians, politics, tragedies, failures, celebrities biting the dust."

"Fallen heroes all," M announced.

He gave her a swift look and frowned. "Someone else once said those exact words to me, but I can't remember who."

A feeling of sick dismay swept over her, and she chided herself, aware that this was one of her brother's standard comments about the play. Changing the subject swiftly, she said, "I'm getting hungry, Larry. Why don't we go to the kitchen and make lunch?"

"Brilliant," he replied, walking back to the chest and the jug of tomato juice and vodka. "I'll make us another, shall I? To help us through the cooking."

"Why not?" she said and went to join him, relieved she'd distracted him.

❀

"I think I'd better make lunch," M announced after five minutes of moving around Larry, bumping into him as he skirted her. "It's a great kitchen, but it's not big enough for two cooks. Anyway, too many cooks spoil the broth, so my mother says."

"But I really want to do it," Larry shot back, frowning at her. "After all, I invited you *here,* not to a restaurant, and I am your host, you know."

M swallowed her amusement at his

seriousness about this and exclaimed, "No, no, no, it's better if I do the cooking. And do be careful, don't drop those eggs."

He was now leaning toward a counter-top, and the egg carton was precariously balanced in one of his hands.

Hurrying across the floor, she took the eggs from him, placed them on the counter, then untied the white chef's apron he was wearing over his black cashmere sweater and black jeans. "I shall put this on instead of you, and that means *I'm* now in charge."

He grinned. "Yes, General, as you say, General." He saluted her, grabbed her arm, pulled her to him, and gave her a quick kiss on the cheek. His eyes were appraising when he asked teasingly, "Have I fallen for a bossy Margaret Thatcher?"

"I'm afraid you have." She eyed him flirtatiously, laughter making her black eyes sparkle. "It's easier if only one person cooks. Now go and sit at the table," she ordered. "We can chat as I cook. What kind of eggs would you prefer?"

"Poached, fried, scrambled, I don't care. There's streaky bacon in the fridge, and Canadian bacon as well. The tomatoes are over there in that bowl. We could have a real fry-up, if you'd like that."

"I do, and we could, but hey, Larry, what about bacon butties? Don't you just love them?"

"I do indeed, they're my favorite, and I always make a beeline for them on an early-morning shoot. The film caterers usually serve them for breakfast. And what about fried egg sandwiches as well?" He grinned at her, enjoying being with her; she was a good sport, and he liked that about her. He couldn't stand pretentious women who put on airs and graces.

"It will be a fantastic repast," she confided, sounding sure of herself, and began to move around the kitchen, getting organized, looking across at Larry, listening to him when he told her where to find the things she needed. She loved hearing that marvelous voice of his, so rich and full of cadences, an actor's voice.

For his part, Larry was thinking that she was probably one of the more adorable women he had met in his life. This morning she looked young and delectable, wearing very little makeup, her hair now pulled back in a ponytail. Yes, she did have a look of Audrey, that was true, but she was also herself and highly individualistic. It suddenly struck him there was something rather exotic about her looks, and he was certain she was photogenic. It was the high cheekbones, of course, the broad brow and hollow cheeks, the perfectly arched eyebrows. Yes, she probably photographed like a dream; no wonder that photographer had been entranced.

He sat back, scrutinizing her as she moved around, energetic, lithe, and so graceful. She paused for a moment to roll up the sleeves of her white cotton shirt, and it occurred to him that she had an elegance unusual in somebody so young. This led him to a question: Was she too young for him? He answered immediately with a resounding *no*. He was twelve years older than she, as she had pointed out, but then she had also said that numbers didn't matter. This was true, he'd always believed that. And M was confident, truly self-assured, and had apparently been well groomed to go anywhere, meet anyone, at any time; there was no doubt in his mind that she would conduct herself with great aplomb and lots of charm. She was unusually engaging.

The whistling of the kettle broke into his thoughts, and he made a move to get up, but M shushed him down, exclaiming, "No, no, no! I'll do it. Do you have a brown teapot?"

"I'm afraid not, love, only my mother's antique silver pot."

"Then I'll have to buy you one."

"Thank you. I accept," he said, smiling across at her. Suddenly he had lost interest in food. What he wanted was to take her to bed and slowly and tenderly make passionate love to her.

"You've got a funny look on your face," M said as she carried over the teapot and a jug of milk, peered at him as she put them down on the table.

"What do you mean?"

She shrugged, laughed, and said, "You were sort of ogling me, I guess." And she laughed again and walked away, murmuring, "Perhaps leering *would* be a better word."

He made no response, amazed at her powers of observation. I'm going to have to watch myself when I'm around her, he thought. I'd better put on my actor's mask and prepare myself to dissemble.

# Fourteen

Lunch in the kitchen had been a splendid success as far as Larry was concerned—warm, cozy, and intimate—and he was loath to break this mood by going out to the movies. He wanted to know more about her, to get even closer to her.

Staring across the table at M, he said, "Listen, why don't we watch a film here? There's a small screening room in the back, which my father created. It's simple but comfortable with a big screen, and we have loads of films to choose from."

"Oh, Larry, I'd love that!" M exclaimed, beaming at him. "We could watch you in

*Hamlet*. That would be brilliant. I loved you in the movie as much as I did on the stage."

"Oh, no," he answered, shaking his head with some vehemence, grimacing. "I have no desire to stare at myself acting. Actually, I rarely do that. I only look at the rushes, the film of the day's shoot. You can gape at my siblings doing their stuff, if you wish, and my parents, but not me. Listen, I've a better idea. Give me the title of one of your favorites; you can be certain it's here if it's a big movie."

"Well, there're a lot I love, so wait, just let me think for a moment. Oh, I know one that's really special to me. Do you have *Julia*? Jane Fonda plays Lillian Hellman in it, and Vanessa Redgrave is Julia."

"I know it well. It's a Fred Zinnemann film, and one of my favorites, too," Larry told her.

"I read something once about Zinnemann. A journalist asked him what it was like directing Vanessa Redgrave, and he said, 'Driving a Rolls-Royce.' Wasn't that cool?"

Larry smiled at her. "He also said something that was most astute. 'The camera's got to love you,' and oh, boy, was he spot-on about that. Come on then, let's go and look for *Julia*. I'm pretty sure we have it—" Larry paused, frowning, obviously listening, his head tilted, and then said, "Do you have a cell phone in your bag? I can hear one ringing somewhere, and it's not mine."

"Oh, God, yes!" M jumped up, ran out into the entrance hall, where she had left her red Kelly and knitted coat on a chair. Rummaging in the bag, she grabbed the phone and pressed it to her ear. "Hello?"

The voice at the other end was far-away, and she could hardly hear it. "Is that you, M?"

"Yes. Who is it?"

"Caresse."

"Oh, Caresse, hi! Have you heard when Frankie's coming back? Is that why you're calling me?"

There was a sudden sound of sobbing at the other end, and then Caresse said in a mumble, "Oh, M, it's terrible, I don't know what I'm going to do . . ."

The voice disappeared, and M shouted into the phone, "Caresse, I can't hear you!"

"Frankie's . . . dead!"

"Oh, my God, no! Oh, God, what happened?" M's voice wobbled and she sat down heavily in the hall chair and endeavored to steady herself. Tears sprang into her eyes. She could hardly believe what Caresse was saying.

"He was in a car crash. In France. On something called grancornish." Caresse's voice faded for a moment, and then she started to sob. Almost immediately static and sizzle took over.

"Caresse, are you still there?" M asked, pressing her ear to the cell.

"Yes." Caresse's voice was back once more.

"Where are you, Caresse? Tell me where you are."

"At Frankie's. At the studio."

"Stay there. I'm coming over. *Now.*"

Larry had not failed to hear the distressed tone in M's voice, and he had rushed out of the kitchen. The moment he saw the dismay on her face he knew something bad had happened, and he stood in the doorway staring at her, filled with concern.

Once she finished the call, he went over

to her. She was unusually pale, and there was a stricken expression in her eyes.

M got up out of the chair. She said, "That was Caresse, Frankie Farantino's receptionist, and she's had bad news . . ." Her voice faltered. "He's been killed in an accident. . . . Frankie's dead."

"Oh, M, how dreadful," Larry responded, his voice quiet, sympathetic. "I'm so sorry. Where did it happen?"

"He was in the South of France. Caresse said it was on grancornish, but I'm sure she was mispronouncing Grande Corniche."

"Yes, she must have meant that," Larry agreed. "I know that road. It's treacherous, especially if someone doesn't know it well."

M stood there looking upset, and Larry put his arms around her, wanting to comfort her as best he could.

She clung to him, but after a few minutes she pulled away. Looking up at him, she shook her head. "I'm sorry," she mumbled. "Very sorry."

"Don't be so silly, M. I know how upset you are, and I don't blame you. It's a terrible shock. Listen, I heard you tell Caresse you were going to go and see her. I think I should come with you, don't you?"

"Yes, I do, Larry. Please."

There was a lot of traffic going downtown, but half an hour later M and Larry were ringing the bell of Frank Farantino's studio.

The huge, nail-studded black door was opened almost immediately. Standing there was a tall, thin man who looked about seventeen, perhaps eighteen. He had a shock of brown curly hair, a saturnine face, and hazel eyes, which looked somewhat teary.

At once M noticed the strong resemblance he bore to Frankie, and stretching out her hand, she said, "Hello, I'm M, and this is my friend Laurence Vaughan. Caresse is expecting us."

The young man shook their hands, saying as he did, "I'm Frankie's son, Alex. Please come in. Caresse is waiting for you."

"We were so upset when we heard about your father's accident, such a tragedy." M touched the boy's arm lightly and added in a warm, caring voice, "I'm very sorry, Alex. It was so sudden, you must be blindsided."

Looking more tearful than ever, he started

to blink and muttered, "Thank you, thanks very much. Yes, it's been a shock." He pursed his lips nervously. It was obvious he was strained and anxious.

Larry now spoke up. "My condolences to you, Alex. This is an awful thing for you to bear, and if there's anything M or I can do, if we can help you in any way, you must let us know."

"Thanks, Mr. Vaughan, thanks."

"Call me Larry, please. I much prefer it."

The young man nodded and took them through the reception area, heading to the main studio. They followed hard on his heels.

M felt slightly dazed; she could hardly believe this was happening. The last time she had been in the vast main studio was the day Frankie had announced she was Audrey Hepburn's twin and promised to launch her career as a model when he got back from the fashion shoot in Morocco. Well, he wasn't coming back now, except in a coffin.

Sorrow swept over her. *Frankie Farantino was dead.* There would be no launch of her career; her big break had vanished in a flash. But none of that mattered. *She* could begin again, find her way somehow. But Frankie wasn't coming back . . . and that was the greatest of tragedies. The world had lost a truly good man and a talented photographer, a brilliant artist.

A wave of memories assailed her as she followed Alex and Larry into the studio. She thought of the fun and excitement of that day of photography, and she couldn't quite grasp that she would never see Frankie ever again. She remembered him moving around with such agility, telling her what to do, how to pose, focusing his camera on her, snapping pictures . . . encouraging her, praising her . . .

All of the lights had been turned on and were blazing throughout; sitting in a chair in the center of the studio was Caresse. She was hunched over, her arms wrapped around herself, her bright red head bent down to her chest.

M's throat tightened. She stood perfectly still, aware that Caresse was heartbroken, and somehow she understood that there had been something important between Caresse and Frankie, that he had been much more than her boss.

Taking a deep breath, M went over to

Caresse, knelt down next to the chair, and wrapped her arms around the young receptionist. "Caresse . . . I'm so sorry, so terribly sorry. What an enormous shock this must be for you."

Caresse did not answer, just let out a long, strangled cry, then sighed several times. But after a few seconds, she lifted her head and looked directly at M. Her eyes and nose were red from crying, her skin the color of bleached-out bone. She leaned closer to M, got hold of her hand, but still seemed unable to speak, or perhaps did not want to say anything at the moment, was endeavoring to recoup somehow.

Eventually, Caresse said in a small voice, "We got engaged the night before he left." Lifting her left hand, she showed the ring to M. "He gave me this ring. It's a sapphire." Tears slid down Caresse's cheeks, and she shook her head, suddenly seemed bewildered. "Why? Why did it have to be Frankie?" she asked, peering at M. "Tell me why."

M had no words for her, and quite unexpectedly she did not know how to comfort this utterly grief-stricken young woman.

After a while, M asked, "When did it happen? How did you find out about Frankie's accident?"

Caresse, taking several deep breaths, focused on M and explained. "Luke called me this morning on my cell. I just happened to be here. I usually come to make sure everything's all right over the weekend. After Luke's call from Nice, I called Alex to break the news. Frankie brought him up; he was a single dad and good at it. Then I called you, M, because Frankie was so excited about discovering you . . . I knew he'd want you to know that . . ." She did not finish her sentence, just burst into tears.

Alex beckoned to M, who got up and hurried over to him.

He was standing with Larry near the small kitchen that opened off the studio. "I can explain a bit more to you," he said, looking at M and then at Larry. "The accident happened about six o'clock in the evening in France. Noon here. Today. Luke Hendricks called Caresse as soon as the police had been in touch with him, at the hotel where he and Dad were staying in Nice—" He stopped all of a sudden, glanced away, swallowing, and once he had control of himself, he went on. "Apparently Dad was driving to Monte Carlo to have dinner with a French photographer he'd known for years. He had . . . a head-on crash . . . with a truck coming from the opposite direction. They were both killed, Dad and the other driver." Clearing his throat, blinking again, Alex announced, "I think I'll go and make some coffee. Okay?"

"Yes, that would be great, Alex, thanks," Larry answered, and turning to M, he put his arm around her and said, "Let's go and sit over there. I'm positive Caresse needs to be alone for the moment, and so does Alex, actually. He wants to have another weep, I think, but not in front of us. He's endeavoring to be brave."

It was an hour later when M and Larry left the studio. Some of Frankie's colleagues had come in, and several other friends had arrived to look after Caresse. M and Larry now felt relaxed about leaving, especially since Alex seemed to have found some inner strength and had taken charge.

Standing outside, Larry took hold of M's hand, and together they walked down the street. It was M who broke the silence between them when she said, "Can we go back to your place, Larry? I don't want to go home, I want to be with you."

This pleased him, since he wanted her with him. "Then let's do that right away. It looks distinctly like rain, and we don't want to get caught in a downpour." He glanced up at the sky, noted the gathering clouds, and hurrying her along, hailed the first cab he spotted.

M was quiet during the ride uptown, and Larry decided to let her sort out her thoughts, not wishing to intrude. It occurred to him that she might be contemplating her future now that the initial shock of Frankie's death had begun to wear off. Her big break, the launch of her career, had evaporated in the blink of an eye. He wondered how he could help her and realized he had no idea. The problem was, he did not know anyone in the fashion business; if she had wanted to be an actress, he could have been very useful to her. He sighed, and she took hold of his arm, peering at him. "Is something wrong?"

"No, no, I'm perfectly fine." A faint smile flickered around his mouth. He continued, "Just worrying about you, darling. You've got to start all over again, go back to square one."

"And that's what I'll do," she responded firmly. "I'm not going to give in or give up the idea of being a model. I have to keep on trying."

"That's the right stuff! Good girl," he exclaimed, his voice full of admiration.

When they walked into Larry's apartment a short while later, there was the sound of thunder rumbling in the distance, and brilliant flashes of lightning were illuminating the rooms overlooking the East River.

Walking over to one of the windows in the library, Larry exclaimed, "My God, look at the sky! It's extraordinary, and any moment there's going to be one hell of a cloudburst."

She went and stood next to him, staring out at the darkening sky. It was filled with bloated black clouds, but oddly, they appeared to be illuminated from behind. Silvery rays of light were streaming across the clouds as if emanating from some source below the far horizon, creating an effect that was otherworldly. Turning to him, she said, "A set designer has been at work here, don't you think? It's like a scene out of *The Ten Commandments,* when Charlton Heston parted the sea."

Larry nodded. "Dead-on, love, dead-on. Now, how about a cup of tea?"

"Why not?" she agreed and asked, "Shall I come and help you?"

"I'll do it. You go and sit down, relax. But it seems a bit cold in here, so perhaps you'd light the fire. It's laid, it just needs a match, and there's a box of them over on the coffee table."

Larry hurried off, and M did as he asked. Once the fire was burning brightly, she sat down on the sofa, took out her cell phone, and dialed Geo, who answered at once.

"Hello?"

"Geo, it's M."

"Hi! How was lunch?" Without waiting for an answer, Geo rushed on. "James is here. He came to look at my paintings, and later we're going to dinner. Are you going to be with Larry this evening?"

"Yes, I am, and I'm happy James is there, Geo."

"So am I, and—"

"I've got some sad news," M interrupted. "I guess you haven't heard?"

"No, I haven't heard anything about anything. What are you talking about?"

M blew out air, took a deep breath, and plunged in. "Caresse called me just after lunch. There's been a terrible accident." Her voice began to wobble, her emotions coming to the surface, but then she took firm control of herself, managed to continue. "Frankie's been killed in a car crash in France."

"Oh, my God! How awful. What happened?" Geo sounded horror-struck.

M told her everything she knew, explained that she and Larry had been to the studio, confided that Caresse and Frankie had become engaged the night before he left for Morocco. "So as you can imagine, Caresse is pretty much devastated," M said, adding, "Frankie's son, Alex, is with her, and a lot of other friends."

"I think I'd better go over. Maybe there's something I can do to help them," Geo said. "What do you think?"

"It would be very nice if you went, comforting. Frankly, I think the two of them are shell-shocked, and what are friends for, if not to be there in a crisis."

"You're right. James will come with me, I'm sure of that."

"Is everything all right with him?"

"Very. Yes, very all right."

"I'm so glad," M answered. "If you need to speak to me, I'm on my cell."

# Fifteen

The fire crackled and burned brightly, the flames flaring up the chimney and giving the room a warm, roseate glow. The thunder and lightning had not abated at all; the rain was falling in torrents, and as Larry had predicted, it was a cloudburst, the rain slashing and rattling against the windows.

As she leaned back against the cushions on the big overstuffed sofa, M's thoughts turned to Larry. She knew that he was smitten with her, he had made that patently clear. And she was smitten with him, totally enamored of him now, as she had been as a teenager. But now it was much more real because she was *with* him, not merely daydreaming about him.

She was also well aware that she had not encouraged him last night; he had intuitively detected her apprehension and had backed off. It struck her that she must endeavor to allay any fears he might have about her reluctance to be intimate with him; otherwise their relationship would never progress.

The Bad Thing hove into view in her head, and instantly she smothered it, stamped on it, threw it away, and so was able to put it out of her mind. *There, it was gone.* She would not think of it again. *Not ever.*

How to explain the way she had pulled away from him and looked scared last evening? I'll stick to a few partial truths, she decided, that's the only way that will work.

Closing her eyes, she allowed her thoughts to dwell on Larry, a habit she had perfected as a teenager. Then something extraordinary clicked in her head, and she sat up with a start. She knew, with absolute certainty, that they were destined to be together. That had been in the cards since she was a child; daydreaming about him had been a prelude to this. In her mind and in her heart she knew him well, knew him truly, as he was at the very core of himself. And she felt safe with him in a way she had never experienced before with a man. He was her destiny.

At this moment Larry walked into the library, carrying the tea tray. He said, "You know, it's a funny thing, M. I feel that I know you, know everything about you, in fact, but then I suddenly realized in the kitchen that there's one thing I definitely don't know about you."

"What's that?" she asked, sitting up straighter, glancing at him with avid curiosity as he came over to the fireplace.

"I don't know whether you take milk or lemon in your tea."

"And I thought you were going to say something world-shaking."

"Here's one of those for you then," he answered as he placed the tray on the coffee table and looked across at her. "Will you marry me?"

She gaped at him, flabbergasted.

"Go on then, give me an answer."

"I can't. I'm stunned, Larry."

"I bet you would have said yes, and with

great alacrity, when you were ten years old."

"That's true."

"So?" He raised a black brow, his blue eyes riveted on hers. "So go on, don't keep me on tenterhooks."

"The answer is . . . *yes*. Very much *yes*."

"The perfect answer, the only answer." He grinned at her and added, "Now that that's out of the way, we can enjoy our tea. Milk or lemon?"

"Today I feel like having it with lemon," she answered, enjoying this lighthearted, teasing conversation. "And a sweetener, please."

Within moments he had poured the tea, which he placed in front of her, then he sat down next to her on the sofa. Immediately he took one of her hands in his. He studied it intently for a moment, his eyes reflective. "I wonder what kind of ring I should give you. Diamond, ruby, sapphire, emerald, or pearl? What's your preference?"

"I'll let you decide. Surprise me."

"That doesn't present a problem. Surprise you I will."

"There's just one . . . *proviso* . . ."

Her voice had grown serious, and he noticed this at once, attuned to her as he had become. Frowning, he asked, "What is it?"

"I think we have to sleep together first. Before we get married, that is."

Larry stared at her in astonishment. He knew she was not joking with him, and she had caught him off guard.

M recognized that he was at a loss, and she said quietly, "I want to explain something, Larry, about last night when we were outside the restaurant. You thought I was frightened, didn't you?"

"Well, apprehensive, yes, that I did. And I didn't want to rush you into bed against your will. That's why I decided to take you home."

"And I was a bit disappointed you made that decision, but I fully understood your reaction."

"I was worried I might do something to spoil things. I didn't want to turn you off . . . me."

She moved closer to him, her eyes never leaving his face, and leaning into him, she kissed him fully on the mouth.

Larry responded eagerly, and then almost at once he pulled away from her, gave her another hard, questioning stare.

"What is it?" she asked.

"You haven't told me what made you afraid of me."

"It wasn't *you* I was afraid of. . . . I suddenly had a bad memory, about someone else. It had nothing to do with you. Honestly, I promise. But when it came back, it threw me for a moment."

"What kind of bad memory?" he probed, his eyes fastened on her face.

"Some time ago I had a horrendous sexual experience with a boyfriend. He got extremely rough one night, and became angry with me when I tried to hold him off. He was violent actually, and he forced himself on me, hurt me. I was a mess for a long time afterward, and I haven't been involved with anyone since."

"What a bastard he must be!" Larry exclaimed, his anger rising. He managed to keep it in check and went on in a lower voice, "I will never harm you in any way. Please trust me on that."

"I do, and I feel really safe with you,

safer than I have for a long time." She meant what she said, and she gave him the benefit of a confident and loving smile.

He nodded, stood up, grabbed her by the hand, and pulled her to her feet. Putting his arm around her waist, he led her out of the library, across the foyer, and down the corridor to his bedroom.

"Since I am rather anxious to tie the knot, don't you think we should get that *proviso* out of the way immediately?"

"At once," she concurred, leaning against him, her arm going around his waist, her eyes full of laughter.

They went into his bedroom, and he closed the door behind them, turned her to face him, and brought her into his arms. "Darling M, oh, darling," he said against her neck. "I know you want to be with me, as much as I want to be with you, but are you sure you wouldn't prefer to wait a bit longer? Until you know me better?"

She smiled against his shoulder. "But I *do* know you, and better than a lot of the people who've been in my life for ages. Anyway, I've known you since I was *ten*, remember? That was when I had my mushy dreams about you."

He had sensed her smile, and he was pleased that she was relaxed and at ease. He knew she was happy being with him, just as he was with her. "Can I now make your mushy little-girl dreams come true?" he asked softly, his breath warm against her neck.

"I wish you would." Standing away from him, she looked deeply into his eyes, reached out and touched his mouth, slid one finger along his cheek. "*Laurence Vaughan.* Do you know, I can't believe it— that I'm standing in your bedroom about to make love with you."

Stepping close to her, Larry smiled as he began to unbutton her white cotton shirt. He took it off, threw it on the floor, removed her bra, and dropped that as well. Then he pulled his black sweater over his head and discarded it.

They both moved at exactly the same moment, stepped into each other's arms. Larry slid one hand down her back, brought it around to cup her breast. Bending over her, he kissed it tenderly, then led her to the bed. They undressed and stood gazing at each other for a moment, before Larry said, "You seem shy all of a sudden. Please don't be shy with me, darling. You're lovely, M, perfectly beautiful. Come on, let's be together the way we want. Let's love each other, know each other in the best way."

They lay side by side on the bed, holding hands, not saying a word. But soon Larry pushed himself up on one elbow, stared down at her. He loved the length of her—she was almost as tall as he was—and admired the elegant lines of her body, her long legs. Her face was finely featured, her dark eyes compelling, and they held his, and somewhere at the back of his mind he had the sudden feeling that he knew her.

Aware that he was studying her, M stared back at him, saw a fine vein beating in his temple, noticed the hollow in his neck just below the chin. How vulnerable he looked, like a child. Before she could stop herself, she lifted her head and kissed that tender hollow, felt a rush of the most intense emotion for him. And in her heart she knew that she loved him.

Larry kissed her on the mouth, let his hand slide down over her breasts. Her skin was silky under his touch; he stroked her stomach and her thighs, and he was gentle with her and tender.

Putting her hand on his neck, M brought Larry's face down to hers, and they kissed deeply. It was a rapturous kiss, and they were lost in each other, enjoying their new-found intimacy.

At one moment M caught her breath, so conscious was she of Larry, of his masculinity and physical magnetism. She was growing more aroused, fired on by his burning desire for her, longing to be possessed by him.

His hands continued to roam over her, fondling, caressing, and when finally they came to rest between her legs, she found herself trembling. Within a few seconds, his expert probing aroused her even more, sent spirals of pleasure rushing through her. At one moment she stiffened slightly, and he murmured, "Relax, darling, just let go." She did as he asked, and a deeper pleasure spread up into her body, filling her with ecstasy.

Now she reached for him, put her hand on him tentatively, let it rest there between his legs. Slowly, she began to stroke him.

Her touch was as light as a feather, and a shiver ran through Larry. He thought he was going to cry out or, worse, explode, and so he swiftly moved on top of her, kissing her deeply, wanting all of her.

Staring up into his face, so intense, so concentrated on her, M thought she was drowning in a deep blue ocean as she gazed into his marvelous eyes, and it seemed to her that she was looking into his soul.

Pushing his hands underneath her, he raised her slightly and brought her closer to him. No longer able to stop himself, he took her to him, entered her, held her in his arms, loving her. Larry's throat was tight with emotion, and his heart was clattering in his chest as they moved together in perfect rhythm, lost in each other as they reached the pinnacle of their pleasure.

Later, sated, they lay quietly, wrapped in each other's arms, not wanting to let go. M sighed against Larry's neck, and sighed again in contentment, and he kissed her cheek, loosened his grip on her slightly so that he could place his head on her shoulder.

And as he lay there next to her, waiting

for his heart to slow to its normal steady beat, he experienced a feeling of perfect peace washing over him and, a moment later, an absence of pain. He was filled with wonder at himself, and then he instantly knew the reason why. It was because he was with the woman he had searched for all his life and had at last found.

❊

"I almost didn't go to Iris's party," Larry volunteered as he and M sat in the library, enjoying a glass of wine and smoked salmon sandwiches. He shook his head. "Imagine that! If I hadn't gone, we wouldn't have met."

Smiling at him beguilingly, a knowing look in her dark, sparking eyes, M said softly, "Yes, we would. . . . It's fate . . . destiny."

"If you say so, my pretty one."

"You know what? I almost didn't go myself," she confided. "I went because I didn't want to hurt Dax's feelings."

Larry gave her a searching look and asked, "Was he, is he, a boyfriend of yours?"

Taken aback by this question, M simply shook her head and also took a sip of wine. Shrugging herself deeper into Larry's silk dressing gown, which he had earlier insisted she wear, she finally answered, "No, he's not a boyfriend, never has been. We met at the Blane Agency, when I first got here, and we kept running into each other. One morning he took me to Starbucks for a coffee, and later he introduced me to Geo, who was his girlfriend at that time. She had a room to rent, I took it, and that's all." She shrugged her shoulders, half smiled to herself.

"There you are! Look what you do to me! You've just witnessed my first flash of jealousy." Larry laughed drily, rose, threw another log on the fire, and stood hovering in front of it, his hands in the pockets of his navy blue dressing gown.

M said, "You've nothing to be jealous about, and incidentally, I've never been seriously involved with anyone." Her head to one side, she threw him a challenging look. Her tone was cheeky when she ventured, "But I don't think I can say the same about you, mister."

"You of all people certainly know that, considering that you've been studying my life for years." This was said in a jocular manner, and he laughed, then said, "But I do have a need . . . *to know about you,* missy."

"How can you say *that*? You boasted that you *truly* knew me."

"The kind of person you *are,* yes, but not much else, no details," he shot back, gazing at her, his blue eyes full of amusement.

"Ask away," she responded, steeling herself for his probing questions and lining up her lies.

"I suspect you have siblings," Larry began, "am I correct?"

"Yes, and I'm in the middle. I have a younger brother," she answered. "They're okay, really, when it comes down to it."

"Are any of them married?"

"My two older sisters are, but one was recently widowed. Her husband died suddenly of a heart attack in his thirties, just over two years ago now. Very sad, actually. My older brother is single, the happy bachelor, just like you."

"Maybe he's not found anyone he wants to spend the rest of his life with, isn't that a possibility?"

"Absolutely. You've hit the nail on the

head. He's very particular. About his *women*."

"Do you have a favorite?" Larry asked. "Most of us usually do."

"Yes, the sister next to me. We call her Birdie. She's the one who's widowed."

"Does she have children?"

"No, she has a job, though; she sells women's clothes, has a boutique of her own. And before you ask, my brother made quite a lot of money in the produce business, supplying food to hotels and restaurants. He built a good business and sold out. Now, I call him the playboy."

"And what about your parents?" Larry stared at her, his eyes narrowing.

Knowing this would be the next question, M was totally prepared. "My father's sort of semiretired these days. He was a builder. He and Mummy are in Australia at the moment, visiting her mother, who's been sick. My grandmother's English, but one of her husbands was an Australian." She grinned at him and raised a brow. "Any other questions?"

"No, no, not really. Thanks for telling me about your family."

"I have one for you."

"Go ahead."

"I know you were named after Sir Laurence Olivier, and that he was a friend of your father's. But did you know him well? And did you like him?"

"I did know him, of course; he was a friend of my mother's and therefore a family friend. Also, my parents worked with him. He was my idol when I was growing up, such a great actor, the greatest actually. I wasn't close to him because of the age difference, but he was always rather nice with me. He died when I was seventeen."

"Yes, I know that."

When she sat back and said nothing else, just sipped her wine, Larry said, "No more questions?"

"Not at the moment."

"I have one. Shall we set a date?"

"A date?" She gave him a puzzled look, but she knew what he meant.

"When shall we get married?"

Deciding to humor him, she said, "November or December? Which do you prefer?"

"I know what we'll do. We'll have a *Christmas* wedding. Here in New York.

Just the two of us. Don't let's tell a soul. . . . It'll be like eloping, in a sense."

"What a fantastic idea! I'll get married in a white wool suit, a white fur, and carry white flowers, and it's bound to snow, and then it will really and truly be a white wedding," she teased.

Filled with laughter, Larry sat down on the sofa and took her in his arms. Against her hair he said, "You're the most adorable girl I've ever met."

And that was how it began, their grand romance.

# Sixteen

Caresse walked around the largest studio within the rabbit warren of the complex called Frank Farantino Photographic Studios. She was endeavoring to see it with cold deliberation, rather than with aching heartbreak. She must not think of her big love Frankie, her fiancé, envision him leaping around like an acrobat in his favorite place, shouting instructions to the models, focusing his camera, shooting his unique shots, and being his impossible but lovable self.

No, that was the wrong thing to do. She must think in terms of money. Not for her but for Frankie's kid, Alex. In a certain sense, he was her responsibility now, because Frankie's older sister, Theresa, a diabetic, had become sicker than ever since his fatal car crash. So it was up to Caresse to do right by "the kid." Alex would soon be eighteen. But that's the way Frankie had always referred to Alex. She must get as much money as she could for the complex. Not only was it an entire building, a vast former warehouse, but Frankie had designed the various studios himself. Aside from the soaring rooms the photographers used for shoots, there were hair and makeup rooms, bathrooms, and an eat-in kitchen fully equipped with the latest appliances. And then there were dozens of klieg lights, various cleverly designed and beautifully rendered backdrops, which rolled around on wheels, plus an extraordinary collection of cameras and other equipment. *Yes, money, money, money for the kid*. That was her theme song at the moment. No bidders yet, but she could hope. She suddenly asked herself if she had given it to the wrong agency. Bentley's was not such a big agent; perhaps she should seek out a more important real estate company.

Walking back to the reception area, Caresse sat down behind the desk and looked at the bookings. Five photographers would be working here today, three doing fashion shoots for magazines and two working on shoots for fashion catalogs. She nodded, grateful and relieved that Frankie's pals were still using his studios, touched that they were being loyal to him. She was proud of that, the friendship Frankie had inspired in others.

Caresse glanced down at her sapphire engagement ring. She still wore it because she couldn't bear to take it off. She was engaged to Frankie Farantino, and that was that. Her eyes filled. He had always been good to her, considerate and very, very loving. It would be hard to find another man like him . . . she couldn't even bother trying.

The jangling phone brought her up with a start, and she answered it with a simple "Farantino Studios, Caresse speaking."

"Hey, Caresse, how're you doing, honey?" Luke Hendricks asked. "Holding up, I hope, sweetie pie."

"Doing my best, Luke. Where are you? What's happening?"

"I'm stuck in Paris, finishing the shoot for *Vogue,* but I hope to get back to New York next week. But hey, listen up, honey, where's M? What's she doing these days?"

"Oddly enough, she was in here yesterday to see me. She often drops by. She's great, cool. She's still working at that cheesecake place, still doing the rounds of the modeling agencies. Poor kid, she doesn't seem able to get that first break. Why are *you* asking about her?"

"Because *I* have that first break for her! A special fashion shoot next week. So try and find her, please, and book Frank's big studio for me, his favorite. Listen, I gotta run. I'm heading out to Versailles to shoot the Coldplay guys . . . sitting in the middle of a gaggle of blond models. Yeah, Chris Martin and his compadres."

"For *Vogue*?" she asked, incredulous.

"No, honey, for *Vanity Fair.* I'll give you a buzz later today. Or tomorrow. Just find her. So long."

"No, wait, don't hang up, Luke. What if she can't do it?"

"Are you kidding? She'll do it no matter what she's doing. She'll cancel out the Queen of England to do this fashion shoot.

It's her first break, for God's sake. See ya, cookie."

Caresse stared at the receiver in her hand, listening to the dial tone. He had hung up on her. Well, that was Luke, always on the run. Banging the receiver into the cradle, Clarisse sat back in the chair frowning, and then a sudden bright smile flashed across her tired face. "Gotta find M, gotta find M," she muttered, cheering up. Life had a purpose again. For the moment.

❖

Dimly, far in the distance, Larry heard a phone ringing. He let it ring, having no desire to talk to anyone. But when the machine did not pick up and it went on ringing, he finally reached for the receiver.

"Hello," he mumbled, still half asleep and half doped up with the pills he had taken the evening before.

"Larry! It's me! *Your mother.* Are you all right?"

Pushing himself up on the pillows, he blinked in the murky light. "Oh, hi, Mother. I think I'm all right. I guess I am. I've got the flu."

"You sound *drugged* to me! Larry, darling, you haven't fallen off the wagon, so to speak, have you? I do hope not, you promised me . . . *no more pills,* you said, yes, that's what you promised. Oh, darling—"

"No! No!" he exclaimed, forcing himself to sit up, endeavoring to be coherent. "Just hold on a minute, I need to get a glass of water . . ." He let his sentence slide away.

"Take your time," Pandora Gallen said in a crisper tone.

Placing the receiver on the bedside table, he turned on the lamp, drank from the glass of water already there, and went back to the phone and his mother. "Okay, that's better. I'm a bit dehydrated, what with all the cold pills and cough mixture I've taken. That stuff does you in, even if it also kills the germs."

"I know." There was a silence, and then his mother continued, "You are sure you have the flu, aren't you? You'd tell me the truth, wouldn't you?"

"Mum! Come on. You know I've never lied to you. Ever. I've had a really bad dose of it, and I'm still under the weather."

She sighed and said, "Perhaps I ought to call you back later."

"No, not later. Let's talk *now.* I'm fine." He glanced at the clock, saw that it was eleven, and therefore four in the afternoon in London. "Anyway, how are you, Ma? And how's Dad?"

"That's the main reason I wanted to speak with you," Pandora answered. "About your father."

He caught a hint of concern in her voice. "Is something *wrong*? You sound funny, Ma. What is it? Is Dad ill?"

"No. Well, not that I know of, but he's out there in Canada all by himself, with the most grueling time ahead of him, and I think somebody ought to be with him. You see, I *detect* this *need* in him when we speak, and the problem is I can't go to Toronto because I start a film tomorrow. But I must admit, I'm genuinely worried about him, my darling."

Larry cursed himself under his breath. He had totally forgotten that his father was about to start rehearsals for a play in Toronto . . . because he had fallen head over heels in love with M. "Send Portia, Mother. You know she loves to travel, and Dad adores her, also—"

"Not possible," Pandora interrupted. "Portia can't leave little Desi. The child has measles. She's been rather sick, actually.

I thought that you could go, stay with your father for a week or two, give him some moral support. *Cyrano de Bergerac* is a tough play, Larry. You're not working, are you?"

"No, I'm not. At least not this week. I'm sick, remember? Anyway, you know very well I don't have a job. But honestly, I don't think I can travel yet, Ma. I'm still a bit wobbly. Besides which, I wouldn't go near anybody, most especially Dad, or any other actor about to go into a play, until I'm absolutely positive I'm completely better. Totally germ free. Doctor Doom I don't want to be."

"I understand that, and you're quite right. But surely by the end of this week you'll be much better. You've always managed to throw off illness very quickly, my darling. You take after me in that. We have great stamina, you and I, the best in the family, actually. Also, you do happen to be the nearest to Toronto."

"What about Edward? He's in Los Angeles. Why can't he go, Ma?"

"Because he's not in L.A. He's here in London, and he can't leave for another week. Horatio is on tour in Australia, in case you've forgotten, and Thomas has a broken ankle and is hobbling around, groaning and moaning like an old man."

"He *is* an old man," Larry shot back, grinning to himself, knowing his mother would refrain from making a comment. To say Thomas was an old man was a sore point with her because it aged *her*. Larry now said, "What about Miranda?"

"My God, Larry, are you insane? I wouldn't wish her on your father, that in itself would make him ill. You know he can't stand her."

Larry burst out laughing. He always enjoyed his mother's forthrightness. She was honest about everyone, her children in particular. And she always said what she thought to a person's face. Suddenly he began to cough and reached for the water. After gulping some down, he asked, "What *exactly* is it that's alarming you about Dad so much, Mum?"

"I can't really pinpoint it, to be truthful, but there's something in his voice that seriously disturbs me. I have a feeling he's a bit trepidatious about this play. But then who wouldn't be? And let us not forget that, even though he doesn't look it, your father is *seventy*."

For a moment Larry remained silent, then said, "Rostand's *Cyrano* is a big piece of theater, Ma, you know that as much as I do, and it can be bloody intimidating—" He stopped, sighing under his breath. "It's a hell of a role to take on, even for a much younger man. Maybe he should just get out of the play—"

"Get out of the play! Are you losing your wits? He signed a contract, Larry, he can't just walk away explaining that he's suddenly afraid of the part."

"That's what it is, isn't it, Mother? And you know it, and so you're afraid. *For him.* If that *is* the case, he should just quit."

"He can't, and he won't, you're aware of that. Look, it would help him if you were with him for a couple of weeks. I know it would."

"No, it wouldn't. He doesn't feel the same way about me anymore. Five years ago he called me the black sheep of the family and added that I was no son of his. Do you think I've ever forgotten his words?"

"No, I'm sure you haven't, but you're not remembering his words exactly. Actually, what he said was this: 'You're no son of mine *if you continue on this downward spi-*

*ral.*' You've conveniently obliterated the last part of his sentence. That has been your problem for a long time."

"Well, he's never retracted his statement that I'm the black sheep of the family. And he should have. He owes me that. I'm a reformed man."

"Larry, with your father, actions speak louder than words, volumes louder. He just gave you the apartment where you are sitting at this very moment. Have you forgotten that you paid relatively nothing for it, and he would have willingly given it to you without an exchange of money, except that your siblings might have objected. Your father loves you, Larry, and he's proud of you. Not only as an actor but as a man. He knows you kicked that habit of yours, that awful dependence on prescription drugs . . ." Pandora cleared her throat, and lowered her voice. "You have, haven't you?"

"You know it, and I do have the flu right now, Ma. I took nonprescription drugs to get rid of it, and I'm not doped up. *Okay?*"

"Yes, all right, don't lose your temper. There's another thing I want to explain. Your father gave you that apartment because he knows you prefer living in New York, and he wanted you to have a proper home, a place of your own. He does care about you, has your interests at heart."

Larry was startled by these words, and he didn't answer for a second, a number of questions spinning around in his fertile brain. But finally he let the questions go, aware his mother was truthful, especially about his father. "I'll make a deal with you, Mum," he said at last.

"What sort of deal?" Pandora asked, sounding suddenly wary.

Catching the intonation in her voice, he said, "It won't break the bank, Ma, so don't sound so cautious and worried."

"I'm neither," she protested. "Why would I not trust *you*? You're my son, and very much like me."

"I know, I know! And more than the others, you're going to say. So here's the deal. Today's Tuesday. I should be back on my feet by Thursday or Friday, and I can fly to Toronto on Saturday. I'll stay with Dad for two weeks, but no longer. After that Edward has to take over."

His mother was silent, weighing his words. Larry could hear her thinking everything out at the other end of the transatlantic line.

At last she spoke. "It's a deal, Larry. I will explain everything to Edward, and I'm sure he'll agree."

Larry thought: You bet he'll agree, the little bastard. He'll salivate at the idea of jumping into my place so he can stick the knife in, bad-mouth me and the others, but especially me, to the old man. To his mother he explained he would check in with her on a daily basis once he was in Toronto, and then he gave voice to the one thought that was troubling him. "What shall I do if I think he's genuinely afraid of doing the play, Mum? Your worries might well prove to be correct. That's my dilemma."

"I don't know. Let's not travel down that particular country lane yet, my darling. I do trust your judgment. And I want you to know that I do have faith in you . . . about the other thing, Larry."

"I've been clean for five years, Mother of mine. I'd never break a promise to you. So let's get down to details, make our plans."

❊

Larry sat staring at the phone after saying good-bye to his mother, pondering their conversation. He loved his father and he wanted to be with him, to help him through his problems. If there were any. . . . There must be; his mother was instinctive about Nicholas Vaughan, knew him better than anyone in the world. It was important to Larry that he was back in his father's good graces, and he wanted to stay there, to prove also that he *was* reliable.

But now there was M in his life, thank God, and he didn't want to be away from her. She had become essential to his well-being over the last few weeks. *He must take her with him.* Yes, that was the solution. But would she go if he asked her? He wasn't sure. But he would invite her.

And what about Edward, his bête noire? Larry had no wish to spend a prolonged length of time with *him.* He wouldn't have to, would he? When Edward arrived in Toronto, Larry would simply leave. That was the deal, wasn't it? Although there *was* a sort of truce between them these days, this did not mean that Edward had reformed. His brother was as two-faced now as he'd always been.

Larry had long been convinced that it

was actually Edward who had planted the idea that *he* was the black sheep of the family in their father's head. Never mind. He would prove to his father once and for all that he was his old self, and to hell with Edward.

Thousands of miles away in London, Pandora Gallen Vaughan sat at her desk in the small study of the family's Mayfair house. Her elegant hand still rested on the phone, and her mind remained focused on her favorite son. No, favorite *child.* That was the truth; he was, and he always had been, although she had striven to hide this from her other children. Larry was the one who was the most like her in character; facially he resembled his father, and of all the children Laurence was the only one who had inherited Nicholas's astonishing blue eyes and classical profile. Where the dark hair and height had come from she wasn't sure. Certainly not her blond, Nordic-like family from the north of England. Probably from Great-grandfather Cornelius Vaughan, the magnificent Edwardian actor with an Irish mother, who had been the favorite of King

Edward VII and Queen Alexandra. Cornelius, in his heyday, had been described as tall, dark, and handsome.

Their children were all good-looking, but it was Larry who was the most handsome, and who had the most talent. That was why some of the others were excessively jealous of him. Funny, though, Larry was the least impressed with himself, his looks and his abilities. He thought the others were much better than he. How wrong he was in that; *he* was the real thing, the genuine star amongst his siblings.

Now Pandora's thoughts focused on Edward. Suddenly she wasn't sure that she wanted him in such close proximity to Larry. Somehow he always proved toxic for his younger brother. Perhaps it would be wiser not to broach the subject to Edward. Maybe Portia could be pressed into service in a few weeks. Surely little Desdemona would have recovered from the measles by then. Did Portia cosset her daughter too much?

Edward might well create problems for Larry . . . Pandora's agile mind raced, endeavoring to envision what mischief he might get up to. Edward was here in London to work out another mess with yet another woman. He'd had three wives and three "live-ins," as he called them, and there were endless children on both sides of the Pond. Oh, God, how would he sort *this* mess out? Only with her help, naturally, and her money. And although she totally disapproved of his behavior in general, she would have to help him in order to protect the family from more scandal. She did love Edward, as she loved every one of her children, in different ways and varying degrees. However, this did not mean she turned a blind eye to some of Edward's less commendable characteristics. It suddenly struck her, on reflection, that it was Edward who was more like the black sheep of the family than Larry. How she regretted that Nick had said that about him. Larry had not forgotten it. But he didn't bear a grudge, did he?

Pandora sighed heavily and looked out of the window. The charming little garden at the back of the town house looked bleak, wintry, even though it was only mid-October. And that was how she felt at this moment . . . *bleak.* And worried about her husband of fifty years.

❋

"Hi, Caresse, it's me, M. I just got all these urgent messages from you. Is there something wrong?"

"Oh, hello, M! Glad you called back. There's nothing *wrong.* I must see you, though. I need to talk to you about something . . . *vital.*"

"I'm all ears," M said, laughing, relieved that Caresse did not have more problems to cope with. There had been so many. "Tell me now."

"I can't. I'm very busy here. Lotta photography going on at the studios. Stop by when you finish at the cheesecake place. Can't you do that?"

"Larry's not well, he's had the worst flu, and he's still rather weak. I've been looking after him. I want to get back to him as soon as possible."

"Please come over. Ten minutes, that's all I need. *Please,*" Caresse pleaded. "It's very important to me."

"Okay, I'll come for ten minutes. You know I'll always try to help you when I can, Caresse. Look, I'll be finishing at the café around five. I'll get there a bit after that."

"Thanks, M, thanks loads. You're cool, we're cool, and you won't regret this, I promise."

Startled, M exclaimed, "Does this have something to do with me?" She sounded curious and suddenly wary.

"No, no! Not at all," Caresse fibbed. "Why do you think it is?"

"Because you just said I won't regret it."

"Oh, that's just a saying I picked up lately. What I meant was you won't regret doing *a good deed.* Honest, that's all," Caresse lied, knowing that she would soon be giving M the surprise of her life. The thing was she wanted to tell her in person because she wanted to witness her happiness when she heard the news. It was about time somebody was happy around here. God knows, she wasn't.

"See you later then," M answered.

"You betcha!" Caresse hung up the phone, a huge smile on her face, the first in weeks, and her step was a little more lively when she went into the big studio to check on what was happening.

# Seventeen

Larry had loved surprises since his childhood—getting them *and* giving them. And now, as he sat at the desk in the library, gazing at the ring in its dark blue Harry Winston box, he wondered if M would be surprised.

He was never quite sure with her. Did she think he was teasing her when he kept making announcements about getting married, suggesting dates and proposing honeymoon destinations? Or did she believe he was being serious?

Certainly she appeared to take everything at face value, responding in kind, going along with him as if he were making real plans. Which of course he was. He had never been more serious in his life. He *was* going to marry her at Christmas, and he couldn't wait to make her his wife because he loved her to distraction. He felt lost and lonely when she was not with him, *bereft* was the best word to use.

He held up the ring to catch the light. And it radiated brilliant blue. It was a superb Burmese sapphire, flawless, cushion-cut and mounted in platinum, with two diamond baguettes on each side. An extraordinary ring. He could only hope she liked it. M had never answered him when he asked her what kind of engagement ring she wanted, because she thought he was joking. But he wasn't. After looking at various stones, he had selected the sapphire because it was one of the most beautiful examples he had seen in years. It would suit her. It was a classy ring for a classy lady, and she had made favorable comments about Caresse's sapphire engagement ring.

Smiling to himself, he placed the ring in the box, slipped it into his trouser pocket, and hurried out to the kitchen. Of course she would be surprised, and of course she would love the ring, what woman wouldn't? After putting a bottle of Dom Pérignon in the fridge, he returned to the library, still thinking about M. He could hardly wait for her to arrive.

Once he had thrown two extra logs on the fire, Larry picked up the film script which his agent had sent over by messenger earlier that afternoon. He began to read, finding himself quickly caught up in the truly superior dialogue and intriguing plotlines.

After half an hour, he leaned back in the chair and laid the screenplay on his lap, looking off into space. He might well do this movie. It was as good as his agent had said it was, and it had immense style. He hadn't worked for over a year, and he wanted to get back in the saddle, was suddenly itching to tread the boards or emote in front of a camera. Besides, he would soon have a wife to support.

A wife . . . what a lovely thought that was. But only because it's my darling M, he added to himself. My beautiful, darling M.

❁

"I don't think I like the way this conversation's going," Geo said in a cold tone, frowning across the table at Dax.

"What do you mean?"

"Oh, come on, don't play dumb with me. You've more or less just said that Laurence Vaughan is a drug addict."

"I didn't say that!" Dax cried vehemently, looking at her askance. "All I said was that I'd heard rumors he had a problem with prescription drugs. Several years ago."

"But why are you telling me this now, if it was *several years ago*? Shouldn't the matter be forgotten? After all, saying things like that can ruin somebody's career."

"I did *not* say he was an addict, or a cokehead, or anything resembling that," Dax hissed at her, leaning over the table. "I only mentioned prescription drugs."

Georgiana was silent. She picked up her latte and took a sip, glanced around the Starbucks café near Eighth Avenue, where they had met a short while before. It was half empty, but Dax had a stage voice that carried. She now wished that she had agreed to see him at her brownstone, as he had suggested. But she was expecting James around five, and she didn't want

Dax there when he arrived. It might look strange, certainly it could be awkward.

Dax put his hand on hers resting on the table. It was a conciliatory gesture. "I mentioned it because, well, because I'm fond of M, and I wouldn't want her getting . . . in over her head."

Geo glared at him and said in a low voice, "If you think I'm going to tell her any of this, you're mistaken. It's none of my business. Nor is it any of yours, as a matter of fact. I just hate it when people gossip. It's dangerous, can cause untold harm and pain."

"Geo, calm down, for God's sake! I wasn't gossiping. I was merely passing on something which came from a reliable source, and—"

"Iris Ingersoll, I've no doubt."

"No, it wasn't Iris. And look, I'm not out to hurt anyone, certainly not M, you know I'm fond of her. Listen up, honey. I was once, and not so long ago, your lover. We even talked about marriage. Now you sound as if you don't trust me. What's wrong with you? Why are you so accusatory?"

Geo let out a long sigh. "I *do* trust you,

Dax, and I'm sorry I was angry just now. I feel very protective of M. I know she gives off an aura of sophistication, and certainly she knows a great deal about everything and everyone. I just have a feeling she's . . ." Geo paused, shrugged. "I have the feeling she's a little inexperienced in certain ways, and I sometimes think that she's been protected most of her life."

Dax nodded. "I've felt the same at times, but I think we're both wrong about her. She can be extremely tough about certain things, I've noticed, and she's got enormous willpower. Anyway, I thought—" He lifted his shoulders helplessly, spread his hands. "What I thought is, Forewarned, forearmed. M once said something to me which struck me as rather clever. I remarked how well informed she was, and she said, with a knowing smile, 'Information keeps you safe.' So there you have it. I was passing information on, and by the way, I never said you should tell her anything. I was talking to you, and sort of . . . looking for your input."

"I know she's tough, and extremely smart, and in a bad situation you can be sure she'll go for the jugular, but there have been those odd moments when I've seen something . . . well, oddly enough, very trusting about her."

"That's it exactly!" Dax exclaimed, sitting up in the chair, staring at Georgiana. "Almost innocent."

"What else did your . . . *informant* tell you?" Geo asked.

"That Larry had lost a lot of work because of his . . . problem. Some producers thought he was a risk, that they might not get insurance on him. . . . I'm talking movie producers, by the way."

"I understood. James and I have had supper with M and Larry a few times and been to the theater, and he seems perfectly normal. Sober, calm, not hyper or on a high, or anything like that." Geo now smiled for the first time and said sotto voce, "And you can be sure she wouldn't put up with it if there was any suggestions of drugs. M would go berserk. She's very intolerant that way. Haven't you noticed she hardly drinks anything, and she appears to be very straitlaced in some ways."

"I think you're right," Dax agreed, relieved Geo had calmed down.

"Who told you about Larry's former—" Geo stopped, made little motions with her fingers and gave him a probing look.

"I don't mind telling you, because I know you will keep a confidence. It was Colin Burke, the English actor I met on the Coast. The one who introduced me to Iris, in a sort of roundabout way."

"I see." Geo sat back, looking contemplative, and after a moment, asked, "He didn't indicate that Larry had any problems now, did he? Or trouble getting work?"

Dax shook his head. "No, and even though Colin's gay, he's definitely not bitchy. I promise you that."

"So basically, all this . . . *stuff* we've been discussing happened some years ago. Right?"

Dax nodded and then went on to talk about his play, realizing this would be a much safer topic.

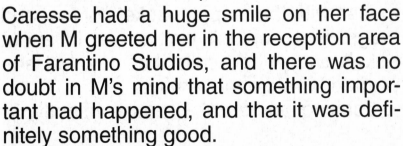

Caresse had a huge smile on her face when M greeted her in the reception area of Farantino Studios, and there was no doubt in M's mind that something important had happened, and that it was definitely something good.

The petite young woman with her elfin features and spiky red hair was more like her old self today. Certainly the gloomy, frequently sorrowful expression she had worn since Frankie's fatal crash had miraculously disappeared.

"You've had good news, haven't you?" M asked. "It's written all over your face."

Caresse nodded, and still smiling, she said, "Come on in, take off your coat, and I'll tell you about it over a cuppa tea."

M started to laugh. "I don't always have tea in the afternoon, you know, so there's no need to have the kettle on the boil every time I come over here."

"I know that, but I'm addicted to your lemon tea. I guess I just picked up your habit, and I have it every day."

The two women walked through the reception area, across the largest of the studios, and into the kitchen. Here M sat down on a tall stool and Caresse started to fuss with the teapot, packets of tea, and mugs. She couldn't wait to tell M about Luke's two phone calls that day, but she wanted to make the tea first.

Looking across at Caresse intently, M

asked, "So, what's happened? Have you finally had an offer for the studios?"

"No. Unfortunately." Taking a deep breath, Caresse went on almost breathlessly, "My good news has to do with you," she cried, no longer able to restrain herself.

"*Me?*" M frowned, looking puzzled. "What on earth do you mean?"

Caresse giggled, then blurted out, "You're about to get your first break, M! This weekend. Luke Hendricks called from Paris early this morning, asked me to track you down. He's coming back to New York on Thursday evening. He wants to do a fashion shoot with you, starting on Saturday. And this afternoon he asked me to tell you that it's a special shoot for Jean-Louis Tremont, the French designer."

"Oh, my God!" M jumped off the stool, rushed over to Caresse, and the two women hugged and began to jump up and down. Still holding each other, then laughing and screaming, they danced around the kitchen like adolescent girls.

When they finally stopped, Caresse ran to turn off the kettle, and M went back to the stool, not quite able to process the news. It seemed incredible to her, and she almost didn't believe it after her last experience. But she wisely said nothing to Caresse, who was obviously over the moon about Luke's intention to use *her* for the Tremont shoot.

"I can't believe this is happening," M said at last, looking over at Caresse. "It's just wonderful! So, tell me what else Luke had to say."

Swinging around, Caresse said, "His first call was about wanting you to do the shoot, and he announced it would be your first break at long last. When he called again at two, he asked me to book Agnes and Marguerite for hair and makeup. He also explained that he doesn't want to start shooting before noon on Saturday, and that you might have to continue the shoot next week as well." Caresse paused, made a face. "Oh, jeez, I bet you won't be able to work at the cheesecake place."

"That doesn't matter," M assured her. "Jody, the manager, understands I have to take time off now and then. It's fine, honestly. Oh, I'm so excited I can't believe it.

Luke must be shooting Tremont's clothes on *me.* Is that what he said?"

"Yes, it is, and listen, before I forget, Luke wants you to bring the things you wore for Frankie's session. It all sounds very serious, don't ya think?"

"I do, and I love Tremont's clothes, they suit me." When she realized Caresse was gaping at her, M explained, "I've never owned a Tremont, just tried his things on occasionally, and once a friend in London lent me a dress of his for a special party." Jumping off the stool, M stepped over to the counter to join Caresse, said, "Oh, God, I must call Larry! Tell him my news. He'll be so *thrilled.*" She pulled her cell out of her red Kelly and started to dial.

Caresse exclaimed, "No! Don't call him! Tell him in person, that's always the best when you have a big surprise to share. He'll take you out to celebrate."

"Not tonight he won't," M answered and put her cell away. "He's had the flu for days. I'm going to make him chicken-in-the-pot again; he likes it, thank goodness, but it must be coming out of his ears by now."

Caresse said, "Jewish penicillin. It works wonders." Handing M the mug, she picked up her own, raised it, and finished, "Congratulations! Here's to the shoot."

❖

"You've been awfully quiet for the last half an hour," James Cardigan murmured, taking Geo's hand in his. "What's bothering you, me darlin'?"

"Nothing, James, honestly. I'm just unwinding after a long day at the easel," she answered and leaned back against the banquette.

"That may be so, but I have a feeling something's troubling you. I know you quite well by now, Georgiana, and I recognize that look in your eyes. A troubled look that doesn't go away." When she did not respond, James lifted his glass and took a sip of his white wine, then glanced around the restaurant. He had brought Geo to Da Umberto on West Seventeenth, a Tuscan restaurant they both enjoyed not only for the food and wine but for the atmosphere. There was a tranquillity about this spot that created a perfect ambience for relaxing, talking, and enjoying the delectable food.

Not wanting to force the point, James

changed the subject when he asked, "How's M? Any breaks yet?"

Geo shook her head. "No, I don't think so. Anyway, she's been very occupied with Larry. He's had the flu, and she's been practically living at his apartment. So I haven't really seen her except for a few minutes. Listen, James, there *is* one thing troubling me, that's true, and it's the safety of my friend Annette Lazenby, who rents the attic floor in the brownstone. I haven't heard from her lately, and neither has her mother, and—"

"Where is she?" James interrupted. "You've only ever mentioned her in passing. So, where is she?"

"She's in Afghanistan on an assignment for her magazine. How dangerous is it out there? In Kabul?"

"Only the most dangerous place in the world, bar none," he responded swiftly. "And no wonder you're concerned about her, I would be. . . . An American woman alone in Kabul, oh boy, is that bad news."

"Actually, it's her mother who drew my attention to it. She called this morning to ask if I'd heard from Annette. And I haven't, not for weeks, and I'm not sure what to do.

Mind you, she's not in the habit of e-mailing me endlessly."

"After dinner I'll help you work out an appropriate e-mail to Annette, making it sound like you're family. That's the first step."

"Why like *family*?" Geo responded, looking baffled.

"You've no idea what's happened to her, and apparently neither does her mother. I want the e-mail to sound as if you're her sister rather than an outsider; that way if someone else has got hold of her computer, if she's been captured or is being held, it will appear innocent."

"But it *is* innocent."

"*I* know that, but others might not."

"I see. So we'll do that, send an e-mail later."

"Annette could be very busy, you know, or traveling. We don't know anything, and we shouldn't speculate."

"Just one question. If she doesn't reply, is there any way *you* can help *me,* so that I can put her mother's worries to rest?"

He was silent for the longest moment, and then he nodded slowly and said in a quiet voice, "I'll do my best to find something out. . . . I still have a few of the right connections. A few markers to call in . . ."

"Thank you, I'm so grateful." Geo squeezed his arm and smiled up at him.

Looking at her, smiling back, James Cardigan realized he would do just about anything for Georgiana Carlson, and he realized yet again that he had fallen for her, very heavily. He kissed the tip of her nose and smiled again, reached for his glass.

For a moment Geo sat staring into the distance, her concern for Annette tantamount in her mind. Yet she knew full well that the troubled look James had noticed a short while ago had to do with the conversation she had had with Dax that afternoon.

Suddenly making up her mind to confide, she leaned into him, put a hand on his arm. "The worried look you just spotted wasn't to do with Annette, actually, James. It had to do with M."

"Oh. Is there something wrong?" His brows drew together, and he appeared puzzled.

"No, I don't think so, not really. It's just

that I had a strange conversation with Dax this afternoon, and I suppose it's worried me a little."

"What do you mean by *strange*?" He peered at her, his eyes narrowing.

Quickly, Geo repeated the conversation about Larry's old troubles. While she was detailed and explicit, she did not reveal that Colin Burke had been the one to inform Dax. She had promised to keep his confidence, and so she did.

James shook his head when she finished and exclaimed, "God, people are terrible! Why did Dax bring it up in the first place? This is old news, bloody old news, in fact."

"So you knew about it?"

"Well, some people did, I suppose. It was about five years ago, and there were rumors that Larry Vaughan was hooked on pills and was losing work because of it. But it was a one-day wonder, basically. It soon went away. Larry immediately cleaned up his act and got on with it. Did a couple of plays, received great notices, and everyone forgot about his so-called drug problem. If there ever was one. In my opinion, it was all a storm in a teacup. I suppose

Dax said he was worried about M, and that's the reason he was telling you?"

Georgiana said, "Yes, that's it. I was pretty angry and told him so, and he immediately let it drop."

"And that's what you should do, my dear. There was no big scandal, and Larry is in good health and perfectly normal, as far as I can see. The past doesn't bear discussing. And who knows whether it was true. Now, let's look at the menu, shall we?"

# Eighteen

Whenever she saw Larry, after even the shortest of absences, M felt a little frisson of excitement, instantly struck once again by his dark good looks, those astonishing blue eyes.

And tonight was no different. She unlocked the door of his apartment and walked into the hall, and her chest tightened at the sight of him. He was standing in the entrance to the living room waiting for her, looking impossibly handsome in a pristine white shirt, black sweater and trousers.

He smiled, obviously pleased to see

her, and took a step forward. She smiled back at him and rushed into his arms, loving him with all her heart. He hugged her to him and said against her cheek, "I've missed you ever so much."

"Me too, you," she answered and stepped away, staring at him. "What are you doing up and dressed? When I left this morning you were a sick man. Shouldn't you be in bed?"

He laughed, helped her off with her coat, and put it in the coat closet. "I'm feeling much better, you've cured me," he answered. "That chicken soup of yours works wonders. Maybe you should bottle it and sell it. As for me, I've had enough of it; it's coming out of my ears. What I want tonight for dinner is a juicy entrecôte and French fries. I've booked a table at Deux Amis."

M exclaimed, "Oh, goody, I won't have to cook!" and walked with him to the library, where a fire blazed in the hearth and a bottle of champagne stood in a bucket of ice on the coffee table.

"How funny that you put out champagne, Larry. It's almost as if you knew," M began and paused, realizing at once that he couldn't possibly be aware of Luke's phone calls to Caresse from Paris.

"Knew what?" Larry asked. He strode across the room, lifted the bottle out of the bucket, and began to remove the metal foil around the cork.

"That I have some wonderful news."

Raising his head, he glanced at her and grinned. "Oddly enough, so do I, hence the champagne. But let me pour us a glass of bubbly first, and you can tell me *your* news. . . . Ladies first."

Joining him near the fire, M took the glass he handed her and waited for him to fill his own before exclaiming, "I'm simply bursting to tell you! I'm so excited, Larry."

"Go on then," he murmured, smiling at her indulgently.

"I've got my first break. *At last!* I'm going to do a shoot for Luke Hendricks. He's got an assignment from Jean-Louis Tremont, the French designer, and I'm to wear his clothes. I think I might be on my way."

"Darling, that *is* wonderful news!" Larry's face was wreathed in smiles, and he raised his glass, touched it to hers. "Congratulations, M! I'm thrilled for you."

Larry was genuinely pleased, knowing how much she wanted to have a modeling career, fully aware of her terrible disappointment after Frankie's death. His happiness showed on his face, and this pleased her. They both sipped from their glasses, but almost at once Larry placed his on the coffee table and put his hand in his trouser pocket. "And my news isn't really *news* but an affirmation of the things I've been saying to you for the last few weeks."

He cleared his throat several times and hurried on. "I think we should become officially engaged." Without another word, and not waiting for her to say anything, he brought out the dark blue box and offered it to her. "This is for you, my darling M."

Slightly stunned, M stared at him and then at the box in his hand. She put down her champagne and took it from him. "Oh, Larry, *darling,* you bought me a ring!" A lump came into her throat, and she thought she was going to burst into tears.

"I did, and I give it to you with all of my love for the rest of my life."

"Oh, it's just gorgeous!" M said, staring at the sapphire ring gleaming against the white leather lining of the box. "It's absolutely beautiful, it really is."

Taking the box away from her, he removed the ring and slipped it on her finger. "Now we're engaged at last, darling." When she just stood there staring at him speechlessly, he searched her face and asked swiftly, "Well, we are, aren't we?"

"Of course we are, you silly thing!" As she said these words, she flung her arms around him, hugged him tightly, then tilted her face to his. It was radiant with joy, which he didn't fail to miss, and this filled him with relief.

After a long, lingering kiss, Larry led her to the sofa, where they sat down together and sipped their champagne, lost for a moment in their own thoughts.

Larry broke the silence when he said in a confiding tone, "I never really knew whether you took me seriously or not. You always went along with me, but occasionally it struck me that maybe you thought I was joking." He paused and looked at her intently. "Did you think that?"

"To be honest, I did once or twice. But

deep down I knew you felt the same way I did. . . . That evening when we met at Iris Ingersoll's was . . . a *coup de foudre,* wasn't it?"

"It was, yes. The minute I set eyes on you I felt as if I'd been punched in the stomach. A more accurate translation of the French would be struck by lightning, of course. *I recognized you.* I knew instantly that *you* were the *one* . . ."

"I've known that about *you* since I was ten," she said with a laugh, then held out her left hand, staring at the ring. "This is so gorgeous, it really is. Thank you, thank you, Larry, it's perfect, and I'm so lucky and I'm so glad you gave me a sapphire, and I love you," she said breathlessly.

"I love *you,* M. And there's something I want to tell you. . . . I've never given a ring to a woman before or been engaged; you're the first woman I've ever asked to marry me."

"Yes, I know that," she responded, glancing at him, a happy expression in her black eyes.

An amused smile played around his mouth. "Of course you do! How could I ever forget that you know everything about me."

"Yes, that's true," she agreed and went on, "Whenever did you get a chance to buy my ring?" She was riddled with curiosity. "It must have been before you came down with the flu."

"It was. About two weeks ago. I just couldn't wait any longer. I wanted my ring on your finger, wanted you to know I was serious about you, and now I want to set a date for our wedding. It's become very urgent to me."

"I thought we were going to have a white wedding at Christmas? Here in New York at City Hall, just the two of us. That was what you suggested, and we agreed it would be like eloping. Isn't that still the plan?" she asked, raising a brow. "It sounded perfect to me."

"To me, too, and yes, that's what we're going to do." He sat back on the sofa, frowning all of a sudden, then turning to her, asked, "Do we need to have witnesses? I'm not sure about the law here."

"Neither am I, but I'll find out, and if we do, we could ask Geo and James to stand up for us, couldn't we?"

"Good idea. Listen, M, I'm afraid I've got to change the subject, something's come up. My mother phoned me from London today; she wants me to go to Canada, to be with my father in Toronto. He's doing a play there, *Cyrano de Bergerac,* and she believes he needs some moral support." Larry related the conversation he'd had with his mother that morning and finished, "So, I'm planning to leave this coming Saturday, and I hope you'll come with me, darling."

"Oh, Larry, I can't!" M exclaimed and rushed on. "I'm starting the shoot with Luke this weekend. At Frankie's studio. It's all set up, hair, makeup, everything. I'll be working all weekend, and most of next week as well, according to Caresse. Oh, God, I'm so *sorry,* Larry. I really do wish I could come, but, well, you know I can't."

Although he was disappointed, Larry took hold of her hand and squeezed it. "Don't worry, it's all right, *really* it is. I understand you can't miss this big chance, nothing must interfere with it, in fact. But I do have to go, give my support to Dad. I hope you understand that; well, I know you do. But I'll sure as hell miss you, sweetheart. I don't want to be away from you . . . and I won't be ever again, if I can help it."

"And neither will I," M said, and she meant this. Sitting up straighter, she hesitated for a split second before saying, in a nervous voice, "Larry, I—" Immediately she stopped, wondering whether to speak out or not.

"What is it? What were you going to say?" he asked, conscious of the worry in her voice.

"You mentioned that you wanted to make our engagement *official.* Do you mean you want to announce it . . . to the world?"

"I wasn't thinking of it in that way, no. *Why?* What's bothering you?" he asked.

"Nothing, honestly," she protested. "But I'd prefer it if we sort of, well, kept it to ourselves for the moment."

"Why?" There was a hint of surprise in his tone.

"Because if we make a formal announcement, my mother will instantly become involved. *Very involved,*" she explained. "She'll start planning a big wedding with all the trimmings, and before you know it we won't be getting married until next year. Big weddings take lots of time to plan, and you know as well as I do that before we can blink, everything will be out of *our* control. The mothers will have taken over."

"Oh, God, you're right about that! *Of course.* Mothers love big weddings. Especially when they involve the favorites, and I suspect *you* are the favorite, aren't you, M? I know I'm my mother's favorite, not that she's ever admitted that, mind you. Okay, you're absolutely right. We'll keep it a secret, our secret, and we'll announce it to the world only when we're well and truly married. How does that sound?"

"Perfect," she answered, filled with relief that she had just averted a disaster.

Awakening in the middle of the night, M found it difficult to go back to sleep. Her mind was racing. She lay very still, not wishing to disturb Larry. He was in a deep sleep, breathing heavily because of his bout with the flu, but she was thankful he was so much better. On the other hand, was he well enough to fly to Toronto on Saturday? He still had a bad cough. One thing she could do was make certain he had plenty of cold pills and cough medicine with him. M wished she could go with him, but there was no way she could cancel or change the date of the shoot, nor did Larry want her to do that. He had totally understood.

She smiled to herself as her thoughts swung to their evening at the little French bistro close by, just off First Avenue. Larry had insisted on ordering more champagne so that they could continue to celebrate their engagement and her big break. And from time to time she had held out her left hand and gazed at the sapphire ring gleaming in the candlelight, admiring it, and Larry had smiled that warm, indulgent smile of his, love for her reflected in his bright blue eyes.

Only one thing had marred the evening as far as she was concerned, and that was hearing that his brother Edward would be joining Larry in Toronto. They were going to spend a few days together with their father, and then Larry would return to New York, leaving Edward in charge.

M was extremely wary of Edward Vaughan, knowing he had mistreated Larry when they were children and had continued to pick on him in their teens and twenties. Now there was a truce between them, at least so Larry said, but she believed a leopard didn't easily change its spots. There was no doubt in her mind that there was a lot of envy still lingering inside Edward. She had recently checked him out on the Internet and discovered, much to her surprise, that Edward's career was successful but not very distinguished. He was the only member of the family who had never won an award. And it was Larry who had been given the most accolades—an Oscar, an Emmy, and two Tonys in America, and in London he had won a BAFTA as well as the much-coveted Olivier for excellence in the theater.

At the time, she'd felt a little surge of pride about that and all of Larry's achievements. Laurence Vaughan, the man she loved with all her heart, was one of the world's greatest actors, and his talent was awe-inspiring. His brother Edward more than likely hated him for *that,* never mind his success. There was no question in her mind that Edward Vaughan was a rascal in his private life—all those wives and women and children. He was quite the opposite of her darling Larry.

Unexpectedly, M shivered, and goose-flesh ran up her arms. *Edward was going to make trouble for Larry in Toronto.* She *knew* this, and she was filled with a sense of foreboding. Try though she might, she was unable to shake off this feeling, and it stayed with her for the rest of the night. It even haunted her dreams.

# Nineteen

If this shoot works for all of us the way I think it will, then it's Frankie we have to thank," Luke Hendricks said, looking from Caresse to M.

The young photographer and the two women were sitting in the kitchen, which opened off the largest of the Farantino studios, drinking coffee and going over plans for the upcoming session.

It was Caresse who spoke first, asking, "But what do you mean, Luke? How is Frankie involved when he's de—" She broke off her sentence, cleared her throat, and finished, "Not here."

"Because it was Frankie who showed Jean-Louis Tremont the pictures of M when we met up with him at Monte Carlo. We were doing a shoot for him there, and when he saw you, M, he was over the moon. I think it was the Audrey thing, your resemblance to her that caught his imagination."

"How sweet of Frankie," M murmured, touched to know that he had kept her in mind when talking to the French couturier.

"You see, he kept his word to you," Caresse asserted, touching M's arm and smiling at her. "That's my Frankie, he's always reliable and—" Once more she stopped speaking, bit her lip, and then said in a sad little whisper, "I mean he *was*."

Catching the hint of despondency in Caresse's voice, Luke exclaimed in a cheerful, somewhat bossy tone, "Now, listen up, the two of you! In about half an hour Kate Morrell is coming over with her assistant and the clothes. She runs the American end of Tremont's business, and he relies on her tremendously. She's bringing a number of pieces, including two coats, two day suits, both with skirts, two short cocktail dresses, and two long evening gowns. Out of that lot we'll choose six pieces for the shoot. So I think Marguerite had better start your makeup, M, and we'll decide about your hair—whether we want it up or in a ponytail—when the clothes are here."

M nodded and jumped off the stool. "I'll go back to hair and makeup straightaway, Luke, and thank you for everything."

"I haven't done anything, at least not yet," he announced with a light laugh and a cheeky wink.

"Just one question, though," M continued, ignoring the leer he threw her. "You say Frankie showed Jean-Louis the pictures he took of me, but then what happened?"

"I guess Tremont spent a lot of time thinking about the pictures, and after the accident he called me from Paris. He'd already left the Riviera. I was still in Nice, doing what I had to do," Luke responded. "Jean-Louis said he wanted to look at the photographs again, and would I come to see him in Paris? Bringing the pictures, of course. And so I did. And voilà! We've got a shoot because he wanted to use you. That's about it."

"Thanks for explaining," M murmured and smiled at Caresse. "You're looking fabulous again," she told her. "I'm so glad you're better."

"So am I," Caresse replied. "I was beginning to feel old, and depressed, wearing so much black. So this morning I thought, It's back to the red or the bright green or the electric blue, so here I am in red, and feeling more like my old self."

"It's also the idea of the shoot," Luke interjected. "And me back here, and M getting her chance, and we're going to do our damndest to make Frankie proud of us. Right, Caresse?"

"Right, Luke! He's watching us, you know."

"I hope he is, honey bun, and giving me a guiding hand long distance." Luke grinned at Caresse and walked toward M. "Listen up, kiddo. Tell Marguerite to keep the eye makeup soft, and I don't want you to have bushy beetle brows. There should be a suggestion of our Audrey, but not an exact replica. Okay?"

"Okay, General." M grinned and hurried out.

Luke turned to Caresse and said, "I want to make her a star, Caresse. For her, for myself, for you and Frankie. He was so determined to launch her, you know. Now it's up to us to do it for him. She's our legacy from him, in a sense, don't you agree?"

Caresse nodded and brushed her hand across her eyes as she unexpectedly teared up. "Frankie told me M was a natural, that he'd never seen anybody so relaxed in front of a camera, never seen a novice so professional. *Skilled* was the word he used. In fact, he kept saying to me that he thought she'd actually been trained to be a model but was keeping it to herself. I agree M does seem to have a lot of self-confidence, a certain kind of composure."

"It's breeding," Luke announced. "I don't know where the hell she comes from or who her family is, but she's got class, and that you can't acquire. You're born with it."

Caresse looked at him through narrowed eyes and murmured, "Frankie said almost the same thing. I'll be honest, he raved about her so much after he'd developed the film, I got jealous. Frankie tried to explain it was only a professional thing; he said he admired her as a model, as an object to photograph, and that he wasn't interested in her as a woman—"

"I am, though," Luke cut in. "I wouldn't mind being entangled with her one bit. Want to know something? . . . I'd enjoy it."

"I think she's seeing an actor," Caresse volunteered.

"Who?"

"Larry Vaughan."

"No kidding!"

"That's what she told me anyway."

"But he's not just an actor, he's a movie star, for God's sake! Do you think it's serious?"

Shrugging and making a face, Caresse said, "I don't know, I don't think so . . ." She gave him a long, hard stare. "So you've got the hots for M."

"Why not, she's gorgeous."

"She's a lot taller than you, Luke."

He burst out laughing. "What does that matter when you're flat on your back?"

"Luke! You devil. . . . I betcha there's no chance with her. Not for you."

"We'll see, won't we? In the meantime, help me roll the Paris backdrops over to the middle of the studio, will you, sweetie pie? We'd better use the Champs-Élysées and the Eiffel Tower scenes to begin with.

That's what Tremont wants, well-known Paris backgrounds for these shots."

The two of them went out onto the studio floor and Caresse said, "Alex wants to help us with this shoot, and he'll be here real soon. That's okay with you, Luke, isn't it?"

"Sure it is, he's a good kid. Anyway, I guess this whole shebang is his now, right?"

"Yes, sure is," Caresse responded and decided not to add that Frankie had left her a thirty percent interest in the studio complex. This was in a codicil he had added to his will about three weeks before they became engaged. She had been so touched when his lawyer told her about it she had cried herself to sleep for three nights, thinking about Frankie, the best man she'd ever known, and missing him like crazy.

Caresse was amazed a short while later when Kate Morrell arrived with her assistant, Janet Gordon, the two women pushing a rack of clothes in garment bags. The thing that surprised her was the way the women handled the rack, especially since they were all dressed up in smart high-fashion outfits and teeteringly high Manolos. She couldn't help wondering why they didn't have an able-bodied young man to do this job.

Caresse hurried forward and introduced herself, as did the two women who worked for Jean-Louis Tremont in New York, and then she opened the double doors to the studio complex and led them over to the biggest studio, where Luke was to do the shoot. They followed her, pushing the rack of garment bags.

❈

Luke and M paused when they reached the rack of clothes, and as he sorted through them, he said, "Since your hair is currently in a ponytail, I think we should start with day clothes, don't you?"

"Absolutely. And I love this pale blue wool coat and the gray flannel suit. Oh, and just look at this black wool dress, Luke, the cut is fantastic." Turning to him, she added, "I've always admired Jean-Louis's clothes. . . . I'm going to enjoy modeling them, I really am."

"That's great, I'm glad you feel that way. Now come on over and meet the two women from the shop. Kate Morrell has a lot of influence with Jean-Louis, but she's very nice, tough but unassuming. You'll like her, and just look at the excitement on her face, she can't wait to meet you."

Luke guided M toward the two women at the far end of the studio, who stood waiting for them. When they came to a stop, Luke said, "Kate, Janet, this is M."

The three women shook hands, and Kate said in an enthusiastic tone, "I think you're going to look wonderful in Jean-Louis's clothes. I can't wait to see you wearing them." Addressing Luke, she continued, "I know you don't like an audience when you shoot, but I would love it if we could see M modeling the clothes before we leave. Is that all right?"

"Course it is, Kate. No problem at all, and I'm positive you'll be thrilled. They look as if they've been designed just for her, don't ya think?"

"I do, yes. They're from Jean-Louis's fall and winter collection, which was shown in Paris this past July, and Janet and I brought along the shoes, gloves, and accessories which go with the different pieces. Janet has the list."

Janet immediately produced this and handed it to Caresse, who had already unpacked the smaller items. Walking over to the rack and signaling Caresse to come with her, Janet explained, "The pale blue pillbox hat goes with this pale blue winter coat, as do the dark beige shoes and matching leather gloves. Now, the pearls work with the black day dress and also the black lace cocktail dress. Every outfit has its own shoes, gloves, et cetera."

"I understand," Caresse said. Glancing down at the list in her hand, she nodded. "Everything's very clear, Janet, and it'll make my job easier."

Luke suddenly announced, in a confident voice, "I don't think Jean-Louis is going to be disappointed."

"Neither do I," Kate shot back, sounding enthusiastic, a huge smile on her face. Seating herself on one of the tall stools and beckoning Janet to join her, she added, "Take your time, Luke, let's work at your speed."

"We'll start in a couple of minutes," Luke responded, and he and M hurried over to the rack. M took the blue wool coat, and Caresse followed them into hair and makeup, bringing the matching pill-box hat, beige shoes, and gloves.

When M walked out into the studio a few minutes later, Kate knew that this young woman was the ultimate, a winner. Her dark exotic looks were eye-catching, and she was beautiful in an offbeat way. An Audrey Hepburn look-alike, no two ways about that, but Kate realized that the makeup had been kept to a minimum, and she suddenly understood why. Luke wanted her to be M, to be herself, not a replica of anyone.

Kate was also struck by the way the pale blue coat looked on her, better than on other models somehow. It had a round neck with no collar, two sets of buttons at the top, and dolman sleeves. An A-line coat with a grand flare at the back. And the pill-box hat was perfect. Jackie O, Kate thought, she wore hats like this.

Oh, yes, this girl has something truly special, Kate decided. What also caught Kate's attention was M's body. She was tall, especially in the three-inch heels, lithe and unusually elegant. She moved gracefully, almost like a dancer, and there was a marvelous self-confidence about her as she walked and turned.

"She'll be at home on a catwalk," Kate murmured to her assistant.

"She'll dominate it," Janet whispered back. "She's a natural, a real find."

Kate nodded. Without a doubt, this young woman, who rather enigmatically called herself M, was going to be a big star. *The New Face of Jean-Louis Tremont,* Kate thought. It would be the banner for their next show. M was exactly what they had been looking for for the longest time. Just what they had needed. And then another thought came to her, a somewhat revolutionary thought. They would make M a star *before* she modeled their spring-summer collection next year. Kate herself was going to make M a star *now.* If Luke's pictures were as great as she believed they would be, they would use them immediately. What a boost for the current collection this would be. A new campaign, with M at the center of it.

I'm inspired, Kate decided. Inspired by the mysterious M.

# Twenty

Several days later Luke had cleared the main studio. Gone were the tall stools, rolling shelves, rolling backdrops, folding and trestle tables. What he wanted was a totally empty space, and once he had it he had brought in six life-size blowups of M, mounted on hardboard.

Strategically placed to complement each other, the black-and-white photographs were stunning. They were arranged in a semicircle and highlighted dramatically by three high-intensity lamps.

He studied the display for a long moment,

finally nodded, satisfied he had achieved the effect he had envisioned.

A few seconds later Kate Morrell came into the studio. As usual she was beautifully coiffed and made up, dressed in a chic Tremont suit. Following immediately behind her was the iconic French designer, tall, elegant, and looking much younger than his sixty years despite his silver hair. In part, his youthfulness sprang from his lithe, slender body, perfect tan, and sparkling brown eyes.

It was Jean-Louis himself who stopped dead in his tracks when he saw the blow-ups. He moved closer, stared at them intently, thinking his clothes had never looked better. This girl was miraculous.

Swinging around, he went to Luke, grabbed hold of him, and kissed him on each cheek in true Gallic style. In his slightly accented, perfect English he said, "Bravo, Luke, bravo! And my many congratulations." Gesturing to the blowups, he added, "*C'est magnifique, ah oui.*"

Luke beamed. "I'm pleased you like the display, Jean-Louis. It seemed to me the pictures looked more dramatic in black and white."

"Fantastic, *mon ami,* fantastic." He turned around as M walked into the studio and he went to greet her. Jean-Louis took her hand, bent over it, kissed it, and gave her a warm smile. "It is nice to see you again. So many congratulations, the photographs are incredible."

"It's the clothes really, monsieur," she replied, meaning this. "You and Luke are the true geniuses here, not me."

"Ah, flattery, mademoiselle, flattery," the Frenchman murmured, his dark eyes twinkling. He liked her a lot, had taken to her instantly when they met a few days ago. He knew Kate was correct about her. She *would* be a star. And his muse, his inspiration. Her style and class were incomparable.

Kate was thrilled with the blowups, and taking hold of Luke's arm, she walked him forward so they were standing directly in front of them. "What do you think about using these in the Madison Avenue store? Mid-December through into the new year? They'd make a wonderful display."

"You and Jean-Louis know best, Kate. And I guess they would lead into the new collection—you'll be showing it in late January in Paris, right?"

"Absolutely, and by the way, we want you to photograph this new collection, Luke, but we'll talk about that later. Right now I have to settle things with M."

"She'll want you to use Blane's, you know. She's very loyal to them."

"No problem, none at all. But she told me yesterday that she'd like to have all the details herself first. Apparently she has a sister in London who owns a boutique, and she wanted to discuss our terms with her before Blane's got involved."

Luke couldn't help laughing. "That's not surprising," he finally said.

Kate stared at him, a look of bafflement on her face. "Why do you say that, and why are you laughing so hard?"

"Because Caresse has always said that M is a tough cookie when it comes to business, although how she knows this I have no idea. Don't misunderstand, she adores M, but then everyone does."

"I can see that, and I understand why, she's a genuinely nice young woman. And I can't say I blame her, wanting to have her older sister, a businesswoman, as a sounding board."

A short while ago Kate Morrell had taken Jean-Louis Tremont to Kennedy to catch the night flight to Paris. But before leaving the Farantino Studios, she had conferred with Luke and M for a few minutes. Something of a mover and shaker in the world of fashion, she always forged ahead undeterred, her heart set on accomplishing her ends. In this instance it was to make M famous *before* the January collections.

She explained this to M and Luke, then told M, "I need you to come to the shop tomorrow, because we have to take your *exact* measurements. Jean-Louis had already designed part of the spring-summer collection; the rest he is going to build around you. And naturally the clothes must fit you *perfectly.*"

Addressing Luke, she had gone on, "And I would like you to be there, because Jean-Louis and I want you to photograph some of the pret-à-porter line, on M, of course, because we do very well with our ready-to-wear collection. Together we will select the pieces."

They had both agreed to be at the Madison Avenue store at two o'clock, and Kate had been as pleased as they were, delighted they were so cooperative.

Luke stood alone in the studio. The overhead lights were out, and it was in darkness except for the three high-intensity spotlights focused on the six blowups of M. She had gone home, Caresse was cleaning up the kitchen, and he had wandered in here to turn off the spotlights but had been momentarily captivated yet again.

Even though he said so himself, it had been an inspired idea to present the photographs like this. The blowups had blown Jean-Louis away, to coin a phrase. As if he had needed convincing; the designer had been enchanted by Frankie's pictures of M when he first saw them in Monte Carlo.

Luke sighed, missing Frankie, as he did every day. What a needless death it had been. A fatal crash on the Grande Corniche because Frankie had more than likely been driving too fast, but there was no doubt in Luke's mind that the driver of the other vehicle had been also. How often he had warned Frankie to slow down, and he had never stopped worrying about Frankie's racing driver mentality; he loved whizzing along at high speed regardless of anything else.

Luke turned off one of the spotlights, and suddenly the mood of the studio was altered. Shadows were thrown across one of M's blowups, giving her an eerie, ghostlike appearance. Luke shivered, gooseflesh prickling his neck, and he had a sudden premonition of disaster. Endeavoring to push this irrational feeling aside, he found he could not.

Luke turned off the second light and was about to kill the last spot, but he did not. Instead he gazed up at the ten-foottall M in the glamorous black evening gown and thought how extraordinary she looked. She was one of the most photogenic women he had ever worked with, and he knew that she *would* be a big star in the fashion firmament. Kate Morrell would see to that. But this was a dangerous world, full of temptations of all kinds, from excessive praise, ego-pumping accolades, and extensive press coverage to sudden celebrity, partying, and frequently soul-destroying drugs. Many a great model had taken a tumble.

He breathed deeply, blew out air, reminding himself that M was practical, business-like, and down-to-earth. He was as positive as he could be that she would remain herself, yet he still felt chilled to the bone, beset by troubling thoughts of the future. . . .

# Twenty-one

M was not only frustrated but worried. And on the verge of becoming really angry. For the past few days she had been unable to reach Larry. Very simply, he wasn't responding to her messages or returning her calls, and she couldn't imagine why.

She sat on the bed in her room at Geo's, staring into space, her mind racing, her cell in her hand. And then she checked her watch for the umpteenth time. It was just past eight-thirty on Saturday morning. Five minutes ago she had tried to get Larry on his cell, but it was turned off. A split second later she had dialed the Four Seasons

Hotel in Toronto and asked to be put through to Mr. Laurence Vaughan's room. The phone had just rung and rung, and she had finally ended the call in exasperation.

She bit her lip, wondering what to do, then realized there was nothing she could do. Anyway, he was coming back to New York later today, after two weeks in Toronto with his father.

Edward, unfortunately, had arrived a week ago, sooner than expected, and the mere idea of this troubled her. No wonder we kept playing telephone tag on Monday, she now thought, Edward is probably giving Larry a hard time, taking it out on him because he was forced to fly to Canada so that Larry could leave. Seemingly, Edward had better fish to fry when it came to being a good son.

So why had he arrived sooner than expected? Don't even go there, she told herself, stood up, pushed her phone into the pocket of her jeans, and went downstairs to the kitchen.

Her mind remained focused on Larry as she made coffee. The first week he had been in Toronto they had spoken twice a day, but since last weekend they had been out of touch. Perhaps Larry wasn't responding because there were problems with his father after all. M considered this possibility for a moment and dismissed it, chided herself for being stupid. Larry had told her that his father was in good shape, so his sudden silence might well have something to do with the arrival of his brother.

The thought of Larry exposed to Edward filled her with dismay. But he *was* due back this afternoon. She would soon know everything, and things would normalize. In the meantime, she would just have to be patient. And she wasn't going to phone him again either, because she didn't want to be perceived as a nuisance. She knew she would hear from him the minute he arrived at the Beekman Place apartment.

Taking her mug of coffee over to the table near the window, M sat drinking it, acknowledging that she was a little disappointed she hadn't been able to share all of her good news with her fiancé. *Fiancé.* Yes, that was exactly what he was, and soon he would be her husband. Her thoughts turned to their marriage; she was well aware she would have to tell him who she really was before they went to City Hall to "tie the knot," as he called it. If she married him under an assumed name, it would not be legal. She wondered what he would say when she told him her name wasn't Marie Marsden—

"Hi, hi, hi!" Geo exclaimed from the doorway, and came bouncing into the room full of energy and vitality, a bright smile on her face.

"Good morning, and you're in good spirits," M answered, smiling back. "I just made coffee a few minutes ago, so it's nice and fresh."

Geo nodded. "I'll come and join you, and incidentally, James stayed over last night, so don't be surprised if he comes wandering in shortly."

"It'll be nice to see him," M replied, meaning this.

As she poured herself a mug of coffee, Geo announced, "I have some great news."

"You're engaged to James," M asserted, hoping this was true.

"No, not yet." Geo sat down opposite M, leaned over the table, and added, "But if he asks I'm going to say yes."

"I'm delighted to hear it, and I'd kill you if you didn't. So what *is* your news?"

"I got a call last night from Annette Lazenby. She's alive and kicking. And in Rome! What a relief it was to finally hear from her."

"I bet it was, and did she tell you why there has been such a long silence?" M asked, suddenly riddled with curiosity about a woman she barely knew.

"She did. She said she'd had a bad case of bronchitis. I think it was only because of James's intervention that she got out of Afghanistan safely."

"I didn't know he'd intervened," M said, looking surprised.

"Sort of. . . . He called someone he knows, who's now based in Pakistan, and asked him to do a bit of checking." Geo shrugged, rolled her eyes. "That's all I know. James didn't tell me anything else."

"Well, he wouldn't, would he? And I bet he's a good man to have in a crisis. I think men like James usually operate on the premise that the less one knows about something problematical, the better off one is. Don't you agree?"

"I do, yes." Clearing her throat and changing the subject, Geo said, "So, from the few little tidbits you've thrown my way, I think you really did get your first break, didn't you, M? It's a big one, isn't it?"

M grinned. "Yes, it is, and I'm *thrilled.* Thanks to Luke and his photographs, I'm going to be under contract to Jean-Louis Tremont. I'll be doing the January–February shows for him in Paris."

"Congratulations!" Geo exclaimed, instantly jumped up, went around the table, and hugged M. "I'm very happy for you. You deserve this chance."

"Geo . . . there's something I have to tell you. . . . I'll be giving up my room in December. I'm going to be living in Paris . . ." M's voice trailed off a little sadly, and she stared across the table at her landlady and friend, then sighed. "I'm so sorry."

"But it's all right, honestly it is," Geo assured her. "I'll miss you, of course. But I have a feeling I'm going to be with James permanently, whether we marry or not, and I believe he'll want to live here with me. Alone. What I'm trying to say is that I don't think I'm going to be a landlady anymore, not after you depart."

"But what about Annette?" M asked, a brow lifting.

"She indicated she may be going to live in Rome, although she didn't explain why. All I know is I'm glad she's safe."

Changing the subject again, Geo now said, "Tell me, how has Larry taken the news?"

"He's happy for me. As pleased as punch, and he's going to come with me to Paris," M confided, without elaborating.

Geo grinned at her. "Hey, I have a great idea! Why don't you get married before you fly away to a new life in Paris? Isn't that a fabulous thought?"

"It is, yes, and I'll consider it."

Geo had gone upstairs to look in on James, wondering aloud, as she left the kitchen, if he was still sleeping. And M sat at the kitchen table, finishing her mug of coffee, lost in her thoughts.

Oddly, she was thinking about Annette Lazenby, whom she didn't know at all, and discovered she was filled with relief that the journalist was going to move out and live in Rome. Annette had proved to be a worry to Geo in the long run, especially

when her distraught mother had kept phoning in tearful desperation, begging Geo to help.

"None of us are our sisters' keepers," M had pointed out to Geo recently, and Geo had quickly agreed. Nonetheless, Geo had been compassionate enough to want to help and had dragged James into the equation.

M *knew* him, and her deepest instincts told her that he was a decent man with a conscience. Apparently he had been able to intervene. As a former agent with MI6, he obviously had a wealth of knowledge and contacts, and so he had done what he could. And he had made this effort because of Georgiana. M admired him for that; she was also happy that these two had found each other.

As for Annette Lazenby, M decided she had behaved recklessly by going to Afghanistan when the country was in turmoil. But then that was what one did as an investigative journalist. M sighed, stood up, went out of the kitchen and down the corridor, and crossed Geo's studio, making for the little garden at the back.

Who am *I* to criticize her? she asked

herself, sitting down in the metal chair on the patio. I have also been reckless; I threw myself into Laurence Vaughan's arms, and he doesn't know my real name; I've lied to him by omission without thinking anything through. I gave myself to him in every way, and I'm in love with a man who has many troubling issues with his family, which can only infringe on our relationship, yet he becomes embroiled with them at the drop of a hat.

M was well aware that Larry lived in New York because he loved it, but she also realized he wanted to keep his daunting family at arm's length. The problem was, Larry believed he was not as good as those of his siblings who were actors. Only Miranda, who was a set designer, did not come into play. M had found herself arguing with him just before he had gone off to Canada, pointing out somewhat forcefully that he was, in fact, better than they, even better than his father, who she thought had become a bit pretentious in his acting, even pompous. He was considered one of the great actor knights, *Sir* Nicholas Vaughan, knighted by the Queen and standing alongside Sir Anthony Hopkins, Sir Michael Caine, and Sir Sean Connery, to mention only a few of that illustrious circle, all of the same generation.

Larry's the best, she thought. No, he's not the best, he's better than the best. Only his mother ranks alongside him when it comes to talent. Why didn't he see it? Why was he so vulnerable to them? So open to hurt?

And he remained bloody loyal. Oh, God, who was she to talk? There was no one more loyal than she herself. She was totally loyal to her lot. . . . Come hell or high water, she would fight for them, die for them, if need be. And this despite anything they might have done to her, any pain they had caused, which was always unintentional. She was one of five, just as Larry was one of six. She closed her eyes, trying to shut out the memories, but they would not go away.

A slight wind suddenly blew up, ruffling through her hair, wafting across her face, and she opened her eyes, sat up, blinking in the brightness of the morning. It was a pretty day with a pale blue sky and golden sunshine; although it was already the end of October, it was more like September, not cold at all . . . an Indian summer kind of day. Immediately M thought of her mother, who basked in delight whenever it was a day like this, a summer's day in autumn, that was the way her mother always put it.

M saw her mother clearly in her head at the moment, and her father as well. And alongside were her two sisters and her brothers. Each of them sharply and precisely defined. She suddenly laughed out loud, thinking of their shock when she told them about Larry. Her siblings had teased her unmercifully when she was ten because of her crush on him after she had seen his memorable *Hamlet.* They would be shocked. No, not that, but certainly surprised, she decided and laughed again.

In a sense she was sad she couldn't confide in her sisters and her mother. Once she and Larry had been married, she would tell them before they found out some other way. That was the only fair thing to do. It was bound to leak, wasn't it? Still, once they were married, it wouldn't matter that her family knew. Certainly they couldn't give her a big wedding, which was a relief.

M was sure they would like Larry and take him to their hearts. He was very engaging, and it was that which would impress them, not his fame, or his looks. Neither would matter to them. After all, they were all famous and good-looking themselves.

She zeroed in on Larry, her mind racing. Where are you? Why aren't you calling me? Are you avoiding me? What's going on? She had no answers, and her frustration and disappointment spiraled into exasperation.

And many months later, when she looked back, she realized that this was the day her troubles began.

# Twenty-two

After she had showered, done her makeup, and dressed, M made a sudden decision. She would endeavor to reach Larry one more time, hoping to ascertain when he would be arriving in New York. Waiting to hear from him was becoming trying, and she was well aware that doing something positive would help to soothe her increasing nervousness.

Sitting down in the armchair near her bed, she reached for the landline and dialed the hotel in Toronto. When the hotel operator answered, she asked for reception, and a moment later a friendly male voice was asking her how he could be of help.

"This is Marie Marsden," she announced in her most businesslike tone. "I'm Mr. Laurence Vaughan's secretary, and I've been trying to reach him, but there's no answer to his room. He was due to check out today, and I wish to know if he's already done so."

"I believe he has, Miss Marsden. Just give me a moment to confirm that, will you?"

"Thank you," M replied, hoping that Larry had indeed left the hotel, and Canada, and was on a plane back to New York at this very moment, as he had planned.

"Miss Marsden, he *has* checked out," the clerk told her. "Do you wish to speak to Mr. Edward Vaughan? Or Sir Nicholas, perhaps?"

"No, no, but thank you. Would you have any idea what time Mr. Vaughan checked out this morning?"

"It was yesterday, actually, Miss Marsden. Mr. Vaughan checked out yesterday afternoon, according to our register."

"*Oh.* Thanks. Thank you very much." She hung up without another word and sat back with a jolt, a stunned expression settling on her face. *He was already in New York, no doubt at his apartment, and he hadn't called her.* Why? What was wrong? Didn't he want to see her? Had the two weeks apart from her made him change his mind about her? Was he dumping her?

All kinds of disquieting questions ran through her mind as she sat, baffled and staring into space, feelings of astonishment, hurt, and disappointment flooding through her. Surely he didn't want to break it off? How could he, after all he'd said and done, the love he had shown her? And what about the sapphire ring from Harry Winston? A man didn't give a woman an important ring like that and not mean what he said about loving her, wanting to marry her. At least a man like Larry didn't, he was too serious-minded, and he was like her brothers . . . true blue. Right from the beginning of their relationship she had felt he was the type of man whose word was his bond. Dependable. Honorable. She sat, wondering what to do and then quickly made up her mind. Going to her clothes closet, she grabbed her black trench coat, picked up her battered red Kelly, and ran downstairs.

Before leaving the house, she went to the kitchen, pushed open the door, and looked in. "Geo, I've got to go out for a while," she said, striving to sound normal.

"All right," Geo answered, smiling warmly. "I'm sure we'll be here when you get back."

James, who was sitting at the table with Geo, grinned and waved. "Good morning, M!"

She waved back and pushed a big smile onto her face, murmured, "See you both later," and was gone in an instant.

Out on the street, she found a cab and got in, was immediately on her way uptown to Larry's apartment. Settling back against the seat, she tried to relax and discovered she couldn't shake her worry. The nearer they got to his place the worse it grew. She had a strange presentiment that there was something wrong, *terribly wrong,* and her chest was tight with anxiety.

Both the doorman and the concierge greeted her pleasantly as she flew into the lobby and took the elevator up to Larry's apartment. He had given her a key some weeks ago, and she used it to let herself in.

The first thing M noticed was the suitcase on the floor of the entrance hall, and his trench coat thrown over a chair. Taking off her own coat, laying it on top of his, she looked in the living room and called his name. There was no answer. When she checked his bedroom and the kitchen and found no sign of him, she went back to the living room and walked through it, making for the library. Before she even reached the door, she heard muffled coughing; she pushed the door open a nanosecond later, found Larry stretched out on the sofa, and saw that he looked ghastly. He was unshaven, and his face was ashen; he wore his pajamas and a dressing gown and was clutching something against his chest.

"Larry! Larry! Whatever's the matter? Oh, my God, you're ill!" she cried. "What's wrong? What is it? Talk to me, Larry." She dropped her handbag on the coffee table and knelt down next to him, took hold of his hand, discovered it was icy cold. Prying open his fingers, she found an empty plastic pill bottle without its top. On the label was Larry's name, as well as the name of the Toronto pharmacy and a doctor. At the bottom it said "Vicodin," and there was a small red label on which was printed a

warning that this was a controlled substance and should be taken only as directed. "Vicodin," she read again, frowning.
Wasn't that a form of codeine? She was
sure it was, and that was a powerful drug,
dangerous if misused, wasn't it?

Putting the bottle in her pocket, she felt
Larry's pulse, then pushed her hand inside
his pajama top, placed it on his heart. She
thought both his pulse and his heartbeat
seemed normal. But he was totally out of it.
He was drugged, she was certain of that.

Leaning over him, she said, "It's *me,*
Larry."

He didn't answer her, but after a moment his eyes half opened. Glazed, they
weren't focused on her, and in an instant
the lids had drooped again.

"Larry," she cried, "try to answer me.
Why have you taken the pills?"

He didn't open his eyes, but somehow
he must have heard her, because eventually he mumbled something she couldn't
quite understand.

"Why did you take the pills?" she repeated. "Do you have pain?"

Slowly, making an effort, he brought his

hand up to his mouth and again mumbled; still she didn't understand what he was saying. Then it struck her that he might have said "tooth." "Did you go to a dentist in Toronto? Did you have a painful tooth?" she demanded. "Is it still painful?"

He was silent, but his hand remained against his mouth for a second before it fell weakly to his chest.

Rising, M ran across to the desk and sat down, her first intention being to call her elder brother in London. She had frequently gone to him when she had problems to solve, and he had always helped her. She trusted him implicitly, and he was smart and worldly wise; he would tell her what to do. She began to dial his number, then stopped abruptly, put the receiver back in the cradle.

She knew that when she explained the situation she was in, he would tell her to get out of the apartment at once. He would want her to protect herself at all costs.

But she loved Larry and wanted to help him, so she couldn't leave him alone. What if he died? He needed medical help. At once. But who could she get to assist her?

She didn't have many friends in New York, only Geo really.

Then another name leapt into her mind. *James Cardigan.* He was a mature man, a former secret agent, head of his own international business, certainly experienced, worldly, and sophisticated. But if she asked him for help, would he keep her confidence?

He will if you're a client, that you can be sure of, a voice in her head told her. Hire him, pay him, and he will be obliged to keep your business confidential.

She hesitated nonetheless, but when she saw that Larry was now shivering excessively, as if chilled to the bone, she knew she must act with great swiftness.

Taking a deep breath, she called Geo. It was James who answered with a cheerful "Hello?"

"James, it's me, M, and—"

"Let me get Geo."

"No, no, I need to talk to you."

"You do?" he answered, sounding surprised, and laughing he added, "I thought it was my lady you were looking for, when I heard your—"

"No, definitely *you,*" she cut in peremptorily and went on immediately. "I want to hire you, James. I need you to help me with something important, but I must work with you as a client and not as a friend."

"But we *are* friends," he countered, sounding taken aback by her suggestion. "I can't accept money for helping you out in some way, that's silly."

"No, it isn't, and yes, you can, and you will. Otherwise I'll have to go, to someone else. And I don't want to do that. *I want you.* Please, James, agree to this. *Now.* At once! It's an emergency."

"All right, whatever you say. You certainly sound upset. What's this about? Talk to me, M, go on, tell me everything."

"It's about Larry. I came up to the Beekman Place apartment when I left Geo's this morning, and he seems ill. He just got back from Canada last night, and I found him in a bit of . . . a mess. I'm pretty certain he's had dental work done there, and he was obviously prescribed strong pills—"

Cutting in, James asked in an urgent tone, "Do you know what they are?"

"Yes. It says Vicodin on the label. I think he might have taken a lot of these painkillers without realizing how strong they are."

"And dangerous," James pointed out,

remembering his conversation about Larry's history with Geo only a couple of weeks ago.

"He's out of it, James. I don't know what to do. I can't get him to a hospital because he's too famous. It will be wrongly perceived, I'm certain. And it'll make headlines. But I need a doctor at once."

"I agree. Tell me what exact condition he's in right now."

"He's woozy, but he did open his eyes, managed to indicate his mouth and mumbled "tooth." I checked his pulse and heartbeat, and they both seem relatively steady, but I'm not experienced when it comes to such things. He's very white. He needs help. *Now.*"

"Keep him warm, and I'll be there as fast as I can. But I can't just disappear, not without explaining to Geo where I'm going. We've made plans to spend the weekend together."

"You can tell her. But just explain we've got to keep this a secret."

"You can trust her. I promise you. She cares about you."

"All right. Just come as quickly as you can. With a doctor. I'm a bit afraid."

"Don't panic, stay cool."

"I'm your client, remember? Promise, James."

"You are my client," James answered and hung up.

Once she was off the telephone, M ran to Larry's bedroom, took the pillows and duvet off the bed, and brought them back to the library. She placed the pillow under his head, propped it up, and wrapped the duvet around him. Then she ran and lit the fire, turned the heat up, and sat down in a chair next to the sofa to wait. Not once did her eyes leave Larry's face.

❋

During the next half hour, M kept checking on Larry, feeling his pulse; she made a pot of tea but did not drink it, threw more logs onto the fire, and continued to wait. She was growing increasingly nervous, and her anxiety was high when the phone rang.

"Miss Carlson is on her was up," the concierge in the lobby told her.

"How's Larry?" Geo asked when M opened the door a moment later and drew her inside.

"About the same. Where's James?" M asked, frowning.

"I dropped him off at Duane Reade on First Avenue. He needed to get something from the pharmacy. He'll be here in a few seconds." The phone began to ring as she spoke, and Geo glanced at M. "That's probably him now," she asserted.

M hurried to answer it, returned at once, and said, "You're right, it *is* James." Crossing the entrance hall, she opened the front door just as James stepped out of the elevator accompanied by a tall, somewhat heavyset young man.

James said, "Here we are, M. This is Dr. Matthew Branden, my own doctor and a good friend. Matt, I'd like you to meet my friend Marie Marsden. We call her M."

The doctor came forward, shook M's hand, and said, "I must see the patient at once. Can you take me to him?"

"Yes, yes, of course," M answered, relieved that James had brought his doctor. A professional was needed now, not amateurs playing guessing games. "I'll take you to Larry," M went on, leading the doctor, James, and Geo through the long living room and into the library.

The doctor went to Larry immediately,

took his stethoscope out of his briefcase, and listened to Larry's heart, then took his pulse and looked into his eyes with a small light.

Geo hung back in the doorway with M, whilst James went to the desk, put down the small plastic bag he was carrying, and asked the doctor, "Is he unconscious?"

Straightening up, Matt Branden shook his head. "No, he's not, thank God. But he *is* drugged." Looking at M, he continued, "I understand that your friend took Vicodin. Can I see the bottle, please?"

It was in M's pocket, and she walked across the library, gave him the bottle, and explained, "It was in his hand, and the top was off."

The doctor nodded and quickly read the label. "James said you believed he'd had dental work, which is why these pills were prescribed. Why did you assume that?"

"Because Larry brought his hand up to his mouth when I was questioning him about taking the pills, and he mumbled something which sounded like *tooth*."

"I see. It's hard to know how many pills he's taken in the last twenty-four hours, but it's imperative that I induce vomiting. I must make him bring up what he has taken."

M bit her lip and nodded. "How can you do that?"

"I filled a prescription at Duane Reade for Ipecac syrup. It's an emetic that works by irritating the lining of the stomach and stimulating the vomiting center of the brain. Because he's conscious, I'll be able to get it into him, then his reflexes will kick in and he'll automatically swallow the syrup. He needs only a tablespoonful. Plus one or two glasses of water afterward. How big is his bathroom?"

"Not very big."

"I will need him to be sitting down, because I don't think he'll be able to stand. How about the kitchen? What size is that?"

"Bigger than his bathroom, and there's a table in there, along with a banquette at one side and a chair."

"Okay, that sounds good. Let's do this. James, will you come here and help me with Larry? I'm sure he's not very ambulatory. We'll just have to maneuver him along as best we can." Glancing at M, he added, "Would you go ahead and find a large bowl or bucket, and put it on the table. And Geo, please take the Ipecac syrup into the kitchen, it's in that plastic bag on the desk."

Both women did as he asked, and James strode over to the sofa. Together he and the doctor managed to lift Larry to his feet. Putting their hands underneath his arms, they held him upright and virtually carried him out of the library.

# Twenty-three

Although she had been extremely worried when she found Larry just over an hour ago, once James and Matt Branden had arrived, M instantly grew calmer. And now that she was actually doing something to help, she was totally in control of herself, as she usually was in emergencies.

As she brought the straight-backed wooden chair over to the kitchen table, she said to Geo, "Could you put the Ipecac syrup down here, and then fill two separate glasses with water, please. You can use tap water, or there's a bottle of Evian in the fridge. Thanks, Geo."

Geo did as she was asked, used the Evian, and then found a tablespoon in a cutlery drawer, saying, as she did, "Don't you think I ought to get a big bath towel to wrap around Larry to protect his clothes?"

"Good idea. The linen closet is in the corridor next to Larry's bedroom," M responded.

Geo hurried out; seconds later James and the doctor came slowly into the kitchen, supporting Larry between them. "Let's get him over to the table," Dr. Branden instructed, and then his eyes swept around the room, noting everything. Once they had placed Larry on the chair and lifted it closer to the table, the doctor went to the sink and washed his hands.

M brought a large square plastic bowl and put it down on the table in front of Larry, who was still woozy, his eyes closed, his chin resting on his chest. "Should I get a bucket as well?" M asked, looking across at the doctor.

"I think it would be wise," he answered as he dried his hands on a piece of paper towel. "And James, please get the syringe out of the plastic bag."

Geo returned with a large bath towel

and handed it to James, who was standing next to Larry, his hand on his shoulder. "Wrap this around him to protect his clothing," Geo said. James nodded and did so, making certain the silk dressing gown was covered.

"I think we're ready," the doctor announced, walking over to his patient. After pouring the Ipecac syrup onto the spoon, he looked at James and instructed, "Please lift his head up off his chest."

James did this, and Dr. Branden opened Larry's mouth, poured the syrup into it, clamped his mouth shut, and tilted his head back slightly. Just as he had predicted, Larry's reflexes kicked in and he swallowed the syrup automatically.

"Let's give him a second or two, and then I must get a glass of water down him. That will be tougher, and I'll start by using the syringe to squirt the water into his mouth," the doctor explained. Once again, James helped his friend, who managed to get the first glass of water down Larry's throat using the syringe; in less than a minute, Larry was vomiting into the bowl. When he finally stopped, the doctor gave him a few minutes to relax before getting the second glass of water down him. Almost immediately Larry vomited it back.

Geo, who was somewhat squeamish, hurried out of the kitchen, but M was determined to stay, wanting to help Larry. She brought a bucket to the table, removed the bowl, and emptied it, while James and the doctor attended to Larry.

At one moment, Dr. Branden gave James a knowing look. "The next stage is a bit difficult. We've got to keep him upright and moving once he's stopped vomiting and his stomach is totally empty."

James nodded. "I understand. We can walk him up and down one of the corridors, or up and down the living room."

"Better make it a corridor," Matt said. "Just in case he starts to vomit again."

❀

By five o'clock that afternoon Larry's eyes were open, the wooziness had dissipated, and he knew what was going on around him. He was as white as bleached linen, weak and debilitated, but all of the Vicodin was out of him, and Dr. Branden was satisfied he would be all right.

"But call me if you need me," the doctor told M. She promised she would.

As she walked him to the front door, she asked, "What should I do about feeding him? He must be awfully hungry, there's nothing left inside."

"Black tea, no milk, a slice or two of toast. Plain, dry, no butter or jelly. A little chicken broth later. Keep it light, no solid food until tomorrow. Okay?"

"I'll do exactly as you say. Dr. Branden. I'm so grateful you were able to come. James and I would have been lost. Thank you very much."

"Call me tomorrow to let me know how he is, and if you need me I'll be right over. I only live a few blocks away."

"Thanks again," M murmured, shut the door behind him, and hurried back to Larry's bedroom. He was fast asleep, breathing evenly. She crept out of the room, not wanting to disturb him, and went to the kitchen, where she found Geo and James.

"I don't know what I would have done without you both," she said. "Thank you so much, James, Geo. I'm so sorry you had to go through this ordeal."

"I'm just glad I could do something," Geo murmured and looked at the kettle as it began to whistle. "I don't know about you, but I need a cup of tea." She went to turn the kettle off.

"I'd love a cup, please," M said and stared at James, then reaching out, she took hold of his arm. "Thank you . . . thank you for getting here so quickly, and for bringing Matt Branden. It was the right thing to do, getting a doctor."

"After I'd hung up with you, all I could think of was that he might die of an over-dose, and then where would we be?" James smiled faintly.

"I understood how lucky it was you'd managed to get hold of your own doctor," M answered and sat down.

Geo brought the mugs of tea over to them, returned with milk and sweetener, and joined them at the table. "While you two were helping the doctor with Larry, I called the pharmacy in Toronto and established that the doctor named on the label is in fact a dentist." She squeezed M's hand. "So you were correct, Larry had said 'tooth' to you earlier."

"I wonder why he took so many pills?" M murmured, baffled. "Maybe there were other things at work."

"Perhaps so," James agreed and hesitated a moment before continuing. "He'll explain everything, I'm sure, as soon as he's a bit better. He must be exhausted, poor sod, after all that vomiting. He's fast asleep, isn't he?"

"Yes, and that's the best thing for him right now. I'm not going to press him for an explanation until he's more like himself," M remarked and took a sip of tea.

Geo said, "I'm sure he should sleep as much as he can. Did Dr. Branden say he could eat something? I bet it's just toast and black tea."

"Nothing else, Geo, certainly no solid food today. Anyway, I doubt he'll be able to keep much down."

"There's nothing, no food in the refrigerator," Geo suddenly pointed out. "Do you want me to do some marketing for you?"

"That would be a great help." M stood up, went to the library, and returned with her handbag. "I'll make a list, and here's a hundred-dollar bill," she said, taking the money out of her wallet. "I think I'll make chicken-in-the-pot. It's soothing, healing. Perfect for tomorrow." She went over to the counter, tore a page from the message pad, and began to make a shopping list.

"Do you want me to go with you?" James asked, turning to Geo.

"No, but thanks for offering. I'll be quicker on my own," she replied, taking the list from M.

❀

Once they were alone, M said, "Let me know how much I owe you, James, and I'll bring you the money on Monday."

"Oh, look, let's not go through that again! I promise you I won't breathe a word to anyone about this . . . incident. Believe me, you don't have to pay me, and I wish you wouldn't even try."

"No, no. That was the deal we made, and a deal's a deal as far as I'm concerned. I insist on paying you, and that's that."

James sighed, shaking his head, and then he said quietly, his voice serious, "You must talk to Larry in a very straightforward way, M. Look, I'm sure you know that without me telling you, but he must explain what he was going through when he started taking quantities of the Vicodin."

"I plan to do that, I promise you," she said in a low but firm voice. "Something like this can't happen again."

"You're damn right," he replied, giving her a cautionary look. For a split second he thought of telling her about Larry's drug history—so called—then changed his mind. He wanted to give Larry a chance to confide in M of his own volition, wanted to be fair to the man. He had never liked playing God, not even when he was with MI6.

They met on Monday morning at his office on Park Avenue, at M's request.

"So he hasn't really explained anything, has he?" James said, sitting back in his chair, regarding M intently.

"Not really, no," she answered swiftly. "But he will."

"I hope so." James continued to stare at her, thinking that, despite her worries of the last couple of days, she looked bloody marvelous. She was wearing a white open-neck shirt with a black sweater and pants, appeared very schoolgirlish in the outfit, her hair in a ponytail, her makeup light and youthful.

M was seated on the other side of his desk, and she had just handed him an envelope containing a thousand dollars in cash. He had protested that it was far too much, but she had adamantly refused to take any of it back. She insisted it was a fair fee for his help on Saturday, his continuing attentiveness on Sunday, and his evident concern for her and Larry.

"You're looking very thoughtful," M said, cutting into his thoughts. Her dark brows drew together in a deep frown. "What is it?"

"I was thinking about Larry and you, your relationship. Listen, are you sure he'll come clean?" James still held her with his eyes.

M was silent for a moment, and then she replied in an even, steady tone. "That's a funny phrase to use, James . . . 'come clean.' He's not trying to hide anything; he'll tell me everything this afternoon, he promised he would. He was still terribly exhausted on Sunday, as you know. All that vomiting did him in. But he did say this morning that he'd had a raging toothache the weekend Edward arrived in Toronto, and that he'd had to deal with it immediately on that Monday morning, which is why we never connected. Then he apparently became embroiled with his father and Edward, over *something*. He didn't say what, merely added he'd been wedged between the devil and the deep blue sea. He must've been referring to his father and brother, don't you think?"

"You're probably right. But he *must* tell you the truth, M." James leaned over the desk, his expression somber. "Matt thinks Larry might well have an addictive personality, which means that if he takes certain pills, such as codeine, for pain, he will become addicted to them at once. Matt explained that Larry should check this out and seek treatment if necessary."

M was startled. "Does Dr. Branden think it's that serious?"

"He's not positive, no, but he has thrown out a number of cautionary words to me, and I trust him. He's a damn good doctor. I rely on him to give me the right advice, and I trust him implicitly."

"I understand." M sighed, still taken aback, and after a moment's reflection, she said, "Once I know everything, I *will* suggest he get help, if that's actually necessary. And I'll tell you what he tells me, so don't worry, James."

"I think that would be wise. I'll help in any way I can. Incidentally, is there someone with him right now?"

"Oh, yes, Mary is there, the housekeeper. She comes in three times a week to look after the apartment, has done so for over twenty years apparently. She worked for his parents, a lovely Irish woman. I told her he'd had a bit of a relapse, another bout of the flu, and she's staying with him until I get back this afternoon. She's going to give him some of my soup and toast for lunch. I told her to keep it light, no solid food yet."

"I'm relieved someone's there. He needs a bit of cosseting. Changing the subject for a moment . . . Geo told me you'll be moving to Paris in December, giving up your room, M."

"Yes, Jean-Louis Tremont has hired me to model his clothes for the spring-summer collection, which he'll be showing in January. It's a wonderful break for me."

"It certainly is, and congratulations, but Geo will miss you, and so will I."

She smiled at him and asked in a slightly teasing tone, "Are you two serious about each other? I'd love to know."

He grinned, his mood growing lighter, his handsome, narrow face becoming animated. "I believe we are. I want to marry her, M. Do you think she'll take on an old reprobate like me?"

"You're not old, and you're not a reprobate, you're a very lovely man, and yes, of course she'll have you. And if she won't, I'll kill her. So there!"

He laughed with her, then asked, "And what about you and Larry? How serious is it?"

**"Very."**

"I see." He rubbed his chin and said thoughtfully, his eyes riveted on hers, "You've got to make it *right* then. You do understand that, don't you?"

"Of course I do, James! I wouldn't want to have it any other way! But I do trust him, you know. There's a lot of integrity in him, and he's the kind of man I've grown up with. He's like the men in my family, that's what I mean." She suddenly sounded indignant.

"Don't misunderstand, I like him, too,

he's a lovely chap," James said reassuringly. "I just want you to be aware of the things Matt Branden mentioned to me."

"I'm grateful." M stood up. "But now I'm afraid I've got to go, James. I'm taking Caresse to lunch. You know, the young woman who runs Frankie Farantino's studio."

"Talk to me later," James said, walking with her to the door.

Caresse sat listening patiently as the man outlined the deal to her, and after fifteen minutes she interrupted him. "Listen, Howard, I'm not interested in your offer, honestly I'm not. It's—"

"It's not *my* offer, Caresse," Howard Dart cut in. "It's my client's offer, and I don't think you should turn down two hundred and fifty thousand dollars quite so fast. That's a quarter of a million dollars!"

"I know it is, Howard. And it's not enough. This place is worth a million or two, not thousands. Listen up, I know how much Frank Farantino spent on the renovations of this warehouse. *A million dollars,* even more. You're coming in too low, so the answer is thanks, but no thanks. I pass. I double-pass."

"Maybe my client will come up in price. He owns property all over the world, and he's anxious to have something like this building here in Manhattan, especially since it's income-producing."

"You bet it is!" Caresse exclaimed, giving the young lawyer a very pointed look. "I'm no pushover. I got advisers," she improvised. "I know what this property's really worth, just remember that. Nobody's gonna steal it."

Caresse was growing increasingly annoyed with him, convinced he was trying to get the studios for nothing since he was considered a bit of a hustler. "Anyway, who *is* this so-called client of yours?" she now demanded, her voice cold.

"What do you mean by 'so-called'? He *is* my client, and his name's S. Herbert Samson. As I said, he's a very important businessman, and you shouldn't be so hasty, Miss Caresse. You'll regret it."

"I doubt that. And on behalf of my seventeen-year-old co-owner, Frankie's son, and myself, I'm telling you that your deal is no deal. And you can tell your client that. As for you, Howard, go fly a kite. Your offer is an insult."

He stood up, his face flushed, and answered in an angry tone, "You're being a fool, Caresse. You'll soon be back to me, and—"

"Don't bet on it," she interrupted sharply.

"I repeat, you'll be back. Nobody's going to offer you more, the place is not worth it."

"Thanks for those nice words, Howard. Please leave the premises. And don't come back."

She watched him as he crossed the reception area, opened the door, and hurried out, almost knocking down M, who was about to enter the studios. "Excuse me," he snapped.

Caresse noticed he didn't even bother to pause. She stared at M and exclaimed, "Don't pay attention to that guy. He's a real jerk."

"Who is he?" M asked as she closed the door behind her and walked over to Caresse's desk, a wide smile on her face.

"Some two-bit lawyer the real estate agent sent over, who thinks he can give me a snow job," Caresse said and grinned. "Imagine him trying to do that to *me*. I told him I'm no pushover, and I'm not. Offering me two hundred and fifty thousand for this place, when it's worth at least a million and a half."

"Oh, much more than that, Caresse," M said, surprised by this low assessment. Shrugging out of her black wool coat, hanging it in the cupboard, she announced confidently, "I'd put the value at around four to five million."

"You gotta be kidding!" Caresse squealed, obviously astonished.

"No, I'm not," M answered, sitting down opposite Caresse. "Property is at a record high in Manhattan these days, whether it's commercial real estate like this or residential."

Caresse was still staring at her, total shock reflected in her eyes. She shook her head and said, "Maybe I should go to a bigger real estate company. What do you think?"

"If I were you, I would get the Farantino Studios evaluated immediately, and then I would go to a bank, take out a loan to pay operating costs, and run this place yourself."

"You've gotta be joking, M! What bank would give *me* a loan?"

"A number of them, in my opinion," M answered in a businesslike voice. "You could put up the studios as collateral against the loan, and hey, listen! I've just had a brilliant idea, Caresse. Why not talk to Luke Hendricks? Maybe he would become a partner with young Alex, put up money himself. How about that?"

Caresse nodded, looking at M with greater interest, remembering how she had always told Frankie that M was smart. She had been right. She said slowly, in a low, confiding voice, "I've never told you this, M, but Frankie left me thirty percent interest in the studios. I also have guardianship of Alex until he's twenty-one. And he's cool, you know, he'll do anything I say, well, within reason, you know what teenagers are." She grinned, ran a hand through her spiky red hair, jumped up, went around the desk, and hugged M, exclaiming, "I haven't yet told you congratulations! Or even said hello because of that awful jerk. So, how does it feel to be the New Face of Jean-Louis Tremont?"

"It hasn't really sunk in yet," M answered truthfully and stood up. "I'd love a glass of water, and listen, just show me around the studios again before we go to lunch.

I'd like to get a proper perspective on this place."

"Come on then, Miss Supermodel, let's do it."

Taking hold of her arm, Caresse led M into the main studio. She was suddenly filled with enthusiasm for M's idea and anxious to talk to Luke. She hoped he'd agree to this fabulous plan, which was what it had already become in her mind.

# Twenty-four

After lunch with Caresse in the MePa, M
took a cab uptown. Her anxiety about Larry
and her need to see him had grown more
pressing, and she had instantly agreed
when Caresse suggested they skip des-
sert and coffee.

"I've just got to get back to the studios,"
Caresse had explained. "There's a big
shoot this afternoon." And so M had swiftly
paid, and they had left, each taking a cab
in a different direction.

Now, as the driver pushed his way
through the heavy traffic, M sat back, her
thoughts turning inward. She couldn't help

wondering what Larry would say when he heard her news. During his first week in Toronto, she had spoken to him every day, confided how well the shoot was going; he had sounded genuinely pleased for her. But he knew nothing about the unexpected events of last week and Kate Morrell's extensive plans for her because he had not returned her calls the second week.

*Six days of silence.* Far too long, wasn't it? They were engaged to be married, after all. Her thoughts raced, zeroing in on him. Had she made a dreadful mistake about Laurence Vaughan? Wasn't he the man she believed him to be? Was she so influenced by her girlhood crush on him that she had been swept away, caught up in the glamour of him? And finally, very simply, had she misjudged his character? She didn't believe this was so, yet his behavior had been bizarre, even questionable.

Still, he had gone to Canada to investigate a problem for his mother, and maybe that problem had been so overwhelming it had overshadowed everything else in his head. That was a possibility, she decided, and reminded herself to keep an open mind.

She began to think about all the things

she had to tell Larry—that she had to leave for Paris in the middle of December because Jean-Louis Tremont had to start fitting the clothes on her, that she was about to sign a multimillion-dollar contract with the designer. It occurred to her that Larry might not want to come to Paris with her. . . . A possible dilemma suddenly loomed.

When M walked into the apartment twenty minutes later, she was surprised to hear Larry's voice coming from the library. That morning she had left him in bed, looking worn-out and damaged, and so she was glad he felt well enough to get up. After putting her coat in the closet, she went to join him.

As soon as he saw her, he murmured good-bye into the phone and hung up, came to her immediately, a faint smile flickering on his mouth. He was pale and gaunt, and there were dark circles under his eyes. He didn't look well after all, even though he was dressed and mobile, bundled up in a navy blue tracksuit and a heavy, knitted-wool cardigan of the same color. Quite suddenly she was aware that he had lost weight.

Without saying a word he wrapped his arms around her, clung to her. "I'm sorry, so very sorry, M. I vowed I would never hurt you in any way, and look what I've gone and done. I've caused you nothing but heartache these past few days."

She drew away from him, saw how bloodshot his bright blue eyes were, and answered gently, "Please, Larry, don't keep saying you're sorry. I accepted your apology this morning, and honestly, I know how contrite you are. What I would like you to do is explain everything from the beginning, if you don't mind. And from the moment you got to Toronto. If you can do this, I think I might be able to understand how you came to be in such a mess, so out of it, when I found you here on Saturday."

"I'll tell you about Toronto. I *want* you to know what happened. Let's go and sit near the fire." Taking hold of her hand, he led her toward the fireplace.

Settling herself in the corner of the sofa, leaning against the soft cushions, M fixed her gaze on him. "I haven't even asked you how you're feeling. Sorry."

"Better. My legs are still weak, and my stomach's sore, but thank God I'm rid of that ghastly headache. It was doing me in. A migraine, actually."

"I'm glad. Let's face it . . . Saturday was something of an ordeal for you."

He nodded but said nothing.

Taking hold of his hand, squeezing it, she went on in the same low, steady voice. "Come on then . . . tell me about Toronto."

"Well, part of it you already know—"

She cut into his sentence, saying swiftly, "I want you to start at the beginning, please."

"Okay, here goes. I thought Dad was perfectly normal when I arrived. He certainly didn't seem ill or out of sorts, and he wasn't afraid of the play, as my mother had suggested to me. In fact, to be honest, he was relishing the idea of playing Cyrano, especially at his age. He's seventy, you know. I went to a few rehearsals with him, and I knew at once that he had a good grasp of the part; after all, he'd played it a number of times before. And I was mystified by the worries my mother had expressed during her phone call."

"Did you bring that up to him?"

Larry looked at her swiftly, a horrified expression settling on his face. "God, no!" he exclaimed, shaking his head. "They're a bit competitive, those two. He'd be furious if he thought she doubted his talent. I said I'd come to see him because I needed a break and wanted to spend some quality time with him. One thing I did notice, though, was that he was irritated Mum was filming and couldn't join him in Canada. But this aside, he was on an even keel . . . very normal as far as I was concerned." Larry paused, rose, went to the drinks tray, and opened a can of Coke. He filled a glass, and looking at M, he asked, "Do you want anything, darling?"

"No thanks."

Returning to his place next to her on the sofa, Larry took a swallow of the Coke, then said, "Suddenly, Edward arrived, sooner than expected. Dad was pleased, because he always loves having his sons around him. He enjoys showing off a bit to us and always expects us to give him over-the-top accolades. Anyway, my teeth were troubling me that weekend, and I missed out on a few meals with them. I finally did get to a dentist on Monday morning, and apparently I had two abscesses and needed immediate surgery. The dentist put me on antibiotics and painkillers, and because I was in agony I didn't pay much attention to them, just took them as instructed, and went about my business . . ." Larry stopped, stared off into the distance. Finally he turned to her and said in a voice that was almost inaudible, "Although I didn't realize it at first, Edward set out to make trouble from the moment he arrived. Trouble for me and, perhaps in a certain way, for Dad as well."

Larry fell silent again, sat looking reflective, and after a moment, M said, "That doesn't surprise me. In my opinion, your brother is your enemy."

"I think you're probably right," Larry agreed. "Edward started to verbally attack me on Monday afternoon, shouting at me that I should share the role with Dad, do it on alternate days to ease his burden, and then Edward dropped a real bombshell on me that night. He told me that my father believed my mother was having an affair with another man, and that was the reason she hadn't come to Canada."

"But she's making a film, isn't she?" M asked, her eyes narrowing.

"Yes, and Edward said Dad's positive she took the film in order to stay in London. To be with her lover."

M looked at him askance. "Do *you* believe that?"

"No. But if you really think about it, how would I know? I live in New York, she's in London. I suppose it could be true. On the other hand, I don't think infidelity is quite her style." He broke off, shaking his head. "All I know is that Edward insisted my father believed this but that I couldn't, mustn't broach it to Dad because it had been a confidence between them, not to be repeated to me. However, Edward has always loved to upset me by saying mean things about our mother. He's always been a bit of a bastard, and he's jealous of me, of my success as an actor, that I do know.

"In any case, everything got out of hand after that. The next day I went back to the dentist, and much later, when I returned to the hotel, Edward and Dad were having a terrible row. It was all about Edward's messy private life, the ex-wives, the live-ins, his kids. And Dad was also *really* furious because Edward had asked for a loan of twenty thousand pounds to solve his personal financial mess. I'll spare you the details because none of it was pretty. Then Edward turned on me, for no reason at all, said I was a no-talent, spoiled brat and Mum's favorite, that I hadn't produced any grandchildren to carry on the great Vaughan theatrical dynasty, whilst he had and yet was punished for it. All his babble genuinely upset Dad, and he became even more enraged when Edward blurted out that I didn't believe the story about Mum's so-called affair. Edward announced that I had actually pooh-poohed it. Dad saw this as some kind of betrayal on my part, and he told me so in no uncertain terms."

"Where was all this happening?"

"Mostly in Dad's hotel suite, where else? Dad is a stickler for decorum, so our differences were put to one side when we were in public. But it was pretty bloody awful, and I think Edward was really off the wall last week."

"Do you think it was an act? A ruse to get money out of your father, and also to punish you by insulting your mother? And he was setting your father against you, wasn't he?" she pointed out.

Larry simply shook his head, looking as puzzled as M.

She then asked, "There's one thing I'm not clear about. . . . Did your father ask you to share the role of Cyrano with him?"

"Not exactly. He vaguely mentioned it when I first got there, said what a wonderful thing it would be for the producers if we did that—two big names, father and son, all that crap—but when I said I wasn't interested, had to be back in New York for my own work, he just dropped it, laughed, and said he'd only been kidding."

"But was he?" M now gave Larry a penetrating stare, convinced that his father *had* needed help, no matter what Larry believed.

"I just don't know," Larry eventually responded. "But he mentioned the same thing to Edward, and Edward took it seriously, very much so."

"Don't tell me Edward's actually sharing the role of Cyrano with your father?" M sounded astonished, and she couldn't help marveling at the duplicity of Larry's brother.

"For the next month. Then Edward's taking it on by himself, and he will play the part until the end of the run. After that one

month in the play, sharing the role, Dad will be let out of his contract, and he'll go back to London. Edward will be the star."

"And the producers accepted this?"

"Why not? Don't forget, Edward's had the lead in a very successful American television series for years, and now it's finished it's gone into reruns. Listen, it plays in Canada as well as the U.S. and the U.K., and Edward's a big name as far as the Canadian producers are concerned. Therefore, no problems."

"Edward's pretty devious, isn't he?"

Larry grimaced. "And then some. As for my father, I do think he was serious when he asked me to share the role, but when I refused, he dismissed his offer as a joke, not wanting to appear foolish or needy."

"So he does require help with the part. Is that what you're saying? And that's why Edward is in the picture?"

"No, I'm not saying that at all. Dad doesn't need help with the part; he practically knows it by heart by now, he's done it enough times. What he wants is *company*. He's *lonely*, M. Very much so. You see, he's used to being surrounded by his family. My mother, Thomas, and Horatio

in London, and also Portia and her little girl, and his brother Jack, and Jack's brood, his daughters, Eloise and Diana, and his son, Maximillian. Our uncle and cousins. I'm sure you know that my uncle Jack and his offspring are actors, and very much a part of our theatrical dynasty."

M nodded. "Yes, of course I do, and they're all marvelous, by the way."

"What I'm getting at is that, on reflection, I do believe my *mother* should have been with him in Canada."

"So why did she take the film?" M asked, a brow lifting.

"Money. It's always about money with my parents. They have a big overhead, and Dad's tried hard for years to put money away for us. I keep telling him to stop, that we can fend for ourselves, but he won't listen."

"Is he going to lend money to Edward?"

"I don't know; it never seemed to get resolved when I was there. But I doubt it. Dad simply can't spare it, I'm sure. I guess they made a deal about the play, though. Edward's probably getting *all* the money, and Dad'll take this loss just to get home to Mum."

"To find out what's going on with her?" M suggested pithily.

"That as well, yes, but mainly I think he's motivated by his loneliness. He's lost when he's away from our bunch. *His lot,* as he calls us."

"I can understand that," M murmured. "I come from a large family myself."

Larry sat back, his expression thoughtful. He said, very slowly, in a low voice, "The point of that whole story is *this,* M. I was so aggravated and nervous because of the rows, my father's upset, and Edward's lousy treatment of me, and in terrible pain with my teeth, I just kept popping pills. Unfortunately, I became hooked on them again."

M sat up, stared at him blankly, frowning, wondering what he meant by "hooked on them again." She didn't dare ask, afraid of the answer. She held herself still, waiting.

Clearing his throat, Larry hurried on: "There's something I must tell you. About five years ago I had pneumonia, and I became addicted to the prescription drugs I was given, especially anything containing codeine. My mother was the first to become aware of it, and she got me into a rehab clinic in London at once. I had eight weeks of treatment. There were some rumors about me being hooked on pills at the time, but Mum managed to keep the lid on the story. Fortunately, through a great PR woman, the rumor was soon well and truly squashed. I survived with hardly a blemish to my reputation, and went on to do some good work. I won a few awards and stayed clean. And I knew I must never touch prescription drugs ever again."

"I see," M murmured, then asked, "So why did you?"

"Truly it was the extreme pain with my teeth, and the horrendous aggravation Edward caused, his battering of me. I don't blame my father at all. But Edward's a menace."

"Then you can't go near him ever again. You must keep him at a distance." Leaning closer, M continued in a steady voice, "You *must* go into a rehab clinic here, Larry. I honestly believe you need help, and so does Dr. Branden. He told James Cardigan he thinks you have an addictive personality, and obviously you do, in my opinion. You must get help."

"Yes," he said, throwing her an odd look, and quickly asked, "By the way, how did you find Matthew Branden? Through James?"

"That's right. When I discovered you on Saturday, at lunchtime, and couldn't rouse you, I didn't know who to ask for help. I was afraid to call an ambulance because I knew your presence in a hospital would leak out, be perceived as a drug overdose, especially in view of your fame. But I was terrified you were going to die if I didn't get assistance. I was really scared and at a loss. So I called James, asked him to bring a doctor, and he showed up with Dr. Branden, who's his own doctor and a friend."

"Thank you, M, thank you for saving my life."

"I think we all saved it, Larry, in fact I'm sure of it. And that's why it can't happen again. Listen to me, heed what I say. What if you took prescription drugs again when you were alone? You might accidentally kill yourself. You must promise me that you'll go into rehab. *At once*," she said forcefully. She stared at him, her face set, her voice tough when she added, "I do mean this week. You must go and see Dr. Branden, and he'll get you into the right place. Immediately."

"The right place is Silver Hill in New Canaan. I'm sure he'll arrange for me to go there."

"Do you know it?"

"Only by reputation."

"And you will go? *Definitely?* Do you promise?"

"Yes, I don't want to die. I don't ever want to get into that kind of mess again." He took hold of her hand. "I promise you I'll get myself cured, and as fast as possible. It's the first of November on Wednesday. I'll have the whole month to clean up. You see, I'd still like us to get married in December." He smiled at her, but the smile slipped when he saw how unresponsive she was.

"You're still angry with me, aren't you?" Larry asked, continuing to stare at her.

"No, I'm not, in fact I was never angry with *you,* Larry, certainly not about the drug overdose, because that's what it was," she replied in a businesslike tone. "I was only angry, frustrated, and exasperated when you didn't return my calls. Looking back, I can say that I was furious, and also hurt."

"I should've called," he murmured, filled with regret. "I tried, but there was always a row, or something erupting, or problems—"

"And late at night," she exclaimed, interrupting, "when you were alone and could've called me, you didn't because you were stoned, knocked out flat by the Vicodin, no doubt."

Ignoring her sarcasm, he said, "Yes, you're correct. I was. All I wanted, needed, was to sleep. Also, my teeth were troublesome." He took a deep breath, unexpectedly changed the subject. "Anyway, I want to hear your news. I know the shoot went well, so what was the final result?"

She had to resist the temptation to say something nasty to him and instead remained silent, gazing at him through accusing eyes.

He saw the hurt in them, reached for her hand, edged closer to her, and said in a genuinely contrite voice, "I'm sorry, honestly I am. And I'm very delinquent. I've been so busy talking about myself and my problems with my brother and my father, I never even asked you about your news. Oh, M, I'm so sorry."

"My news is that I'm about to become the New Face of Jean-Louis Tremont. He's building half the haute couture spring-summer collection around me, and I have to be in Paris by the middle of December for my fittings. I'm planning to sign the contract later this week."

"Hey, darling, this is wonderful news! Congratulations! He must have been thrilled with your pictures."

M nodded, but she wasn't prepared to give an inch at this moment. "Jean-Louis flew over to New York because Kate Morrell, who runs the American end of his business, was convinced I should be his 'new face,' as she calls it. It did go well, very well indeed. Luke took marvelous shots, and I guess I'm on my way."

"I'm so happy for you, and very *proud*. So, can we get married before you leave for Paris? And can I come with you? It could be our honeymoon, couldn't it? That would be wonderful . . . Christmas in Paris, together on our honeymoon. Oh, M, please don't look so angry, please say yes."

She sat staring at him, her face still cold,

closed, thinking of the past week. At last she said in her quietest voice, "It was six days, Larry. I didn't hear from you for *six days*. I called you every day, sometimes twice, and left messages, and not a word from you."

Unexpectedly, against her volition, she burst into tears, all of her pent-up emotions coming to the fore . . . her frustration, anger, worry, and fear for his life converging and overwhelming her.

He brought her into his arms and soothed her, hating himself for what he had done, stupidly, unthinkingly. He was instantly filled with guilt and shame, and he was afraid . . . afraid of losing her, this wonderful, marvelous girl who had become his whole life. What a blasted fool he had been, letting Edward get to him. He should have just packed and left Toronto. Instead, he'd fallen off the wagon, as his mother called it, fallen into the role of victim once more, and he was appalled at himself.

M sobbed and sobbed as if her heart was breaking, and he didn't know how to calm her down, so he just held her tightly, endeavoring to soothe her, promising her he would never let her down again, never hurt her in any way. And eventually there were no more tears to shed; she lay limp in his arms, still heaving. Eventually he lifted her face, looked into her eyes, and told her with absolute sincerity, "I give you my word I'll see the doctor tomorrow. I'll go into rehab at once. I'll be clean for the rest of my life. I'm so sorry I did this to you, M. Please believe that." He sighed deeply, then went on, "I should have told you about the problems I had five years ago. By not telling you I was lying by omission. And we mustn't do that to each other. There must only be truth between us."

"Yes," she agreed. "Only truth. And it's all right, Larry, honestly. I do love you . . . with all my heart."

# Twenty-five

Her hands were wet, and the crystal glass slipped out of them. She watched it as it dropped to the floor; it appeared to be falling in slow motion. Stupid, M thought, I'm stupid to handle delicate objects with wet hands.

She reached for the towel, and as she did the starched cuff of her white shirt caught on the edges of the two plates balanced on the counter. They slid off the marble top and crashed down, joining the fragments of glass on the floor. She stared at the mess surrounding her feet, shaking her head, silently remonstrating with herself for being so clumsy.

Her head was spinning, and her eyes were narrow slits in her face, puffy from crying earlier, but she had been unable to hold the tears back any longer. Her emotions had been pressed down inside for days. Quite suddenly, a few hours ago, they had erupted like a volcano spewing out its lava.

M went and sat down at the kitchen table, wanting to calm herself. Her hands were shaking slightly, and she felt drained, as if everything had been sucked out of her. How unsettling the last few days had been. . . . She leaned back, closed her eyes, drifting for a few moments with her myriad thoughts.

Shattered crystal, shattered china . . . and a shattered man sitting in the library. Yes, Larry *was* shattered at this moment, but unlike the china and crystal, *he* was repairable, absolutely repairable, thank God. She was now going to take charge, look after him, get him well, make sure he was never exposed to his brother again. Edward was a bastard, vengeful and spiteful and a menace to be around. Larry was vulnerable and insecure. The perfect target for a rotten bully. Whatever it took, whatever she had to do, she would keep them apart.

Things broke, she thought, people could be broken, life itself was an easily breakable possession, wasn't it? But not Larry's life. She would make sure he mended it, whatever it cost her.

Rousing herself, she swept up the debris. Once she found a clear plastic bag, she emptied the shards of china and glass into it and added a piece of paper on which she had written "broken china." After sealing the bag, she laid it on the floor to be put next to the garbage bin on the service landing later.

After washing and drying her hands, M took another crystal goblet out of the cabinet, filled it with Gatorade, and left the kitchen, heading for the library.

Larry was immersed in the film script his agent had sent him several weeks ago, more taken with it than ever. But when he heard her step, he lifted his head, his face lighting up at the sight of her. His darling M, his fiancée, the woman who made his life complete. How he loved her.

"I'm definitely going to do this film, darling. The more I reread it the more I like it. Love it, in fact. And it could have been *written for me,*" he told her, sounding excited. "So whilst you were busy chucking china around the kitchen, I phoned my agent and told her I was on. And, this will please you, I also called Dr. Branden's office and made an appointment to see him tomorrow afternoon."

"I'm glad you want to do the film, and genuinely relieved you're going to see the doctor," M answered, handed him the glass, and then explained, "Dr. Branden said you have to drink two or three glasses of this a day. Where's the film being made?" She sat down on the sofa opposite him, settled back against the cushions.

"That's another good thing about this project. We'll be shooting in Paris, Versailles, and London." A grin surfaced, and he raised a brow. "How do you like them there apples?"

M smiled for the first time in days. "I'm thrilled. I was just having visions of being separated from you for months on end."

"Not on your life, my darling girl. You're not going to get rid of me that quickly. By the way, we start shooting in Paris in March, finish in London two months later, and we'll be doing postproduction there as well, London, I mean." He drank the Gatorade, placed the glass on the end table.

"It works perfectly, doesn't it?" she said.

Looking across at her, Larry smiled lovingly, and there was a hint of mischief in his blue eyes as he added, "And I am quite aware that I will, in short order, have a wife to support, so it's back to work for me. I've had enough time off, actually."

M sat back on the sofa and gave him a long, careful look, her mind working rapidly. Now was the time to tell him the truth. She was dreading it. Finally, after taking a deep breath, she began to speak. "Earlier this afternoon, you said that by not telling me about the problems you had with drugs five years ago, you lied to me by omission. I'm so sorry, Larry darling, but I've done the same thing to you, I'm afraid. I've lied to you."

Sitting up straighter in the chair, he threw her a sharp look. "What exactly do you mean by that?" His eyes remained on her face.

Having plunged in, M knew she must be

forthright and must get to the point at once. "I haven't been honest with you, Larry. I've been hiding my true identity from you."

"Have you now?" he said, a note of curiosity echoing in his voice. "I often thought there was something rather odd about you, and I also felt I knew you. I do, don't I?"

She shook her head. "No, you don't, not exactly. But you do know my brother."

"I do?" He frowned, his puzzlement evident. "Who is he?"

She told him.

For a moment Larry seemed startled, then disbelieving, even nonplussed. Finally he nodded. "So I do know you then, don't I?"

"No, you don't," she insisted. "We've never met actually."

He sat studying her. "You're correct, I don't think we have been in each other's company. And I remember something now. I did see a picture of you once, when you were much younger. At your brother's apartment; he was giving a cocktail party. I asked him who you were, and he said his baby sister, and I made some idiotic remark like 'When she grows up she'll be some babe.'"

Larry sat back, an amused smile flickering.

"My real name is Emma, but my nickname has always been Em. I simply used the single letter *M*."

"Well, well, well, so that's who you are. My goodness." He suddenly chuckled. "No wonder you want to keep our marriage a secret. I can well imagine how your mother would take over if she knew our plans. And with her in combination with my mother, we'd be done for before we started," he finished on a note of hilarity.

M laughed with him, happy and relieved that he had taken her news so well.

"Listen," he said a moment later. "I'm curious about one thing. Why the duplicity? Why not use your real last name instead of Marsden?"

"I didn't want the baggage that comes with my family. . . . I wanted to reinvent myself, be me and not part of that whole scenario of . . . well, their success . . . their celebrity and all that stuff."

"I can understand that. I've had to cope with the same kind of thing. But here's another question, Why did they allow it? I mean, let's face it, a woman of twenty-three alone in New York . . . weren't they worried about you?"

"I don't think so, and if they were, they didn't say anything. And I suppose because they know me inside out and upside down, and reared me, they do trust me, trust my judgment. And they understood that I needed to reinvent myself, that I wanted to do it on my own terms, and they respected all those things."

There was a little pause before M asked softly, "You're not angry, are you? I mean because I didn't tell you who I really was immediately."

"No, I'm not, and actually I don't care who your family is either. I'm marrying you, not them. But I'm glad about your brother because I admire him tremendously, he's a fabulous guy."

Rising, Larry went to sit next to her on the sofa and took hold of her hand. "My hat's off to you, my darling, for doing it on your own. Alone. It's your success, and nobody else's, and I know what that must mean to you. But I do have one final question."

"What is it?"

"Were you ever going to tell me the truth?"

"Of course I was, silly! I would have had to tell you when we got to City Hall, because our marriage wouldn't have been legal if I'd used a false name."

Putting his arms around her, he drew her close, nuzzled her neck, and whispered against her hair, "We've discussed a lot of things, you and I, but we've never talked about babies."

"Babies," she repeated, surprised, pulling back, staring up into his face.

"Yes, *babies*. Our babies, our children. You do want babies, don't you?"

"Yes, and especially yours, but not yet. I'm just about to walk the walk, start my career as a model. Do you think we could wait for a couple of years?"

"Certainly. But I think we ought to get a bit of practice in, perfect our skills in the meantime." He kissed her neck and whispered, "Let's go to bed, M. I've missed you so much, and I do need to practice and practice and practice . . ."

She smiled and asked sotto voce, "Are you sure you're up to it?"

"Can't you tell?" he responded, gently

pushing her down on the cushions, stretching out on top of her. He began to kiss her on the mouth as he opened the buttons of her shirt.

❖

James Cardigan stood up as the maître d' led Geo to his table at "21," his favorite in the center of the long back wall, facing the entire room. Once she was seated next to him on the banquette, he kissed her cheek, murmured, "Hi, darling," and then asked, "Where's M? Isn't she coming?"

"Good evening, James, and yes, she's coming, but straight from Frankie's studios. She had something to do there late this afternoon. I'm sure she'll be here fairly soon."

He nodded, reached for her hand, squeezed it, and went on softly, "I'm so glad you like your ring."

"Oh, I do, I love it!" she exclaimed, lifting her hand onto the table, staring at her engagement ring, an emerald with two diamonds on either side. Then she took hold of his hand again and leaned closer. "I'm so happy, James. I've never been happier in my life."

"And neither have I," he answered,

meaning it. "What do you want to drink, Georgiana? A glass of champagne?"

"I'd like that, thanks."

After ordering two glasses of champagne from the waiter, James told her, "I spoke to my mother today and confirmed that we would spend Christmas in England with her and Dad. Naturally she was thrilled. And I'm sure he is, too. Obviously, they can't wait to meet you, their future daughter-in-law."

Geo smiled at him, her eyes sparkling. She felt a rush of warmth spreading through her, a lovely glow she hadn't experienced in years. And it was all to do with James. There were moments when she couldn't believe her luck, that they had fallen madly in love and wanted to spend the rest of their lives together. The timing had been just right for them both. Although she had vaguely known him for well over a year, it was only at Iris Ingersoll's party for Dax that they had actually clicked. Luck indeed, she thought, my very good luck.

James said, "I spoke to Matt Branden this afternoon, and seemingly Larry is doing very well at Silver Hill, thank goodness. Has M said anything to you?"

"The same . . . that he's feeling better, and very much likes the psychiatrist who's working with him. And that he is adamant about her *not* going to New Canaan to see him. Don't you think that's a bit strange, James?"

He shook his head. "Not at all, darling. If I were in his position, I'd want to battle it through by myself. I'd want to concentrate on getting my head straight, without any feminine distractions."

She laughed. "I'm glad you think of me as a feminine distraction—"

"And a very beautiful and talented one, I might add."

"Thank you." She touched his arm. "There's M. In the doorway."

"I see her." James pushed the table out and stood up. He greeted M warmly as she came to the table and ushered her onto the banquette next to Geo, taking the outside chair for himself.

"Sorry to be late," M apologized once they were all settled. "But I had this meeting with Luke and Kate Morrell, and I thought it would never end."

"No problem. What would you like to

drink?" James asked as he motioned to a waiter.

"The same as you, a glass of champagne," M replied, and when she turned to greet Geo, she noticed the emerald ring. "Oh, Geo, oh my God! You and James got engaged, didn't you?"

Smiling and nodding, Geo said, "Yes, last night. James gave me the ring last night."

"Congratulations, Geo, and you, too, James. Thank goodness I won't have to kill her now."

Geo was baffled for a moment, looked quizzically from M to James.

It was James who explained. "When I asked M if she thought you'd accept an old reprobate like me, she said if you didn't she'd kill you."

They all laughed, and M asked, "When are you getting married?"

"Not sure yet, but we're going to England for Christmas," James confided. "Geo thought it would be nice if we came to Paris to see you after the holidays. What do you think about that?"

"I think it sounds wonderful! And again, I'm so happy you two got together." Turning to Geo, she went on, "Just think, if we hadn't gone to that party for Dax, you wouldn't have run into James again, and I wouldn't have met Larry."

"Too true, and perhaps that's an example of the randomness of life," Geo announced, then wondered aloud, "Life is random, isn't it?"

"Maybe. But it could be fate. Destiny," M ventured. "You know, what will be, will be. *Que sera, sera.*"

Changing the subject, James focused on M and said, "Matt Branden is really very pleased with Larry's progress, and he's confident he'll be as good as new, if not indeed better than ever, once he's finished his treatment at Silver Hill."

"That's the way Larry feels," M remarked. "His attitude is very positive. And I know he was as frightened as I was. Actually, I was terrified he was going to die, and Larry understands I can't live through anything like that ever again."

"Did he ever tell you what went on in Canada?" James probed gently, riddled with curiosity.

"Yes. It was all to do with his brother Edward," M said. "There was a lot of back-

# Twenty-six

Kate Morrell sat in the auditorium on the top floor of the Jean-Louis Tremont store on Madison Avenue. It was a large, airy room with a catwalk, and the store usually showed their latest collections here. It could hold a hundred people, including the press, on small gold-painted ballroom chairs.

On this cold November day, a week before Thanksgiving, M was modeling a show-stopper for Kate. It was a navy blue silk organza cocktail dress with a lace coat from the new spring-summer collection, and she was commanding the catwalk with great panache.

stabbing, and terrible aggravation for Larry, and I've told him to stay away from his brother, who wants to do him in."

"There's nothing like sibling rivalry, you know, it's even been the death of kings," James reminded her.

M burst out laughing. "Too true. Many a head has rolled because a brother has coveted the crown." She eyed James. "And what about you, James? Do you have siblings?"

"I do indeed. I have a younger brother, and a sister. Thank God we don't covet anything the other has."

When the champagne was placed in front of her, M raised her glass and toasted Geo and James. "Here's to you two love-birds. May you have a long and happy marriage, and I hope all your troubles are little ones."

This old-fashioned English toast cracked James up, and he grinned, then took a sip of his drink. "And what about you and Larry? Where is your relationship heading?"

"Probably in the same direction as yours. Eventually," M replied evasively.

Kate was the only person watching as M glided along, swung around, strode out again, and moved with a style all her own.

Suddenly Kate stood up and walked over to the catwalk.

M paused, looked down at her. "Is everything all right?"

"Where did you learn to parade down a catwalk like that?" Kate asked in a soft voice, but her eyes were slightly narrowed. There was an appraising look on her face as she gazed up at M.

"Nowhere. What I mean is, I *didn't* learn, not really."

"What do you mean by 'not really'? Did your sister teach you? Did you model at her boutique? Because in my opinion, you have been on a catwalk before, and you *have* been trained."

Without answering, M hurried along to the stairs, walked down them, and joined Kate. She said quietly, "I did do a bit of modeling for my sister, that's true, but she didn't teach me anything. However, my other sister, who's been to many of the couture shows in Paris, sort of, well, showed me how top models walk. I wasn't trained, though, honestly, I wasn't. Besides, who would train me?"

"That's what I'm wondering," Kate said and then laughed lightly, not wanting to antagonize this young woman, whom she considered their biggest find in years. Jean-Louis had needed a boost for some time now, and M would be that boost, she was convinced about that. Not only was the girl beautiful but she had a unique style, a wonderful way of handling herself, and she moved like a dream. Moved like a professionally trained high-fashion model who'd been at it for years. And that was why Kate was skeptical about her story. But why did it matter? It didn't even matter who she was or where she came from. What mattered was that she was under contract to *them*. And she was dating a famous man. A good-looking actor who was also a movie star. That would help them when it came to publicity. A dream couple, Kate thought, and made a mental note to play this up with the press.

"I can only add this," Kate now said, taking hold of M's arm and walking with her to the dressing rooms at the other end of the auditorium. "Jean-Louis will be even more thrilled when I tell him how great you are on the catwalk. He wanted me to check that out now, just in case you needed guidance when you arrived in Paris. But obviously you don't. Time saved. Oh, and by the way, when are you planning to go to Paris, M?"

"In the middle of December . . . about a month from today."

"Is Laurence Vaughan coming with you?"

The mention of Larry's name startled M for a moment, and she wondered how Kate knew she was involved with him, then realized at once that Luke would have told her. "Yes, Kate, Larry's coming to Paris with me," M finally answered. "We want to be together for Christmas, and also he's going to start shooting a movie there in early March."

"Oh, how wonderful that you can be together!" Kate exclaimed, genuinely meaning this. She liked M and wanted only the best for her, personally as well as professionally.

"He's away at the moment, otherwise I would have introduced him to you," M thought to add. Clearing her throat, she said slowly, "Do you think Glenda Bailey is going to agree to use me on the April cover of *Harper's Bazaar*?"

"Yes, I do. With one proviso. She will have to be impressed by the photograph of you in the wedding gown. But I'm sure that Luke will pull out all the stops, and that the picture will be great. If the plan works, it'll be quite a coup for us, you know."

"I realize that. When will the dress arrive from Paris?"

"Claude Allard, one of Jean-Louis's dressers, will be bringing it in this coming Monday. It's currently getting the finishing touches from Jean-Louis. Claude's sister lives in New York, and she's coming for Thanksgiving. With the dress. Luke will do the shoot the first week of December, otherwise it'll be too late."

"Because of the magazine's three-month lead time, I guess," M said in response and wished she hadn't opened her mouth when Kate threw her the oddest look.

Quickly changing the subject, M continued, "I'm so glad you were able to find the right lawyer for Caresse, Kate. I'm happy that she, Alex, and Luke will become partners in the studios. It's so much better,

more profitable, for them to run it themselves."

"It was smart of you to suggest it," Kate
remarked, wondering yet again who on
earth M was. She seemed to have a handle on a lot of things. And how the hell did
she know about magazine lead times? It
doesn't matter, Kate reminded herself. I'm
going to make her into a star. She'll be the
greatest supermodel of all time. That's all
that counts.

M was well aware that Kate Morrell wanted
to promote her as their discovery, the girl
from nowhere who'd never been trained.
Their creation. The girl they had turned into
the world's latest supermodel. That was
why Kate was always probing, wanting to
know about her past, her beginnings in the
business. It was transparent. Basically Kate
was anxious to know whether M had ever
modeled clothes for anyone else. Obviously Kate didn't want to have egg on her
face if others came forward to claim that
the mysterious M had once worked for them,
and that they had turned her into what she
was today.

She hadn't been a model before, she

had told Kate the truth about that, and M didn't mind the questions because she had nothing to hide on that score. She *was* a novice. Nor did Kate's publicity plans trouble her. She would take everything in her stride, do everything that was asked of her, within reason, to become the New Face of Jean-Louis Tremont. She would make herself accessible. And she would be professional. Her brother had always emphasized this to her: "Be a true professional, that's all I ask," he had said to her before she left for New York.

Now, as she went up the front steps of the brownstone and let herself into the house, M smiled, thinking of the woman who *had* trained her, taught her the little bit she knew about modeling. Her elder sister, the first-born. The one who was known as the most beautiful woman in England, if not the world. And she was indeed gorgeous, a dream-like creature of whom M had been in awe most of her life. It was she who had demonstrated the model's way of walking, the swift swinging around, the *strutting* really, and the mannerisms.

Her elder sister had been very strict and tough with her, and M had rebelled one day, exclaimed, "You're too bossy, you're becoming another Napoleon! No, better still, another Bismarck. Yes, that's it, getting lessons from you is like going on German war maneuvers. Hey, that's funny, isn't it?" M had said, and they had howled with laughter, fallen about, making silly faces for a few minutes. After several more lessons, M had been informed she had graduated, and her sister had left her to her own devices, told her to do her own thing now.

After taking off her coat, M went into the kitchen. The little chandelier over the table was turned on as usual, but the house was empty. M knew that Geo and James had gone to the theater, to see Dax's performance again, and were taking him to dinner afterward. *A Streetcar Named Desire,* the play by Tennessee Williams, which he was starring in, had been a limited run, and it would close immediately after Thanksgiving. They had wanted her to go with them, but she didn't feel up to it, still far too preoccupied with Larry, their upcoming marriage, and their move to Paris. Anyway, she had a lunch date with Dax next week. To celebrate. He'd been offered a film and was thrilled.

After putting the kettle on, she wandered into Geo's studio, glanced at the pictures lined up against the walls. What an accomplishment, M thought as she strolled around, gazing at the paintings. Geo had finished quite a lot of them, but apparently not enough. The gallery in Chelsea where her paintings were to be shown had asked for more, and the show was now going to be much later. Next year, in fact. One thing was certain, though, Geo's talent was amazing. The piercing whistle of the kettle cut into her reverie, brought her back into the kitchen. M made a pot of tea, then went up to her room.

She pulled the suitcase out from under the bed, unlocked it, and took out her small briefcase. Groping around inside it, she found the Harry Winston box, opened it, and admired her engagement ring for a second, then put it back. She took the envelope of traveler's checks out, slipped five hundred dollars into it, and returned this to the briefcase as well. M was determined to replace the thousand dollars she had used to pay James so that she could give Birdie *all* the traveler's checks back when she next saw her. The money had been a "safety net," according to her sister, but she hadn't needed it. She *had* made it on her own.

Sliding the suitcase under the bed, M ran downstairs, poured a cup of tea, and sat down at the table, thinking about Larry. She had missed him terribly and was glad he would be leaving Silver Hill early next week. They were going to spend Thanksgiving here at the house with Geo and James, and she and Geo were going to cook. Suddenly she jumped up, went to the small set of bookshelves at the end of the room, and found the big American cookbook Geo swore by. Taking it to the table, she started to look at recipes. M found cooking very therapeutic and was looking forward to making a sumptuous meal for her darling Larry and their friends. And the following day she planned to move to the apartment in Beekman Place.

There was something extremely likable about James Cardigan, Larry thought, watching his fellow Englishman opening a bottle of champagne at the far end of the kitchen.

Larry sat on a tall stool at the long counter, and it was a great vantage point. What he liked about James was his open, straight-forward manner, and his politeness despite his frank way of speaking. James was genial, a genuinely nice chap, and Larry had trouble imagining him as a spy. Yet M disagreed and had said she'd smelled "cop" on him the moment they met at Iris's party.

Larry swung his head, focused on the center of the kitchen. There she was, his lovely girl, her black hair in a ponytail. She was wrapped in a big white apron, cooking like the expert chef she was, one of her talents he had discovered. Geo, her abundant blond hair piled on top of her head, was standing alongside M, making the gravy and keeping an eye on the cranberry sauce on the stove. The smells floating around him made his mouth water. He knew he and James were going to be treated to a very special Thanksgiving dinner.

"Here you are," James said a moment later, bringing him a silver tankard of champagne. "I like Geo's idea of serving the bubbly in these antique mugs. Somehow they seem to make the stuff taste better."

"I know what you mean. A friend of mine does exactly the same thing. It's the silver, it keeps the champagne cold. However, I'm still on the wagon, James. I learned a lot at Silver Hill." He rose, took his tankard over to the table at the far end of the kitchen, and returned with another filled with water.

The two men clinked tankards, and Larry said, "I'm afraid I've been a bit remiss, James. I haven't actually thanked you properly for helping M to look after me when I was out of it. I might well have died if it hadn't have been for you."

"That young woman cooking her heart out over there wouldn't have let such a catastrophe happen, I can assure you of that, Larry. She was being very protective of you, in every way. She's quite remarkable . . . but then you know that."

"I do, yes. I've never met anyone like her before. She's absolutely unique."

"M told us the other night that you're going to do a film in the new year, and that it's shooting in Paris. Nice and convenient, eh?"

"It is indeed. I couldn't be happier, and I love this. It's the best I've read in a long time."

"What's it called? What's it about?" James asked.

"It's about Coco Chanel, and it's called

*Coco in Love.* It's romantic and rather touching, and it has a lot of meat to it. It's a period piece. At the beginning of her career, Chanel fell in love with a handsome young Englishman called "Boy" Capel, who supported her before she became well known. He was very much in love with her and wanted to marry her, but Chanel refused. She insisted she had to repay the money she owed him before she could marry him. Anyway, he eventually married an English aristocrat, and according to the script, he broke her heart by doing so. He died in 1919, which is when the film ends."

"And you're playing 'Boy' Capel," James said, making it more of a statement than a question.

"I am indeed, and looking forward to it."

At this moment Geo and M took off their aprons and came to join them. "How about a jugful of Dom Pérignon?" Geo said, coming to stand next to James. "All this cooking has made me thirsty."

"Coming right up, and one for you, too, I hope, M?" James said, turning to her, smiling warmly.

"Yes indeed, I'm parched. Thanks, James."

Once the two women had silver tankards in their hands, James said, "Can I now prevail upon you both to come and sit down in the den for a few minutes, in order to cool off. I find it quite warm in here."

Geo laughed. "It is when the oven's going, but you might feel better if you took off your heavy sweater, and you, too, Larry."

Both men laughed and did as she suggested, and the three of them trooped into the den across the hall, following M, who was exclaiming, "Let's make our plans for Paris. Decide what the four of us are going to do on New Year's Eve."

James soon realized this wasn't a very restful period in the den for the two women. They were forever running to the kitchen to check on the turkey, the sweet potatoes, and all of the other dishes they were making. And so he finally stood up himself and said to Geo, "Let's all go and join M in the kitchen, shall we? I think that will make life easier for the two of you."

"Agreed," Geo exclaimed, pushed herself to her feet, picked up the silver tankard, and left the den.

The two men walked after her, and as

they went into the kitchen, James turned to Larry and said, "Let's park ourselves here at the counter, where we're out of their way." He sat down on one of the barstools and took a long swallow of champagne.

James, who had been studying Larry surreptitiously for a few minutes, suddenly said, "You're looking awfully pensive. Is everything all right, old chap?"

"Sure, sure, I'm fine. I was thinking about you, actually." Larry grinned at him. "I just can't imagine you as Double O Seven."

"That's because I don't look like Sean Connery, Roger Moore, or Pierce Brosnan," James shot back, a faint smile playing around his mouth.

"Ah, but you do have a hint of Daniel Craig about you, James, my boy. He's the *new* Bond, in *Casino Royale*. He got raves."

"I expect he's lean, wiry, and fair-haired," James remarked, a sandy-colored brow lifting.

"Indeed he is, and he's going to be the fair-haired boy of Barbara Broccoli, the producer, I can tell you that. The movie's going to make big money."

Larry sat back, watching James walk to the end of the kitchen, pleased that he was becoming a good friend. There was something stalwart about James Cardigan. He was trustworthy, Larry felt certain of this. A quiet man, with a lot of depth and inner strength.

The two men continued to sit at the counter, occasionally chatting, sometimes falling silent, but they were at ease with each other, and relaxed. Suddenly Larry leaned closer. "Silver Hill was such a good experience for me. I'm glad I went, and I wouldn't have done so if Matt Branden hadn't advised me to check myself in. So thanks again for Branden. He's a very clever doctor. Anyway, I learned a lot about myself, my problems with my brother, and why I react to him the way I do. According to the psychiatrist there, Dr. William Fowler, I revert to my childhood role when Edward starts hounding me, become the little-boy victim. I really responded to Dr. Fowler, and I feel better than I have for a long time."

James, pleased that Larry had confided in him a little, nodded his understanding.

"I'll never be like that again," Larry added. "I have M to consider. . . . I would never want to scare her like I did when I got back from Canada. Not ever."

"She'll keep you on the straight and narrow, no doubt in my mind about that!" James chuckled. "She's a bit of a Margaret Thatcher at times, don't you think?"

"Very bossy, she is, my bit of trouble and strife."

# Twenty-seven

The bride did not wear a white wool suit with a white fur as originally planned. Nor did she carry a posy of white winter roses. It didn't even snow. But it was a beautiful day, cold but sunny, with a pale blue sky that echoed the color of her Tremont coat and matching pillbox hat.

The groom was smart in a dark blue suit, pale blue silk tie to match her coat, and dark overcoat, which matched his dark glasses.

They were the best-looking couple in the line at City Hall. Several people glanced at them curiously, but they paid no attention, just stood quietly together, holding hands and waiting their turn. When it finally came, they were asked to fill in papers, to date and sign them, which they did. When they handed their sets of papers back to the clerk, they were told they were now a married couple.

They were still holding hands as they left City Hall and hurried to the car which was waiting for them. They were laughing hilariously, and Larry said, "That was as easy as renewing my driver's license. And hardly a ceremony."

"Oh, who cares!" M answered and flashed him her cheeky smile. "Gosh, I'm now Mrs. Laurence Vaughan!"

"You are indeed, and don't ever think you'll be anybody else's missus either, because you won't. This is for life."

"You can bet on that," M shot back, squeezing his hand.

Once they were inside the car and the driver was pulling away from the curb, Larry brought out a wedding ring; taking hold of her left hand, he slipped off the sapphire, put on the plain gold band, replaced the engagement ring, and kissed her cheek. "There we are! It's all legal and proper, my rings are on your finger, and we're well and truly married, my girl. My very best darling girl."

She threw her arms around him, hugged him tightly. "I *am* your girl, and you're my boy, and I've never been so happy, not ever . . . Larry. Today we're starting a new life, our life together. I think it's wonderful."

"So do I. And now I'm taking you to lunch at La Grenouille to celebrate."

"That's a nice surprise, you didn't tell me." M gave him a huge smile and asked quietly, "It *is* just the two of us, though, isn't it? You haven't invited anyone, have you?"

"Of course not," he answered, put his arm around her shoulders, and held her close to him. All he wanted was her. Forever. She made his life complete, was his reason for living. He thought he was the luckiest man on earth. He counted his many blessings, of which she was the best of all.

❧

On their way uptown to the restaurant, M fell into her private thoughts. In particular, her mother and father were on her mind, and she had to admit that in a sense she had cheated them by marrying in secret. She felt a little sad about that. It had always been her mother's dream to have a big family wedding for her, since she was the youngest daughter, and now that would never be.

Neither she nor Larry had wanted a splashy marriage. But perhaps later, in the coming year, there could be a small ceremony at her parents' home, just for the two families, with a little reception afterward. If Larry would agree, and she felt sure he would if *she* wanted it to happen.

Quite suddenly she wished her mother and her sisters had been with her today, and for all of the sentimental reasons she had grown up with, all the English traditions which were upheld within their family. They were a family who had always shared things, done things together, and they enjoyed being with one another; there was great camaraderie and love among them. Never mind, she thought, looked down at her left hand, and smiled inwardly.

She was married to Laurence Vaughan, the hero of her childhood. Whoever would have thought that this would come to pass? Certainly not she herself. It seemed quite extraordinary. But then everything had been extraordinary in the last few weeks.

After those first frustrating months of waiting, hoping, tramping around the agencies, and working at the cheesecake café, she had finally *stumbled* into her first big break. Almost by accident. Was it randomness or destiny? She didn't know. But it was thanks to Geo, Frankie, and Luke Hendricks, who had carried the ball forward. It was his incredible photographs shown as huge blowups which had sealed the deal with the French designer in her opinion. And so suddenly. She was on her way to becoming a supermodel. And she was also a married woman. *Mrs. Laurence Vaughan.* She had to pinch her arm from time to time, to remind herself she was not dreaming. This was her life.

Unexpectedly, she thought of her elder brother, who constantly claimed that Lady Luck played an integral role in everybody's journey to success. He was right. It seemed to her that Lady Luck had been with *her* of late.

When she had come to New York to reinvent herself, she had been a little apprehensive, and she wondered what would have happened if it had been another man she had met and become involved with and not Larry. *Nothing would have happened.* She knew that only too well. Somewhat traumatized, she would have been on her guard, holding back, unable to take the relationship forward. But Laurence Vaughan was known to her, a man she had idolized since childhood. And so she had not been afraid of him . . . and had relaxed because of his tenderness and caring, his genuine love for her. She was safe with Larry, and she had known that from the first. She would always be safe with him.

"I want you to stand as still as you possibly can, M," Luke Hendricks said and then glanced across at Caresse hovering near the doorway to reception. "Please come and help, Caresse. Fix the edge of the dress, there at the bottom." He pointed and added, "The hem seems a bit bunched up. I want it straight, and skimming the floor."

"Right away!" Caresse did as he asked, then remained on her knees, looking at the entire dress, making sure the hem was perfect on all sides.

Kate Morrell came to join her, walked slowly around M, nodding, then told her,

"You look superb, M, and the dress is magnificent on you."

"Thanks." M gave her a faint smile. "When are you putting the lace veil on me?"

"In a few minutes. Luke's going to get some shots of the gown without the veil first. And we're waiting for the team from the magazine."

"Okay," M said and pushed her elbows back to stretch her shoulders but did not move otherwise.

Kate thought that this haute couture wedding gown was one of the most spectacular pieces Jean-Louis Tremont had ever designed. It resembled a ball gown with its huge bouffant skirt and strapless bodice above a narrow waist. The white silk taffeta hung beautifully from the waist; the boufancy of the gown was created by underskirts of white silk net. The strapless bodice was decorated on the front with a fan-shaped piece of finely pleated white taffeta, and it gave just the right finishing touch.

Because of her height and slenderness, M carried the gown well, and as he began to shoot, Luke said, "Stay perfectly still, honey! Let me do the moving around today. Hey, I love that smile, M, keep it! Hold it. Move your shoulders slightly, just a hint, hey, right on, kid. That's great. Twist your waist, face me. *Great!*"

After fifteen minutes Luke stopped shooting, put down the camera, and said, "If you're stiff or getting a cramp, why don't you move within that boundary I showed you? Just don't take too many steps, okay?"

"I'm fine, I really am, Luke, thanks anyway."

Caresse had left the studio, and she now returned from reception with the fashion editor of *Harper's Bazaar* and her assistant. The moment the two young women set eyes on M, they looked at each other, smiled, and clapped their hands. M waved, smiled back at them.

Kate went over to greet them, and they stood chatting together; after a few moments the women crossed to say hello to M and Luke, and then they retreated to the back of the room, sat down next to Kate.

The shoot continued for another half hour, and then Luke asked Kate to bring the net-and-lace veil; the two women helped her place it on the top of M's head, slightly to the back. Her hair had been swept up into a marvelously chic chignon by Agnes, and at the front, just above her bangs, the hair had been smoothed into a flat coil. It was just behind this coil that the women fastened the rosette attached to the veil.

It took them a few minutes to arrange the long veil over M's shoulders, so that it floated down her back and around her feet, but eventually they were satisfied it was perfectly arranged and went back to their chairs.

A few times Caresse peeped in around the door and smiled to herself when she saw Luke leaping about, circling M, whom he needed to be absolutely stationary. He suddenly reminded her of Frankie, who'd been a real prancer. He had always insisted the models remain in the same place. "I'll do the walking and the jumping," he used to tell them. "You do the smiling and the posing." It seemed that Luke was following suit today, but then he had no choice. He had to work this way with this gown. Closing the door, Caresse went back to the reception area to wait for Howard Dart and his client, who'd insisted on coming to see her. She had tried to dissuade Howard but to no avail.

At the behest of Kate and the magazine, Luke shot both color and black-and-white film. He stopped occasionally to move a light or turn one off, and he worked alone, which he much preferred on certain shoots. Finally, at the end of three hours, he walked over to M and said quietly, "Thank you, honey, you've been fantastic, and I know the shots will be super. You look fabulous. I'll get Marguerite to come out and pat your face. I don't need Agnes, though, your up-do's marvelous, not a hair out of place."

M threw him a cheeky smile and said swiftly, "I shouldn't think there is, Luke, I haven't moved an inch."

He laughed. "I think the veil should come off. And when Marguerite's touched you up, I'm going to do the final shots. Let me reload some of the cameras, and once I'm ready to start I'll tell you. It's then, and only then, that I want you to walk toward me. I want your head held high, in that elegant way you have, and your back straighter than you've ever made it. This gown is so impeccably cut and tailored it would stand on its own. So just move forward, don't think about the gown, it'll be perfect."

Once Marguerite had flicked a brush over M's face and renewed her lipstick, Kate went over to M and unpinned the veil, carefully carried it away.

When Luke was ready, his camera focused, he said, "Okay, M, start walking, very slowly, small steps, come toward me. Don't look down at the dress! It's fine, it's skimming the floor beautifully. Come on, slowly, smile, M. Give me that gorgeous smile of yours. Now, slowly turn. Oh, God, that's great! This is it, M, you've got it. Turn again, slowly. Now do a swirl. I promise you the gown will move with you and without . . . flinching."

At four o'clock the shoot was finished. Kate, Agnes, and Marguerite helped M to get out of the gown, and several minutes later she was sitting down, relaxing in her comfortable uniform of black trousers and sweater. Taking deep breaths, she sipped a glass of water; finally looking across at Kate, she asked, "Do you think it went well? Was I all right?"

Kate looked back at her for the longest moment before a huge smile spread itself across her face. "Not well, *superbly,* M.

You were just out of this world. God knows how you managed to stand so still for so long, but you did it."

"Discipline," Agnes announced. "M's the most disciplined model I've ever worked with, disciplined person, I should add."

"Oh, Agnes, you're so sweet to say that, but I'm not really," M said, laughing, and stood up. "I'll be back in a moment. I want to give this to Caresse before I forget."

As she hurried through the studio making for the door, M heard a male voice and hesitated for a moment before going into reception. Then she recognized it as the lawyer's. *Howard Dart.* Suddenly anxious for Caresse, wondering if she needed moral support, M pushed open the door.

Howard Dart was standing in the reception area with another man, but they both looked as if they were on the verge of leaving, were already wearing their overcoats. Ignoring them, M stepped over to Caresse's desk and placed the envelope in front of her. "I believe you wanted this," she murmured, smiled at Caresse, and raised a brow questioningly, silently indicating her worry.

Caresse smiled confidently, wanting to

reassure M, and looked across at the two men. "Thanks for coming in, but as I told you on the phone, Howard, Alex and I are keeping the studios. I also explained that Luke's becoming our partner. The three of us are now running it." She shrugged. "That's it."

Howard said, "Have it your way, Caresse. But I think you've made a mistake. If you change your mind, or get into trouble, let me know."

"We'll be available," the other man said in a clipped tone.

M swung around to look at them.

Both men stared at her intently. Howard inclined his head, then followed his client through the door.

Staring at Caresse, M said, "Who's the other man? Howard's client?"

"That's right. His name's S. Herbert Samson; he's a property developer. And he sure was anxious to buy the studios. But their offer was lousy, and the guy is a bully. And so is that sleazeball Howard Dart. What's in the envelope, M?"

"My address in Paris, and various telephone numbers I want you to have."

"But we're having lunch tomorrow."

"We are indeed, a festive lunch to celebrate everything. And so I'm getting rid of my bits of business today. It's fun for me from now on, until I start working for Jean-Louis in Paris."

Caresse nodded and felt her eyes filling with tears. Turning her head swiftly, she blinked them away, not wanting M to see. Her heart felt suddenly heavy as she realized she was not going to see M for quite some time. Caresse had grown attached to her and valued her friendship. She would miss her so much.

❖

With great speed, S. Herbert Samson managed to disengage himself from Howard Dart. "I've got to make a few of my European calls before it gets much later," he said. "I'm gonna grab a cab, Howie. I'll be in touch."

"I'm sorry the deal didn't work, S.H.," Howard answered. "I'll continue looking for prime real estate, and something'll come up, never fear."

"Great. Keep at it, Howie," S.H. replied and jumped into the cab which had miraculously drawn up next to him. After giving the driver the address of his office on Madison Avenue, he settled back against the seat, reliving that moment in the Farantino studios when the black-haired woman had walked into reception. She had knocked the breath out of him. He focused his mind, assessing everything, and eventually knew he was right in his conclusion. Also, he knew exactly what to do.

Once he had paid off the cab, he rushed through the lobby of the building, went up in the elevator to his fifth-floor office, a rented space that was more than adequate for his needs. He had no employees because he didn't need any. He had a laptop, which he was skilled at using. He prided himself that he didn't have one scrap of paper in this office. All of the filing cabinets were empty. Everything was in the laptop or in his head.

Once he was in the office, he locked the door and went to his desk. Taking out his cell phone, he was about to dial, then remembered how dangerous cell phones were. There was so much "chatter" these days, "chatter" picked up by hundreds of surveillance organizations, investigation companies, the FBI, the CIA, MI5 and MI6, and other U.S. and U.K. government agencies, not to mention foreign agencies like the KGB. He slipped the cell back into his jacket pocket and pulled the landline toward him. A landline was a bit safer but not much. He would talk in riddles, as the Boss preferred.

After dialing the number, he sat back in the chair, waiting patiently.

"Hullo?"

The voice was faint, but S.H. was positive he had reached the person he wanted. "It's me, Boss."

"S.H., I presume."

"Correct," he answered, relief flooding him as he recognized that posh voice.

"It's rather late here. This must be important," the upper-class voice intoned.

"It is. I've found her."

There was a silence. "Found who?"

"You know *who*. The lady who ran away."

"Aha, aren't you the clever one! How did you manage that?"

"You know I've been looking for her for months, and with no luck. But my luck changed, I found her this afternoon, Boss. What do you want me to do?"

"I don't know. Fill me in. What has she been doing? Where has she been hiding?

And exactly where did you . . . *find her,* if one can call it that."

"Stumbled over her at the Farantino photographic studios. I admit it, Boss, it wasn't cleverness on my part. She's become a model. I don't know much, but I can find out more tomorrow. When I was up there a few weeks ago, I heard the woman who runs the place talking on the phone. She was telling someone that Luke Hendricks, the photographer, was tied up for a week doing a big shoot for Jean-Louis Tremont, the French designer. And that their new model, whom they had discovered, was going off to Paris to work for him. I *know* it's the girl . . . she's going to Paris to become a supermodel, Boss."

There was a silence and then a soft, amused chuckle. "A *supermodel,* eh? Fame is the spur. So our little girl is going to become famous. Well, well, well, this is an unusual turn of events."

"Boss, what do you want me to do?" S.H. pressed. "Shall I pay her a visit? Get it over with?"

"Tut, tut, S.H.! Why would you want to do that? It's far too soon to leave your calling card. Let's wait, shall we? Once she's famous, if that does indeed happen, we could have a bit of fun with her before completing the mission. Or at least you could."

"Shall I stay on in New York, Boss?"

There was a long sigh. "Find out as much as you can about her in the next few days and then move back to Europe. Permanently."

"Okay," he answered. "How's Bart?"

"He's getting better. I would prefer not to talk about Bart. I'm afraid he blew his chance with me. Watch your step, Sam. I wouldn't want you to follow in *his* footsteps."

"How can you think a thing like that? I'm smarter than him."

The chuckles that flowed down the line from across the Atlantic were louder. "Good night, Sam," the man said, still chuckling as he hung up.

# Part Two

# DODGING THE ENEMY
## January–April
## 2007

Unnatural deeds do breed unnatural troubles.
William Shakespeare, *Macbeth*

# Twenty-eight

She felt different.

Was it because she was head over heels in love? And marvelously loved in return? Was it because she was now living in married bliss with the man of her dreams?

Or was it because she was about to be launched as a supermodel by one of the greatest fashion designers in the world? Then again, perhaps it was because she was in Paris, a city she loved more than any other in the world. Yes, it could be that. Paris had forever cast its spell over her. The very thought of it made her drool.

Perhaps she felt different because all of these wonderful things were rolled into one big ball of absolute perfect happiness. Whatever it was, she felt fabulous. And free as a bird . . . liberated.

She clutched Larry's hand tighter and stole a surreptitious look at him, smiled to herself. He was in disguise. So was she. They weren't really, they had no reason to be, but what they were wearing felt like a disguise. Pants, heavy sweaters, and boots, covered by bulky quilted coats, wool caps pulled down over their ears, scarves around their necks, woolen gloves on their hands, and dark glasses. All of this clothing was to combat the icy January weather, and the chill wind. Nonetheless, it was a beautiful day, with a bright blue sky without a cloud and shimmering sunlight. A perfectly lovely day except for the freezing cold.

They walked at a steady pace down the Avenue Montaigne, heading for the Champs-Élysées. When they turned onto it, they were both surprised how busy it was, chockablock with people, and Larry said, "I think this is a city where people never worry about the weather, unlike London and New

York. Paris is so bloody beautiful the weather doesn't matter one bit."

"You're right, darling, I've always thought that. Isn't it funny how we often think the same thing? Anyway, it's the wind that's a bit of a problem. It comes down from the steppes of Russia, blows right across Europe to Paris, where it seemingly stops."

He looked at her swiftly, grinning. "I bet you just invented that, you clever little minx! A wind down from the steppes of Russia! What an imagination you have, M, and how clever you are."

"Neither. I just have a good memory, and that was what I was once told by a very famous concierge in a very famous Paris hotel. And as you well know, being a seasoned traveler in La Belle France, concierges know everything."

"Touché, my little chickadee."

"Well, it's true! I'll call him at the hotel later, and if he's on duty you can speak to him, and he'll confirm what I just said. His name's Vincent, and he's a very good friend of mine."

Larry tightened his grip on her hand, laughing, and they walked on, in complete harmony. She pinched herself every day to make sure she wasn't dreaming all this, and he thanked God that he had found her when he had.

Once they got to the bottom of the avenue, they waited for the lights to change, then crossed the road to the other side, going toward the Rond-Point des Champs-Élysées. They hurried on, heading for the Rue du Faubourg-Saint-Honoré, and they didn't slow down until they arrived at Hermès, which was their actual destination.

"We can't go in, not looking like this!" M suddenly exclaimed.

"Don't be so silly, of course we can. Who cares about clothing these days?" Larry gave her a puzzled stare.

"I'm sure *they* do. How awful we look, Larry." She jabbed his arm. "Just look at our reflections in the window. We resemble huge bumblebees."

"No, we don't. We're not yellow and brown, we're almost all black, actually."

His sudden hilarity was infectious, and she laughed with him, then said, "I'm going to take this ghastly woolly cap off. There, that's better." As she spoke she shook out her glossy black hair, smoothed her hands over it, pushed it back from her face. "At least I put some makeup on before we left the hotel."

"You should have done an Audrey in the makeup department, and they'd let you in no matter what. They'd be convinced you were her, that you'd suddenly come back to life or been reincarnated, something like that."

"But if you take your woolly cap off, and your dark glasses, they'll know you're *you,* and they'll let me in with a handsome, very much alive actor who's a big number in France."

"Only in France," he shot back, faking a pout, and pulled off his red-and-black striped cap, stuffed it in his coat pocket.

Reaching up, M smoothed his hair and nodded. "You look divine, my lad."

"Oh, shucks, you're just prejudiced, babe."

Searching in her pocket, M found her lipstick, took it out, and staring in the window of the shop, she outlined her lips. "There, that's better."

"It sure is. The lipstick makes such a difference," he teased. "Come on, let's go in. I'm determined to buy you a brand-new Kelly to call your own."

"I don't mind the old ones, you know," she answered. "After all, they *were* passed down to me by some very chic women."

"What color do you want?" Larry asked, pushing open the door.

"I don't think I'm going to have my pick, you know. The store has a waiting list, and it's usually full of Japanese tourists buying up everything."

"A waiting list for a handbag?" Larry threw her an incredulous look. "That's unbelievable."

"I know it is. But I didn't invent the rules. They did."

They walked around the store for a few minutes, looking in the display cases at belts, silk scarves, gloves, enameled bracelets, all sorts of things, including a few handbags. But there wasn't a Kelly in sight.

M took hold of Larry's arm and whispered, "See, I told you. My sister says they keep the Kellys and the Birkins hidden in the basement. You're going to have to pull rank and play the movie star. But listen, darling, it doesn't matter if they don't have a bag available. Honestly, I have the one thing I want in the whole world, and he's standing next to me."

He kissed her cheek, squeezed her arm.

At this moment an elegant, well-groomed saleswoman came hurrying over to them. After smiling at M, she looked at Larry, and in a reverential voice she said, "Good morning, Mr. Vaughan. My name's Ginette, can I be of assistance?"

Larry gave her one of his dazzling smiles. "I'm sure you can. I was wondering if we could look at some Kellys and Birkins, Ginette?"

The saleswoman let out a small, almost inaudible sigh and made a tiny moue. "I'm not certain we have any in stock at the moment, Mr. Vaughan."

"How disappointing," Larry answered, focusing his improbably blue eyes on her. "Perhaps you could check. I'd be ever so grateful . . . Ginette."

The saleswoman smiled, murmured, "Let me ask the manager," and disappeared.

"Talk about butter melting in your hand. I thought she was going to swoon at your feet."

"A little charm doesn't hurt," he said, grinning. "Especially if it's going to get my darling her Kelly."

"It would be nice to have one of my very

own that's brand-new, but basically it doesn't really matter, as I just told you."

"I know that. But I wanted to give you a gift, darling. To celebrate this coming Monday. *D Day.* How do you feel? Are you nervous?"

M shook her head. "I don't think so. Neither am I frightened, which Kate asked me the other day. I told her I was impatient, and I guess that's exactly what I still feel now. I'm itching to put my feet on that runway."

"You get to do that tomorrow, don't you?"

"Yes. A rehearsal. Kate wants me to walk down it a few times, just to get the feel of it, to be sure of myself. You can come with me if you want, she said you could."

"Naturally I'm coming. Try and stop me."

Ginette returned carrying two orange cloth bags with the Hermès insignia stamped on the front in brown. "Only two Kellys, I'm afraid, Mr. Vaughan, and definitely no Birkins in stock. However, we can put you on our waiting list if you wish."

Larry threw her a lovely smile and turned to M, raising a brow.

M shook her head. "But I would like to look at the Kellys, please, Ginette."

Ginette smiled. "Here is the black one," she said, taking it out. "And the other one is this interesting tan color. Both bags can be worn with many colors." The tan bag also came out of the orange cloth cover and was placed on the counter.

As decisive as she always was, M knew immediately which one she preferred, and she looked at Larry. "I like the tan bag best."

"So do I," he replied and took out his credit card.

Patience was a virtue. Her mother had always told her that, and Kate Morrell had believed her. And so she had trained herself to be patient. As a child, as a teenager, and as a young woman. Now, at the age of thirty-eight, she considered herself the most patient woman on the planet. But she was about to demolish her record. She was going to go berserk. At least with Peter Addison when he arrived. If, indeed, he ever did. She had been waiting for him for four hours, and he was still not here . . . here being her suite at the Plaza Athénée hotel on the Avenue Montaigne.

When he had called her last night from London, he had said he would be at the hotel no later than eleven. It was now three o'clock. She had checked her cell phone constantly for missed calls, there were none; she had checked with hotel reception, and yes, they said, Monsieur Addison was expected but had not yet checked in. And of course she had tried to call him on his cell. It was turned off.

The phone rang again, and she snatched it up, realizing she was feeling more impatient than ever. "Hullo," she snapped.

"It's me, Kate."

"Who's me?" she demanded, knowing full well who it was.

"Please, Kate, be nice. It's Peter."

"Where the bloody hell are you?"

"In my room. I've just checked in."

"To this hotel?"

"Of course this hotel. Where else?"

"God only knows where you might check in, you're so undependable."

"Can I see you?"

"You'd better come and see me immediately if you know what's good for you!" she shouted and slammed the phone down.

A moment later there was a knock on the door of the suite. "What now?" she muttered and went to answer it.

Peter was standing there, looking extremely troubled.

"That was certainly quick," she said, ushering him inside.

"I'm across the corridor," he mumbled and walked into the sitting room, sat down in a chair.

"Where the fuck have you been? I've been waiting here for four hours. Not a word from you, that's the worst. If you'd only called me or left a message, everything would have been fine. But you let me hang, and I've been worried about you, frustrated, and growing bloody angrier by the minute. I've actually lost my patience. *Finally.*"

"For the first time in your life, I've no doubt," he said, very softly.

"What's that supposed to mean?" she demanded, her voice rising.

"Exactly what I said. . . . There's no hidden meaning or double entendre."

"What happened, Peter? Why are you so late? And *why* didn't you get in touch?"

"Where have I been? Sitting in the bar of the Ritz Hotel on Rue Cambon in a blue funk. Not knowing what to do. What to say to you. I needed to come to you, to tell you what's been going on in London in the past week. But . . . well, to be brutally honest, I lost my nerve . . ."

Kate knew him extremely well, understood him completely, and had been intimately involved with him for six years. He was her big, huggable teddy bear of a man, who constantly neglected himself, forgot meals, and was an unrepentant workaholic.

Now, Kate frowned, sat scrutinizing him, suddenly growing conscious of the strained look in his usually sparkling brown eyes, the tautness of his face. He was not himself; in fact he looked drained and tired.

"What's happened, Peter?"

"A devastating thing occurred this week. But before I go there, I just need to say that everything you wanted me to set up for M's launch and the spring collection for Tremont has been done. I have all the material in my briefcase, I'll give it to you later. But just so you know, I have the entire British and American press coming over, all the major national newspapers and magazines— *Hello!, OK!, Vogue, Harpers & Queen, Tatler, Elle*—and all the major networks, including the BBC, ITV, CNN."

"You're a genius, darling, and I'm thrilled.

You've obviously done a great job yet again, and thank you. But I want to know why you're disturbed, what happened? Please tell me."

Peter pulled all of his diverse thoughts together. "Allegra has done something completely foolish and selfish. It's disastrous. And I'm not sure how to make it right."

Kate stared at him intently, not daring to say a word. She had always liked his daughter but had known from the first day she met her that the girl was a walking time bomb. Self-involved, impulsive, irrational at times, and so gorgeous every man fell for her instantly.

"So what's the beautiful blond bombshell done now?" she finally asked in a careful, level voice.

"She's run off to Australia with a man fifteen years older than herself, and taken the two children with her. She's left Jim, says the marriage is over and that she will file for divorce. Or he can."

Kate sat back with a jerk, stunned by the news.

"I'll see you through the spring collection, Kate, and keep to the terms of my contract, but then I'll have to go to Australia."

"What for? I mean, why would you go to Australia?" She threw him a puzzled look.

"To bring her back."

Gaping at him, Kate exclaimed, "That's the most ridiculous thing I've ever heard! She's twenty-four, if I remember correctly. She won't listen to you, Peter, and neither will the new man in her life. She can do what she wants, darling, she's of age. Anyway, she's stubborn to a fault. Also, surely it's Jim's place to go and bring his wife back, not yours. Now listen to me, and I'll tell you how to handle this."

"All right. I'm listening."

"It's simple. You are going to step away from Allegra's mess and let her handle it with her husband and her lover. It's none of your business."

He nodded, knowing she was absolutely right.

"I want you to know that I'm here for you, Peter, and I'll help you in any way I can. Let's put Allegra and her problems to one side for a moment."

He nodded, looked suddenly more at ease, less taut.

"You're under contract to the House of Tremont, and that contract will be extended for as long as you want. Especially now that we are about to launch the New Face of Tremont in the shape of M. Also, I have a secret to tell you, and I know you won't breathe a word to anyone."

"Who the hell am I going to tell?" he asked, sounding slightly combative, more like himself.

This sudden change in his manner pleased Kate, and she leaned closer to him. "M told me last week that she's married, and this is going to be one helluva story for us. It'll boost the PR campaign in a fantastic way."

Peter frowned and asked, "Why? Who's she married?"

**"Laurence Vaughan."**

"*The* Laurence Vaughan? The actor? The gorgeous movie star?"

"You've hit the nail on the head, honey."

"Jaysus! That *is* a great story! Oh boy, Kate, they're going to be the new 'in' couple, and overnight. I guarantee that. It's all going to work beautifully for you. This really opens up the coverage, because it takes us away from fashion, beyond it. I can place lots of human interest stories. When did they get married? And where?"

"In New York in December. At City Hall. And in secret. And she was clever enough to wear a Tremont coat and hat. Clever, clever girl."

"I'll say."

# Twenty-nine

"They called her the Avenue of the Grande-Armée, you know," M said, turning on her side and looking at Larry.

"Who?" he asked, sounding sleepy.

"Margaretha Zelle MacLeod."

"Who on earth was that?" he asked, pushing himself up on the pillows, staring at her.

"She was also known as Mata Hari. She was an exotic dancer, and she got her nickname because of the extraordinary number of army officers she slept with during the First World War. She was a demimondaine, which, as you know, is simply a euphemism for prostitute."

"Why are you telling me all this?" Larry asked, puzzled but intrigued.

"Because I was just thinking about her. She lived here at the Plaza Athénée for a time, in January of 1917, to be exact, and this was her suite."

"You've got to be kidding! Now, why do I say that? Of course you're not kidding."

"That's right. Anyway, she checked out toward the end of January and went to another hotel, where she was later arrested for espionage. She *had* spied for the French, but she was accused of being a double agent, working for the Germans."

"The famous spy, now I remember. I once saw an old movie about her, starring Garbo. Or was it Dietrich?"

"Both of them made Mata Hari movies. But she wasn't a double agent, at least not according to British MI5, who believed the charges against her had been trumped up. Anyway, she was executed for treason later that year. In October."

"And tell me, M, how do you know all this?" An affectionate smile played around his mouth, and he leaned into her, kissed her brow, as always amused.

"I read a book about her, and I remembered certain things."

"And you do have an exceptional memory, that I'm aware of, and how do you know this was *her* suite?"

"The concierge told me. I asked him which one had been hers, and he said, "You are occupying it, madame." I told him I'd read this interesting book and gave him the title. Guess what? He'd read it, too. It was translated into French."

Larry started to laugh and said, through his laughter, "There's nobody like you, M, and I guess if you ask a lot of questions you get a lot of information."

"That's true. Oh, my God, Larry! Look at the clock. It's already eight-fifteen. Aren't we meeting Luke in the bar at eight-thirty?"

"That we are, we'd better get a move on, sweetie." He jumped out of bed, exclaiming, "I just need to wash my face and comb my hair. It'll only take me a few minutes."

"Me, too," M answered and went to the dressing table. After brushing her hair and tying it back in a ponytail, she smoothed the merest touch of makeup over her face and added pale lipstick. Within a couple of minutes she had dressed in a white cashmere turtleneck, a black satin waistcoat, and wide black satin trousers. She found a small black purse and stepped into high-heeled black satin shoes.

"Ready!" she called out and grinned as she turned around. Larry had dressed in a similar fashion, was wearing black jeans, a black blazer, and a crisp white, open-necked shirt. "I keep telling you we think alike," she said.

"So I see, and you look gorgeous, my girl." Taking hold of her arm, he led her out of the suite and down the corridor to the elevator. "Am I relieved you're not one of those women who mess around with their makeup for hours."

"Call me Swifty. That's me."

A moment later they stepped out of the elevator and into the hall. It was exactly eight-thirty, and Luke Hendricks was standing there waiting for them.

There were hugs and kisses, and Luke said, "My God, you two look fantastic. I wish I had a camera."

"Not tonight, Josephine," M murmured, and seeing Luke's baffled expression she explained, "That's a famous phrase of Napoleon's, supposedly uttered once by him to Josephine, his wife. I guess he was feeling too tired."

The two men were still laughing at M's comments as the three of them walked down the Galerie des Gobelins, heading in the direction of the Bar. It had recently been redone and was colorful, glamorous, modern, and the "in" place in town. And very busy.

Luke ushered M through the door, led her toward the far end of the room, and she suddenly spotted Caresse sitting with Geo and James, and let out a small whoop of delight. Rushing forward, she left Luke and Larry to follow in her wake.

Caresse jumped up the moment M reached the table, her perky little face filled with excitement. "I got in this morning, and I've been dying to see you ever since," Caresse explained, beaming at her.

"I can't believe you're here!" M answered, hugging her redheaded friend, of whom she had grown so fond.

"I wasn't going to miss your first walk down the catwalk," Caresse replied, sitting down and still grinning. "It's an *event*."

Geo stood up and hugged her, and so did James; Geo said, "We didn't want to miss your debut either, so we came over for a few days."

"I'm so happy you did. I'm thrilled the three of you are here, really happy to see you all."

"It's also our honeymoon," James announced, rather proudly. "We got married a few days ago at City Hall."

"Congratulations!" M sat down, her expression one of genuine happiness. These three people had become very important to her in New York, and she considered them dear friends. And she was delighted James and Geo had married.

"This is going to be a real celebration tonight," she said. "Let's have some champagne, Larry. You remember Larry, don't you, Caresse?"

Larry shook Caresse's hand, greeted her with genuine warmth, and sat down at the table. Turning to M, he said quietly, "Shall we tell them *our* news?"

M was silent for a moment, thinking quickly, and then she said, "Why not? It's going to be announced this coming week anyway."

All eyes were on Larry as he said in a low, confiding voice, "We got married, too. Also at City Hall in New York, just before we left in December. We did it in secret, and we'd like you all to keep it a secret for a few days, because Kate Morrell wants to make a big splash when she announces it. After the spring and summer collection has been shown."

Everybody promised to keep quiet, gave their congratulations in hushed voices, and Luke asked, "No photographs?"

"Of course not!" M threw him an amused glance. "However, I was married in the pale blue Tremont coat and pillbox hat, and there's no reason *you* can't take our 'wedding' shot, so called. We can stage it next week."

"What a clever little thing you are." Luke laughed.

"Not so little, Luke." Reaching out, M took Geo's hand in hers. "I'm so happy you married James, and that you, James, married Geo. You're the perfect couple. Congratulations again, and isn't it nice that the four of us are celebrating our nuptials together tonight."

"It is." James agreed, then grimaced all

of a sudden. "I'm afraid I won't be too popular with my parents when we tell them we got married without them being present. I think they were hoping we might tie the knot in England so they could be there." He shook his head and continued, "What about yours? How did they take it?" James looked from M to Larry, a questioning expression on his face.

M said, "I never know what to think when it comes to my parents and their reaction to the things I do. They regard me as a bit of a kook, I guess. They were sweet and congratulatory, then wanted to know if we'd like to get married again. In England, at our family home, where I grew up, and I said why not, and that seemed to satisfy them. They sounded happy when they hung up."

"And mine are in the middle of the most monumental row since that strange little man the Prince of Wales announced he was abdicating to marry the love of his life, Wallis Simpson, long ago. And don't ask me what my parents' row is about. I don't really know. However, because of it, they were sort of . . . well, offhand. Preoccupied with their own drama. But my mother said something about being certain my new wife was lovely, and that I was a very lucky chap. It was as if I'd been married before, the way she spoke."

"So basically we're off the hook," M asserted.

"Only for the moment," Larry announced and motioned to the waiter, asked for the wine to be served, then said to the others, "Earlier I ordered Billecart-Salmon pink champagne, and it'll be here in a moment. I hope you all like pink champagne?"

"Oh, I've never had it," Caresse said and then blushed, wishing she hadn't said this. "I'm sure I will though," she added, still pink in the face.

Larry continued, "I booked a table here at the hotel, at the Relais Plaza. We happen to love it, and who wants to go out again in this cold? M and I were frozen stiff today."

"It's my favorite spot," Luke said, and James agreed and went on, "And it's my dinner."

"Oh, no, not this time. It's mine," Larry argued.

"No fisticuffs, chaps," M said and was glad when the waiter arrived with the champagne.

Once they had toasted each other several times, and sipped their champagne, Larry said, "I've got to tell you this amazing thing I just learned from M. It's a marvelous story. Better still, let her tell you herself."

"What amazing thing?" M asked, playing dumb and gazing at him over the rim of her glass, her eyes loving.

"Your story about the Avenue de la Grande-Armée."

M burst out laughing and immediately recounted the tale of Mata Hari. They were all agog, listening attentively.

When she had finished it, Luke said, "Listen, kiddo, you've just given me a great idea for a magazine spread. Featuring you, naturally. I'd love to transform you into different famous women for a series of pictures—"

"Perhaps you could transform me into an Audrey," M suggested.

Luke, who was deadly serious about his sudden idea, ignored her teasing. "It would have to be done with wigs most probably, but the makeup would be easy. Some good artists could make you over to look like some of the famous women who've stayed here. I bet the hotel has a record."

"They do," M responded, understanding now that he was indeed serious. "They'll show you their albums. Many big movie stars have come trotting here over the years; it's always been popular with the movie crowd. The Plaza is also considered the Pantheon of the haute couture world, because all of the famous fashion designers are located around here, on Avenue George-V, Rue François 1$^{er}$, and Avenue Montaigne. Actually, Luke, I think you've hit on a fabulous idea, even though it's probably been done before."

"Everything's been done before," Luke shot back. "There's nothing new under the sun." He paused, gave her a long look. "But do you really think the idea will work, M?"

"I do. Ask the others what *they* think."

He did. They all talked about it for a while, drinking their champagne and enjoying themselves. And they laughed a lot when they came up with the names of famous women who would challenge Luke's artists' inventiveness when it came to hair and makeup for M.

"That was fun," Luke said later to Caresse, as they left the Bar and trooped down the galerie, across the lobby, and into the side door of the Relais Plaza.

Larry preferred the second level of the Relais, and Werner, the maître d', greeted them warmly and led them up the steps, over to a roomy table in the center. Once they had been seated, had studied the menu and ordered, M said to Geo, "I want to show you something. Something really special. Come on."

They both stood up, but as M pushed her chair back she noticed a sad look settling on Caresse's face. Not wanting her to feel left out, M exclaimed, "And you too, Caresse! I want you both to see this wonderful work of art."

Suddenly full of smiles again, Caresse rose, and she and Geo followed M down the three steps into the other part of the restaurant. Although it was busy, M managed to maneuver them closer to the bar.

"Just look at that," she said and indicated a panel on the wall above the bar. "That dates back to the 1930s. It's a bas-relief depicting Diana the huntress, and I think it's so unusual. I've always admired it, and it was recently regilded, so it looks better than ever."

"It's certainly unique," Geo agreed, "and if I'm not wrong, the panel has actually been sculpted on the wall, hasn't it?"

"Yes. And what I love about it is the sense of movement it depicts, it looks so . . . alive, with Diana and the dogs chasing the stag."

Caresse agreed and added, "The restaurant is . . . gorgeous. Did you see those two stained-glass panels of 1920s women? I hadn't noticed them when we came in. I think—" Caresse cut herself off and grabbed hold of M's arm. "I can't believe it, M," she whispered urgently. "Look, over there at that table where the blond woman is sitting. She's with that awful guy Samson, Howard Dart's real estate client. The guy who was badgering me to sell the studios. He's a jerk, just like Howie."

M followed the direction of Caresse's gaze and saw that she was correct. It *was* Samson, and he was staring across the room at them.

M shrugged and muttered to Caresse, "Don't pay any attention to him, just walk straight ahead. Follow me." As she spoke she led the way, her nose in the air, heading down the room.

Caresse and Geo did the same thing, appeared oblivious to Samson. But seeing him had upset Caresse, and she hadn't liked the way he had focused his gaze on M. She shivered involuntarily. There was something odd about Samson. He seemed sinister to her.

# Thirty

The scene was a hive of activity. Very well organized activity, M decided. She was sitting in a chair at a dressing table, watching everything with undisguised interest and enjoying every moment.

Dressers were moving about, coordinating shoes and accessories, sliding garments along racks to be certain all were labeled accurately and matched the models' names written large on big cards attached to the racks. Hairstylists and makeup artists maneuvered through the group of assistants from the House of Tremont with ease and grace. All were intent on ensuring every girl looked perfect, beyond perfect, if that were possible.

And of course a bevy of the most beautiful girls were at the center of this activity, sitting around in cotton robes like M, waiting for the magic hour when they would step onto the catwalk to do their stuff. M identified a couple of top models, as well as others she did not know. They were all occupied: on cell phones, reviewing their makeup, reading newspapers or magazines, checking date books, searching through carryalls. They didn't do any fraternizing, she noticed, and this did not surprise her. Everyone here was preoccupied with herself and her upcoming performance on the runway.

As M swung her eyes around, she noticed that some of the models looked bored to death, others were lost in thought, yet others were daydreaming. But still, there *was* a sense of tension and excitement. Jean-Louis Tremont was soon to present his spring-summer collection. It was the last Monday in January 2007, a day M knew she would never forget.

As usual, the great French fashion designer was showing his latest line of haute couture clothes at the Grand Palais on Avenue Winston-Churchill, the venue he preferred the most. He was showing at three o'clock for the same reason—preference; he liked an afternoon event best, mostly because it catered to the press. The show would last forty minutes, and from four o'clock on the photographers could shoot away to their hearts' content. They could stay until midnight, as far as he was concerned.

M became introspective, which she usually did when an important moment in her life drew closer. Today most especially she wanted to remain focused on what she was about to do, which was to walk down a runway in front of hundreds and hundreds of people for the first time in her life. Very shortly it would be her moment of truth. Her stomach tightened, and she felt a little ripple of nerves.

She was glad Kate had insisted on the rehearsal yesterday. She had walked the walk here at the Grand Palais, with Kate and Jean-Louis in attendance, and she had benefited from their advice. They had pointed out a number of things to avoid, and she had paid attention to every word they said.

Now it was D Day, as Larry called it, and the action was about to begin.

Glancing into the distance, M spotted Kate Morrell talking to Peter Addison, the head of public relations for the collection. She had met him last night with Kate and had liked him at once. He reminded her a little bit of an absentminded professor, and he had kind eyes, a gentle manner, but she knew that behind this likable facade was a tough PR man, one more exacting than most, according to Kate. And brilliant at what he did.

Suddenly, Kate was heading her way, looking purposeful, and M sat up straighter and took a few deep breaths.

"We're okay, aren't we, M?" Kate asked as she drew to a standstill. "No last-minute nerves?"

M forced a laugh. "A few I'm afraid, something I didn't really expect."

Kate nodded. "It would be inhuman if you weren't a bit nervous, sweetie. But you have great self-confidence, and that is the *key* to everything. *Your own self-confidence.* Forget the clothes, your beauty, just remember that one thing: *the confidence. Tell yourself this: I can do it. I'm the best. I'm going to strut my stuff.* Many a beautiful girl, a potential top girl, has failed because the confidence fled once she was out there. Got it, sweetie?"

"I've got it," M answered, sitting up even straighter, lifting her head higher, remembering who she was.

"And one other thing. Larry is sitting out there, and Caresse and your other friends from New York," Kate said. "They're right up front, I made sure of that. Take this advice from an old hand like me. Don't look for them, or at them if you spot them. Ignore their presence. You're not on that catwalk for *them.* You're out there for the audience, and the press, and to show Jean-Louis Tremont's clothes brilliantly. *You are the New Face of Jean-Louis Tremont.* Don't ever forget that. I decreed it. And you must not let me down. Understand?"

"I do, yes, Kate. And I want to thank you for everything you've done. You've been very good to me, and I will be okay."

"Better than okay. You're going to be the best. Right?"

"Absolutely."

"Now, let me give you the once-over." Kate stepped away, leaned into M, and studied her hair and makeup for a few moments. "They've done a great job. A hint of Audrey, well, more than a hint, but not too much to overshadow *you*." Kate nodded, then looked around as Luke stepped up to join them, carrying a camera.

"What do you think, Luke?" Kate asked, glancing at him. "Makeup is great, and so is the hair."

"She's perfect," Luke said. "And Jean-Louis prefers a neat head as you well know. I'm glad we kept it to a simple chignon." Luke drew back, leveled his camera at her. "Okay, smile, kiddo! I want a nice casual shot of you sitting here in your little cotton wrapper before you wriggle into those gorgeous clothes made just for you."

M laughed and gave him a little wave, and he caught that shot, then said, "Come on, stand up here next to your rack." He took some shots and then motioned to Kate. "Join the fun, Kate! Come and stand near the rack, and do me a favor, please. Point at her name, point to the M." He grinned. "Some name. So short."

Kate did as he asked, remarked, "I understand from Peter that the press turnout is staggering."

Luke threw her an odd look. "And why does that surprise *you*? If anybody's ever stage-managed anything, it's you, Kate."

Before she could think of an appropriate answer, Kate spotted Jean-Louis and turned around to face him, smiling broadly. "There you are, J.L. I was just wondering what happened to you."

He inclined his head graciously, smiled at her, murmured, "Kate," turned to look at M. Taking her hand, he kissed it. "Mademoiselle. You are looking . . . *superb.* I know you will be the grand success. I have no doubt at all. And I will be applauding you the loudest."

"Thank you, monsieur, I won't let you down."

He smiled at her, his admiration showing in his eyes, then shook Luke's hand, and said, "*Bonne chance* with the photography, Luke. I owe Mademoiselle to you. *Merci beaucoup.*" He nodded and strolled off to speak to the other girls, as always the most courteous of men. Unexpectedly, he swung around and beckoned to Kate.

"Excuse me," she said and left.

Luke said, "You're not frightened, are you, M?"

"No, I'm fine, honestly. I had a flutter of nerves earlier, but Kate kind of put the fear of God into me. I don't dare have any nerves. I've got to go out there and be . . . nerveless."

"No, fearless," Luke corrected and squeezed her shoulder. "Here comes your dresser, Claude. I like her a lot. She'll get you into the clothes with the greatest of ease." He grinned. "See ya out there, kid! Break a leg!"

❁

Suddenly Peter Addison was at her side, and he said, in a quiet voice, "I won't keep you, M, I know the dresser's waiting to help you into your first outfit. But I did want to wish you the very best."

She gave him a huge smile. "Thanks so much, Peter, that's kind of you."

"A word of advice," he now said. "Be prepared for the flashbulbs going off. The best thing to do is to keep your head up high, look toward the back of the room, staring straight ahead. That way you're not blinded *too* much. There's a lot of photographers out there, I must warn you, waiting for that first glimpse of you . . . so be ready."

"I will, and thanks for the tip, Peter."

A moment later Kate was taking hold of her arm. "Let's get you into the hot pink, sweetie." As they walked over to Claude, who was waiting with the outfit, Kate added, "Jean-Louis is contradicting himself again. I know last night he said he wanted you to go out first, but he's now changed his mind. He feels we need the audience to be warmed up a little, and also, if they don't see you immediately, there'll be more anticipation out there. So you'll go third. Be relaxed, M, don't worry, it'll all be fine."

M could only nod; her mouth was dry, her chest tight.

Waiting in the wings, M watched the first two models go onto the runway, both walking at a relatively steady pace. She felt slightly sick to her stomach, nausea rising, and then she stood up straighter, pushed the peculiar sensation away. She was taut, and she knew she would be until her feet hit the catwalk. It was impatience and pent-up excitement which were making her so tense. But she was certain the moment she was out there she would be perfectly fine.

Kate whispered, "*Now!* Go! Knock 'em dead!"

As M walked into the middle of the stage, she thought of her mother, her elder sister, and Birdie. *She had to succeed.* For the three of them. She had to make them proud of her. Then she erased all thoughts, wiped the slate clean, focused entirely on the job she had to do.

Adopting a rapid pace, stepping boldly onto the runway, M did not hear the music or the number of her outfit being announced. The only thing she heard was the applause. It was deafening.

She moved with her usual grace and fluidity, slowing slightly at times, then turning, swirling, strutting, showing off the impeccably cut hot pink wool coat, making sure it flared out behind her for full effect. And all the time she kept her head high, stared into space, avoiding eye contact with anyone. The flashing camera bulbs did not stop, but they did not bother her.

Sliding the coat off her shoulders but holding it tightly to her chest, she turned, walked slowly back, again turned, and took the coat off completely, held it in one hand, now displaying the purple silk dress and its flurry of pleats. The smashing color combination and superb tailoring were impressive. And so was she. They let her know that, clapped until she left the catwalk, dragging the coat behind her as Jean-Louis had shown her last night.

Claude, full of smiles, was waiting for her with a white silk suit and a black-and-white polka-dot blouse. "*Fantastique,* M," she said, admiration glowing in her dark eyes. "You have the knack," she added. M was out of the purple dress, into the white suit, and out on the runway again, everything done in record time.

And so it went. All manner of day suits, coats, dresses for afternoon, and cocktail outfits were shown, and applause for M and the clothes was overwhelming. During this time she held one thought in her head: *self-confidence.* That's the key, she reminded herself, and she kept hers. And was happy she had always had enormous self-assurance, which she attributed to her upbringing. It stood her in good stead.

Time was running on, and M knew that

they would probably run late, but it was not her fault. There had been a snag with another model which had delayed them briefly. Still, they might catch up.

Soon it was the moment for her to appear in her first evening gown, and the crowd went wild when she literally flew onto the catwalk amidst swirls of pastel chiffon. The gown was a confection of spring colors, which looked as if they'd been borrowed from a bunch of sweet peas. Pink, lilac, white, pale blue, yellow, and rose were combined in the delicate floral pattern, and she appeared to be a dreamlike creature in clouds of chiffon skirts below a strapless top and pale pink pearls.

Suddenly it was the finale. When M appeared on the edge of the stage before gliding forward onto the catwalk, she received a huge round of applause. She was wearing the extraordinary white silk taffeta wedding gown in which Luke had photographed her in New York for the cover of the April issue of *Harper's Bazaar*. The net-and-lace veil, pinned on the crown of her jet-black head, was draped over her shoulders and fell gracefully to the floor. Holding herself as tall as she could, she moved forward slowly, not wanting to trip, and knowing that this particular gown seemed to have a life of its own.

M was elegance personified as she stepped down the runway, her back straight, her head high. She was regality itself.

M received a standing ovation at the end of the show. And so did Jean-Louis Tremont when he stepped onto the stage to join M and the other models. The show had run twenty minutes longer than anticipated, for a full hour, but nobody seemed to care. In fact, everyone seemed to be carefree.

And Jean-Louis Tremont knew that he had a triumph on his hands. Two triumphs if he counted his collection of clothes.

Larry, slightly dazed, still sitting in his chair, had been mesmerized by his wife's *performance.* Because that was what it had been. She had all the qualities that make a star: beauty, self-assurance, utter belief in herself, and a hauteur that was undoubtedly bred in the bone. Kate Morrell may well have stage-managed everything for months, but it had worked only because of what M herself was.

"So be it," he said to no one in particular.

It was Geo who answered him. "That's right, Larry, she's going to be a star. An overnight sensation. That's what you meant, isn't it?"

"You hit the nail on the head, my love," was his response. He looked at James and murmured, "I have a feeling we're going to need some security, and as quickly as possible. Unless I'm mistaken, there's going to be a feeding frenzy with the press. I need her protected at all times, and I don't care what it costs."

"I agree," James responded. "She was absolutely magnificent, and the press are already crazy about her. You can see in their behavior that she's 'it.' I'll get onto it right away. The best plan is for us to get you your own car, and I'll provide a proper driver and an assistant, the second chauffeur. Both are ex-SAS. They'll shoot first and ask questions later."

"Oh, my God!" Larry exclaimed, looking at James in horror. "Are you serious?"

"I'm only kidding. But they're as tough

as steel, and that's what you need. Experienced operatives who have the training
and the guts, and can spot danger before
anyone else is aware of it."

Caresse hugged M and clung to her arm.
"You were the dreamgirl, the supermodel,
and I was bursting with pride, as if I was
your mom. Congratulations."

M hugged her again and laughed. "I'm
glad I made you proud, Caresse. And I'm
proud of you, the way you're running Farantino's."

Looking pleased by this unexpected compliment, Caresse grinned. "Luke's pleased,
and a bit surprised. He said he'd no idea I
was such a good businesswoman."

"I'm glad he realizes just how valuable
you are. You'll do well with the studios,
Caresse, and Kate is keeping him on to do
all the photographs of me for this collection and pret-à-porter, that I do know."

"Yes, he told me. Here's Kate now."

"There you are, sweetie!" Kate exclaimed,
drawing to a standstill. "What are you doing hiding away in this corner of the salon?
Jean-Louis wants you to come over and

have a glass of champagne, perhaps something to eat. Also, he would like to introduce you to a few people."

"Of course, Kate. Oh, is that my lot? Over there." She waved to Larry, Geo, and James, who were hovering near the window. "Oh, look, isn't he a darling? He's blowing kisses to me. I'd better go and give him some real ones."

"It's nine o'clock, darling," Larry said after she'd hugged and kissed him. "Aren't you done in?"

"Not really," M responded, linking her arm through his. "More like exhilarated, on a big high. Surely *you* know what I mean, my lad. Isn't it like that after a first night?"

"It is indeed, and you were fabulous, my darling M. A real star."

"Not a star, no. That's you, and only you, Laurence Vaughan. I am just a model."

Changing the subject, Larry said, "Peter Addison is a nice chap, and he seems to have the press eating out of his hand—"

"But what?" she interrupted.

He laughed. "You know me too well already, Mrs. Vaughan. I was going to say I just hope he's not working you too hard. You've been photographed nonstop from four-thirty to eight-thirty, first at the Grand Palais and now here at Tremont's salon. Aren't you tired?"

"No, I'm fine. Honestly, darling. Anyway, they've a right to get something for all that money."

"What money?"

"The money they're paying me. But I can't go into it now. Later, I'll tell you later. Let's go and rescue Geo from that plump chap who's almost but not quite making her his dinner."

# Thirty-one

On Tuesday, January thirtieth, M was hailed as the biggest new supermodel in years, guaranteed to join the ranks of the top girls. The day after this showing of the Tremont Spring-Summer Collection her picture was in every newspaper across the world.

Two days later, on February first, Jean-Louis Tremont and the House of Tremont invited the entire press corps to an afternoon champagne reception. The idea was for them to meet M on a more casual basis, talk to her and take candid photographs. It was soon after the arrival of the press that

Kate Morrell announced that their new discovery, M, had been recently married. Within minutes, she entered the reception room holding hands with her groom, Laurence Vaughan.

The press went wild, took the couple to their hearts, and in a sense sent them spinning off into the stratosphere. Overnight they became the new international "in" couple. The interview was glamorous, charming, and also touching because they were so much in love, and it immediately went online. After just ten days, that interview had been viewed by a hundred million people on YouTube. Remarkably, M and Larry remained calm, coped with everybody in a pleasant way, were never impolite, nor did they show any temperament. In other words, they were highly professional and took everything in their stride.

M's family were happy for her immense and sudden success, and somewhat amused by all the fuss. Certain members of Larry's family acted in a similar way; however, a couple of them were nasty about it. Miranda called it a disgusting display of vulgarity; Edward, eaten up by jealousy, said that his brother had found his true forte at long last—being a celebrity married to a model girl.

Larry, as independent as always, did not care what his family, or anyone else for that matter, thought. All he cared about was the wife he adored and keeping her safe. He was more than satisfied with James Cardigan. From the very first, James had been capable, devoted, and efficient, and he had put two crack officers in charge of them: tough, experienced, and dedicated. Fortunately, M and Larry found them compatible. They genuinely liked Stuart Nelson and Craig Lowe, who were always on the ready but also polite. Most important, their presence made Larry feel secure about M's safety.

❖

By the end of February, a number of things had become their daily routine. M was busy with the last of the pret-à-porter shows and completing Luke's photographs of her in those clothes. Larry had finished learning his lines and was impatient to start filming at the beginning of March, tired of having too much time on his hands.

On the last Sunday in February, Larry

and M were relaxing in their suite at the Plaza Athénée. M was going over her schedule for the week, and Larry was flipping through the script, looking at his margin notes. Suddenly a thought struck him, and he looked across at her.

"Will you be able to come to London with me when we move the production over there in April?" he asked.

"Yes, I will, Larry," she answered and began to turn the pages of her engagement book. "I just have one thing outstanding, and that's the charity fashion show I promised Jean-Louis I would do. It's on the twenty-second of March, and then I'm free as a bird."

"I'm glad, darling. I couldn't bear it if I had to leave you here and go alone to London."

"Neither could I, and listen, after that I'm actually free until July. That's when Jean-Louis will be showing the fall-winter collection, both haute couture and pret-à-porter, and incidentally, Luke told me the other day that Kate Morrell wants him to photograph the shows. He's thrilled, so you can imagine how Caresse feels. Except that she misses him, I think."

Larry's dark brow lifted, and he asked, "Is there something developing between those two?"

"I'm not sure," M answered with a laugh. "Maybe it's too soon after Frankie's death, but then again, maybe it isn't. And I would think she's a bit lonely in New York, although the studio is booked solid, Luke says, and there's Alex to look after."

Larry burst out laughing. "He's turned eighteen, for heaven's sake!"

"I thought he was younger," M muttered, and closed her engagement book. Changing the subject, she said, "Will you mind living in a very girlie-girlie flat in London?"

"No, as long as it's *your* girlie-girlie flat." He threw her a skeptical look and asked, "Is it really like that? All frilly and full of pink? I don't think I believe you, M. You're not the type."

"What type am I?"

"The delicious type," he answered, flirting. He put the script down, stood up, walked over to her, and put both hands on her shoulders. Bending down, he kissed her on the cheek and said, "How about a little siesta, pretty one?"

"When you say 'siesta,' are you using it as a euphemism for a little of the hot stuff?"

"Absolutely and most definitely."

"Then I'd love to have a siesta, mister."

❀

"I wish we could have a siesta every afternoon," M murmured a short while later, snuggling up to Larry, putting her arm over his body. "I always feel wonderful afterward, so relaxed and happy. Do you think that's how the Spanish feel after their siestas?"

Larry chuckled, held her close to him, loving her so much. She could be so quaint at times. He said, against her hair, "I think the famous Spanish siesta is a little different than ours, my love. But I can't be certain, of course."

"Neither can I. Well, never mind. Listen, Larry, I've been meaning to ask you something. How long will Stuart and Craig be with us?"

"Funny you should ask, I was discussing that with James yesterday afternoon. He agreed with me that we should keep them on for the next few months, until everything normalizes. If it ever does. James has the feeling there's always going to be enormous press interest in us, paparazzi chasing us, that sort of thing. But the excitement will probably taper off by the end of the year. The chaps don't bother you, do they?"

"No, not at all, and they're ever so discreet, unobtrusive actually. I was just curious, that's all."

"I can only say I'm glad we've had them around this past month, M; it got chaotic at times with the press turnouts wherever we went." Putting his hand under her chin, tilting her head, he looked into her face and asked, "So, how does it feel?"

M stared back at him, looking puzzled, and asked, "I'm not sure I know what you mean."

"Being you. The famous, mysterious M. The supermodel, born literally overnight. Some are even calling you the new Gisele Bündchen. Tall, thin, gorgeous. The rage of the paparazzi. The most photographable woman in the world. The favorite face on magazine covers." He grinned at her a little cheekily. "I'm glad to see it hasn't gone to your head, missus. *Yet.*"

"Gone to my head? It's actually gone to

my feet! Which I'm standing on for twelve to fourteen hours a day at the moment."

"You must be tired, sweetheart, it's been pretty tough," he said sympathetically, even though he knew she had tremendous energy and stamina.

"Yes, it has. And yet it hasn't, because I've . . . *enjoyed* it. Enormously. Anyway, what about you? You've had quite a month yourself, Larry. But I suppose it's a bit different for you, because you're used to fame. You come from this famous family, theatrical royalty they call you, all of you great Vaughans. And have you forgotten that you became a star overnight? When you played Hamlet on the stage, when I was ten and you were twenty-two. Younger than I am now, actually."

He burst out laughing. "By a year, that's all."

"And your first movie was a huge, fantastic hit, and you became a film star overnight. And you've never looked back. So how did *you* feel then?"

"I guess I felt sort of surprised, M," he answered honestly. "I was a bit taken aback after the success of *Hamlet.* I thought, Bloody hell, what's happened to me? And then I thought, This is bloody amazing. Because, you see, I hadn't put fame into the mix when I became an actor. Because you don't do it for the fame, do you?"

She remained silent.

He gave her a long, questioning look, a brow lifting. "Or did *you* do it for that?"

"Don't be silly! I did it to *prove* something."

"*Exactly.* That's why I did what I did. What I still do. And for the joy of doing the work. It's never fame or money, although the latter's useful. I've often pondered on my work. I act because I love it, and I want to meet the challenge of it every day. I have to sort of . . . grab it by the scruff of the neck and shake it, and say, I *can* do this job. And I will succeed. And so I do." He paused, released her gently, pushed himself up on the pillows, and continued, "Anyway, you come from a famous family, too; you're accustomed to attention."

"It's a different kind of fame, though, and it was never *mine.* It was, and is, theirs."

"That's right, but it's still fame."

"You began this conversation by asking me how I felt, and you know what, I feel great, Larry. I wanted to prove to my family that I could make it without them, and I did. And without the use of their name. I feel a lovely sense of gratification because I did it all by myself. Well, look, I know I had help from Luke and Kate, and Frankie before them. But I've done the actual work, and I didn't rely on the family name."

"Correct. But did you really think it would be so big and so fast?" he now asked, marveling that she had been so normal, so cool about everything.

She shook her head. "No, I didn't. And thank you for being there, and for watching my back."

"I'll always watch your back, my darling. And thank you for watching mine."

"What do you mean?"

"When I had lunch with James yesterday, he told me that you'd insisted on hiring him and paying him. I was so touched you wanted to protect me, made such an effort."

"I love you, and I certainly understood that if you turned up drugged in a New York hospital, everything would be misinterpreted. That there would be a scandal. I wasn't going to let *that* happen."

"He still has the cash in the envelope. He wants to return it."

Taken aback, she exclaimed, "Tell him to put it in the bank. It was his fee. I was happy to pay it. Anyway, I'm sure he gets more than that for his services."

"Probably. I said we'd take them to dinner tomorrow night."

M looked at him in surprise, her face filling with excitement. "*Them?* Is Geo coming to Paris?"

"Yes, she is, tomorrow afternoon. She's been staying with James's parents in London."

"Oh, that's wonderful. I can't wait to see her."

"They're only staying for a couple of days, and then they're going to Berlin on business. After that it's apparently back to London. He's doing some revamping of his company and expects to be around until the middle of April. That should please you."

"Oh, it does! But what did he say about Geo's show? The exhibition of her paintings at the gallery in Chelsea?"

"She's having everything framed at the moment. All of the new paintings are finally finished, and he told me the show will now be in September."

"It'll be a big success," M asserted. "Whenever it is. But why the delay, do you know?" A dark brow lifted.

"Because Geo started a series of brilliantly colored, offbeat portraits of women, and the gallery owner wanted to include them," Larry explained. "And also, from what James told me, Geo wanted to be with him in Europe."

"I think I've seen two of those portraits," M murmured, looking suddenly reflective. "They're half finished, at least they were last November. And one of them looked a bit like me . . . in an Art Deco way. She's very gifted."

# Thirty-two

Geo glanced around the grand salon of the Hôtel Cygne Noir, not far from the Louvre and newly opened, thinking how beautiful the room was. Traditional in style, it smacked of Marie Antoinette and Louis XVI; the latter's name was given to a decorative style she happened to like, even though it was sometimes a bit rococo.

The runway opened from the stage, ran straight down the middle of the salon, and stopped almost at the end, where it branched out to make a T shape. She couldn't wait to see M gliding down it, "strutting her stuff," as M called it, and she was thrilled to be here. She and James had flown to Paris last night, after two weeks in London, so that she could come to the fashion show and spend a few days with M.

Hearing her name, Geo turned around and immediately jumped up when she saw Luke heading her way, camera in hand as always.

The two of them embraced, and Luke said, "You look fantastic, Geo. Marriage definitely agrees with you. And how's James?"

"He's great. Somewhat busy with all this reorganization of his company. But anyway, you'll see him tonight; on the way over here M told me we're all having dinner together."

"I know, and hey, that's great, kiddo. By the way, I'll be shooting M from around about here once the show starts; it's a great vantage point for me. And after the show is finished, I want to get some casual shots of the two of you together. Okay?"

"That's fine, Luke, just as long as I can have copies of the pictures."

"It's a done deal," he said, his puckish face lighting up. "I'm going backstage to get some candid shots of M. See ya later, honey."

Geo sat down on the gold ballroom chair marked with her name, then turned to her right as the woman sitting next to her spoke.

"I hope you don't think I'm being rude, but I couldn't help overhearing the photographer when he was speaking to you. He was standing so close to us. Let me introduce myself. I'm Rebecca Byam."

Geo smiled at the tall, blond, rather attractive woman who had walked into the salon a few minutes before Luke arrived. She stuck out her hand. "I'm pleased to meet you. My name is Georgiana Carlson."

"I'm happy to meet you, too, and this is my friend Ann Molloy," Rebecca answered.

Ann Molloy stood up, went to shake Geo's hand. "Hello. Lovely to meet you, Ms. Carlson."

Geo nodded. She was another tall, good-looking woman, with thick chestnut hair and unusual greenish blue eyes. Both women were wearing smart clothes, and Geo realized they were American. She now ventured, "You said something about the photographer. Did you have a question about him?"

"Not exactly," Rebecca replied. "But he did start talking about M, and we couldn't help overhearing. We weren't eavesdropping, you know, it's just that he was so close. And we wondered if you *knew* her. We're such big fans of hers."

"Actually, I do, yes," Geo answered but volunteered nothing more. She was fiercely protective of M and her business, as were Larry and James, and also Luke Hendricks. There was far too much curiosity about M these days, and they all knew to keep their mouths shut.

"We read that she's totally unspoiled by all this sudden fame and success. Is that true?" Ann asked quietly.

Geo thought there was no harm in answering this perfectly innocent question, and she nodded. "She's the same as she's always been. Fame hasn't even made a dent."

"Isn't that nice to know! Success often goes to people's heads," Ann remarked.

Wanting to change the subject, Geo now asked, "Do you go to many fashion shows?"

Rebecca was the one to reply. "Yes, we

enjoy them. And when we had the opportunity to come here today, we thought it would be wonderful. Especially since it was advertised that M was going to be showing the clothes."

"You'll really enjoy it," Geo said and opened her program. The two women followed suit, and they were all three soon engrossed. At one moment, Geo glanced around and saw how fast the salon was filling up. Looking at her watch, she realized the show would be starting soon. She settled back in the chair, excited about seeing M on the runway again. She was tremendously proud of her friend.

❖

M settled her body down, making herself comfortable in the pastel chiffon evening gown, her "sweet-pea dress" she called it, and turned to thank her dresser, Claude. As she did so she spotted Philippe Tremont heading her way.

She had met Jean-Louis's brother earlier in March, when he had returned after almost three months of traveling. Philippe ran the export division of the House of Tremont, except for the States, which was Kate

Morrell's domain, and he had been on a worldwide trip.

There was a smile on his tan, handsome face as he came to a standstill next to her. Philippe was a younger, slightly more dashing version of his brother, with a great sense of humor and a much more relaxed demeanor than Jean-Louis. He said, "This was my first chance to see you on the runway, M, and you are fabulous. It belongs to you. Some models, even top girls, can't always do that . . . take it for themselves. Congratulations."

"Thank you, Philippe, it's nice of you to say so. I guess it's just a knack I have. My elder sister taught me certain things about modeling, and she used to instruct me to do what you just said . . . take the runway for myself. She likened it to a path in our mother's garden, and constantly reminded me to make it a familiar place. In other words, she told me not to be afraid of it."

"She was a good teacher, I believe, this sister. Well, I am so glad you are with *us* . . . as the New Face of Jean-Louis Tremont. Kate is brilliant, the way she launched you."

"She is, and so is Peter Addison. I think they have done a fantastic job." She suddenly giggled and added, "They made me a supermodel overnight. Can you believe *that*? I still can't."

Philippe laughed with her, thinking what a lovely, unspoiled young woman she was; according to Kate she was not at all temperamental. He had a good feeling about her, and he believed she would always remain just as she was today.

Claude waved to her, and M excused herself, hurried over to her dresser, who said, "You will go on next, M, in only a moment."

"Thanks, Claude," M answered and got ready to move forward as the other two models were coming off at the opposite side.

She glided onto the wide stage, paused dramatically, spun around, walked forward, paused again, and then pranced out onto the runway, moving down it with ease and grace and total self-confidence.

M and the gorgeous summer evening gown inspired instant applause; she turned and swirled in the middle of the runway, then strutted on, walking up and down on the T at the very end. A moment later she was coming back up, moving gracefully, showing the lovely chiffon frock to advantage, loving every moment of what she was doing.

M was extremely lighthearted this afternoon. Everything was good. She and Larry were so much in love, and they had a perfect marriage, compatible in mind as well as body. Thanks to a lot of luck, and Kate and Luke, she now had the career she had long wanted. And her dear friends Geo and James were in Paris . . . Paris in the spring. Well, almost, she thought, and what could be better than having them here *now* with me and Larry? My life is so great . . .

Walking on at her normal fast pace, M covered the catwalk once more before stepping onto the stage. She swirled again and headed into the wings, knowing she would be going out again in a few minutes. She had just enough time to change into the next gown.

But as she rushed toward the dressing area, she fell flat on her face. M went down heavily, tried to break the fall with her hands, and managed to keep her face from hitting the floor. Thank God, she thought. She knew at once what had caused her fall. Her left high heel had caught on something.

*"Mon Dieu! Mon Dieu!"* Claude cried when she saw M fall, and she rushed forward to help her. Philippe, who had been talking to Claude, swiftly followed the dresser.

"Are you injured?" Claude asked urgently. "What happened?"

"It's the heel of my shoe, it's caught on something," M said and tried to move her foot with no success.

"Please, M, remain still," Philippe said. "I must release the heel. It is stuck in a . . . *crack* on the wood floor. Is it possible for you to slide out the foot?"

She said, "I can't. My foot is trapped, and the shoe is at a funny angle. Claude, you'll have to get somebody else to go on in my place. I think I've done my ankle in; it's either broken or very badly sprained."

*"Oui, oui, bien sûr,"* Claude replied and hurried away.

Kate arrived with Jean-Louis. They were horrified when they saw M on the floor, with one foot trapped at such an awkward angle.

Jean-Louis knelt next to his brother and took hold of M's hand. "Is anything broken? Are you in pain, mademoiselle?"

M smiled at him faintly and shook her head. "I think I've sprained my ankle, but there's nothing we can do at the moment."

Kate, practical as always, also knelt down, looked at the shoe, a satin pump, and said, "I need a sharp knife, a box cutter if possible. I have to cut the shoe off M's foot. Her foot is very swollen, and I'm afraid to even *attempt* to get the shoe off any other way."

"*Oui, oui,* Kate, cut it off!" Jean-Louis exclaimed, and after squeezing M's hand and smiling at her encouragingly, he stood up, as did Philippe.

Kate crouched next to M, touched her shoulder. "Are you really all right, sweetie?"

"I am, honestly, Kate, except for my ankle. Well, I've got a bit of a pain in my side because I twisted my body so I wouldn't hit my face on the floor. But I'm okay."

"You didn't hit your face, luckily. And we'll get you fixed up in no time, don't worry, sweetie. Either Angelina or Sophie can finish showing your clothes. Oh, here's Sophie now. Claude's put her in the pale blue chiffon. I guess she'll have to wear the wedding gown also, since she's about your height and size."

"Oh, God, the wedding gown. I'd forgotten that for a moment," M cried, grimacing. "I could try to go on, Kate. Listen, if Claude gets me into the gown, Philippe and Jean-Louis could carry me to the catwalk. I could just stand there—"

Kate shook her head, but a smile touched her mouth as she said, "You're such a good sport, M, you really are. We'll manage. Sophie's okay. Oh, here's Philippe with a box cutter."

Philippe knelt down with Kate, and he held M's foot steady as Kate carefully slit the satin vamp from the rim to the toe. Pulling the fabric back, she was able to slide M's foot out fairly easily. "Very swollen, darling," Kate informed M. "I'm afraid you won't be able to stand on it for a couple of days. And you'd better see a doctor. It could be broken, and it's best to be sure."

"Thanks, Kate, for getting me out of the shoe," M said.

Philippe and Kate got M to her feet, and they each put a hand under her arm and helped her as she hopped to her dressing table.

Georgiana had an exacting eye. Now, as she sat waiting for M to reappear as the fashion show drew to a close, she noticed something odd. The runway seemed to shift slightly and ripple.

How could that be? Geo frowned, blinked several times, then looked at it again. She must have been imagining things. Now it was as steady as a rock; she wondered if she needed glasses.

Two of the top girls were finishing their pirouetting and parading, and left the catwalk, and Geo leaned forward, peering at the runway very intently now that it was empty. It seemed that there was nothing amiss after all.

Glancing around, she caught Luke's eye, and he nodded, grinned at her, went on reloading one of his cameras, seemingly undisturbed. And then Geo sat straighter in her chair, amazed to see the six bridesmaids coming onto the stage. Their arrival signaled the finale. It was too soon, wasn't it? Part of the show was missing. Or perhaps

Jean-Louis had simply edited it down for the charity event.

The six models came onto the runway, turning and moving gracefully, showing off their pink and yellow organza bridesmaids' dresses with their usual consummate skill. Within seconds they tripped back to the stage to join the groomsmen and the groom, who had just stepped onto the stage. All of the male models were handsome in black tie.

A moment later a wide smile spread across Geo's face when M glided onto the stage; then it immediately fled. She stared in astonishment. It wasn't M wearing the wedding gown. It was another girl. Sophie. Geo's eyes flew to Luke. He shrugged, shook his head, indicating that he was also baffled.

Now the bride and groom, the bridesmaids and groomsmen were moving down the runway. They were followed by the whole troupe of models wearing the evening gowns they had just shown. The catwalk and the stage filled. The audience went crazy. They clapped and cheered, some even stamped their feet and waved their arms. Jean-Louis stepped out onto the stage, smiling, bowing, acknowledging this great accolade.

Geo was watching everything, wondering where M was when she saw it. The runway rippled, just as it had earlier. It began to tremble, then literally crumbled before her eyes. Metal supports were collapsing, wood crashing. It was a catastrophe.

Chaos. Screaming. The male and female models falling off the disintegrating runway. Falling on one another, on the audience, on the floor. Chairs being turned over. People pushing. People running. Blood everywhere. People hurt. People dead.

Appalled, Geo was frozen to the spot.

She felt someone grab her arm, heard a voice urging her to move. It was Rebecca Byam, the American. Her friend Ann Molloy had picked up Geo's handbag and was shoving it into her hands. They were pulling her away from the scene.

Geo saw Luke, blood all over his face, coming toward them, beckoning. Luke, Geo, Ann, and Rebecca made it to the exit door where the runway ended.

Someone had grabbed the mike, was asking for calm. Security men from the hotel were everywhere. Outside, police sirens were screaming. Ambulance signals were blaring.

Luke opened the emergency exit door and hurried the three women out of the salon. They found themselves in a corridor and took a moment to catch their breath.

"What happened?" Ann asked. "How could the runway collapse like that?"

Luke said, "God only knows! But it's the biggest disaster I've ever seen. Unbelievable. The underpinning just crumpled away like it was made of cardboard."

"I saw it ripple earlier," Geo said at last, her voice hoarse with emotion. "Then I decided I'd imagined it. Obviously I hadn't. I should have told somebody. I could have prevented this." Tears came into her eyes.

Luke took hold of her arm consolingly. "Who would you have told? And who would have listened? Or believed you? Tell me that."

Geo said, "You must be hurt, Luke. You've got blood all over your face." She opened her bag, took out some loose tissues. "Here," she said, handing them to him. "They're clean."

He wiped his face and reassured her. "I'm not hurt. But someone near me was badly cut by a piece of metal . . . that's how I got blood on myself."

"We have a car and driver outside," Rebecca said. "Can we take you somewhere?"

"Thanks, that's so nice of you, Rebecca, but I have a car," Geo murmured and hugged her and Ann. "Thank you so much for helping me. I was sort of . . . *frozen.*"

They chatted for a moment longer, and then the two women walked down the corridor. Geo said, "They were terrific." She looked at Luke. "Do you think we should go back inside, try to help?"

He shook his head vehemently. "There's nothing we can do, kiddo. A lot of the hotel security men were rushing in as we were getting out, and we heard the sirens. Proper help is in there now. We'd only be in the way."

Geo said slowly, her voice shaking, "Thank God M wasn't on the runway. She could have been killed."

"She's just had a narrow escape." Luke shuddered. Taking hold of Geo's arm, he led her swiftly down the corridor, explaining, "I'm going to sit you down in the hotel lobby, and then I'll go and see what's happening, look for M."

"But everything must have been all right backstage, don't you think?" Geo said, her face filled with anxiety.

Luke nodded. "I think so. I hope so. Which one of her security men was with her?"

"It was Stuart. Craig stayed with the car. He's parked nearby. I have his cell number. I'm to call when we need him."

Nodding, Luke opened another emergency exit door, and they found themselves walking into the lobby. There were many people milling around, but Geo saw Stuart almost immediately. He was taller than most. She hurried over to him, dragging Luke with her.

Relief spread across Stuart's face when he became aware of Geo approaching. "M sent me to look for you," he said. "But they wouldn't let me into the salon. Security's very tight. Police are in there already."

"M's all right, isn't she?" Geo asked, peering at him.

"Yes. She's already in the car. Waiting for us. She sprained her ankle earlier, that's why she wasn't on the stage or the runway when it collapsed."

"I'm glad she sprained it," Luke exclaimed. "That's why she's still alive."

Stunned by the disaster which had just occurred, Jean-Louis Tremont was managing to hang on to his self-control. Despite the hysteria rising inside, he spoke in a steady voice to Inspector Raymond Letort. The inspector had been one of the first policemen to arrive on the scene from the nearest *gendarmerie*.

"*C'est un catastrophe,*" Jean-Louis said, his expression dour. "Never in my entire career have I known anything to happen like this. *C'est incroyable.*"

Inspector Letort nodded and escorted the designer to a quieter corner backstage. He said sympathetically, "It is indeed horrendous, Monsieur Tremont, an overwhelming tragedy. Now, monsieur, tell me exactly what occurred, from your point of view. *S'il vous plaît.*"

"It happened in an instant." Jean-Louis shook his head, still disbelieving. "I came out onto the stage. It was the end of the show. I was going to thank everyone, say a word. I did not open my mouth. The runway—" Jean-Louis paused as his voice began to shake, then he continued more steadily. "I saw the runway collapsing. I became paralyzed. My girls, the models, were falling off. And the male models. Panic. Screaming. It became a chaos. I saw people hurt, blood everywhere. I rushed off the stage into the grand salon, to help. I did my best. It was horrific."

"I understand, monsieur. And your brother?"

"Philippe had been standing in the wings. He heard the commotion, came to investigate. I saw him rush away. I understood he was coming here, to the dressing and makeup area. Our model M was waiting for her car, and Philippe wished to be sure she was all right."

"She was not on the catwalk?" the inspector asked, a brow lifting in surprise.

"*Ah, non.* M had had a small accident backstage. She sprained her ankle."

"She was lucky, *n'est-ce pas*?"

"That is true," Jean-Louis agreed.

"Monsieur Tremont, I have sent for our top antiterrorism unit," the inspector announced, his voice lowered. "There is something peculiar about this most tragic accident. Runways do not collapse on their own. Not in France. Fashion is big business. *I am suspicious.*"

Jean-Louis was silent for a second before asking, "Do you think it was *contrived*?" He sounded astonished. There was a frown on his face. "Why would someone wish to sabotage my fashion show? Surely not *terrorists*?"

"Why not, monsieur? Why *not* hit a big show like yours? A few hundred people are killed or injured. *Extraordinary publicity ensues.* Success for the terrorists. Every public event is vulnerable these days, I am afraid." Inspector Letort's eyes were sorrowful. "We live in bad times."

Before Jean-Louis could respond, Philippe came hurrying over to them, accompanied by two men. Inspector Letort greeted one of them. "Ah, there you are, Arnould," he said, and looking at Jean-Louis, he explained, "This is my colleague Inspector Henri Arnould."

Jean-Louis nodded. The two men shook hands, and the designer greeted the other man next. He was the hotel manager, Thierry Marchand, and Jean-Louis now introduced him to Inspector Letort; then he brought Philippe forward, explaining, "This is my brother, Inspector, Philippe Tremont."

Once all of the introductions were over, Inspector Letort gathered the group in a far corner where it was totally quiet. They discussed the situation in detail. Inspector Arnould explained that the police had discovered that the metal underpinning of the wooden scaffold had been tampered with. *Extensively.*

Arnould continued: "The bolts and nuts securing the metal parts which held the wooden platform had been loosened, and many had been removed in strategic places. The weight of the models walking on it for over an hour and then the weight of twelve people on it together brought the structure down."

Letort turned to Thierry Marchand, and asked, "*When* was the runway built, monsieur?"

"Last night, Inspector. And I must point out that security is excellent in the hotel. When the construction company hired to do the job finished, they immediately left. The grand salon was locked. It was secure, Inspector Letort."

"But somebody entered that room," Arnould announced, sounding positive. "In my opinion it was a terrorist. Or a terrorist group."

"I agree," Inspector Letort said. "There is no other possible explanation."

At this moment Jean-Louis noticed Kate Morrell and Peter Addison walking toward him. Excusing himself, he went to meet them. He was appalled by Kate's appearance. She had blood all over her clothes and face and looked as distressed as he felt. Peter was also disheveled and grim-looking, his suit covered in dust and blood.

"Kate, Peter. Thank you. It was good of you to go into the salon. You are not hurt in any way?"

"We're both fine," Kate answered, her voice slightly hoarse. "Which is more than I can say for a lot of other people. There have been many casualties, Jean-Louis."

"How many have been killed?" the fashion designer asked. "I can't bear to think about it."

Kate was silent, shook her head.

"How many people have been injured, Peter? How many are dead?" he asked again, staring at the PR man.

"We don't know yet, J.L. The ambulances took part of the audience away. And all of the models. Sophie has been injured, but not killed. It's a catastrophic situation."

Jean-Louis remained silent. He appeared beaten down.

Philippe came to join them, looking gray under his tan.

Kate filled him in, but he already knew most of it since he had been helping out at the other end of the salon. "It beggars belief. I don't know how such a thing could happen in Paris," he said. "The fashion industry employs thousands and is a big moneymaker. Also, the construction companies who specialize in building the runways are skilled and responsible. *How could such an accident happen here?*"

"You know the police don't think it's an accident," Jean-Louis finally said wearily. He looked at Kate and told her, "The construction was tampered with. Nuts and bolts were removed from the metal underpinnings."

"The police believe it's an act of terrorism," Philippe interjected. "And perhaps it is."

"Oh, my God!" Kate exclaimed, her face turning white.

# Thirty-three

James Cardigan stared at Larry when he opened the door of the suite, then exclaimed, "Good God, you're as white as a sheet. Are you all right?"

"Almost, now," Larry replied, ushering James into the sitting room and closing the door. "But I wasn't earlier. Come on in and sit down, and I'll explain."

The two men sat opposite each other, and Larry continued, "I got frightfully sick on location this afternoon, started to vomit. Immediately after lunch. The nurse attached to the production unit is convinced I ate something that was contaminated. I couldn't stop vomiting for ages, but when I was a bit more stable and able to leave the set, the assistant director brought me back to the hotel."

"What did you eat?" James asked, still regarding him intently. "Shellfish can do it, you know, or eggs, which are frequently tainted. They can give you salmonella."

Larry shook his head, grimaced, and then laughed hollowly. "I had both, I'm afraid. I had Parisian eggs; you know what they are, you like them, too. Hard-boiled eggs with mayonnaise and anchovies. After that I had a shrimp salad. Bad combination, no?"

"I concur with *that!*" James answered. "Have you seen a doctor?"

"Yes, the doctor for the production company, who's on call, came over about two hours ago, when I first got back, and confirmed what the nurse said. He gave me a prescription, which the concierge had filled, mainly because he was worried I might get another attack of diarrhea. As all the vomiting has ceased, he says the best thing for me is to do nothing. Because everything bad is out of my stomach. He prescribed hot black tea, no milk or lemon. Or water and dry biscuits or dry toast if I get hungry."

"How are you feeling now, old chap?" James peered at him, his eyes narrowing as he said, "You look a bit done in, I'm sorry to say."

"I am. But listen, funnily enough, I'm beginning to feel better. *Empty* inside but better."

James threw him an odd look and opened his mouth to say something, then stopped abruptly. He sat back in the chair, let out a long sigh, crossed his legs.

"What is it?" Larry asked. "You've got a funny look on your face."

"I just hope M doesn't think you took something, such as prescription pills, earlier."

"Oh, come on, James, she won't think that! I was at work, for God's sake, and she is well aware I am the most serious and professional of actors. In any case, I promised I'd never take any kind of pill ever again, and I don't break my promises."

"Sorry, Larry, I didn't mean to suggest you'd fallen off the wagon. Look, I must digress. Just before you called me, I was about to ring *you* on your cell. I didn't know whether you were back from the set or not. I wanted to let you know that M had sprained her ankle earlier and wasn't able to finish the charity fashion show. So she—"

"Is she all right?" Larry cut in swiftly, leaning forward, fixing those staggeringly blue eyes on James. "Oh, God, she must have been attempting to reach me on my cell. I've had it turned off all afternoon. I wasn't able to cope with answering it."

"She did try to reach you several times, and rang me, asked me to get in touch. About fifteen minutes ago. She also wanted me to tell you she was okay, and to explain about the catastrophe at the hotel."

**"Catastrophe?"**

James realized Larry had not heard anything, and he explained, "Something horrifying happened at the end of the fashion show. Around six o'clock." In his usual precise way, James relayed to Larry as much as *he* knew about the incident at the Hôtel Cygne Noir.

A shudder passed through Larry, and he said, "What a terrible tragedy. How many people have been hurt?"

"I don't know yet. I got my information

in bits and pieces, first from Stuart, then Craig, and a short while ago from Geo, who was there when it happened. Sophie, the top model, did get hurt, but she's alive. Fortunately Geo and Luke are okay. They managed to get out through an emergency exit. They are in the car with M and your security chaps, en route to the hotel as we speak."

Larry sat back, closed his eyes for a moment, and then, sitting up straighter, staring at James, he asked, "How could something like that happen? In Paris, of all places, the home of the catwalk and the center of the world's fashion."

"I don't know," James replied. "But the police seem to suspect a terrorist act, according to Craig, who was talking to some of them outside the hotel."

Larry simply gaped at him.

The two security men helped M into the suite, one on each side of her, their hands under her armpits. She hopped forward, smiling broadly at her husband, and then her smile slipped when she saw Larry in his bathrobe and pajamas and realized he was pale as a ghost.

"Darling, what's wrong?" she asked as he came toward her looking anxious.

He took hold of her, kissed her cheek, and said, "I managed to get food poisoning on location. At lunchtime. The assistant director brought me home this afternoon, and the doctor attached to the production has been over to see me. I'm fine, sweetheart, it's nothing serious, but what about your ankle?"

"I'll have to get it X-rayed tomorrow morning. However, I'm certain it's only a sprain. What did you eat that made you so ill?" She stared at him intently and lifted a brow.

"Eggs first, and then I had a shrimp salad."

"You only need to eat one tiny piece of contaminated food to get sick as a dog, at least that's what Daddy has always told me," M remarked and sat down in the chair. Looking up at Stuart and Craig, who were hovering over her, she said, "Thanks so much for looking after me and Geo, and Luke. Let's order a drink, shall we? We all need one." Glancing at Larry, she exclaimed, "Oh, sorry, darling, perhaps we shouldn't be crowding in on you like this. You should be resting."

"I'm glad of the company, and I can always go and lie down in the bedroom if I feel suddenly done in again. Right now, well, I'm glad to say I'm not too bad. Luke, Geo, you two were really lucky from what James has just told me."

Luke said, "Damn right we were lucky, and fortunately we were both near the end of the catwalk and, more important, close to an exit door. But the person who is truly lucky is M, Larry. If she hadn't had the accident backstage, done her ankle in, she would have been on the runway. She would have been thrown off when it collapsed, like all of the others were."

"I can't bear to think of what might have happened," Larry said, a rush of apprehension turning him cold. Swallowing hard, squeezing M's shoulder, he thanked God she was safe.

Geo, who was standing with her arm tucked through her husband's, looked from Larry to M and said quietly, "You must have a guardian angel sitting on your shoulder, M."

M pursed her lips together, stared at Geo, and said, very slowly, her eyes reflective, "Once, when I was quite small, I fell into a deep ravine. I rolled, tumbled, rolled and tumbled, until I got to the very bottom. When my panic-stricken mother reached me, I was totally intact. Not a scratch or a bruise on me. All I had was a dirty face. It was a miracle I hadn't been killed, and *she* told me that day that I had a guardian angel watching over me. I guess I do, Geo. I hope I do in the future, too."

Larry said, "James, would you be kind enough to call room service. Let's get a couple of bottles of white wine up here and a bucket of ice. There's a drinks trolley over there with the usual on it—scotch, vodka, and gin, and here're Cokes, tonic, and soda in the minibar. I won't have any alcohol, but I'm sure you all need a drink after what you've been through."

James did as Larry asked, and once the order had been given, he walked over to Stuart and Craig. "Give me your take on the disaster. Tell me what you found out, Craig. You were in the street, weren't you? Come on, chaps, let's sit over there." As he spoke, he indicated a second seating area against the back wall; the three of them walked over and sat down.

Geo took the chair next to M; Larry positioned himself on the sofa next to M's chair and took hold of her hand. Luke sat down next to Larry, asking him, "Do I still have blood on my face?"

"No, you're as clean as a whistle," Larry responded, and looking affectionately at his wife, he murmured, "I shall have to get you a pair of crutches tomorrow to help you get around."

"*A crutch will do. And thanks, darling.*"

After a few moments talking together, James, Stuart, and Craig joined them, all three of them settling down on the opposite sofa in front of the fireplace.

James said, "We all want to know as much as we can, to understand what happened, and I think the two people who know the most are the eyewitnesses: Luke and Geo. After that, M can give us details about the activity backstage. Luke, start telling us, would you, please?"

"I will, if you want. But actually, James, Geo should really start this off, because she saw more than I did."

Before James could utter a word, Geo said, "That's right, I did see everything." She steadied herself and began by saying, "The funny thing was, right near the end of the show, I saw something really strange. I thought I saw the runway *shift* slightly. It appeared to *tremble.* Then when I looked again, I thought I'd dreamed it, or that I needed glasses. In the end, I decided I'd been imagining things." Suddenly afraid that she might start to weep, Geo took a moment before continuing her story.

After Geo, Luke spoke for several minutes, mostly explaining what had happened when people started to panic, how they pushed past one another and upturned chairs in their haste. With emotion he said he actually saw the models falling off the catwalk and into the audience, how some people were injured when this happened, others hurt in the crush of the crowded area. He finished by explaining how he, Geo, and Ann and Rebecca, the two American women, had managed to make such a swift and relatively easy escape.

James now looked at M and said, "You were backstage, so Geo told me. How *did* you find out about the collapse of the runway?"

"It was Philippe Tremont who came rushing backstage. He looked alarmed, told me to pull my things together and to come with him. I asked him to bring Stuart over, and within seconds the two of them had virtually lifted me outside. I then persuaded Stuart to try to get back into the hotel. To find Geo, extract her and Luke. First, Stuart called for the car, and once I was in it he went to the front entrance of the hotel."

"Anything to add, Stuart?" James asked.

The ex-SAS officer shook his head. "That's about it, James. Craig was the one who had a bird's-eye view of the events outside."

Craig nodded. "That's true. Not much to tell, though, James. There were any number of cops milling around. Their cars and vans were blocking the area. The traffic jams were building, so there was a great deal of shouting, blaring of horns, and foul language being spouted out of windows. I did manage to have a few words with two different cops at one point, and both told me that counterterrorism units had been summoned. They were naturally very anxious. Some were wondering if there were bombs planted inside the hotel. I tried to get more information from others but wasn't able to do so."

At this moment the doorbell rang, and James went to open it. The waiter wheeled in a trolley, immediately opened a bottle of the white wine, and poured a small amount for James to taste. He did so, and the waiter hurried off, telling James to ring if he needed anything else.

James asked, "Who wants what? Geo? M? Luke?"

"I'll have white wine, and I suppose Geo will, won't you?" M said.

Geo smiled at James. "That's fine, darling."

Stuart and Craig also elected to have white wine, as did Luke. After pouring the wine, James opened the other bottle. Craig handed the glasses around, and then they all settled back in their seats to continue the conversation.

It was Larry who spoke first. Glancing at James, he said, "As you're the expert here, in view of your last position, working for Her Majesty's Secret Service, why do *you* think the *flics* called in the counterterrorism unit or units? I mean, why would the police think terrorists would target Jean-Louis?"

"*If* the tragedy at the hotel this afternoon

*was* an act of terrorism, I'm *certain* it wasn't aimed at Jean-Louis Tremont . . ." James lifted his glass of water, said cheers, took a sip, and continued. "This disastrous act was directed at the Hôtel Cygne Noir. It is an American-owned hotel, by the way, and also the new preferred destination for American movie stars and celebrities. And the act was also aimed at one of the biggest industries in France."

"The Fashion Business, with capital F and B," M exclaimed and looked pointedly at James. "And an industry which makes billions a year, one of the two top export businesses in France . . . Wine and Fashion spell France." She paused, drank a little wine, then said, "I know haute couture is not as big as it used to be, that the wealthy customers for it are diminishing, but haute couture is still the great symbol. Pret-à-porter and ready-to-wear are big and sell well, and so do the toiles of the couture clothes, which are bought by manufacturers from all over the world. They buy the right to copy the originals. And then there are patterns and fabrics, all from the haute couture range, which are sold worldwide. It employs thousands of people. So here's how it probably breaks down: damage an American hotel, damage a French industry, damage the Western democracies by slaying people. *I believe it was a terrorist act,*" M finished and looked at Craig and Stuart, who she knew agreed.

Luke said, "I absolutely concur with M, especially about fashion being such a huge business. So many people dismiss it as a vanity, and shallow, but they don't realize all its different moneymaking aspects. Fashion photography, fashion magazines, fashion public relations . . . it is just endless. And—"

"Oh, my God, I must call my sister!" M cried, struggling to her feet. "She knew I was doing this charity show today. I have to phone her in London before she sees the news on television. Larry, please help me into the bedroom. Excuse me, back in a minute."

❖

Once they were alone in the bedroom with the door closed, Larry took M in his arms and held her close to him. Against her hair, he said, "Thank God you weren't hurt, my darling. You're my life, you know. Without you I would have nothing."

"I feel the same way, Larry, and perhaps my mother was right all those years ago when she said I had a guardian angel. . . . I had a narrow escape today."

"I think so, yes." Looking down at her, his bright blue eyes riveted on hers, he said in a low and very serious voice, "I do have food poisoning, M. I haven't taken any pills. All the vomiting I had earlier today was due to something I ate. When I promised you I would never take a pill ever again, I meant it."

"I know you did, and it never crossed my mind that you might have taken pills. I know you, Laurence Vaughan, and you're a serious, dedicated actor. You would never do anything to jeopardize your career. I do have one question, though. Was anybody else ill after lunch?"

"As a matter of fact, yes. Two members of the camera crew, and the woman who runs the catering company for the film locations, Chantelle Valbonne. And perhaps her assistant, although I'm not sure about that."

"Will you be able to go to work tomorrow?" she asked.

"Yes, but thank God I'm not on call."

"And neither am I, not with this ankle. I know it's not broken, but I will go to the doctor."

"Please, darling. And I'll come with you."

"That's great. I'll treat you to lunch. In the meantime, I must call London town."

"Come on, sweetheart, I'll help you over to the chair." Larry put his arm around her and lifted her to the desk chair. She pulled her cell phone out of her jacket pocket and dialed her sister.

"Hullo, darling, is that you?" M asked, knowing it was.

"Yes. Where are you, M? I just heard the news on television about that dreadful disaster at the Hôtel Cygne Noir. I was starting to worry about you, because you'd told me you were modeling there today. You were, weren't you?"

"I was, yes, Birdie—"

"Have many people been hurt?" her sister cut in.

"From what I understand, yes, but I don't have many details. You see, I fell backstage and sprained my ankle. It was a flukey thing, but I was unable to go onto the runway again. It saved me, the sprain, I mean."

"I'll say! Anyway, I was just going to phone you, so it's quite a relief to hear from you, little one. How's Larry?"

"Great, except that he had a mishap today, too. He has food poisoning, caused by something he ate at lunch on location. But basically we're both okay, I promise."

"When are you coming to London, darling? I can't wait to see you."

"In ten days. We'll be arriving at the beginning of April. Larry has to shoot there; he has about a week's work and he'll be down in the country. Once those scenes are in the can, he's finished, except for postproduction. But all of that will be done in London. We'll definitely be there for a couple of months."

"Whoopee! That's wonderful news, M. Everybody's going to be thrilled. By the way, did you call our big sister? To tell her you're all right."

"I didn't even know she was in Paris. I thought she was away with the children. So no, I didn't." M took a deep breath. "Could *you* phone her for me, Birdie, please? I just don't want to talk to her yet, or go and see her."

"I will, if you stop calling me Birdie. However, I don't understand you, M. Why are you avoiding her?"

"Oh, Birdie, I'm not! It's just that I need a bit longer to be *me* and not part of . . . all of you."

Her sister burst out laughing and said, after a moment, "All right, I'll call her. Bye-bye."

"Why don't you want to speak to the Beautiful One?" Larry asked, using one of his nicknames for her sister. There was a note of bafflement in his voice.

M looked across at the bed, where he was stretched out resting. "Because she can be a bit . . . *peculiar,* and also I want to get the Jean-Louis Tremont campaign over with, at least this first part of it. And I want us to be more . . . settled down before I launch you into the middle of my family."

"We *are* settled down. At least I am. I certainly feel like a very much married man, and incidentally, I love that feeling! So hop over here and give your old man a big smacker."

"Certainly. I'll be right over, mister."

"Oh, no, better not do that, you'll fall," he exclaimed. "I'm coming over to you."

Later that night, M fell into an exhausted sleep, but around three o'clock she suddenly woke up. She was filled with a strange apprehension, worried about Sophie, who had taken her place and been hurt, and a sense of guilt settled inside her. Endeavoring to shake this off, she focused on Larry, who slept soundly next to her. In a way, she was angry with herself for suspecting him, initially, of taking those deadly prescription pills. But the thought *had* leapt into her mind, no two ways about that. Now, in hindsight, she knew he would never go back there, never take a prescription pill again. He was chastened after his experience in Canada. And more important than anything, he had made a promise to her, and she now realized, and accepted, that he would never break that promise. She trusted him.

# Thirty-four

Philippe Tremont stared at Jean-Louis in astonishment, wondering if his brother had taken leave of his senses. Clearing his throat, sitting up straighter in the chair, he now said, "But why in God's name would you think Rafi is responsible for the sabotage? My God, that's *ridiculous,* Jean-Louis! He wouldn't even have the resources to do such a thing."

"Yes, he would. There is a lot you do not know about our cousin. What is that odd expression our mother used so frequently . . . the water that is still and deep has the devil resting at the bottom. Some such thing."

"All right, maybe he does have a bad streak running through him. But please explain two things to me. Why would he want to sabotage your charity fashion show? And how would he have managed to get into a secured room to dismantle the underpinnings of the runway, and all by himself?"

"Maybe he was not alone, maybe he is part of a group of terrorists and—"

"Now you are really stretching it!" Philippe cried, his voice rising. Hearing a noise, he stood, crossed the room, opened the door, and looked into the secretary's office. Louise's chair was vacant, and there was no one in sight. No one had been eavesdropping. Closing the door and returning to his chair, Philippe added, "Rafi is not a terrorist. You are exaggerating because of your constant anger toward him."

Jean-Louis settled back in the chair behind his desk, steepling his fingers, and looked over them at his younger brother. "Perhaps he is not a member of an organization specializing in terrorism, but he is a *hothead.* He always has been. And let us not forget that he may bear the name Tremont, because his father was our father's brother, our uncle, but his mother is an Algerian." Jean-Louis grimaced, shook his head, and concluded, "And a *putain*."

Philippe sighed. "She's not a prostitute. But I know you believe all this, Jean-Louis, and I've never been able to make you change your mind. Answer this. Why would he want to strike at *you*?"

"Because recently I have asked him to start paying back the money he owes us, and I do not think he is happy about that." Jean-Louis sighed. "Why did I bother to ask him? He has no money, he is a beggar."

"All right, maybe he has a vendetta against you. Tell me something, though. How did he get into a locked room? And how could he dismantle the underpinnings himself?"

"I told you, he may not have been alone. I believe it is obvious he had help. And I cannot explain how he got into the grand salon to do his dirty work. Unless . . . he was part of the construction crew. Perhaps he managed to hide in the room and then let his cohorts in later."

"Anything is possible," Philippe conceded. "However, I think you are attributing too much intelligence to our cousin. I have always thought him to be dim-witted myself."

"Not his wife. *She* is quite the operator," Jean-Louis remarked, giving Philippe a knowing look, wondering why his brother didn't understand the setup.

"So what you are saying, in effect, is that you think the police are wrong, and yesterday's disaster was not an act of terrorism," Philippe asserted, staring at his older sibling.

"That is correct. Well, terrorism in one sense, by Rafi against me."

"I don't think the DST would agree with you, *mon frère*." Philippe smiled. "Those guys who occupy number one rue Nélaton appear to have other ideas altogether, from what I read in the newspapers today."

"Perhaps. And I do believe that the intelligence agency has some brilliant operatives. But in this instance, well, I have come to my own conclusions, and with good cause."

"And yet there is nothing we can do—"

"Oh, yes, I can do something. I am going to see Rafi—"

"Oh, no, you're not," Philippe interrupted most forcefully. "I'm not having you wandering around Belleville, it's not safe. If necessary I myself will go and talk to him."

"Perhaps that would be better, Philippe, *merci beaucoup.* I might lose my temper." Jean-Louis smiled ironically at the thought.

Philippe announced, "I will go. *This afternoon.* After our meeting with our lawyers and the director of the insurance company. Now, *mon cher frère,* let us go and have lunch."

Belleville was on the opposite side of Paris, and Philippe knew that it would take him a good forty minutes to get there. Once he had finished the meeting with their lawyers and the insurance people, he hurried to his apartment on Avenue Montaigne, quickly changed into more casual clothes, and gave his driver the address of their destination.

The traffic was heavy at the end of the afternoon, and he cursed himself under his breath, realizing he should have gone out there in the early evening, when it was less congested.

But it was too late. He was on his way, and he wanted to get the meeting over with; he had toyed with the idea of ringing his cousin Raphaël and discussing the matter on the phone. But instantly he had changed his mind. Nor did he wish to call to announce that he was coming out to see him. Better to arrive when he was not expected.

Although he did not harbor the same troubling thoughts and grudges his brother did, Philippe nonetheless knew that their cousin was a disreputable character who mingled with crooks and criminals; the lowest of the low seemed to be his preference. Raphaël Tremont had had many advantages in his youth, yet he had thrown them all away, had gone from disaster to disaster all of his life. He has larceny in his heart, Philippe suddenly thought, my brother is right about that. And he is a loser.

Philippe glanced out of the window as the car finally arrived in Belleville. It was an ugly area of Paris that hardly lived up to its name. Even though it was growing dark, Philippe could see that the streets were more scruffy-looking than ever, and depressing. He had always thought of it as an odd part of the city, a disreputable district. It was the Arab quarter, where most of the North African and African immigrants lived. He was well aware that there were many decent, hardworking people amongst them, yet somehow the place had managed to get a peculiar reputation in the last few years.

The car turned off the Boulevard de Bel-leville, and Philippe directed his driver to the small street off the boulevard where his cousin lived with his wife and son.

When the car arrived at the front door of the modest apartment building, Philippe told the driver to wait if that was possible, adding, "If you have to move on, do so, Marcel. If you're not here when I leave, I will call you on your cell."

*"Oui, monsieur,"* the driver said, jumping out to open the door for him.

Philippe rang the bell marked tremont. There was no reply. But after a moment a youth came out; Philippe nodded to him, held the door open, and slipped into the building.

He took the stairs two at a time until he reached the third floor, where his cousin lived. He rang the bell, and when no one answered he banged on the door. Finally a gruff voice demanded, "Who is it? Who's there?"

"Rafi, open the door! It's Philippe. Your cousin Philippe."

"Get lost! I don't want to see you!"

"I have something for you," Philippe said. "Money. I know you need it."

"Just shove it under the door."

"No, no. That is not possible. I must see you, speak to you."

Much to Philippe's amazement, the door opened at once. He stared at Raphaël, barely recognizing him. "In God's name, what has happened to your face? You look as if you've been hit head-on by a truck going at top speed."

"Two bastards going at top speed," Rafi answered and stepped back, opened the door, beckoned for Philippe to come inside.

"You've been beaten up, is that it?"

"Several times, by several shitheads."

"When did this happen? It looks as if the wounds are fresh."

"A few days ago. I got in a brawl. Over money." He tried to grin, but it obviously hurt his face too much, and he mumbled, "Okay, Philippe, where's the cash?"

"I need a bit of information first, Rafi."

His cousin looked at him suspiciously. "Information about who? Or what?"

"First tell me this . . . Where were you two nights ago? The twenty-first of March, to be precise."

"Today's Friday, so we're going back to Wednesday, right?"

Philippe nodded.

"That was the night I got the shit kicked out of me. I was in the bar. Down the street. Why?"

"The following afternoon, which was yesterday, there was a horrific incident at the Hôtel Cygne Noir. The runway collapsed at a fashion show, and many people were hurt."

"I saw it on the news. Your fashion show. Jean-Louis's fashion show." He threw Philippe a sullen look and added, "Tell your brother *sorry* from me."

"It wasn't an accident, Rafi. It was a deliberate act of sabotage. Did you have anything to do with it?"

"*Me?* Why me? Hey! Come on! What's all this about? I told you what was happening to me. Trying to get me into trouble, are you?" He stepped back. "Go on, get out. I don't want the *flics* coming around here."

"You know, there is a suggestion this sabotage was the act of terrorists. You're not a member of any extreme political or radical religious group, are you?"

"You're insane to think that!"

"But you used to be very militant, and fanatical . . . about Algerian politics."

"When I was a kid, days long gone. No time for that shit now. Got to earn a living."

"Are you working, Rafi?"

"No. Not this week. I can't go to work with this face."

Philippe was certain that Rafi had as much to do with the sabotage of the runway as he did. His brother was all wrong about their cousin, at least in this instance. Reaching into his pocket, he took out a wad of euros and handed them to Rafi. "I hope this helps," he said. "And how's Chantelle?"

"Same as always. Working hard, running her company. The catering company she started. Little good it does me, I don't see a sou."

"Take care of yourself, Rafi," Philippe murmured and let himself out.

As he went down the stairs, he felt a wave of sadness and depression flow over him. He always experienced this feeling when he had been here to see their cousin. It was unbearable for him to think of the waste. That Raphaël Tremont, once so good-looking and a brilliant musician, had become this . . . *derelict* . . . beaten to a pulp, wearing ragged old clothes . . . dependent on handouts . . . a lost soul.

Rafi sat staring at the door, an expression of bitterness setting on his face. *Handouts.* That was all his cousin ever gave him. But Philippe was a decent man; Jean-Louis, filled with his own importance, was a bastard. Rafi sighed, put the money in his pocket. Later, he would go out to the bar and drown his sorrows in red wine. Cheap Beaujolais was his solace these days. Certainly he found none with his wife. When he had married Chantelle Valbonne, some years ago now, his expectations had been high: a life of married bliss. Well, that had never happened. And now she was too busy running her catering company, mixing with movie stars and doing the bidding of that weird character whose parties she catered. He was loaded and paid her well, but Rafi often wondered what *exactly* she did for the guy with the exaggerated English accent. He would never know that; she rarely confided in him. But she was still a beautiful woman, if older, and she kept a roof over their heads, such as it was. Who was he to complain?

# Thirty-five

There was nothing girlie-girlie about M's London flat, even though that was the way she had described it in New York. In fact, it was just the opposite, Larry thought, because of its innate simplicity and its lack of folderol. It also displayed wonderful taste, the taste of someone who had a superior knowledge of antique furniture and fabrics, paintings and objects of art. He had not been at all surprised when M told him she had decorated it herself, because he saw her signature everywhere.

Essentially, it was a two-room flat, if you discounted the pristine gray-and-white-tiled kitchen, designed for serious cooking, and the large master bathroom. There was a medium-size bedroom and a living room, and it was this room, where he was now standing, that made the place so unique. He had been gobsmacked when he first saw it.

On this cool, slightly drizzly morning at the end of April, Larry meandered around the room, coffee mug in hand, taking stock of everything once more, always discovering something new to admire.

M had gone off to have a business meeting about a special project, but he was quite happy to be alone, to relax and have a bit of quiet time. He had finally finished filming, now had only the looping to do. Larry had enjoyed making *Coco in Love,* had found it a happy experience, with some great actors supporting him and a brilliant director at the helm.

His strange bout of food poisoning had been all but forgotten, except that he was now more careful what he ate wherever he was.

At the moment he was wondering whether to accept a play in the West End, which he had just been offered, and he was mostly hesitating because he didn't really want to be tied down this summer. He wanted to have a holiday with his adored wife, a honeymoon was the way she put it.

Walking toward the French limestone fireplace, Larry stood gazing at the painting hanging above it, one of his favorites in the flat. It was of a young woman sitting on a stool in a sun-filled room, half turned away so that her face was partially obscured, a shawl draped over her nude back. Painted by Bernard Taurelle, a French contemporary artist, the picture displayed a marvelous mixture of colors. The pinks and peaches, cream and yellow, various tones of terra-cotta, blue, and mauve were most alluring. It seemed to Larry that if he reached out to touch the woman in the picture, her skin would be warm from the sun, so realistic did she look.

Turning away at last, seating himself on one of the big cream sofas in front of the fireplace, he sipped his coffee, glanced around, liking the banana color of the walls, the French country furniture, Provençal in style, which M had used throughout this extraordinary room. "Mostly chosen for the mellow woods," she had explained.

What made the room different was its size. It was big and had a twelve-foot-high ceiling; the size and proportions reminded him of one of those Great Rooms so often seen in houses of the Elizabethan period.

In essence, M had divided it into three areas: the central seating arrangement in front of the fireplace; a dining area on the left side of the room, near the kitchen door; and on the right side, where a huge window dominated, she had lined the wall with floor-to-ceiling bookshelves loaded with books and decorative objects. A desk, a sofa and chairs, and a TV set made this area an intimate corner to watch television and movies.

The ringing of the phone brought him to his feet, and he went over to the library corner, picked up the phone on the desk. "Hello?"

"Larry, darling! Can we make our lunch a little later?" his mother asked, obviously in a hurry since she hadn't even greeted him.

"Good morning, Mum, and yes, of course. You sound harried. Is everything all right?"

"Oh, yes, yes, I'm just a trifle pushed at the moment, my darling."

"Anything I can do?"

"No, no. I'll be fine. I've managed to let the morning slip away from me somehow, and now I'm late for an appointment before I meet you."

"How's Dad?"

"He is now back to normal, I'm happy to say. I shall tell you all about it when we meet. You did say the Caprice, didn't you?"

"I did. And at twelve-thirty now, instead of noon?"

"Yes. See you anon, my darling." She hung up abruptly.

He stared at the receiver, smiling, and placed it in the cradle. His thoughts stayed with his mother as he took the coffee mug to the kitchen and rinsed it. She was an enigma, but then so was his father.

He went down to the bedroom to shower and get dressed. It was already eleven, he noticed as he glanced at the clock on the chest of drawers in a corner of the room. Walking over to the chest, he looked at the photographs M had arranged there, all of them her family, her siblings and her parents.

He had met them all now except her oldest sister, who lived mostly in Paris. Her parents had given a dinner when they first arrived in London at the beginning of the month, and he had fallen in love with her mother, who turned out to be the exact opposite of what he had anticipated. He knew beforehand that she was good-looking and clever, but what he had not bargained for was the innate natural charm, the sweetness, the lack of pomposity and pretension. When he had said this to M, she had given him an odd look and then laughed. "She's just an ordinary woman who's very, very special."

"And brilliant," he had murmured. "Let's not forget that."

Seeing her elder brother again had been a bonus for him; they had always been good friends, had so much in common. Her family were a good-looking bunch, just like his lot, some of whom M had met.

He had done a bit of editing when his mother had invited them to come to dinner and had crossed off Miranda and Thomas, keeping only Horatio and Portia, along with his parents, of course, the hosts. Fortunately, Edward was in Los Angeles, and Larry soon discovered nobody wanted Miranda or Thomas. His mother had explained she had been trying to be polite by putting them on the list.

As for his parents' constant rowing, it seemed to have ceased, and his mother had promised to explain everything today at lunch. Hopefully, he said under his breath, as he went into the bathroom to shower. She had already broken this promise twice since he had been back in London.

M stood outside the famous store in Knightsbridge, staring up at the name. HARTE'S. Founded by Emma Harte in the 1920s. Her namesake. She felt a rush of pride as she pushed open the door and went inside. As she traversed the fabulous cosmetic floor, that great sense of pride was replaced by a rush of gratification. She had done it herself, created a big career as a supermodel without help from her family. She had made it on her own, just as the first Emma had done so long ago. A smile of happiness slipped onto her face, and she acknowledged some of the greetings from various assistants behind the counters, who knew her only as M, the famous supermodel.

"Is she in, Connie?" M asked.

Connie Wayne immediately swung her desk chair around and exclaimed, "M! You startled me! I didn't hear you come in."

"I crept in on silent feet," M answered, smiling at her.

"Yes, you certainly did, and congratulations. You're *the* famous one in the family now." Connie jumped up, came around the desk, and the two women hugged. Her sister's personal assistant then said, "Yes, she *is* in her office, and she's expecting you. Shall I tell her you're here?"

M shook her head. "No, let me startle her, like I did you." Again smiling at Connie, she moved forward lightly, paused at the door and opened it quietly, slipped into her sister's office.

M stopped in the doorway, saw that Birdie was standing in the middle of the office, facing the fireplace, speaking on her cell phone. Closing the door as quietly as she could, M took several steps, thankful for the thick carpet. She hadn't made a sound; her sister had no idea she was standing a few feet behind her.

M waited until the phone call ended, then spoke. "Hullo, Birdie darling."

Her sister jumped, and as she turned she cried, "If you don't stop calling me that I'm going to start calling you by a name you won't like either."

"Oh, you wouldn't do that, would you, lovey?" M grinned and added, "I would hate that."

"As do I, and I'm talking about the nickname you gave me when you were all of four, or some such tender age."

They both began to laugh and hugged each other tightly, clinging a bit longer than usual. "God, I've missed you, M. Every time I see you I realize how much. Having you drop in like this is so wonderful, just knowing you're back in your flat down the road fills me with relief and happiness. But come and sit by the fire. It was so damp and drizzly when I arrived at six this morning, I knew it was going to be one of those days . . . when I needed a fire going until I go home."

"You were here at six! I can't believe you're still doing that early shift."

"I don't, well, not every day. But there was a problem this morning, and I had to come in."

"A problem at six? Who on earth was here before you?"

"One of the managers, but don't let's waste time talking about a problem I've solved. How's Larry?"

"He's great. Glad the film is in the can, but he liked the cast and crew. I think he had a really good time making it."

M sat down on the sofa, and her sister went and stood with her back to the fire, a habit of hers. "I've gone over the figures you gave me last week, M, and all of your ideas, and I think you can create something great, very commercial. But I do have a few questions."

"There is something I missed out," M said. "I should have explained that I can't possibly introduce this line of products until 2009 or 2010, because I will be under contract to Jean-Louis Tremont all of this year and next year as well. Aside from being legally bound to him, I'll be making around ten million dollars over these two years."

"You've just answered one of the questions. I thought—"

"You grow to look more like *her* every day," M interrupted, staring at her sister. "The likeness is remarkable. How old was she when that was painted?"

"In her thirties I think, a bit older than I am now. Mummy would know how old Grandy was when she sat for this portrait. Before Mum was born, of course, but she *is* the expert around here."

M didn't speak for a moment, her eyes resting on the painting of their very famous great-grandmother, a beauty with her red hair and green eyes. Her sister was the spitting image of her; it was actually uncanny the likeness. Clearing her throat, M asked, "So what were the other questions you had?"

"I was wondering if you had made a long-term plan, and by that I mean do you have any other products up your sleeve beyond the perfume, the toilet water, and the body creams? Any thoughts about a cosmetics line?"

"I have come up with some good ideas, and not to digress, but what do you think of the name, M Is Magic?"

"I like it. I also like M, just the one initial, because you have made it so famous. But I also like Magic. The simple packaging is also great. The black or clear glass bottle, the plain labeling. It's chic, different. I suppose *youthful* is the word I'm looking for."

"I'm so pleased, Birdie."

"I'm glad you are, *Emsie.*"

M groaned. "Okay. Truce, Lin. Okay?"

Linnet O'Neill nodded. "There's something else I want to talk to you about, darling, but I'm not sure this is the right time to do it."

Frowning, M said quietly, sounding worried, "You look ever so serious. Is there a problem in the family? Or something wrong?"

"No, not in the way I believe you mean. But I *am* worried about something, in fact it's beginning to preoccupy me."

"And what's that?"

"The succession. . . . Who's going to succeed me, M? Who's going to run Harte's?"

"But you're not old, you're not going to retire," M cut in peremptorily. "You're in your thirty-second year, for heaven's sake. You've twenty more years in this job, if not longer."

"What if something happened to me? Who'd take over . . ." Linnet let her voice trail off and stared hard at her sister. "Would you? Would you take the responsibility of running the stores *she* created?" As she spoke, Linnet looked up at the portrait of

Emma Harte. "We can't let her down, you know."

"I would do it, Linny, yes, if I had to, obviously. I'd never let the side down. But what about our cousins? They both worked here, ran the stores with you and Mummy. What I mean is, they have more experience than I do. And there's the Dorf . . . the Dauphine. Tessa might come back from Paris."

Linnet shook her head. "I've talked with them all, the three of them, separately, of course, and at different times. But they've got their hands full, what with their husbands and babies galore, and running various homes. None of them are interested. In fact, there is only you."

"Look here, Lin, I don't like the way you're talking, no, not at all. Are you thinking of retiring?" M got up, went and stood next to her sister, took hold of her arm. "Are you?" she repeated, staring into her eyes.

"Certainly not."

"Do you have some awful illness, God forbid?"

"Don't be daft," Linnet answered in her blunt way.

"Then why this talk of succession now? When you're still in your thirties? It's so silly, and—"

The first blast was so forceful Linnet and M were both thrown onto their backs. Several small paintings fell off the walls, chairs toppled, vases of flowers tipped over and rolled onto the floor. The second blast had even more force than the first, and all the windows shattered, as did every glass item in Linnet's office.

Scrambling to their feet, staring at each other fearfully, Linnet and M ran to the door, got there just as it burst open.

Connie, looking as white as chalk, cried, "Some kind of explosion."

Linnet simply nodded, ran past her, wrenched open the door of Connie's office, and went out onto the floor of the store. M was close on her heels.

People were milling around; some were getting up from the floor, others remained prone. Linnet saw the first of the security men running forward, and she followed them, heading in the direction of the Bird Cage, the restaurant where there had been a problem that morning at six o'clock. All she could think was how fortunate it was she had ordered it closed for the day, and the rest of the week if necessary.

The glass windows and door that fronted the famous restaurant were shattered, smoke was billowing out, and toward the back of the first dining room Linnet could see flames shooting toward the ceiling. Ten of the store's security men were inside, spraying foam onto the flames from fire extinguishers, and another six were handling hoses, dowsing the interior with water.

Simon Baron, head of security for the Harte stores, was already outside the Bird Cage, and he ran toward Linnet and M as they came to a standstill, his face strained, a worried expression in his eyes. Both women were out of breath, and it took them a moment to recover.

"Are you all right?" Simon asked, taking hold of Linnet's arm solicitously, peering at her. "I was just coming to look for you."

She nodded.

Staring at M, showing the same concern for her, Simon said, "How do you feel, M? No problems?"

"None," she answered and added, "Probably lots of bruises, though. We were thrown to the floor by the blast; it was terribly forceful. What happened? Was there some sort of gas explosion in the kitchen?"

"We don't know," Simon said. "The fire brigade and the police are on the way, and we'll only know then. But I got our own chaps onto it immediately because I was fearful this end of the floor, and the executive offices, might go up in flames."

"Thank God you did," Linnet exclaimed. "Good work, Simon. And how fortuitous that I decided not to open the restaurant today."

"You told me earlier that there was a drainage problem," Simon said, giving her a questioning look. "A bad smell in the kitchens. I know this is probably a stupid question, but are you sure it wasn't gas leaking somewhere?"

"Absolutely. And so were the manager of the restaurant and our maintenance department. There was a blockage in the drains. A bad blockage. But fortunately the plumbers had most of the drains cleaned out by ten o'clock. However, I'd made the decision not to open at six o'clock because I knew the smell would linger." Giving Simon a direct look, she asked carefully, pressing down on her anxiety, "Were there any plumbers working inside the restaurant when the explosion occurred?"

"No. By some stroke of luck the three plumbers who were still working in the kitchens decided to take their lunch break at eleven. There was no one inside at the time of the explosion. But some people have been injured, Linnet."

"Harte's employees?" she asked swiftly.

"Mostly. Unfortunately, several shoppers passing at the time were knocked down by the force of the blasts. But there are no fatalities and only minor injuries."

"Are you telling me that no one has been seriously hurt?" Linnet asked, a look of incredulity settling on her face.

"To my knowledge, not one person is badly injured. But I do think some people will need help. There may be a few with broken bones, some people in shock, others badly bruised, that kind of thing."

"Ambulances are on the way, I'm sure," Linnet asserted, her gaze still lingering on Simon Baron.

"Yes, everything's been done. We just have to wait now. Oh, look, Linnet, here are some of the firemen and the police."

Taking hold of Linnet's arm protectively, Simon led her and M away from the smoldering restaurant, firmly guiding them toward the linen department close by. "Let's get the professionals in there as fast as possible. I'll be back soon," he promised.

Linnet nodded and took hold of M's arm, pulled her farther into the linen department. To Simon she said, "We'll just wait here. Come and get me when you need me."

Once they were alone, M said, "I know this is a dreadful thing to happen, Lin, but aren't we fortunate you'd closed the restaurant? A lot of people would have been badly hurt, maybe even killed, if you'd kept it open."

Her sister nodded. "I've been thinking that for the last fifteen minutes," she said, sounding hoarse. "It's almost a stupid thing to say, under these circumstances, but we've been lucky."

❖

Within fifteen minutes, Simon Baron came back to see Linnet, bringing with him two policemen. One was Inspector Yardley of Scotland Yard, the other Captain Gibson of the Yard's Counter-Terrorism Command. After being introduced, Captain Gibson explained to her that two bombs had exploded in the Bird Cage, and that they suspected this was the work of terrorists.

Inspector Yardley now said, "We've been expecting one of the big department stores to get hit, Ms. O'Neill. All the stores are targets these days, for obvious reasons, and I'm sorry it had to be Harte's." He shook his head and gave her a sympathetic look as he went on, "Unfortunately, we will have to check the entire store to make certain there are no other bombs here. I'm afraid you will have to close Harte's down. As of now."

"I understand," Linnet said quietly. "How long will the store have to remain closed?"

Inspector Yardley glanced at Captain Gibson. "What's your estimate, Bill?"

The captain looked at her. "It's a big store, Ms. O'Neill," he said. "But we can get a few more units in here immediately, and we can work all night. And part of tomorrow morning, if that's necessary. Today's Wednesday. Shall we say tomorrow afternoon? Or Friday morning at the latest?"

She nodded. "Thank you, Captain Gibson, and my thanks to you, too, Inspector

Yardley. Mr. Baron will give you any help you need to get the store cleared of people."

The two policemen left, and Linnet couldn't help thinking that she was relieved she had her own policeman in Simon Baron. She always felt safer when he was close by; her head of Harte's security was the best in the business, trained by the unbeatable Jack Figg.

# Thirty-six

She made an entrance worthy of a Hollywood movie queen, except that she wasn't up to any of their tricks. She didn't wear sexy or revealing clothes and piles of jewelry, nor did she flaunt herself. In fact, she was the epitome of decorum.

Tall and elegant in an impeccably cut dark blue suit, she was an eye-catching, glamorous blonde who looked twenty years younger than she actually was, and as she glided gracefully across the room, every eye was on her.

She was a legend in her own time.

Pandora Gallen, one of England's greatest actors.

Smiling and standing up as the maître
d' led her toward his table, Larry couldn't
help admiring his mother. She had that
special something that could not be bought
or acquired. You had to be born with it . . .
charisma, star quality. Yes, she was certainly a star, acclaimed the world over. He
had to take his hat off to her. She dominated this restaurant just by being in it,
sucked all of the oxygen out of it.

After kissing her and getting her settled
in her chair, he said, "Mother, you look absolutely gorgeous. Have you had something done? You haven't got a line on your
face."

Pandora laughed heartily and gave her
favorite child the benefit of a huge smile.
"Of course I've had something done, lots
of things. I'm an actress, remember, and I
want to look good on a stage or in front of
a camera. Looking good helps me to meet
every day with a smile on my face and
gratitude in my heart, despite this ghastly
world we live in today. And since I was
meeting you here at the Caprice, I went to
the hairdresser's first. After all, you never

know *who* you're going to run into, do you, my darling?"

"Bravo, Mum, you're the best, and *congratulations.* You look simply divine."

"Well, perhaps not quite that, Laurence. Shall we have a glass of champagne?"

"Why not, it's a great idea." He motioned to the waiter, ordered two glasses of pink champagne, and then turned to his mother again. "I want to ask you something, Mum, and—"

"Oh, Larry, dear heart, let's have a drink before we discuss your father and his ridiculous accusations."

"I wasn't going to ask you about Dad. I wanted to know how your lunch went with M the other day. She didn't say much when she came home, and you haven't mentioned it either when we've spoken on the phone."

"We had a nice time together; we get on very well, you know. And we understand each other perfectly. M makes everything extremely clear, speaks her mind. In fact, I don't think I've ever met anyone quite as forthright as she is, and I must admit she took my breath away several times."

The waiter had brought their flutes of

champagne, and Pandora picked up hers, raised it to her son, and said, "Here's to you and M. Happy days."

He touched his glass to hers, took a sip, and then stared at his mother intently. "Why did she take your breath away, Mum? Did something happen?"

"Naturally something happened, but it wasn't anything bad."

"But what did she do? Say? Please tell me. I don't want there to be any ill feelings between the two of you."

"Oh, Larry, don't be so dramatic, there are no bad feelings between us, and she took my breath away because of her insight into this family of ours. Plus she gave me my orders, nicely, because she's very polite, but they were presented in no uncertain terms." Sitting back in her chair, Pandora drank her champagne, looking totally untroubled.

Yet Larry could not let it go, and he pressed, "Tell me what she said, what orders she gave you."

Pandora smiled at him, then reached out and patted his hand. "She gave me the rules about Edward, in relationship to you. Let's cut to the chase, shall we? She absolutely does not want you to be alone with him. Not ever again. At first she said you and she could not attend any family gatherings if he was going to be there, but eventually I persuaded her to relent a little about that. However, she doesn't want you to have any interaction with him, or sit next to him if you are at the same event. M believes he's your enemy and that he wants to do you harm any way he can."

"Oh." Larry stared at his mother and grimaced. "She can be tough, especially about anything that might affect me."

"So I realize, and aren't I glad about that! I understand her perfectly, Larry. She loves you very much, and she'll go for the jugular if anybody tries to hurt you."

"Yes, she would. But banning us from family gatherings . . ." He let the sentence slide away, his dark brows drawing together in a puzzled frown.

"I told you, she relented," Pandora murmured and added, "In any case, we don't have many of those gatherings these days. Incidentally, she did say she thought your father had been weak in Canada, the way he had let Edward get at you. Do you think that's true?"

"Dad was taking a battering from Edward, especially about money, but perhaps he was a bit weak-kneed when Edward was hitting on me."

"Let me just say this, Larry. I wholeheartedly approve of M. She's terrific, and I can rest easy knowing you have such a marvelous wife."

"So all is well between the two of you?"

"It is indeed." All of a sudden Pandora began to laugh, shaking her head. After a moment she said, "She adores Portia but thinks she fusses too much about little Desi, is overprotective of her. And she believes it's time Horatio gets married before he becomes too set in his ways, turns into a grumpy old bachelor." His mother shook her head again, amusement flickering in her eyes. "I told you she was forthright."

"She certainly is. And you didn't mind?"

"No, I didn't. I thought it was refreshing that she spoke her mind so openly, and actually, she does happen to be right about everything she said. I know your father can be very weak-kneed at times, and Edward is a bad penny. And she certainly put her finger on the problems Portia has, and Horatio, too, if the truth be known. So again, congratulations, you've got yourself a winner for a wife, my darling." Picking up the menu, Pandora glanced at it, looked across at her son, and said, "I'm going to have asparagus first, and then that marvelous fish cake they do here, with chips, of course."

He grinned. "I'll have the same, and Mum, I just want to say this, I'm thrilled you like M."

"*Like*? That's too puny a word to use, my darling boy. I *love* her. And I might add I think her parents are lovely, especially her father. My goodness, what a handsome man Shane O'Neill is. If only I were a few years younger . . ."

He gaped at her and said, "Really, Mother."

"I'm just joking, Larry, just joking."

Once they had ordered lunch, Larry stared at his mother and said, "Well, you did promise to explain about all the rows with Dad. So go on."

Pandora was silent, not wanting to discuss this matter, but she grew uncomfortable under her son's fixed scrutiny, accepted that she had no alternative but to explain.

❀

The asparagus vinaigrette was served, and Pandora started to eat immediately. Larry did the same. He knew she did not eat much for breakfast, just a slice of toast and coffee, so she genuinely enjoyed lunch. It was her favorite meal, dinner being a nuisance for her, especially when she was working in the theater.

He was very attuned to Pandora, had been all his life, and he knew better than to probe further now. It would be better to wait until after their main course to discuss her problems with his father. Larry very much doubted Edward's story about his mother being involved with another man. His brother was a troublemaker; he had been since they were children and had only grown worse as he had grown older. Larry was relieved his brother was back in Los Angeles and not floating around London causing havoc everywhere he went.

After finishing his asparagus, Larry said, "My agent sent me a copy of *The Winslow Boy*. There's going to be a revival of it, but

I can't work up any enthusiasm. What do you think, Mother?"

Pandora gave him a long, thoughtful look. "My advice is to take your wife on a honeymoon, which I know she wants very much. Therefore, don't take the play."

"Thanks," he said, smiling. "I just knew I had better fish to fry."

"Absolutely, and here come the fish cakes. After we eat I'll endeavor to explain about your father's accusations that I am out there screwing another man."

"Mother!" he exclaimed, looking at her aghast. "Everybody heard that at the next table."

"Oh, good. Now they'll know there's still life in the old gal yet."

He stared at her and burst out laughing. She had said this with such glee, and such total disregard for public opinion, he couldn't help but admire her. There was nobody like his mother, she was truly a one-off. No, he was wrong about that; there *was* somebody just like her in certain ways. His wife. No wonder he loved M, and no wonder M and his mother got on so well. Two peas in a pod. Sort of.

Once the plates had been cleared and Pandora had finished her third glass of champagne, she said in a low, steady voice, "Before I get to these awful rows your father and I have been having, I must tell you a story, Larry darling. All right?"

"Yes, that's fine, and take your time. I'm not in a hurry, Ma, I'm all yours."

"Do you remember I once said to you that you can know somebody all of your life and never truly know them? And yet, conversely, you can meet someone and know who they are and what they're all about in an instant. I think I likened it to being part of the same tribe."

"I do remember. In fact, I've never forgotten what you said. And actually, that's exactly the way I felt when I met M."

His mother nodded and continued. "That happened to me, Larry, a long time ago. Thirty years ago . . . I was just forty. And I had a happy marriage, a good husband, and six beautiful children."

"When I was five years old," he said, suddenly remembering something, although he wasn't sure what this was, something hidden at the back of his consciousness . . . a memory, forgotten . . . and yet not.

"That's right . . . you *were* five years old. And I met a man at a dinner party. I wasn't working at the time, your father was in a play, and so I went alone to the dinner. It was one of those instantaneous things. He looked across the room at me, and I looked back, and my whole world was turned upside down. I forgot everything. It seemed to me there was only him. And I knew at the end of the evening that he was mine, that I was his."

"Who was he?"

"I can't tell you."

"You mean you won't, Ma."

"I do mean that, yes. I will never tell you who he was. Nor will I ever tell anyone else, for that matter."

"He's still alive, isn't he?"

"Yes. But let's not get ahead of ourselves. All those years ago . . . he asked me to meet him for lunch the next day. It was a Wednesday, matinee day, and so I could. Your father was at the theater. I knew at the end of the lunch that I had met my true soul mate. I *knew* him, Larry, knew who he was, what he was. It was as if I'd known him since the day I was born. And he felt the same way. We knew we had fallen madly in love before we'd even left the restaurant that Wednesday."

"And so you had an affair?"

"No, we didn't. I saw him whenever I could, but I was fearful of sleeping with him. . . . I just knew it would be fatal if I did."

"So you didn't sleep with him. But what happened?"

"We became close friends, and saw each other quite a lot over a couple of weeks. But we never embarked on an affair because I knew it would destroy my family if I left your father for him. He knew that, too. I loved this man deeply, to the core of my soul, and he loved me, but he had his obligations, too."

"Was he a married man?"

"Yes. With children. And he was well known."

"Another actor, Mum? He was, wasn't he? *Who was he?* You can tell me. I'd never betray a confidence."

"No, Larry, I won't tell you. I really mustn't, darling. I will only say this, he was a politician, a man who was going far, and I didn't want him to destroy his career. Thirty years ago that could easily have happened, you know. Things were a bit different then."

"And so you never saw him again, and once more became the dutiful wife and mother?" Larry gave her a sympathetic look.

"That's more or less correct. It was terribly hard for me at times, but I loved you all *so much.* And although your father was difficult, he was a decent man, and I had no intention of hurting him. So obviously, since I'm sitting here with you today, I stayed. I never saw . . . *him* again. At least not alone. We did run into each other from time to time at public functions and quickly removed ourselves from each other's company."

"God, that must have been a bloody tough thing to do, Ma. How could you stand it?" Larry asked, thinking of how he would feel if he had to give up M. He looked hard at his mother, admiring her loyalty to his father and then to her children.

"It *was* tough, but we did it. We had no other choice."

"So what's all this got to do with Dad's accusations? Oh, my God! You met him again. Last year. That's it, isn't it, Mother?"

"We did bump into each other, yes. But

look here, Larry, we only had one lunch and one dinner in restaurants. After that we saw each other at his house. Anyway, to cut to the chase once more. Your father found out that I'd been seen with *a man,* having lunch, looking intimate and supposedly involved. And because I'd taken the film around the time your father was going to Canada, he decided I'd made a point of being in London in order to be with this man whilst he was away."

"But did Dad know he was *the man* from the past?"

"No, of course he didn't. Because he had never known about that friendship. Your father was in *Caesar and Cleopatra* at the time. It was a difficult role, and it was a huge hit. He was suddenly a bigger star than ever. He was involved with work, publicity, and all that other stuff that comes with fame. I had been extraordinarily discreet. Nobody knew about this . . . soul mate of mine. I hadn't felt the need to confide in a friend, and neither had he."

"So why has Dad been so suspicious? And anyway, how did he find out?" Larry asked, bafflement echoing in his voice.

"Someone told him I was seen with a

man whilst he was slogging away in Toronto. Who that was I might never really know. But someone *did* pour poison. And I have my suspicions."

"Mum, listen to me! I bet he was that two-faced bloody brother of mine. *Edward.* He was here in London before going over to Canada when Dad was rehearsing *Cyrano.* Remember?"

"I don't think Edward is the culprit, Larry. Besides, he knows which side his bread's buttered on. He wouldn't do anything to upset me, because—"

"You're giving him money, aren't you, Mother?" Larry interrupted. "Giving him thousands so he can support all those women, all those kids. You're enabling him to behave badly."

"I am giving him money, Larry, yes, because all of those kids, as you describe them, happen to be my grandchildren. I can't see them starve just because my son, their father, behaves like a juvenile delinquent." Pandora shook her head. "I don't believe Edward was the one who told your father, but somebody definitely did."

"So, Dad must know the name of this . . . soul mate of yours, Ma, think about that.

Since you've obviously been seen in public, *they* must have passed on a name."

"What are you getting at, Larry?"

"You can tell *me* his name, can't you? Since Dad must know, why the big secret?"

"Such curiosity, darling, but no, I can't reveal the man's name, because whoever it was who gossiped to your father didn't know the name of my old friend. He hasn't been in office for years, he's someone from the past, he doesn't look the same. Only someone of my age might recall who he actually is—"

"Are you saying a younger person told Dad?"

"Yes, I am."

"Who, Ma? Someone we know?" He threw her a searching look.

"I think it might have been Miranda," she finally confided.

"*Our* Miranda? Your daughter? My sister? Ma, you must be joking."

Pandora bit her lip, looked suddenly saddened as she murmured in a low voice, "The first time I had lunch with my soul mate— Oh, God, let's just call him the politician, that's easier. Well, that day, I was sitting facing the door in a little restaurant in Chelsea, and I suddenly saw Miranda rushing out. It was as if she had come in, seen me, and hurried off. Embarrassed. She looked embarrassed."

"God, I can't believe it! Why would she tell Dad she'd seen you with a man having lunch? And so what? You have male friends in the theater with whom you lunch and dine. Do you think Miranda would gossip to Dad? I mean really? And they don't like each other, Ma."

"But who else knew where to get in touch with him? Only someone in the family, and she's the only person who saw me that day, as far as I know."

Larry sighed, leaned back in his chair, staring at his mother thoughtfully. Taking a deep breath, he said softly, "Maybe you're right. Perhaps Miranda wants to curry favor with Dad, stroke his ego. She might be thinking of that last will and testament."

"Larry, *please.* Don't be ghastly. I can't stand it when you're like that. However, to be fair, there is a point to what you say. And regarding my friend, the politician. He's a widower; one daughter is dead, the other lives abroad; he's rather lonely. And once, long ago, we cared about each other. He wants us to be friends, and that's all there is to it. He just needs a friend."

"You said you meet at his house? *Why?*"

"I didn't want to run into anyone I knew a second time, because your father was acting up so much once he'd heard the story. I was simply trying to be discreet." She paused, took hold of his hand. "I was being kind to both of them."

"I understand. But where's it at now, with my father?"

"I've finally convinced him the man is just an old friend, someone from when I worked in Los Angeles, a man who'd been kind to me when I was filming there from time to time. I also managed to convince him that my old friend was only over here on a short trip and then confided that the man was gay. And there the matter rests. The rows have stopped; your father is more like himself. And just think on this, dear heart. I managed to do all this simply by telling a little lie about a man's sexuality."

"I'm glad you did, since it makes life easier for me, for the family, when the two of you are not at loggerheads."

"Glad to hear it, Larry."

"Ma?"

"Yes?"

"Who is the man? Please tell me."

She looked into his extraordinary blue eyes and sighed. He was her favorite, she loved him unconditionally; she trusted him implicitly. And so she told him who her soul mate of long ago was.

"Jesus Christ!" Larry exclaimed, looking thunderstruck. "The true seat of power. Oh, Ma."

"Quite," Pandora murmured, opened her bag, took out her lip gloss, and ran it over her beautiful mouth.

The moment he walked into the flat after lunch Larry knew that something was wrong. M was standing in the library corner, intently focused on the television screen, and when she heard him and swung around, he saw how pale she was, and there was a worried expression in her dark eyes.

Hurrying toward her, he asked anxiously, "Darling, what is it?" What's wrong?"

"I thought you probably hadn't heard, Larry. The store's been attacked. Two bombs exploded there this morning when I was having my meeting with Linnet. At around noon. In the Bird Cage—"

"Oh, my God, how horrendous!" he cut in, joining her in front of the television, putting his arm around her, drawing her close to him. *"Lunchtime."* He groaned. "How many people have been killed?"

"It was closed. Fortunately, Lin had closed it because of a drainage problem, so it was empty. Even the plumbers had gone to lunch. But there were a number of casualties." Turning off the set, taking hold of his hand, she explained everything as she led him toward the kitchen.

"Obviously Lin is going to be at the store for hours with Simon Baron and Scotland Yard. And the antiterrorism chaps. But I've asked her to come over for supper, and Simon, too. I hope you don't mind. She needs me at a time like this."

"Of course she does, darling, and I'm glad they've accepted. And thank God you're both all right."

"Yes. We are, although we're bruised a bit. The blast threw us across the room. We were in Linnet's office, and we could've had a few broken bones."

Once they were in the kitchen, Larry realized M was making his favorite Bolognese sauce. Chopped beef, tomatoes, and onions were spread over the central island counter, and she had already taken out various bowls, pots, and pans. "I can see we're in for a treat," he said, sitting down on one of the tall stools, still feeling shaken by her news.

"It's the easiest thing for me to make, and I had all the ingredients except for the meat." As she returned to her work with the food, M went on. "The store will remain closed until tomorrow, late afternoon, or Friday. The bomb squad have to check the entire building just in case more explosives were planted on other floors."

He stared at her, worried, shaking his head. "It's unbelievable this has happened. There's such enormous security at Harte's."

"Yes, I know. Scotland Yard believe it's a terrorist attack, and Inspector Yardley told us they'd been expecting a hit on an important department store for a long time. Public places are very vulnerable, you know. Remember the 7/7 bombings two years ago? The public transport system was attacked during the morning rush hour, and the damage was horrible, so many hurt. Fifty-two people killed, and an additional seven hundred injured altogether."

"I do remember it, M. I had a friend who was injured on that bus."

"It's extremists, I'm sure. And I have a theory. I think whoever did this hid in the store until it closed, planted the bombs, and then waited until the store opened the next morning in order to leave. I know that place inside out. I have since my childhood. Believe me, there are many corners to hide in without being spotted."

Her cell suddenly rang, and M snatched it up off the counter. "Hullo?"

"It's Lin," her sister said. "A bit of news."

"I'm listening," M replied, pressing the phone closer to her ear. Once Linnet had finished, she said, "Thanks for letting me know, and we'll see you tonight around eight-thirty then. Bye."

Looking at Larry, M told him, "The police have found two unexploded bombs in another area of the Bird Cage. They didn't go off, just fizzled and died. Thank God."

Larry was aghast. "Thank God indeed. I hate to think of the carnage if *four* bombs had exploded."

M gave him a knowing look, went to the stove, put the chopped onions in a pan with a little butter, and let them cook slowly over a low flame. Next she poured hot water on four large tomatoes so that the skins would drop off easily.

Larry continued to watch her, admiring not only the deft way she worked but her calmness and self-control after the explosion. She was a wonder.

At one moment he said, "I don't know much about Simon Baron. Tell me about him, darling."

"He's Jack Figg's nephew. Well, he's not really. By that I mean he's not actually a blood relative. Jack's sister Sarah and her husband, Alistair, adopted Simon when he was a baby, maybe six months old or so. Jack's close to him, and Simon worked for Figg International before taking over day-to-day security for the stores." M let out a sigh, shook her head. "I wish Jack were here right now. He makes me feel safe."

"Where is he?"

"He went to Hong Kong. Apparently he had business there. Even though he's sort of semiretired, he goes in to the Knightsbridge store three days a week, and I know it makes Linnet happy to have him around. They're as thick as thieves, those two."

"Jack told me at the dinner your parents gave for us that Linnet's Emma Harte reincarnated."

"He should know; he worked for Grandy from the age of eighteen." Changing the subject, she now asked, "How was lunch with your mother?"

"Fascinating."

"Really? What did she want to talk to you about?"

"I was the one who wanted to talk to her, actually. By the way, she told me she adores you, and she's thrilled we're married."

M smiled for the first time that day. "And so am I. What did *you* wish to discuss with your mother that was so important?"

"The vulnerability of the human heart."

# Part Three

# WINNING THE GAME
April–August
2007

They laugh that win.
William Shakespeare, *Othello*

Winner takes all.
Anonymous

# Thirty-seven

The meal had been an incomparable feast, and Jack Figg fully understood that it had been prepared especially to please him. One after another, sumptuous dishes elegantly arranged on platters were presented to him, then served with consummate skill. They were his favorites and the most delicious he had ever tasted . . . at least since he had been in this house several years ago.

Looking across the highly polished rosewood dining table at his host, Zhèng Wen Li, Jack said, "Thank you for this splendid treat, and my compliments to the chef. He has outdone himself tonight, and I feel most honored, Wen Li."

"I am gratified you enjoyed the meal, Jack," the respected Chinese banker murmured, inclining his head graciously. Settling back in the carved mahogany chair, he added, "It is I who am honored that you are here in my home. And I thank you for coming to see me. It was vital that we meet, and I am too frail to travel. Now that we have dined, let us go into the library, where we can enjoy jasmine tea or a digestive, and we shall speak of many things."

Jack rose and followed the refined and dignified old banker out of the dining room, thinking how elegant he looked in his red-and-gold brocade ceremonial robe. A family heirloom of great antiquity, it was magnificent, and Jack was fully aware that Zhèng only wore it with his family and intimate friends. This in itself was a compliment to him, and he was flattered by this relaxation of formality.

A long, wide gallery, where priceless Chinese scrolls, paintings, and objects of art were displayed, separated the dining room and the library. Out of the corner of his eye, Jack noticed a few new pieces of exquisitely carved jade on display on the glass shelves, and he hoped Zhèng would show them to him later.

Stepping briskly after his host, Jack caught his breath when he entered the library. When he had first arrived, the mist had been rolling down the Peak, and outside the vast plate-glass window the panoramic view of Hong Kong, Victoria Harbour, and Kowloon had been obscured by smog.

But now all were visible, and the view was spectacular under the ink-black sky scattered with shining stars. Hong Kong glitters, he thought. But then it always had for him, and in so many ways; if he had to pick a favorite city in the world, this would be it. What a mixture it was: skyscrapers and squalor; jewels and junk; big money and stark poverty . . . rich and poor living cheek by jowl in this great melting pot of humanity, where anything and everything was possible. He had come here as often as he could when he was younger, and he had once even contemplated living here. But he had known all those years ago that this would never happen. England was his country and his home.

Moving forward, Jack joined Zhèng at

the window, and his friend turned to him, murmured, "There is no view like this in the world, is there, Jack?"

"There surely isn't, and it's different every hour of the day, or so it seems to me . . . constantly changing."

"As life is constantly changing . . . the only thing that is permanent is change." Zhèng sighed and indicated with a wave of his long, slender hand that Jack should be seated. He took the chair opposite this Englishman whom he considered the best friend he had ever had.

Almost immediately one of the Chinese houseboys appeared, carrying a silver tray of jasmine tea; another followed sharp on his heels with glasses of iced water; a third boy brought a brass tray holding a bottle of vintage Napoleon cognac and brandy balloons.

Jack took a small, paper-thin porcelain bowl of the jasmine tea, as did Zhèng, and when they were alone, the banker said, "I am quite certain you understood that I had an important and confidential matter to discuss when I asked you to come here . . . because it was imperative that I speak to you face-to-face."

"I did, Wen Li, and knowing you the way I do, I had no intention of ignoring your request, or questioning your judgment."

"We have known each other a long time, haven't we?" Zhèng said, slipping his hand into the pocket of his robe, bringing out a small green-jade pebble, smoothing his hand over it, turning it slowly. A smile touched his eyes. "My talisman, Jack. For good joss."

Jack nodded. "I remember it. And we've known each other for thirty-five years, to be exact."

"And the first time we met, all those many years ago, you introduced me to your friend Mallory Carpenter, then head of the Hong Kong Police, when this island was still the British Crown Colony. Thanks to you, he helped me to solve a terrible problem. He became a wonderful friend, as indeed you did."

Jack sat back, listening carefully to his wise Chinese friend, wondering what he was leading up to.

Leaning forward, Zhèng said in a low voice, "You risked your life to save mine. At the time I told you I owed you a debt of honor, but that I hoped and prayed I never would have to repay it. I explained that I didn't want *you* to *need* my help because you were in danger or in trouble. Do you remember, Jack?"

"I do indeed, Wen Li." Jack spoke quietly. He was startled and wondering what this was all about, and he returned Zhèng's long stare, waiting. When he had flown here two days ago, he had done so on the assumption that Zhèng needed *his* help. Now it appeared that the boot might be on the other foot.

Rubbing his hand over his mouth, Jack straightened his back, moved to the edge of the chair, decided to plunge in. "Am I in some kind of danger, Wen Li? Is that why you asked me to come here?"

"I am loath to be the bearer of bad news; however, in this instance I must be. A man you and I detest has surfaced in Hong Kong, although he is not here at this moment. I am aware he bears you ill will. I had to warn you, Jack. You must protect yourself."

Jack frowned in perplexity and shook his head. "I'm sure there are a lot of people who'd like to do me in, but in Hong Kong? I don't think so." He was certain of this, and his voice reflected his confidence.

"I am sure of it."

"So tell me who it is."

**"Jonathan Ainsley."**

Thunderstruck, Jack gaped at Wen Li.

Jonathan Ainsley. That dreaded name from the past, the evil man who had vowed to destroy Paula and her daughters: Tessa, Linnet, and M. Her whole family, in fact, including her sons, Lorne and Desmond, and her husband, Shane O'Neill. Emma Harte's grandson, who believed that he had been cheated of his due and that his first cousin Paula had inherited what was rightfully his . . . the great Harte emporium in Knightsbridge and all the other stores as well. And to think that his father, Robin Ainsley, and Paula's mother, Daisy Amory, were brother and sister. How had such evil come about in one man? He was not like the rest of the Hartes at all. That old saying "Blood is thicker than water" did not hold true. . . .

"It is apparent you don't believe me," Zhèng eventually murmured, adding with some insistence, "but it is the truth."

"He's dead. He died in 2002!" Jack exclaimed. "He was in a car crash in France. His car was hit by a lorry head-on. We all know this. The car was demolished and so was he. He's dead. I'm telling you he's dead. And buried."

Zhèng shook his head.

"It's a silly rumor somebody's spread around. It's not true, it can't be," Jack persisted.

"I did not believe it. I reacted as you have. However, apparently his American wife took him to a clinic in Switzerland and they healed him. It took a long time, but they pumped life back into him."

"I just can't accept this! I can't!" Jack muttered.

There was a long silence between the two men, and finally Zhèng said in a carefully measured voice, "Surely you believe *me*. In any event, I have the benefit of my own eyes. An intermediary brought a message to me, asking me to come to Ainsley's office. I was flabbergasted, as you are. But I went, I met with him. Ten days ago. He invited me to do business with him again."

Jack remained silent, stricken by the news, which he realized he now had to believe.

The banker continued. "He is a dangerous man, and he has not changed. He is still vindictive, and that is why I had to warn you. He will endeavor to destroy Paula, as well as you. He still hates her with his whole being. The hatred goes back to their childhood."

"Did he mention me? Or Paula?"

"No, he did not. But I know, Jack . . . *I know it here,*" Zhèng said, putting a hand over his heart. "And I know it in my frail old bones. . . . I was compelled to send for you. . . ."

*Jonathan Ainsley. Back from the dead.* The words floated before Jack's eyes. How this was possible he did not know; they must have worked a miracle at the Swiss clinic. He said, all of a sudden, "What does he look like?"

"I did not recognize him," Zhèng replied. "And neither would you if you were to see him."

Jack did not answer.

Zhèng sat studying his old friend, and after a moment he drew closer to Jack, placed a hand on his knee.

Jack looked at him, his expression quizzical.

Zhèng said in a voice so low it was almost inaudible, "There is another reason

I needed to see you in person. I have many things I must share with you about Ainsley." The Chinese banker paused, held Jack with his eyes, said at last, "We must discuss ways to render him powerless. That is an imperative. Let us start planning. There must be a way you and I can defeat this odious man."

It was long after midnight when Jack got back to his hotel in Central. As usual he was staying at the Mandarin Oriental, and although it was his habit to have a nightcap in the Captain's Bar, tonight he went straight to his room.

As he went in, he immediately saw the blinking red light on the telephone, and he closed the door and went over to the desk in front of the window. Checking his hotel voice mail, he discovered that Linnet had called him, and so had Simon. A third message was from Linnet, explaining that she and Simon were in her office at the store. Until eight. After that they would be having supper at M's flat. Jack checked his cell phone, which he had left on the desk recharging, and found messages from the two of them left about half an hour ago.

Sitting down heavily, he knew at once there was some kind of problem. Five years of peace and tranquillity. Now the tension was back. The thought of Ainsley made his blood run cold. Gooseflesh spreckled the back of his neck, and he shivered. *Somebody walked over my grave,* he thought, remembering an old saying from his childhood.

He pulled the phone toward him, glancing at his watch as he did. It was almost one o'clock in the morning in Hong Kong; six o'clock in London. Since there was a seven-hour time difference, Linnet and Simon would still be at Harte's.

After dialing her private line, Jack sat back and started to worry about her mother. How to protect Paula O'Neill from Ainsley? That was going to be some task.

"Linnet O'Neill."

"Hello, Beauty. It's me."

"Jack! You got our messages?"

"I did, Linnet, yes. Has something happened? *I hope not.*"

"I'm afraid so, Jack. I guess you haven't

seen the news. Turn on CNN. We've been attacked by terrorists. The Bird Cage blew up around noon today—"

"Jesus Christ!" He went cold all over and closed his eyes, then snapped them open. "Tell me the worst."

"I'd closed it, Jack. At six o'clock this morning. Brenda Powell had called me at five about trouble with the drainage system. She was in early because she was running the power breakfast today. She acted fast. Jack, some good news. Nobody's dead. Staff and customers injured by the blast, but it's not overwhelming."

"I shall come back straightaway, Lin, don't worry. I suppose Simon called everybody. Brought in the Yard, all that lot."

"Yes, he did, and here he is. He wants to tell you everything. But we're both fine, Jack. And we've got matters under control."

Jack Figg listened to everything Simon had to say. He had trained Simon himself and knew what a brilliant security officer he was. There was nobody more alert, responsible, and efficient. But Jack became alarmed when he heard that the counter-terrorism squad had discovered two unexploded bombs in the Bird Cage. He knew that if they *had* gone off, the damage would have been horrendous. The executive offices, he suddenly thought, Linnet could have been killed. She'd had a narrow escape. A chill ran through him again.

After a few more minutes on the phone, he told Simon he would be back by the weekend, Monday at the latest, and hung up. Once he had found the remote control, he stood in front of the television set, zipped around until he found CNN. Then he sat down on the end of the bed, waiting for the coverage of the terrorist attack at Harte's to show up on the screen. He saw mention of it on the crawl first, and suddenly there it was, his beloved store, and his beloved Linnet, the managing director, being interviewed about the attack on the most famous department store in the world.

He awakened in the middle of the night, and for a moment he thought it must be morning. After glancing at the illuminated electric clock, he learned it was only four and groaned.

Jack lay there, listening, wondering what had woken him. And within seconds he understood. His own brain had dealt a solid blow to sleep; his thoughts had intruded, and so had M's voice. Two weeks ago she had said to him, "I had a narrow escape, Jack. If I hadn't sprained my ankle, I'd have been on the runway. And I could have been a goner. I think my namesake is watching over me. . . . Mummy has always said Emma's my guardian angel."

M had had a narrow escape. Linnet had just had a narrow escape. Both incidents, in public places, were considered terrorist attacks. But were they?

Throwing back the bedclothes, Jack got up, put on a robe, and went over to the desk. He found a piece of hotel writing paper and drew an oblong shape on it. He then drew three squares next to one another and wrote in the squares "Bird Cage," "Linen Department," "Linnet's Office." All three adjoined one another. He knew they did; he had just needed to see them set out like a floor plan.

Had Linnet's office been the real target? Maybe. But it was impossible to get into the executive offices without setting off a series of alarms. If somebody wanted to do damage to Linnet's office, why not place bombs in the linen department next to it? Because it didn't have any doors, was open to the entire floor, and therefore likely to be checked at night by patrolling security men. The Bird Cage was the obvious place to hide bombs. And to hide the perpetrators themselves until they could leave the next morning.

Jack leaned back in the chair, wondering if M had been the real target in Paris. And what about her husband? Larry had eaten contaminated food the day the runway collapsed. Or had he been poisoned? Running his hand over his face, Jack asked himself if he was becoming paranoid now that he knew Jonathan Ainsley was alive.

He had no answer. But he did know he had to watch his back, and Paula's, and the backs of her daughters.

Jack didn't even bother to go back to bed. He sat at the desk, wondering where the hell to begin. Jonathan Ainsley was a psychopath, there was no question in his mind about that. And a billionaire, so money was no object. He had to be stopped. Whatever it took.

Jonathan Ainsley. Alive not dead. Bad joss. *His* bad joss.

When he hit the streets at ten o'clock that morning, Jack caught his breath in surprise. For a moment he had forgotten what it was like to move on foot here. He was quickly engulfed in a cacophony of sound, blinded by swirls of color and brilliant light. Everywhere there was movement, noise, and tumult, as he was instantly caught up in the crowds rushing about their daily business.

Jets soared in the skies above the Peak; junks, sampans, ferries, and yachts plowed the waters around Kowloon and Central. Yet there was a distinct rhythm to all of this flow of humanity. Normally, Jack reveled in the teeming life of this island where space was at such a premium. But this morning he was irritated as he hurried to his destination in Central, dodging the trams, buses, rickshaws, and cars that surged through the streets.

He was intent on his purpose, making for the offices of Zhèng Wen Li, where he was expected in a short while. Last night, as he was leaving the banker's grand house on the Peak, Zhèng had invited him to come to the private bank so that they could finish their business.

Within fifteen minutes Jack arrived and was immediately shown into Zhèng's inner sanctum. The respected banker, smiling at the sight of his friend and rising at once, came around the desk and shook his hand. He said, "I am saddened that Harte's has been hit by the terrorists, Jack. I am sure you have spoken to Linnet. From the information I garnered from the television news, it appears that the damage was not as enormous as it might have been." He sat down at the desk; Jack took a chair at the other side.

"That's correct, Wen Li. And I did speak to Linnet, and to Paula. They both send you greetings and their good wishes. The store is closed until tomorrow; antiterrorism squads have been checking every nook and cranny, making sure there are no more hidden explosives. Fortunately, there have been no fatalities, although a number of people were injured. Nevertheless, it could have been much worse."

"The special terrorist branch of Scotland Yard are calling it a terrorist attack,"

Zhèng murmured, eyeing Jack pointedly. "But what is your opinion? Could this crime have been perpetrated by . . . an *individual* with extraordinary resources?"

"Yes, it could. And that thought had crossed *my* mind. Ainsley could have set everything in motion with no trouble at all. He's done similar things in the past, and we know he is unconscionable."

Zhèng simply nodded.

Jack said, "I have several other appointments today, various things I want to put in place, and a couple of meetings tomorrow. But I am flying back to London on Saturday, Wen Li."

Leaning across the desk, the banker said, "I shall proceed as we discussed last evening, Jack, and keep you abreast of all matters."

"Thank you, and I'm sure you understand my urgent need to go back to London."

"I do indeed. Now, I have a few more items to clear with you, and then I wish to introduce you to a most brilliant young man, whose expertise might be helpful to us at some point in the future."

Jack nodded and listened as the banker passed on additional useful information about Jonathan Ainsley, before finishing, "And that is everything I know, Jack. For the moment." Zhèng picked up the telephone, dialed a number, spoke quickly in Cantonese, and hung up.

A moment later there was a knock on the door, and it opened to admit a man who looked to be in his mid-twenties.

Jack stood, stepped forward, and took the hand that was instantly offered to him.

The young man said, "I am very pleased to meet you, Mr. Figg. I am Richard Zhèng, but everyone calls me Richie."

"How very nice to meet you, Richie," Jack responded and added, "You have been educated in America, I am assuming."

"Yes. At the Wharton School of Business, among other institutions. But now I am back in Hong Kong, where I belong. And to stay."

"I am proud to inform you that Richie is my grandson, Jack," Zhèng announced, and his smiling face told Jack that the banker was besotted with the young man. And what a specimen he was. Jack had been startled by his looks when he walked in. Richie was tall for a Chinese, and staggeringly good-looking, and Jack suspected there might be Occidental blood in the young man because of his height and skin tone.

As if he had read Jack's mind, Zhèng said, "My son married a beautiful Englishwoman, Jack. After his parents died, I raised Richie, and he has proved to be the most devoted of grandsons. He is my sole heir, and he has been learning about banking here with me. One day, China Zhèng Private Bank will be his, and I know it will be safe in his hands. But I think you should also know that there is another area in which Richie excels."

Jack looked at Zhèng expectantly, but when he sat there smiling, saying nothing, Jack turned to Richie and asked, "And what else do you excel at besides banking?"

"I'm a computer whiz," Richie replied.

"No, not a whiz," Zhèng corrected sternly. "You are a *genius* with computers." Looking across at his grandson, the banker said something in Cantonese, then turning back to Jack, he murmured, "An invaluable asset, Jack. Do you not agree?"

Jack's mind was racing so fast he simply nodded.

As he walked back to the hotel, Jack's mind remained focused on Ainsley. How fortuitous it was that the man had never known how close he was to Zhèng Wen Li, as Emma had been until she died, and then Paula afterward. This gave them an advantage now. Nor did Ainsley know that the Chinese banker had always detested him. As Wen Li had once said to him, "You don't have to like those with whom you do business, Jack." It had been a cynical remark, but then, like most bankers, Zhèng Wen Li was a pragmatist, and he had made money with Ainsley at different times.

# Thirty-eight

Jack Figg sat in Linnet's office, drinking a cup of coffee as he waited for her to finish a phone call, which had started a few minutes after he arrived. He studied her surreptitiously, as he so often did, thinking that she looked better than she had for a long time. He was positive that this was because M was back in London, and that she felt less lonely with her sister around. Thank God she and M had not been injured in the explosion. "Only a few bruises," Linnet had explained. "M and I are none the worse for wear and tear, or explosives!"

He brought his gaze back to the fireplace, where as usual a fire was burning brightly. He was glad of it this morning. It was May Day, pouring with rain, rather cool and windy. Some spring day, he thought.

Lifting his eyes, he stared at the oil painting of Linnet's great-grandmother Emma Harte, a woman he had revered, and still did. She had been on his mind a lot these last few days. He suddenly thought of the time he had decided to leave Harte's because he wanted to start his own company. Emma had fought him at first, and then, relenting, she had cleverly persuaded him to compromise. She had said she would help him to finance Jack Figg International, a company he would own, with the understanding that Harte's would be his first client.

He smiled to himself now, remembering how cunning she had been. His second client had been Blackie O'Neill and O'Neill Hotels International, his third Sir Ronald Kallinski and Kallinski Industries. He hadn't needed any other clients once he was representing the three clans: head of security for three major tycoons and three successful companies. Emma had managed very skillfully to keep him bound to her for most of the time on an exclusive basis. One day, some years later, she had drawn up a document that gave him total ownership of his company; when he tried to return her initial investment, she had told him that it was a bonus for his devotion, that he owed her nothing. But he knew he did. He owed her everything, the life he had today, the life he, in turn, had helped Simon to have.

Linnet was so like her, not only in her looks but in a variety of ways. She could be just as loving and charming, clever and devious, and surprisingly ruthless when this was necessary. He was relieved she was now coping with her grief so well. Julian Kallinski's unexpected death two years ago had knocked her sideways. It had been a shock to them all.

There was a knock on the door, and it flew open as M came hurrying into the office, a little out of breath. Blowing a kiss to her sister, she glided over to Jack, sat down next to him on the sofa, and planted a kiss on his cheek.

Sitting back, she asked, "Have you seen the mess? The Bird Cage is virtually destroyed, Jack. I couldn't believe it the day it happened. We had a lucky escape. Just imagine if those other two bombs had gone off in the restaurant. The linen department would have been demolished and possibly this office."

"Not possibly, M, it *would* have been. And an inferno would have ensued with all this wood paneling," Jack answered, glancing at the beautiful polished pine walls dating back to Emma's day. "It's a great relief to me that you're both all right. We had good joss in that, at least."

"Good *joss*?" M repeated, sounding puzzled.

"Good joss means good luck; it's an expression the Chinese use." He put his hand in his pocket, brought out his beautiful jade pebble, and showed it to her. "A friend gave me this. It's a talisman, and it's supposed to bring *good luck.* And you and Lin *were* lucky last week."

"I know you've spoken to Linnet and Simon on the phone over the past few days, so you must know everything. And I suppose Simon brought you up to date this morning, right?"

Jack nodded.

M gave Jack a direct, penetrating stare.

"Do you think it strange that no terrorist group has come forward to claim responsibility for the bombing? Don't they usually love to do that? Take bows?"

"Not always. But I agree with you. Quite frankly, I thought some group might make an announcement, because of the importance of Harte's."

"Anyway, we're open again," M said, assuming a cheerful tone. "I suppose that's because we've made sure everyone knows the store was thoroughly checked. Also, that we've increased security."

She raised a black brow, grimaced. "I couldn't move for all the extra security men this morning. They're swarming all over the place. Thanks to Simon. Anyway, on to other things. How was Hong Kong, Jack?"

"Interesting," he answered noncommittally. "And still one of the most extraordinary places in the world."

"I'd love to go there one day, but only if you were along. Nobody knows it like you, and I bet we'd have a great time."

"Just let me know *when,*" he said, smiling at her, even though his heart was heavy. Black Irish, he thought, studying her. With her dark good looks, she's as much a throwback to Blackie O'Neill as she is to Emma Harte.

"I'm sorry. That was an interminable call." Linnet apologized as she put down the phone and came to join them.

M jumped up, the sisters hugged, and Linnet held her away and said, "I know I've said this many times lately, but I'll say it again . . . it makes me so happy that you're back in London."

"Me too, Linny."

As usual, Linnet sat down in the straight chair next to the fireplace. Jack knew she felt the cold just as her great-grandmother had and preferred this warmest spot in the room. Smiling at him, she said, "Sorry I had to take that call just after you arrived, but it was important."

"No problem. However, I have something vital to discuss with you both, and I think it would be best if you asked Connie to hold any phone calls, Linnet."

Throwing him a curious glance, she went to her desk, spoke to her personal assistant on the intercom, and then rejoined them around the fire.

Linnet said, "Is this something to do with your trip to Hong Kong, Jack?"

"It is. As you know, I went to see an old friend of mine, and of your mother's, a very good and loyal friend, the banker Zhèng Wen Li. He needed to talk to me confidentially, and in person. He's very cautious and didn't wish to speak to me on the phone or send a letter or an e-mail." Jack paused and realized that Linnet and M were staring at him intently.

"Wen Li had some news for me. As it turned out, it was bad news. For all of us." He paused, then said in a low voice, "Jonathan Ainsley is alive."

"That's not possible!" Linnet cried, shaking her head. "Everyone knows he died in that horrendous car crash." She realized her voice wobbled on the last few words.

"Apparently not. According to Wen Li, Ainsley's American wife took him to a clinic in Switzerland . . . his American wife being Angharad, of course."

"Jack, this can't be true! It just can't be!" M exclaimed, her voice shrill. "There was a funeral, we all know that. Oh, my God, did they have a *fake funeral*? To *deceive* us?" M, her face as white as chalk, was staring at him, her black eyes wide. "That bitch was bad news from the moment she stepped into our lives. She's as evil and as vindictive as Ainsley. And she hates all of us."

Linnet, endeavoring to overcome her shock, asked, "How does Wen Li know Ainsley is alive? Has he seen him? It could be just some strange story, an invention."

"I thought that, too, Lin, but Wen Li *has* seen him, and he said I probably wouldn't recognize Ainsley, because he hadn't, not at first."

"So how can the banker be sure it *is* our fiendish cousin?" M said. "It might be an impostor."

"I posed all the same questions to Wen Li, believe me I did, M. Because it seemed so improbable. I'm afraid he was able to give me answers that I had to accept. At first, Wen Li didn't recognize Ainsley facially. I suspect there was a lot of plastic surgery, because of the burns from the crash. However, Wen Li did recognize the voice, which is very distinctive. He said it was the eyes, the aquiline nose, and the height that also confirmed his identity. Wen Li remembered Ainsley's brownish blond hair. And incidentally, Wen Li told me he has a limp, walks with a stick."

"How the hell did they do it?" M wondered aloud and then turned to Jack. "Where is the clinic? Where was Ainsley treated?"

"Wen Li didn't know that, but I had one of my European operatives on it over the entire weekend. I heard from him last night. Ainsley was in the Wendkettern Clinic in Zurich. He was there for a full year, then in and out for long periods for another year. Later he spent six months as a day patient. Altogether I think he has been treated at the clinic for three years, and has lived in Zurich all that time."

"And is he now living in Hong Kong?" Linnet asked.

"Wen Li thinks he is not, even though he still has the flat he bought there in 1970. That's when Ainsley moved to Hong Kong, after your grandfather David Amory fired him and your mother kicked him out of the family because he was cheating Harte Real Estate, a company he ran. He had good joss in Hong Kong; he made a fortune in real estate at a time when you could. According to Wen Li, Ainsley's now a billionaire."

"Why did Wen Li see him? I mean, what was *that* all about?" Linnet leaned closer to Jack. "Were they friends before? Or colleagues?"

"As you know, Wen Li owns one of the oldest private banks in Hong Kong, inherited from his father. The China Zhèng Private Bank is very highly thought of, renowned actually. Over the years he has done business with many people, including your mother, and before her your great-grandmother, as you're aware. And he also did business from time to time with Ainsley. But they were never friends, in fact Zhèng never liked him. According to Wen Li, about two weeks ago he received a message from Ainsley via an intermediary, asking for a meeting and—"

"He must have been gobsmacked!" M cut in. "Shocked as we are, no?"

"Absolutely," Jack replied. "He couldn't believe it either. He was tremendously puzzled but knew he must investigate because of me, and the Hartes."

"All a ruse, eh?" Linnet muttered to no one in particular. She tried to remain calm, but she was shaking inside, suddenly understanding what Jack probably suspected.

Jack said, "I think you're correct, Linnet. To my way of thinking, Angharad was the mastermind behind this. When she got to him, she realized Ainsley was still alive in that French hospital, if only just, and she decided to get him to one of the Swiss clinics. And then later, she dreamed up the idea of a funeral. She held a bogus one in order to throw us all off."

"But why?" M asked.

"Ainsley has a vendetta against your mother," Jack told her. "He believes that Paula was left the Harte stores in Emma's will because she had used great influence on your great-grandmother. Not true, I can vouch for that. Just so you know, Emma Harte had always planned to leave the stores to your mother, and she divided up the rest of her holdings, properties, and companies among her other grandchildren. Jonathan Ainsley has ranted against your mother for years. He's tried all manner of tricks to get the stores, and at one moment he even owned a lot of the shares. But he also has a virulent hatred for your mother because she kicked him out of the family. So, there's a lot of emotion there."

"I still don't understand," M said, looking from Linnet to Jack. "Why did Angharad let us all believe her husband was dead?"

"To throw us off the track," Linnet exclaimed. "So Ainsley can attack us without us knowing that it's him doing it."

"Attack us how?" M leaned in to Jack. "Does he want to kill us? Is that what Linnet means, Jack?"

"Yes, he does . . . using others to do his dirty work, of course. Cast your mind back in time. . . . Don't you remember the bomb in the church in Pennistone Royal village? When it went off, that could have killed the entire family. He's ruthless, relentless."

M had gone paler than ever, and she nodded vehemently. "I hadn't forgotten . . ." She looked at Linnet and burst into tears.

※

It took M only a couple of seconds to calm herself. Reaching for her tan Kelly, she pulled out some tissues, blew her nose, and dried her tears. "Sorry about that, chaps. I suddenly remembered that day so vividly. So sorry," she said again and took a deep breath, thinking of her family home in Yorkshire, her favorite place in the whole world.

Jack said, "Listen, to cut to the chase, I honestly believe you're all at risk. Your mother, the two of you, and also your sister, Tessa. I believe Ainsley is a psychopath and that he's out to destroy the Harte women, especially those with high profiles."

"What about our cousins?" Linnet asked.

"I don't think *they* factor into the equation. It's all about Paula in Ainsley's sick head, and since he hasn't managed to maim or kill her in thirty-five years, he has now added you two to the mix, and Tessa, of course."

"Did Ainsley tell Wen Li this?" Linnet asked, and then instantly she shook her head. "No, of course he didn't, he wouldn't tip his hand. This is a scenario you've worked out, Jack, isn't it?"

"It is. But getting back to Wen Li for a moment, he himself said the same thing, more or less. He told me Ainsley seemed as vindictive as ever, that he hadn't changed, and that he, Wen Li, felt it in his heart, in his old bones, that Ainsley was quite likely to go on a rampage. Against Paula."

"With us as the other targets," Linnet asserted and grimaced. "Out of curiosity, did Wen Li agree to do business with that bastard?"

Jack had to smile, she had sounded so like Emma at that moment, pithy and very angry.

"He was smart as a fox. He indicated that he was interested, very interested, but that he had to mull it over for a few days. Wen Li's thought was to talk to me at once, to get my input, and to ask me if he could be of use to us by doing business with Ainsley."

"And what did you say, as if I didn't know," M muttered, giving him a shrewd look. "You said he should do business with him so that we'd know where Ainsley was. Well, not exactly that, I guess, but that we would have . . . *access* to him. Right?"

"Right. The problem is, Wen Li doesn't know where Ainsley is living. We know that when he was in Hong Kong, Ainsley was staying at his flat on Victoria Peak, because he boasted about how valuable it had become to Wen Li, and how beautiful it was. Since he's not in Hong Kong now, nor has he been seen there for years, until last week, he must be living at his Paris flat."

"He sold the Yorkshire house," Linnet informed Jack and went on. "And the London flat has gone as well. That was all handled by Angharad, I'm sure."

"Don't worry about these minor things,"

Jack said. "I have an operative working on Ainsley's homes and real estate already. We'll soon know where he hangs his hat on a permanent basis. Now there is another thing I discovered from my Swiss operative. Angharad has had Ainsley's child. It's a girl, and she's about four years old."

Linnet started to laugh somewhat hollowly. "Oh, my God, that must have done him in! He was always after a son and heir. A girl, eh? Well, they certainly run in this family. He should have known better."

M stood up, walked over to the window, and stood looking down at the traffic in Knightsbridge. After a moment she said slowly, "Don't you think it's odd that the British police, the great Scotland Yard and antiterrorist squads, and the French police and DST haven't come up with much regarding the two attacks, here at Harte's and at the Hôtel Cygne Noir?" She looked at Jack, then Linnet, and continued, "Because I do. Everything's gone silent because they've found nothing. Is it possible that those attacks are somehow linked, and that you and I are the links, Linnet? Because of the fluky things happening we both had narrow escapes, but you know as well as I do we could easily have been killed."

Linnet stared at her, frowning, and made no response.

Jack said, "I thought of that when I was still in Hong Kong, M. I also wondered about Larry. Was *he* targeted on location because he's your husband? It is a possibility, you know."

"I agree. But actually, Jack, there were other people who had food poisoning on the film."

"Oh, just a couple, M," Jack said dismissively. "Larry told me it was two guys from the camera crew and the caterer herself. So what? If I wanted to poison one person in a group, I'd make sure several others got sick as well, just to throw everyone off the scent."

M nodded. "Maybe. Do you have a plan, Jack?"

"A lot of ideas. I want to put plenty of security around all of you."

"But Larry and I have two security guards already. My friend James Cardigan arranged that. However, I'm sure Mummy doesn't—"

"James Cardigan, you say?" Jack interrupted. "Is he in his mid-forties, sort of wiry, good-looking with sandy-auburn hair?"

"Yes, that's him. He's married to my friend Geo. He has a big company something like Figg International, and he used to be with MI6. Do you know him? The look on your face tells me that you do."

"Yes, if he's who I think he is. Oddly enough, I met him some years ago in Hong Kong."

M pricked up her ears and exclaimed, "James and Geo are in London for another few days. Actually, I'm meeting them for lunch today. Linnet was going to join us. Why don't you come, too?"

"I'd like to, but I did tell Simon I would have a bite to eat with him. We've a lot to go over, as I'm sure you can imagine."

"Bring Simon. Six heads are better than one, Jack. Anyway, I know one thing. I'm not going to sit around waiting for Ainsley to kill me! I have an idea, and I think we should put it into operation immediately."

"And what idea is that?" Jack asked cautiously.

"Let's hire a hit man. Or a contract killer, or whatever you call them. Let's get that

Jonathan Bloody Ainsley before he gets one of us. Or all of us. I bet James could find me a hit man, and I've got plenty of money. I can pay for the contract killer myself."

Linnet exclaimed, "My God, I do believe you're serious!"

"Naturally I'm serious," M shot back, suddenly glaring at Linnet. "Why shouldn't we take matters into our own hands? Let's get rid of that bugger now!"

"*We* live by different rules," Linnet reminded her.

"Rules are meant to be broken," M said and added, "And I'm all for breaking the rules. When those you love are at risk, you'll do anything to save them. I know I would. So let's break the rules and go after that *swine.* Because that's what he is, and a *sicko.* I don't want him hurting my husband or my sisters or my mother. Or me, for that matter. Come on, Jack, let's get a hit man."

Jack, amazed by this outburst, said, "Not quite yet, M. First we must see if we can find a way to demolish him without resorting to criminality."

"I bet we can't!" M asserted in a tough

voice and came and sat down on the sofa. "Sometimes we have to take big chances, take risks."

Observing her for a moment, Jack found that he was still startled by her toughness, her passion, and her bluntness, but then Emma had been as blunt as they come, as was Linnet.

Funny how he remembered M as a girl, always pottering around with horses in the stables at Pennistone Royal. Out of the blue he said, "Do you still have that gorgeous gelding of yours? Wasn't his name Gypsy?"

"Jack! Gosh! I can't imagine how you remembered, and yes, I still have him, my good old Gypo." Memories of the incident last March came rushing back unbidden. Her face crumpled as it struck her that she had more than likely been targeted then. Oh, God, no! No! No! The Bad Thing loomed. She brought her hands to her face, and her body began to shake. And she thought, I must tell them about what happened, how I was assaulted in the woods, how I escaped from that man called Bart.

Jack said, "M, darling, whatever's the

matter?" He put his arms around her, and Linnet stood up, came over to the sofa, asking, "M, what is it?"

"He raped me," she sobbed. "That man, he raped me, Jack."

# Thirty-nine

I know I should have told you, Linnet," M said, catching her breath as the dry heaves began to slow. "But I just couldn't."

"I'm your sister, and I love you," Linnet answered softly, squeezing her hand. "You're not supposed to keep a terrible thing like that to yourself, darling. You needed help and comfort, and loving support."

M shook her head, sat up a little straighter on the sofa, and murmured, "I suppose I was . . . well, a little embarrassed, maybe even ashamed, I don't know really . . ." Her voice trailed off, and she turned to Jack. "I hadn't thought of this before, but perhaps I was a target that day because of who I am. Because I'm a Harte."

Keeping his expression neutral, Jack said in an even voice, "You might well have been, M. But unless I know the details, I can't really make an assessment. Do you feel up to talking about it?"

M bit her lip, looking thoughtful. She had hidden this ghastly attack for a year, dealt with it in her own way and somehow managed. She had put the Bad Thing behind her. At least so she thought, and especially after becoming involved with Larry; he had helped to heal her without even knowing he was. His love had been her salvation. It was Jack's mention of her beloved horse Gypo that had triggered the vivid memories of that day in the woods. And she had fallen apart. She felt a bit better now, most probably because she had told them. She swung her head, gave Jack a questioning look.

Noticing this at once, he said, "What is it, love? Don't you want to talk about it? I know it's a difficult thing to discuss with anyone. Just remember this, M darling, I've known you all of your life. I want to help you and protect you in every way I can."

"You've known me since *before* I was born," she said, managing to give him a faint smile. "And you've always been like a surrogate father. I've always been able to talk to you about anything, Jack. It's just that, well . . . I don't want anyone else to know." She glanced at Linnet. "You've got to promise you won't tell Mummy and Dad. *Nobody can know.* Most especially Larry."

"I won't tell anyone, darling," her sister promised. "You have my word. You know I've never wanted to play God. It's your life, and you live it your way."

"And certainly I shall keep your confidence," Jack assured her. "I'll do whatever you want."

"Okay." M took a deep breath and began to tell them about the day she was assaulted. "It happened in March last year. I went for my usual afternoon ride on Gypo, in the woods at the foot of the moors. Just outside Pennistone Royal village. I was on the wide part of the trail when I was stopped by a heavyset man. He was standing next to a parked van. He asked me to help him, said that his friend was ill, he'd had a heart attack. He asked me if I had a mobile phone on me. I told him I didn't. At his request I jumped off Gypo and went to look at his friend. The other man was slumped over the wheel, not moving, breathing oddly. As I turned to say something to the heavy-set man, he grabbed me, dragged me into the woods. I struggled, screamed, but he was too strong for me. He threw me down, ripped my shirt, pulled my jeans off . . . and flung himself on top of me. I struggled so hard—" M broke off, shaking her head. She brought her hands to her face, trembling.

"Take your time, darling," Linnet said soothingly and glanced at Jack, her expression worried. He gave her a sympathetic look, which had reassurance in it. "She'll be all right," he mouthed.

"Could I have a glass of water?" M asked her sister after a few moments. Linnet immediately jumped up and went to open one of the small bottles on the tea trolley. Filling a glass, Linnet brought it to M, who thanked her and took a long swallow.

"Suddenly, I heard somebody barging through the bushes, shouting," M continued. "The man holding me down was distracted. He instantly shifted his body and looked around at his friend, who was still shouting at him as he reached the clearing. I knew it was the moment to act. I grabbed a rock, bashed him on the side of the head, and as he fell over backward, I pulled on my jeans and ran. I could hear Gypo snorting in the trees. I got away. That's it."

"Thanks for telling us, M. Now I have a few questions, if you're up to answering them," Jack said.

M nodded. "I think so."

"Could you tell where they were from? Were they locals? Foreigners? English? What?"

"Not locals, no, but English . . . probably from the London area."

"Were any names used?"

"Yes. One name. When the other man came rushing through the woods, he was shouting the name Bart, telling him to get off me."

"And that's all?"

"Yes, it is, Jack."

"Would you recognize either of them?"

"The man who assaulted me, yes. Not the other one. I didn't see his face when he was slumped in the car, and when he was running into the woods I was busy freeing myself, and then I ran away without looking back."

Jack nodded, now asked, "What did you do next, M? You obviously didn't call Linnet. And where were your parents?"

"I didn't tell anybody anything. Mummy and Dad were in the South of France, there was only the staff, Margaret and Joe, at Pennistone Royal. I had a shower, later Margaret made supper for me, and then I packed. I came up to London the next day. Over the next few weeks I scoured the newspapers, watched TV, because I thought that maybe I'd killed that man when I hit him with the rock. I needed to know that I hadn't. I did go to a clinic and see a doctor. Obviously, it was too soon to tell if I was pregnant. Anyway, I wasn't. I also soon knew that I didn't have a sexually transmitted disease." M looked at Linnet and shook her head. "Don't be angry with me, please, Lin. I really did want to handle everything myself."

Linnet was staring at M in amazement, tremendously proud of her younger sister but also saddened that she hadn't realized she could tell her anything, that her love was unconditional. "I think you're extraordinary, M, and very courageous, but you should have confided in me, darling. I could have helped you get through the ordeal, given you comfort, even found you a counselor."

"I guess I kind of . . . toughed it out," M said and forced a laugh. She said again, more forcefully, "I don't want anyone else to know."

"I understand that," Linnet reassured her.

Jack said, "What did you think about the attack later, when you could think straight?"

"That they were sexual deviants, something like that, and in cahoots with each other. It never occurred to me that they might have been sent to kill me. Do you think that was it, Jack?"

"It's hard to tell. Sexual perverts roaming around the countryside, looking for a young woman to attack, it's not beyond the realm of possibility. The world is full of sickos. On the other hand, they were parked in a spot where *you* ride every day, which suggests to me that they were stalking you. I think you might well have been a target, but not for rape. It's just possible the man called Bart was a . . . hit man but that he couldn't resist sexually assaulting you first."

"You're right!" M exclaimed. "Because that other man who came barging through the woods shouting that he should get off me sounded angry, now that I think about it."

"Are you suggesting Jonathan Ainsley is behind that attack last spring?" Linnet said.

"Yes, I am," Jack responded. "I wouldn't put anything past that man."

"I see. Aside from giving us all extra security, what else are you planning to do, Jack?" Linnet now asked, wondering what he could do. And before he could answer her, she said, "I mean, how does one fight a phantom? We don't know where he lives, what he's up to, where his business offices are. It's like grasping for smoke, isn't it?"

"It may seem that way to you, Linnet, but not to me," Jack replied. "Wen Li is working on a plan to get a mole inside Belvedere, that's the name of Ainsley's new company in Hong Kong, the one he wants Wen Li to become involved with. I think Wen Li will succeed in doing that, which will be tremendous for us. He does have an excellent candidate. We will immediately know a lot more than we do now. Also, I have all of my operatives in Europe trying to track Ainsley down." Rising, going over to the tea trolley and taking a bottle of water, Jack went on talking. "It is obvious that we have to stop him. He has to be dealt with immediately, this can't drag on, because he *is* terribly dangerous."

"Why can't we hire a hit man?" M asked, giving Jack a hard stare.

"No, no." Jack shook his head. "The Hartes don't operate like that, M. There are other ways to destroy a man like Ainsley."

"We have to target his soft spots," M pointed out. "Find his vulnerabilities . . . like his wife, his daughter, his money, his businesses. I wonder if he has a mistress? *We* could target *her.*"

A grin spread itself across Jack's face, and then he began to laugh. "I know this is serious business, not a laughing matter, but I just can't help it, M. You're absolutely priceless. When you get bored with being a supermodel, come to me, I'll give you a job as one of my independent operatives. You've just hit the nail on the head. Wen Li and I agreed that we had to seek out Ainsley's soft spots in order to finish him off completely. Short of committing murder, of course."

Linnet asked, "When are you going to explain everything to Mummy? Oh, and what about Tessa?"

"I have a date for tea with Paula this afternoon, and I suppose the best thing would be to speak to Tessa on the phone. I think she'll understand what I'm getting at even if I speak in riddles, don't you? But I could pop over to Paris."

Linnet nodded. "Our sister the Dauphine, or the Dorf as we call her, is very fast, she'll pick up on it without you having to say too much. Do it on the phone."

"Jack, do you think Ainsley is actually in hiding?" M said as she stood up.

"Not in hiding, no. I would say he is being very secretive about his whereabouts. Neither is he flaunting his wealth and success. He's definitely keeping a low profile. Better to remain hidden in order to do your dirty work without facing retaliation."

"Clever, eh? He's a clever bugger," M muttered, and turning to Linnet, she said, "Can I use your bathroom to wash my face and dab on a bit of lipstick?"

"You don't have to ask, you silly girl," Linnet answered. Once they were alone, she said to Jack, "M is amazing, isn't she?"

"Why do you sound so surprised, Beauty? She's a Harte, isn't she?"

Simon Baron sat in his office at the store, staring at his notes but not really seeing them. His concentration had fled. He was facing the biggest dilemma of his life, and he didn't know what to do.

Simon had fallen in love with the wrong woman. Passionately, hopelessly, madly in love.

He had known a number of interesting women over the past few years, and intimately, but the relationships had not been particularly serious. In fact, he had characterized them as flings.

This time it was different. He knew that he was seriously in love. The problem was, the lady in question was unaware of it. What was even worse, he worked for her. Linnet

O'Neill was the object of his affection, the woman he wanted to spend the rest of his life with.

Although she was widowed, he knew she was still unattached after two years; lately he had come to believe that her grief for Julian Kallinski had abated, that she had put it behind her to a certain extent. On the other hand, he kept hesitating about asking her out to dinner, then chastised himself for being a fool, even a coward. Very simply, he kept losing his nerve when he was on the verge of issuing an invitation.

The situation was growing unbearable, seeing her every day and wanting her, dreaming about her. He had thought of moving on, finding another job, but he had not had the guts to do so because of Jack, who would be hurt, disappointed, and angry if he left Harte's. And now, with the disaster of last week looming over them, he couldn't leave. His presence was vital. And he wanted to be there to make sure she was safe. A chill ran through him when he thought of how easily she could have been killed in the explosion. Life without her,

even if she was only a boss, would be unbearable. He closed his eyes, not wanting
to think of this.

He was thirty-eight years old and ready
to settle down. He wanted marriage and
children, a traditional life, with Linnet—

There was a knock on the door. He
glanced up, said, "Come in." And was totally
taken aback to see Linnet O'Neill standing
there. Smiling and walking into the room,
his lady boss said, "Jack asked me to come
and get you, Simon. He told me the two of
you were going to lunch, and I invited myself along. I hope you don't mind."

Simon was already on his feet; he came
round the desk, bent down, and greeted
her with a quick kiss on the cheek. "Of
course I don't mind. I'm glad. And where're
we going?"

"Jack decided he didn't get enough Chinese food last week in Hong Kong, which
as you know he loves. So he's taking us
to China Tang at the Dorchester. Connie
made a reservation."

"Hey, one of my favorite places! Come
on then, let's go and pick him up," Simon
exclaimed as he opened the door of his
office and ushered her out, lightly holding

her arm. Although he was nervous, it did not show, and he felt a sudden rush of happiness.

"He told me he would meet us there. He's still chatting with M in my office. She's having lunch with friends, a couple from New York, and Jack thinks he knows the husband, whom I gather he'd like to see again. Let's grab a taxi, shall we?"

Simon simply nodded, guiding her to a bank of elevators. He said, "Jack told you about the *new development,* I'm sure. I know he wanted to explain everything to you and M."

As they stepped into the lift, Linnet said, "Horrible news, almost unbelievable. We'll have to do something drastic, and pretty damn quick, Simon. I'm particularly worried about my mother. She's going to take this to heart, and she's a bit frail these days."

"Try not to worry, Linnet. Jack's got some clever plans, and so do I. And I agree it has to be dealt with at once."

Out in the side street, Simon hailed a taxi, helped her into it, told the cabbie to head for the Dorchester, and took the other corner of the cab.

There was a sudden awkward silence

between them, and after a second Simon cleared his throat several times, finally said, in a hoarse voice, "I think we must get security for M and Larry—"

"Oh, but they have it," Linnet answered and looked at him quickly, then glanced out of the window. She was so conscious of his close proximity, she could hardly bear it. She had fallen in love with him months ago, much to her amazement. Even though she tried to tell herself it was mostly physical desire, an overwhelming sexual *need* for this tall, blond hunk, she knew deep within herself that it was more than that. *Much more.*

Simon Baron was one of the most intelligent and sensitive men she had ever met; she had been drawn to him for years, long before he had worked at Harte's, always finding his company pleasant. She found him compatible, considerate, and charming. He had a good sense of humor; it was a little dry and certainly self-deprecating. On the other hand, she knew he was catnip to women and that he played the field. So why would *he* be interested in *her,* when he could have a twenty-two-year-old hanging on his arm and sleeping in his bed? On the other hand, the reality of the cruel world they lived in had brought her to a decision. Why not let him know how she felt? What did she have to lose?

The cabbie swerved to avoid a car drawing too close, and Linnet was flung across the seat, landing almost, but not quite, in Simon's lap. He grabbed hold of her, endeavoring to steady her, and she clung to him tightly.

"Wow!" she exclaimed as the cabbie righted the vehicle and drove on. She stared up at Simon. "Sorry about that—" She couldn't finish her sentence. Her mouth went dry, and her heart started to pound. He was looking at her so intensely, and there was such desire in his light blue-gray eyes, she was in no doubt how he felt. Oh my God! The same way she did. "Oh, Simon, Simon, darling," she whispered and reached up, brought his head down to hers, kissed him fully on the mouth. He kissed her back and passionately so, then drew away, looking slightly stunned.

She smiled, her eyes dancing with

laughter. "I've been wanting to do that for months, Simon Baron. And finally I *did.*"

Staring into those mesmerizing green eyes, Simon realized that she most definitely shared his feelings. He grinned and said, "And so have I, and I want to keep on doing it, don't you?"

"Absolutely." Linnet shook her head. "I'm not quite sure how I'm going to get through this lunch with Jack."

Simon groaned. "I know exactly what you mean. But we have to, there are some very serious matters to discuss."

"Oh, God, yes." Linnet sat up straighter but remained close to him, leaned against his body, took hold of his hand, gave him a very pointed look. "Is there any possibility of seeing you later, Simon? Much later, I mean. Like this evening. Could you come to dinner at my house?"

"Try and keep me away. But I do think you should know I have serious intentions."

"I'm glad to hear it. And, you know what, so do I. Very serious intentions."

They had arrived at the Dorchester Hotel, and Simon alighted first, paid the cab, helped her out, squeezing her hand as they headed up the front steps together. "We'd better play it cool," he murmured. "Jack knows us both extremely well, he'll spot something if we're not careful."

"Yes, perhaps he will, but does it matter?" she asked.

# Forty

I think I'd like a drink," Linnet said, once they had been seated in the library area of China Tang, the popular Chinese restaurant downstairs at the hotel.

"What would you like?" Simon asked, reaching out and placing his hand over hers on the table, filled with joy that he could actually touch her.

"A glass of pink champagne, please."

"*Champagne,*" he repeated, raising a blond brow.

"Yes. To celebrate."

"Celebrate what?"

"Kissing you," she murmured, looking

at him flirtatiously out of the corner of her eye. "As far as I'm concerned, that was something special, and therefore something to celebrate. That's what champagne is for."

He laughed, enjoying her, as he always had when there had been occasions for them to see each other on a social level with Jack, her parents, and the rest of the family. He had known her for many years, *forever,* it seemed like to him, had always found himself attracted to her. But she had only had eyes for Julian, her childhood sweetheart. It was different. At last. Now she was alone and available, and she obviously had strong feelings for him, as he did for her. It was up to him now to make her well and truly his. For always. That was what he wanted.

When the waiter appeared at their table, Simon ordered two glasses of pink champagne, and once they were alone again, he leaned into her, kissed her neck, muttered against her ear, "Got to make the most of it before Jack gets here."

"Yes, we do," she replied and stared at him, her face turning serious. "We're in danger, aren't we, Simon? From Ainsley?"

"Yes, and we have to pinpoint his whereabouts as fast as we can. I agree with Jack, though, who thinks it'll be like looking for a needle in a haystack."

"These last few years have been so peaceful, not having to look over our shoulders all the time. Now it starts again."

The waiter returned with their drinks, and Linnet lifted her flute, as did Simon. They touched glasses, and Linnet said, "Here's to that very special kiss I've waited so long to give you."

He smiled at her, his eyes loving. "It was special for me, too." After taking a swig of the champagne, Simon said, "Before Jack gets here, I would like to ask you something."

Linnet nodded. "Yes, ask me."

"Did you mean it when you said you had serious intentions?"

"I did. Why?" She frowned, her auburn brows drawing together.

"Because I know how *I* feel about *you,* and I have known for a very long time . . . I'm serious about you."

"I'm glad we feel the same. Aren't we a couple of fools? Harboring the same feelings for each other for so long and never saying a word."

"We've wasted a lot of time, Linnet."

"But we'll make up for it, and then some—" Linnet stopped abruptly, removed her hand, placed it in her lap, and murmured, "Here comes Jack."

A second later he was being shown to the table, greeted them both, and sat down. "That looks good," Jack said, eyeing the champagne. "Very refreshing. I think I'll have a glass." Motioning to the waiter, he ordered and then said to Linnet, "M got James Cardigan on his cell, told him about me, and yes, we did meet in Hong Kong. But this is the thing, when she was talking to him she said the Hartes had a serious problem and did he know any hackers. I couldn't believe my ears, she's very clever."

Simon exclaimed, "That's what I said to you this morning. I had the same idea. Let's get some hackers working. Maybe it would be tough to hack into Ainsley's computers, but they might be able to get into the computers of some of those chaps he does business with. Possibly we could get information about him through a few leads."

"That is exactly what I discussed with Zhèng in Hong Kong last week. However, it sounds a lot easier than it is, and remember one thing, the Hartes can never be involved in anything criminal."

"But we can break a few rules, don't you think?" Linnet said. "I bet Emma broke some, and what about my great-grandfather Blackie O'Neill? I'm sure he must have stretched things a bit at times. And David Kallinski, their willing partner, too. M is prepared to break the rules all the way, and so am I."

Jack laughed. "But that was then, and this is now, and we're going to toe the line. Understood?"

Linnet nodded and winked at him.

Smiling, Simon said, "For the time being anyway." He moved his leg closer to Linnet's, slipped his hand under the table, and found hers resting on his thigh. He removed it gently, since he felt the first signs of arousal, an unexpected reaction at a lunch table for him. He was usually in control of himself in every way.

"Linnet, I want to discuss something," Jack began. "But I decided to wait. And it's about the things we can do through Wen Li."

"What things? How can he help?" she asked.

"He has a grandson, Richie Zhèng, a wonderful-looking young man, a Eurasian of about twenty-five. He went to the Wharton School of Business and spent some time in the States. Anyway, he's very Americanized and a computer genius, also a brilliant banker, according to Wen Li. Extraordinarily talented with figures. Wen Li is going to propose to Ainsley that Richie Zhèng work with Ainsley as Wen Li's representative."

"But why would Ainsley agree to have Richie Zhèng in his company?"

"Because Wen Li is planning to invest a hundred million dollars—American dollars—with Ainsley. The proviso is that Richie be brought into the company. In a sense, he would be looking after Wen Li's money, although Wen Li's not saying that."

"Good God!" Linnet exclaimed. "That's a fortune."

"However, he won't invest that amount if Ainsley says no deal regarding Richie being part of the company."

"A piece of cheese to catch a rat, eh?" Linnet laughed grimly.

"You could call it that, Beauty. Anyway, Wen Li wants Richie to work at Belvedere, that's Ainsley's new company in Hong Kong, and it can't do us any harm."

"I understand everything," Linnet said, "and it's an awful lot of money to invest. Wen Li must believe he can double or triple it with Ainsley."

"I believe he does think that, although one of his chief motivations was finding a way to get Richie inside Ainsley's organization. Belvedere is a holding company, and although it's based in Hong Kong, it's an umbrella for Ainsley's worldwide investments. And there is another reason." Jack paused. "He wants to help *us*."

Linnet stared at Jack in disbelief. "M is going to be really surprised when I tell her all this. Why would he risk all that money for us, Jack? *That* I don't understand."

"He isn't risking it, not really. Wen Li knows what he's doing, he's a shrewd banker. Anyway, let's hope the rat eats the cheese, to borrow a phrase from you."

Simon said to Linnet, "Shall we order?" And turning to Jack, he added, "Actually, Jack, I think it might be a good idea if we let you order lunch, since you're such an old Hong Kong hand."

Picking up the menu, Jack scanned it and said to Linnet and Simon, "How about wonton soup to start with? Soup's nice on a damp day, comforting, wouldn't you say? Then I love their minced squab wrapped in lettuce leaves. They also make delicious shrimp dumplings, and another thing I enjoy are the spring rolls. Any preferences?"

"Whatever you say, Jack," Linnet answered. "But I do happen to like wonton soup and minced squab."

Simon said he'd have the same, and that Jack should order whatever else he thought they would like. As Jack conversed with the waitress, who had come to take their orders, Simon squeezed Linnet's hand under the table and gave her a long, loving look.

Paula O'Neill stared at herself in the cheval mirror, straightened the skirt of her tailored, navy blue silk dress, and adjusted the string of pearls around her neck. Satisfied with the way she looked, she went over to her dressing table, where she picked up her pearl earrings and put them on.

She smiled to herself as she turned away from the dressing table, thinking that she was dressed in what she termed one of her "uniforms": Today it was the simple dress in a dark color.

When she had run Harte's, she had always worn a well-cut black suit with a white shirt or blouse. Her daughters Linnet and M had followed in her footsteps, choosing similar "uniforms" to wear during the day. Not Tessa, of course. She had her own inimitable style, favoring white mostly.

Paula's mind focused on M, her youngest daughter, and the one who looked the most like her. She was proud of her, the way she had gone off to New York and done it on her own, without their help. But then that was a Harte characteristic, wasn't it? In many ways M had always been the most independent of her three daughters, sure of herself and what she wanted to do with her life. And to think the world's new top supermodel on every magazine cover had once protested about putting on makeup and washing her hair, had had no desire to look smart, preferring instead to muck out the stables and care for the horses.

Seating herself at the desk, Paula opened her appointment book and looked at the day's engagements. Tea with Jack was the most important date. He was coming at four o'clock. She hadn't seen him for a few weeks and was curious about the impending visit. Was he simply coming to catch up with her on certain matters? Or was he about to impart bad news? After the bombing at the store, she was certain he was not the bearer of good tidings. On the other hand, he had been in Hong Kong, and perhaps he was bringing gossip and greetings from mutual friends he might have seen on the trip.

Well, whatever the reason for his visit, she was pleased she was going to see him. They had been friends for over forty years. She frowned. Where on earth had all that time gone? It just disappeared in the blink of an eye . . . it didn't seem possible to her.

She had first met Jack Figg when she had gone to work for her grandmother at the store. Emma Harte had adored the young Jack, had seen enormous potential in him, and as usual, Emma had been right. He had turned out to be a superlative head of security, loyal and devoted. He had also become her best friend, and a member of the family as well, loved by all.

Sometimes Shane teased Paula about Jack and his extraordinary devotion to her, and hinted that Jack might have been carrying a torch for her for many years. She always shrugged off that suggestion, because there had never been any indication of it. Jack was always the perfect gentleman.

Sitting back in the chair, Paula thought of what had happened in all those years which seemed to have passed with such speed: her marriage to Jim. The birth of the twins, Tessa and Lorne, and then the slow but terrible disintegration of her marriage to Jim Fairley. It was her love for her childhood friend Shane O'Neill that had been a wondrous revelation. And then had come a terrible sorrow and a mantle of guilt when Jim and her father had been killed in a fatal air crash in France. But this tragedy had been followed, eventually, by her marriage to Shane. From this she had drawn great peace as well as immense joy. The birth of their sons and daughters,

Patrick, Linnet, Emma, and Desmond, had brought untold happiness.

She suddenly remembered the way she and Shane had ruefully admitted to each other that there could be only *one* Emma in the family. They had belatedly understood that her famous grandmother completely overshadowed the baby Emma. And so she had become Emsie, then Em, and finally M. Paula smiled in delight, thinking of her grubby little horse-loving child, who had become this startlingly beautiful supermodel. And Larry. What a blessing he was, and M was safe with him.

She sighed, and a sadness crept into Paula's heart as memories of her darling Patrick rose to the surface . . . their beloved little boy born with brain damage, who had been the sweetest and most loving child, beloved by all. When he had died, and so suddenly, everyone in the family had been devastated.

Ah, yes, so many losses over these years, which she and Shane had shared: the death of his grandfather Blackie O'Neill, and of her grandmother Emma Harte; then Shane's father, Bryan, had passed, as had so many other family members. She thought of Great-Aunt Edwina, Emma's firstborn child, and then laughed, remembering her. They had all likened her to a general, but they had truly loved her, the genuine eccentric in the family.

And what of the terrible mistakes she had made in business? Paula cringed at the thought. Once she had put the stores at risk. To think that she had almost lost them to her cousin . . . but she had outwitted and defeated Jonathan Ainsley. And so very cleverly, thanks to Ronnie Kallinski, the man she had always addressed as Uncle Ronnie, referred to as her wise rabbi. Ainsley was dead and buried, and she had survived those troubles and moved on.

Despite all the mistakes, the losses, the deaths and tragedies, there had also been marriages and births, and new beginnings . . . more children to carry the banner of the famous name of Harte, to run her grandmother's empire. There had been so many blessings, as well as troubles.

The happiness she had shared with Shane all these years, and still shared, that was truly something to treasure and to enjoy. How lucky she had been to be part of this man's world. Life had often punched her in the face, but never mind that now. She had so much to be thankful for, had had more than most.

Rising, Paula left the bedroom and went downstairs to wait for Jack, still thinking of all the happenings that had marked the years.

Sometimes she had wondered if the Hartes were cursed, but she had inevitably dismissed this idea. They were truly a large family, and life had spared none of them, and that was all there was to it. She didn't believe in curses. Like her grandmother, she was far too much of a pragmatist for that nonsense.

"You've come to tell me we have more trouble, haven't you, Jack?" Paula said as she walked across the sitting room to welcome him.

"I'm afraid so," he replied. Coming to a standstill next to each other, they embraced; Jack kissed her on the cheek, held her away, his eyes searching her face. "No matter what's happening, you always look wonderful, and you're positively blooming today."

"Thanks, darling, and I'm feeling very well, although Linnet fusses over me far too much. Well, never mind, she means well, and I must say I'm proud of the way she runs the store, takes everything in her stride." Sitting down on the sofa, giving him a questioning glance, Paula said, "So give me the bad news."

Blowing out air, shaking his head, Jack took the chair opposite her. "Steel yourself for this. . . . Jonathan Ainsley is not dead and buried as we believed. He's alive."

Jack was watching her carefully, worried about her as usual, and he saw her flinch, but otherwise there was no visible reaction. Then a deep sigh escaped her, and she gave him her full attention.

Leaning back against the cushions, Paula said, "I know you must be certain of the truth of this, but naturally I'm curious. How did you find out?"

"Through your old friend, and mine, Zhèng Wen Li. He contacted me, said he had something important to tell me, something *vital,* but that it must be face-to-face. That's why I went to Hong Kong last week."

"I see. And how does Wen Li know about Ainsley coming back to life, so to speak?"

Jack told her everything, and finally explained Wen Li's idea of putting his grandson inside Belvedere, Ainsley's holding company in Hong Kong. "The bait is the vast amount of money he's going to invest with Ainsley," Jack finished. "A hundred million dollars."

"I understand everything, Jack, and if Wen Li's plan works, we'll have somebody on the inside, a spy in the house of Ainsley. Then at least we'll have an idea of what's going on."

"Correct, Paula, although Ainsley might not be in Hong Kong at every moment. Nevertheless, Richie Zhèng will have access to a great deal, and I just pray that Ainsley does take the bait."

"So do I. It's good of Wen Li to do this for us."

"And also for himself, Paula. You know he hates Ainsley as much as we do, and he does stand to make a lot of money on his hundred million. But yes, he has proved to be very loyal, a good friend."

"When is all of this going to happen?"

"Imminently, I think. In the meantime, there's not much we can do. Obviously, I've got to put a lot of security around you

and Shane, M and Larry and Linnet, and
Tessa and her brood in France. He's a dan-
gerous man. Also *elusive*." Jack frowned.
"I've absolutely no idea where his base is."

"So it's not Hong Kong?" Paula raised a
brow.

"No. He still has an apartment there,
and a business office, but that's the same
as before. It's just a new name, that's all."

"He could be living in Switzerland, you
know, especially since you said he was
treated at a clinic in Zurich."

"That's true, he was, but somehow I doubt
that he lives in Zurich. Geneva maybe."

"You mentioned security guards for
my girls, Jack, but what about my sons?
Shouldn't Lorne and Desmond be protected?"

"Absolutely, and I will talk to them both.
Lorne has fought it in the past, but this
time he'll have to listen. How's Desmond
going to take it?"

"Not too well, I'm afraid, but I'm sure
you can persuade him . . ." She gave him
a small smile. "You're very persuasive, you
know." Leaning forward, she now asked,
"Once Richie Zhèng is inside Belvedere

and gets information about Ainsley for his grandfather and you, what then?"

"I am hoping we will be able to pinpoint Ainsley's permanent location and keep track of him at all times. However, even as we speak, I have many of my European operatives trying to track him down. I'm leaving nothing to chance. I want to find him quickly and deal with him."

"But how will you deal with him? You can't just go out and shoot him."

"If I could I would, and I would have done it years ago, you know that. What will I do?" Leaning forward, drawing closer, taking her hand in his, he said, "Wen Li and I must render him harmless to us, Paula. And we will. I promise you that. But I can't tell you what we're going to do because we haven't finalized everything. Anyway, the less you know the better."

"I trust you, Jack."

He half smiled, then went on. "I'm going to insist some other members of the family, some of your cousins, have security, and I think that should do it for the moment. You see, he's mostly out to get you and your daughters—"

"But *why* is he still persisting after all these years?" she exclaimed, her voice rising an octave.

"When a terrible illness is not treated, it does not get better, nor does it simply go away. Actually, it gets much worse. Jonathan Ainsley is a very sick man . . . he's mentally ill. I believe he is a psychopath. Even his own father said that just before he died. Ainsley must be stopped."

"As soon as you can, Jack, please." Her voice sounded suddenly tense.

"It will be done as fast as possible, I can guarantee that, and I *will* keep my promise to you," Jack responded in a reassuring tone.

"Thank you. I don't know what we'd do without you."

"About Tessa, Paula? Do you think her husband will object to having security guards?" Jack now asked, his concern echoing.

"I doubt it. Jean-Claude is rather brilliant, as you well know. Furthermore, he's considered one of the foremost experts on terrorism. So he understands about bodyguards. Anyway, you can ask Tessa about it herself in a very short while. She's here in London, just for the day, with Jean-Claude. She's coming to have tea."

A huge smile crossed Jack's face, and he exclaimed, "I can't wait to see her, it's been ages."

Paula cleared her throat and threw Jack a knowing look. "You're usually a few steps ahead of us all, so I'm assuming you've already thought about what I'm now going to say . . . that Ainsley might have had something to do with the bombing of Harte's?"

"I was just about to bring that up, Paula, and yes, I had thought of it. I feel certain he arranged for it to be done. I also consider Larry's poisoning on location very suspect. And then there's the collapsing runway at the hotel in Paris. I can't help thinking that this was another one of Ainsley's attempts to kill or maim a Harte. This time, M."

At this moment the door opened, and Vesta, the housekeeper, came in, wheeling the tea trolley. "Here I am, Mrs. O'Neill, and Miss Tessa just arrived a few minutes ago. She went up to her old room to freshen up. And she said she'll be down very shortly."

❖

To Jack, Tessa Fairley Deléon was beautiful in a classical sense. She was tall, slender, willowy, with long silver-gilt hair, silvery eyes, and a perfect skin without blemish. Her chiseled features in an oval-shaped face were perfect, and she had an aura about her, perhaps because of her extraordinary taste and elegance, the way she held herself and moved with such grace.

Now, as she walked into the sitting room of her mother's Belgravia house, he caught his breath in surprise. If anything, she was more beautiful than ever, ethereal, and it struck him suddenly that she didn't walk, she floated. Or so it seemed to him.

She was wearing an outfit in different shades of gray and pale blue, and it drifted around her gorgeous legs like some sort of hazy mist. She wasn't movie-star beautiful, that would be a ridiculous analogy because she was beyond that. Tessa was like a being from another world. And to think he had once detested her.

Jack had not been the only one to dislike Tessa. Her entire family, even though they loved her, had found her impossible at times. Because she was a Fairley, through Jim Fairley, her mother's first husband, she was a monumental snob. The Fairleys had been the great aristocratic Yorkshire family in their heyday at the turn of the nineteenth century, and Tessa couldn't stop boasting about that, them, and her remarkable heritage.

What annoyed everyone was the way she looked down on the Hartes and was forever flinging the Fairley name in their faces. She constantly annoyed her mother and Linnet because she called herself the Dauphine, alluding to the fact that she was the eldest child, and therefore Paula's heir to the Harte stores.

Tessa *was* the firstborn of Paula's children, that was true, since she was delivered a few minutes before her twin brother, Lorne. Fortunately, they got on well together, and he never stood in her way, because he had no interest in the family business. His aim was to become a great actor, and he had done that.

Jack suppressed a smile now as he thought of the way Linnet and M had mocked Tessa behind her back, calling her by that

awful nickname, the Dorf, short for Dauphine.

But they had also become her defend-
ers and allies once they discovered that
she was an abused wife. Tessa's first husband, Mark Longden, had beaten her up
on a regular basis and treated her so badly
she had finally left him. None of them had
known the true situation, because Tessa
had put on such a good face for years.

Jack realized what a bastard Mark was
when Tessa's daughter by Mark disappeared several years ago. Little Adele went
missing from Pennistone Royal and was
nowhere to be found until Jack tracked
down her father and discovered that Mark
was the kidnapper of his own child.

Throughout this horrendous abduction,
he had come to know Tessa well and
had become her friend and admirer. She
had displayed true grit, been tremendously
brave, and had confided at one moment
that she was glad she was a Harte woman,
with her great-grandmother's indomitable
spirit.

She had inevitably changed, and had
become the lovely woman she was today
after meeting and falling in love with Jean-

Claude Deléon. The renowned French writer and philosopher was twenty years older than she was, but they had quickly married and had had three children. Tessa now lived in France, where she had flourished, grown into her own skin.

After greeting her mother and then Jack, Tessa exclaimed, "Shall I play Mum and pour the tea?" And Paula laughed and said, "Please do, darling."

Once Tessa had served her mother and Jack, and handed around the small tea sandwiches, she took a cup of tea for herself and settled next to Jack on the sofa.

"Why is it we never see you in Paris, old friend? I do wish you'd come and visit us."

"I will, I promise," Jack answered and looked across at Paula, who nodded, smiled at him.

Jack continued. "As a matter of fact, I was thinking of popping over to see you tomorrow. But now that you're here, there's no reason . . . at least not at the moment."

"Why were you coming to see me?" Tessa asked, looking suddenly intrigued.

"I wanted to talk to you about a rather important matter, Tessa. I'm sorry to have to tell you this, but at this moment, you,

Jean-Claude, and your children are at great risk."

Tessa drew back, staring at him uncomprehendingly for a moment, and then exclaimed, "What on earth do you mean?"

Jack told her, giving her all of the details he had just enumerated to Paula, and she listened attentively.

Once he had finished, Tessa said, "Just tell me what you want us to do, and we'll do it, Jack. I'll do anything on this earth to protect my husband and my children."

At this moment, the door swung open, and as Paula turned around, her face lit up. She rose and exclaimed, "M! How wonderful to see you." She hurried across the room, embraced her youngest daughter.

"Oh, Mummy, you look absolutely fabulous," M said, and then when she spotted Tessa near the fireplace, she cried, "Beautiful One, what are you doing here? You're supposed to be in Paris."

Laughing, tossing back her long hair, Tessa hurried to M, and the two of them hugged.

"Have you grown taller, or am I shrinking?" Tessa asked, frowning, and then grinned. "So you're twenty inches taller because you're wearing your Jimmy Choo shoes. That's it!"

"No, it isn't. See, I'm in flats." M showed her foot clad in a classical Chanel ballet slipper–style shoe. "And I'm only an inch taller than you."

The two of them laughed, and M went on, "I just want you to know that I've talked Lorne into coming to stay with you. He's a bit down in the dumps."

"Why is that?"

"I think he's lonely, if you really want to know. No woman around." She moved across to the sofa and gave Jack a big hug, whispered against his ear, "How did Mum take it—the news I mean."

"With resignation," Jack answered. "In her usual elegant manner."

Paula joined them near the fireplace and asked M, "Do you want a cup of tea, darling? It's still hot."

"I'd love it, and I'm so glad I came over . . . to see you, Mummy, but how nice that Tessa's here and Jack. You've heard the bad news from Jack."

"Yes, indeed we have," Paula answered.

"I'm all for having *him* demolished by a hit man," M announced. "And I'd be willing to foot the bill. Ainsley's a menace."

Paula and Tessa both stared at her in astonishment, and then Paula laughed. "Really, darling, we can't go around killing people, or having them killed."

"Why not?"

"Don't be silly, M." Paula shook her head. "We're not murderers, criminals—"

"Ainsley is," M cut in and said to Tessa, "You'd better agree to have bodyguards."

"I've agreed," Tessa answered. "I've always listened to Jack, you know."

"How long are you staying?" M asked and stared at her elder sister.

"I came with Jean-Claude just for the day, darling. He was flying in on a private plane, so I just hitched a ride to see Mummy."

"I'm glad you thought about that, Tessa," Paula said and looked at M. "What were you saying about Lorne?" She sounded anxious.

# Forty-one

Linnet left the store in Knightsbridge earlier than usual, feeling impatient, nervous, even agitated. As usual, she walked to her small but charming house a few streets behind Harte's, where she had lived since her husband's death.

Once she had let herself in and dumped her carryall in the entrance hall, she hurried into the kitchen and opened the refrigerator, looked inside. She had been right, there was lots of food, including smoked salmon, country pâté, and the makings for a tasty salad. She noticed a cottage pie which Carla, the housekeeper, had apparently made that morning. Enough for dinner . . . to satisfy a hungry man.

Whirling around, Linnet crossed the hall, went into the living room to check that everything was in place, and then strode into the bedroom. She quickly changed out of her black, tailored trouser suit, her uniform for work, put on a pair of beige slacks and a matching light cashmere sweater, and hung up her suit.

As she turned, her eyes caught the bedside table. The telephone sat there along with a message pad in a leather holder, and that was all. Until recently, a photograph of her late husband in a silver frame had stood there—a photograph she had owned for many years.

Several months ago, Tessa had said to her, "I think this has to find another home, Linny darling. Such as the living room or your den."

She had frowned at her sister, had started to protest, but Tessa had held up her hand, shaking her head vehemently. "Listen to me, darling, Julian has been dead for two years, and you've got to move on. Put that photograph somewhere else.

Don't have it in your bedroom, for heaven's sake. One day, sooner than later, hopefully, there'll be another man in this bed, and believe me, there's nothing more offputting than a photograph of a woman's late husband staring at both of you when you're making love."

Linnet remembered now how she had given Tessa a reproachful look and muttered something about there being a shortage of eligible men, and Tessa had picked up the photograph, put it on her hands, and led her out of the room.

"You're wrong, there are plenty of men around, but how would you know? You're always at work. So tell me how you're going to meet any. I'll have to start procuring for you. How about that?"

Tessa had suddenly started to laugh, and so had she, and taking her sister's advice Linnet had put Julian's photograph in her den that day. And as she had done so, she had thought about Simon Baron and the crush she had on him, and had sighed to herself, believing him to be far beyond her reach.

How wrong she had been. Suddenly she thought about the cab ride through the park at lunchtime today, and blessed that cabbie for taking such a big swerve and throwing her into Simon's arms. She also marveled at herself for having had the nerve to kiss him. She smiled. She had known he wanted to kiss her the moment she stared up into his eyes, seen the desire in them, the yearning.

Leaving the bedroom, she went down to the garden floor and the cozy dining room, which opened onto the garden. She had phoned Carla earlier to ask her to set the small circular table for supper for two, and the housekeeper had done so before going home.

Linnet nodded as she glanced around, pleased with the blue-and-white color scheme, and her favorite antique pieces, which fit so well in here. Buying the house and decorating it had kept her busy after Julian's sudden death, and had helped her to cope.

And the house had been a new beginning. As tonight was going to be a new beginning. . . .

Linnet looked at the carriage clock on the living room mantelpiece. It said five-forty.

Twenty minutes before Simon arrived. She had come home from the store far too early, and now she didn't know where to put herself.

She rose, walked across the room, straightened a silk cushion on the dark rose-colored sofa, wandered out into the foyer, saw her carryall, took it up to her den on the next floor.

Seating herself at the desk, she looked at yesterday's mail, dismissed it as not important, stood again, and walked over to the window. After looking down into the street, she went back downstairs, feeling expectant and just a little afraid.

Her mind entirely focused on Simon, she suddenly wondered what he would prefer to drink and flew into the kitchen, looked in the refrigerator. There was a bottle of white wine chilling as usual, and now she added pink champagne, some bottles of water, and noticed to her surprise that her hands were shaking.

God, what's wrong with me? she wondered, realizing that her heart had started to pound. And all because of Simon Baron. Whom she had known for donkey's years and saw every day at work. But it was

different now. Because she had kissed
him in the cab and he had kissed her back,
and they had confessed they were keen
on each other, more than keen. And on
the way back to the store, after lunch with
Jack, he hadn't been able to keep his
hands off her. Nor had she. She wanted to
touch him, kiss him, hold him . . . possess
him . . . and be possessed by him.

The doorbell shrilled, and she jumped,
startled. Linnet glanced at her watch and
saw that it was ten minutes to six. *He was
early.* Endeavoring to keep herself as calm
as possible, she walked to the front door,
looked through the spy hole, and saw that
it *was* Simon.

Opening the door, smiling, she said,
"Hi," and stopped because her mouth had
gone totally dry.

"Hi," he said back and stepped into the
hall.

Linnet closed the door and turned to
face him, shaking so much inside she was
convinced he would notice.

"I'm sorry I'm early," Simon murmured.
"But, well, er, er, well, I couldn't wait to get
here, to see you."

Linnet stood leaning against the front

door, staring at him, thinking how wonderful he looked. He had dispensed with the tie he always wore to work and looked more casual and relaxed in his open-necked, pale blue shirt. She wanted to make love to him. Her mouth was drier than ever.

He cleared his throat, appeared anxious.

She finally spoke. "I know, I was the same. I came home far too early . . ." Her voice trailed off. She took a step forward, and then another, and so did he. Suddenly they were rushing into each other's arms. His mouth was on hers, and he was kissing her with passion, pressing her close to his body. His tongue touched hers, and she clung to him, wondering how she was managing to stand; her legs felt weak, and she was trembling.

Against her hair, he murmured softly, "It was unbearable this afternoon . . . I wanted you so much."

"It was mutual." Drawing away from him, she took his hand, led him into the living room, asking him what he wanted to drink, speaking in a mumble.

"Nothing right now," he replied. "I just want to hold you in my arms and kiss you."

As he spoke they half sat, half fell onto the sofa, and she drew closer to him, and their mouths met again. His hand was in her hair, on her cheek, touching her neck, and then he slipped it under her sweater, unhooked her bra, fondled her breast.

Linnet could hardly breathe. Every part of her ached for him. She wanted his hands on her everywhere, touching, feeling, probing; she longed to touch him, needed the feel of his skin under her hands. Her face was growing hotter and hotter, and the heat suddenly was spreading up through her legs into the pit of her stomach. Then unexpectedly he pushed her sweater up and brought his mouth to her breast, lavishly kissing her until she let out a small moan of pleasure.

Simon stopped abruptly and said, "Let's find a bed . . . *please.*"

Pulling down her sweater, Linnet jumped up, took hold of his hand, and drew him across the room to the front hall and into her bedroom.

Simon closed the door, leaned against it, took her face between his hands, and stared into her eyes. But he remained silent and so did she.

Their clothes were swiftly discarded, and they lay together on the bed, still staring at each other, touching each other's faces. But a moment later they were kissing again, and his passion for her soared. And soared. They found themselves clutching each other; their mutual yearning knew no bounds. When Simon finally entered her, and swiftly so, Linnet caught her breath, and so did he. And as he moved against her, saying her name over and over again, she said his name, and gave herself to him entirely.

❖

Simon pulled her into his arms and brought the duvet up over them, and they did not speak for a while, lost in their own meandering thoughts.

Eventually he murmured, "I could stay like this forever. . . . I feel as if I have the whole world in my arms."

"That's a lovely thing to say. And I have the man of my dreams in my bed."

"Can he stay?"

"Tonight?"

"Yes, tonight, and perhaps other nights," Simon replied.

"Just try and leave!" she exclaimed.

He laughed; she had always had the ability to bring a smile to his face. "What I meant was can I stay the whole night, and have breakfast with you tomorrow?"

"If you really, really want to, I'll consider it."

His answer was to wrap his arms around her tighter and nuzzle the back of her neck. After a moment, he said, "Isn't life amazing, Linnet? Just imagine, if that car hadn't come too close to the cab, the cabbie wouldn't have swerved—"

"I was just thinking that earlier," she interrupted, laughing.

"But it goes backward, actually," Simon went on. "Because if you hadn't asked Jack if you could join us for lunch, we'd have never been in that cab in the first place."

"I'll confess something to you, Simon. I wanted to come to lunch because of *you,* because I wanted to be with you, sitting close to you . . ."

"We've been a couple of fools, considering we're grown-ups," he asserted.

"Yes, we have. But sometimes timing is important, and the time is right for me now, Simon. For you to be in my life."

"I'm so glad to hear that. And it is for me, too."

"Are you . . . *free*?" she asked softly and wanted to add, *to be mine* but resisted the temptation.

He said, "I broke up with someone almost a year ago, and there's been nobody since. . . . But I don't know that I'm *free.*"

Linnet struggled in his arms and turned around to face him. "What does that mean?" she asked, her expression fierce.

"Don't look like that! What I meant is that I'm not free because I'm so involved with you, Linnet. I don't suppose I'll ever be free again."

"And neither will I," she said, touching his face lovingly.

Linnet stood staring at her wedding photograph, which was on a chest in the living room, her throat tight with emotion. What she saw was herself gazing into Julian's face, he into hers. It was a marvelous picture of them both, taken at Pennistone Royal. For a moment she felt sad, but she had to let sadness go.

There was a slight noise, and she straightened, swung around. Simon was standing in the doorway, obviously not wanting to intrude. She forced a smile and said swiftly, "Simon, don't stand there, darling. I came in here to turn on some lamps and noticed my wedding picture as I passed the chest. We weren't married very long before he suddenly died, but as you know, we'd grown up together—" She stopped, wondering why she was explaining. He knew about her life.

Simon nodded, walked into the room. He took hold of her arm and led her over to the sofa. As they sat down, he said quietly, "You were childhood sweethearts. I understand how you feel, Linnet. At least I think I do. . . . It's hard to let go, in a way."

"How perceptive you are," she murmured, looking up into his face, noticing that his blue-gray eyes now looked bluer, a reflection of his shirt, she decided.

"You spent most of your life with him," Simon remarked, "and he's part of you. He's deep in your heart, and he always will be, I realize that. No one can, or should, completely erase the past, especially if it was a happy past, and memories are very important, Linnet. You loved Julian, you were married to him, and naturally it's going to seem . . . well, perhaps a bit strange being with me."

"I know what you mean," she answered. "But oddly enough, it doesn't seem strange. I feel very at ease with you, and that's because I've known you so long . . . and I trust you, Simon, feel safe with you."

"You can, and you are. I'll always look after you," he answered, his sincerity apparent. "I just need to say this. I don't think you should suppress your feelings about Julian because of me, or attempt to hide them from me. You have your memories, and you should cherish them. Look, we're both in our thirties, bringing our pasts to this relationship, but we mustn't let that stuff get in the way. Things happened before you and I were involved. I wasn't married to anyone, but I did have a couple of relationships which were meaningful. However, they don't have anything to do with . . . *us.* Nor does your marriage to Julian."

Simon searched her face, his eyes full of concern, his expression serious. "I suppose what I'm trying to say is that what *we* have together has nothing to do with anyone else or whatever it was we had with them."

"I agree with you," Linnet was quick to say. "And I'd like us to be truthful with each other." She leaned closer to him, her eyes focused intently on his. "I don't want to pretend to other people either, pretend we're not seeing each other. Anyway, it's nobody else's business, is it?"

He pulled her toward him, kissed her on the cheek. "We are of like minds, Linnet, and I just want to tell you that this is the happiest day of my life, knowing you feel the way I do, and that we're going to be together."

"Oh, you mean this is not a one-night stand?" she teased, an auburn brow lifting coquettishly.

"No, it's not, you little minx!" he exclaimed, grinning at her. "It's a rest-of-my-life stand, that's what this is."

She gave him the benefit of a huge smile.

Simon stood up, pulled her to her feet, and started to walk out of the room, saying as he did, "Shall we go and make supper? I'm ravenous."

Linnet caught hold of his hand, stopped

him in his tracks, and he turned to look at her, his expression puzzled.

Drawing closer, leaning against him, she said softly, "When you saw me earlier, looking at the picture, I wasn't comparing or anything like that. . . . I was saying good-bye to him. . . . And I know he would be happy for me, Simon. . . . Julian wouldn't want me to be alone."

Touched by her words, Simon took her in his arms and held her close, his heart overflowing with love for her.

# Forty-two

James Cardigan threw Jack Figg a look that mixed curiosity and bafflement, and asked, "But when you have found Ainsley, what do you actually plan to do, Jack? Kill him?"

Jack looked thoughtful for a minute and then said, with a small, wry smile, "I don't think murder in cold blood will be necessary in this instance. There are other things we can do to him . . . in cold blood."

A look of eager expectancy flashed across James's face, and he said, "That sounds a bit bloody mysterious to me, Jack. What exactly are you getting at?" His eyes were riveted on Jack's face.

"From the things I told you about Ainsley last week, you know what makes him tick. I also gave you a list of his weaknesses. Basically he has three: his hatred of Paula and her daughters, his addiction to women who are beautiful and clever but genuine ball-breakers—those women whom he likes to break before they can cut off his cojones—and money. *Very big money.*"

Jack straightened up in the chair, and staring at James across his Georgian partners' desk, he added, "I'm going for the money."

"Thank God for that! I'd visions of having to get you out of some sweaty, flea-bitten jail in some moldering third-world country, but I should have known better. So, before we get to your real plan, why are you so anxious to pinpoint him on the map of the world?"

"Basically, just to know where he is, James, what's he doing, and get details of his daily activities, his modus operandi, his friends, colleagues, visitors. I want my operatives tailing him, but believe me I'm not going to take him out. I don't think it's necessary."

"Neither do I. However, if need be, I have a handful of skilled guys who'll do the job for you. They always deliver on a contract."

"Thanks, James. What we do need are some really brilliant hackers. We might have to hit his computers in the not too distant future, and we want the best chaps available. Maybe my Chinese friends have some contacts."

"No problem. Now, a bit of good news. I think I can pinpoint his whereabouts at this moment, at least within a few hundred miles."

As he spoke, James got up, crossed his private office overlooking Mount Street in London, and pressed a button at the end of the long wall. The mahogany panels slid back to settle at each end, and a battery of television screens were revealed. When he pressed a remote control, which he pointed at the TV screens, they instantly came alive. One showed CNN, the next BBC World News, yet another *Frost over the World* on the Al Jazeera English network, the fourth an illuminated map of the world, the fifth the world financial markets.

James brought up Russia on the map,

pinpointed the area of St. Petersburg, and turned to Jack. "Ainsley is currently in Russia. I'm not sure where *exactly,* but my Moscow operatives are certain he's in Peter the Great's impressive city of St. Petersburg, built on stilts by Peter as his new capital in 1703."

"That's *great!*" Jack said, playing on the repeated word, and beamed at James. "I knew I could count on you when we talked last week. You were one of the best damn agents MI6 ever had. Out of curiosity, how come they lost you?"

"Greed for one thing. I wanted to make some real money, then get married. And stay alive to do both." James shot back and grinned. "A bit of information from my agent in Zurich, by the way. Angharad Hughes, Ainsley's wife, owns a villa there, and has since the time of Ainsley's car crash in France. She obviously lived there then, when he was in the clinic, and still does. *Occasionally.* The other bit of information I got is that Ainsley has no particular interest in his only child."

"No, he wouldn't. She's a girl, and he hates girls in business. By that I mean *business* business, and not shady business, because he does apparently still have a predilection for whores. The pricey ones."

Jack rose and walked across the room, joined James in front of the screens. "This is fabulous. Good to see you have all the up-to-date mod cons."

James nodded and went on. "I got to thinking about my Hong Kong days over the weekend, Jack. I must admit I had a helluva time there, loved every moment of it. Well, almost. And I remember *our* nights in the Chinnery bar with Mallory Carpenter. We did have a ball, the best of times. Bachelor days. Well, a lot of water under the bridge since then. And listen, Jack, you're in good nick, I must say that."

"I'm getting old."

"No, not old. *Older.* And an older chap who's in good nick can still make it with the gels."

Jack began to laugh, shaking his head. "Not so much interested anymore. Now, back to business. I want to explain something. It's about Richie Zhèng, the grandson of Zhèng Wen Li, whom you said you did meet with Mallory."

"Yes, and what about him?" James probed, intrigued by these extraordinary machinations going on around M, her sister Linnet, and the Harte family in general.

"Let's go and sit on the sofa, and I'll tell you before M and Linnet get here. It's an odd story, and it goes like this . . ." Jack stopped, looked thoughtful and then continued. "Wen Li has had a vendetta against Jonathan Ainsley for years, and his grandson positively detests Ainsley. He can't wait to have his revenge on him because of what Ainsley did to his mother. So—"

"She was one of Ainsley's women, was she?" James interrupted.

"Sort of, but hold on, my lad, and listen carefully, because I'm also going to tell you my basic plan of action. But it must remain confidential, James. Geo cannot know—"

"Geo's in New York, working on additional paintings for her exhibition," James cut in swiftly, his eyes not leaving Jack's face. "And you must know I would never reveal anything."

"I do. But this has to be top secret, otherwise it won't work."

"I get it, Jack, but you're going to have trouble with M. She's very dogged, and she won't let go. She told me yesterday that she wants to look for Ainsley herself, have him arrested."

"I know, I know, she's very determined, and very clever, make no mistake about that. But I can't have her wandering the world with a Kalashnikov in her arms, dragging Linnet along for the ride and all set to have a shoot-out. *I* have to deal with the elimination of Ainsley, or to put it a better way, I have to render him harmless to them. I know we can do it. Now, I need your promise, James, before I can continue confiding in you."

"You have my promise as a former secret agent. I know the importance of keeping my mouth shut. What's that old saying from World War II—Loose talk costs lives."

"You're damn right there, and that's why you're still standing upright. So, here we go. . . . Many years ago there was a very beautiful woman who came to see Wen Li."

James leaned forward, listening attentively as Jack Figg told a strange tale, one of the strangest James Cardigan had ever heard, and it held him fascinated.

Linnet and Simon stood outside the building where James had his office in Mount

Street. They were waiting for M and Larry to arrive for the meeting M had insisted on.

"I'm still not quite understanding," Simon said, turning to Linnet, taking her arm, and walking her a few steps up the street. "Is M planning to invite the entire family on this yacht? Or just us?" He stopped walking and focused on Linnet.

"Not the entire family, no," Linnet responded. "Just us, if you'll agree to go. Oh, and Lorne. She *was* thinking of inviting Jack, and possibly James and Geo."

"Jack won't go!" Simon asserted, staring at her askance. "Can you see *him* cruising around the Mediterranean, taking it easy?" He shook his head. "Because I can't."

"Oh, darling, you're right about that," Linnet conceded. "But I wouldn't mind going. Still, I don't think I'd enjoy it much if you weren't along. Can't you go?"

"It depends on Jack, whether he needs me at the store."

"I understand, but if he were to say it's okay, would you like to go? Would you *enjoy* it?"

"I'd enjoy being anywhere with *you*," he murmured, his eyes twinkling, and kissed her on the cheek.

"No, be serious. Could you really and truly cope with being a week or two on a yacht?"

Simon thought about it objectively for a moment and then nodded. "I could manage a week; in fact, I think I'd like it. I'm not sure about *two weeks,* though. And look here, Linnet, I'm not sure Jack is going to agree with this at all. I don't think he could stomach M and you floating around the world on a boat. I think he wants you right under his nose so that he can personally protect you if that is required. He's very adamant about that . . . and I can't say I blame him."

"I know, I know, he worries and fusses, and he's always been like that. . . . There's just one thing, Simon. I am going to back M on this because she's really been longing to get away with Larry on a—"

*"Honeymoon!"* he cut in peremptorily and gave her a pointed look. "So why does she want company on their honeymoon?"

"I suppose because she's smart enough to know that Jack won't let them go off alone."

"Right on the nose, Lin, right on the nose."

A moment later a cab drew to a stop,

and M jumped out, followed by Larry. M looked smart in a navy trouser suit and a starched white shirt, with her hair in a ponytail and an old quilted Chanel bag thrown over her shoulder.

"Hey, didn't that Chanel used to be mine!" Linnet exclaimed in mock annoyance as she ran over to her younger sister and hugged her. "I shouldn't have given you *that,* it looks brand-new."

"You said you hated it, and hey, don't you look scrumptious! And so happy." M looked past her sister at Simon, saw the adoring look on his face, pulled Linnet closer to her, and said, "Oh, how delicious! Are you and Simon having—"

"Sssh. The answer is yes, and I don't want any cheeky comments from you. Because this is serious with a capital *S.*"

"Oh, Linny, darling! How fab. Are you, I mean have you . . . ?"

"I don't want to discuss this on the street with him standing only a few yards away. But yes, yes, yes," Linnet hissed in M's ear, then gave her a beatific smile.

Lorne Fairley was the last to arrive at the meeting in James Cardigan's office. Once they had all greeted Paula's elder son, Jack said, "James has made some progress. His Moscow operative has pinpointed Ainsley's whereabouts."

He looked across at James, who came to join him in the central seating area of the room. Turning on the television set which displayed a map of the world, James zeroed in on St. Petersburg. "We believe he's in a hundred-mile radius of the city, and I should have more information within twenty-four hours. But we know that Russia is his new base and that he probably has a Russian partner."

There was some discussion about Ainsley; M asked a number of pointed questions, as did Linnet. Jack and James answered in careful, precise language and promised to keep them all updated. Jack then focused on M. "I understand from Linnet that you plan to charter a yacht in Italy. When are you thinking of doing this?"

"In about ten days, Jack, for two weeks. I have found an appropriate ship. Lorne knows the Greek Islands and Istanbul very well, and I thought that would be a great area and we should be very safe there. I know that's what's worrying you . . . our safety. But Linnet thought that Simon could accompany us, and I would like to invite you too, Jack." She smiled at him.

"It's very kind of you, M, and perhaps I will pop down for a few days. Have you discussed this with your parents?"

"Yes, and they seem to think it'll be all right, but they informed me that you must have the last word."

"The last word is that I'll let you know tomorrow."

❁

Once he and Jack were alone again, James brought up the cruise M wanted to take. "I think it would be safe, Jack. You could provide plenty of security onboard, and Simon's presence would be reassuring, wouldn't it?"

"Yes, it would. Anyway, he wouldn't let Linnet go without him. They've become involved, romantically involved, I mean." He grinned. "I'm pleased to inform you."

James nodded and grinned back. "He seems like a nice bloke, aside from being a helluva great cop."

"He is. I spoke to M's mother about this cruise, and she made a very good point, which was that Ainsley wouldn't attempt to attack a moving target, especially one that docks in a foreign country every night. That would have to be a proviso, that the yacht was anchored in a harbor and not out at sea, where it might be vulnerable."

Jack now stood, paced for a few seconds, and then said, "Today's Monday the seventh of May. In a week's time Richie Zhèng should have some very important information for me. That brings us to the fourteenth. I don't think we can knock Ainsley out of the box by then, but I do want him neutralized before the end of the month. He's got to be gone and forgotten in short order."

"How in God's name are we going to do that?" James wondered aloud.

"I shall tell you how," Jack answered. "And by the way, I would just like to say I'm glad M suggested you and you agreed to work with us, James. It's great to have you onboard."

# Forty-three

M, Larry, and her brother Lorne cut quite a swath when they entered Harry's Bar on South Audley Street. As they were led to a table for three at the end of the room, their presence could hardly be ignored.

Larry and Lorne were both six-footers, and M, wearing high heels, was the same height. This aside, all three were wonderfully good-looking and extremely famous.

Once they were seated, Lorne said, "I don't know about you chaps, but I'm going to have one of their fantastic Bellinis." Glancing at his sister, he said, "I know you don't drink at lunch, but go on, have one, darling. I hate to drink alone."

"I'll certainly join you," Larry said. "But promise to stop me after I've had two. I'm afraid that once I start, I drink 'em like pop."

M began to laugh and nodded. She said to Lorne, "Count me in. Why not?" As Lorne motioned for a waiter to come over, M's eyes swept around the room, and she said to Larry, "Not a soul I know. How about you?"

"None of my friends here," he replied and half shrugged. "But it's Monday, sweetheart, and a lot of people are only just getting back from the country." He paused, then asked, "Do you think Jack's going to agree about the yacht?"

"I hope so," she said. "Linnet thinks he will, and I hope James and Geo will come, too. Jack's worried about our security, you know. He needs reassurance that we'll be safe."

Larry directed his attention to Lorne. "I wish we could think up a way to stop this bloody guy Ainsley. He's a menace, and he obviously has tons of money to finance his murderous schemes."

Lorne agreed. "He does, and he's as mad as a hatter . . . psychotic, in my opinion. Jack thinks the same thing. But look here, if Simon and James are along for the trip, then Jack should feel more at ease. As for you two, you're surrounded by security already." He chuckled, glancing from one to the other. "The two of you have become a couple of rock stars. And almost overnight. And why not? You're both gorgeous."

Larry and Lorne, stars in their own right, had been good friends for years and felt even closer now that they were brothers-in-law. And it was to Lorne that Larry turned when he needed to know anything about the family. Especially Jonathan Ainsley. This morning was no exception. "Why hasn't anybody been able to stop him before now?" Larry asked, staring at Lorne, a brow lifting.

"I guess Jack and his guys have tried for years. Then there was this horrendous car crash five years ago, and Ainsley was killed, and there was a funeral. But as you know, all that seems to have been a load of drivel, the funeral, not the crash, I mean.

I'm all for making the trip to Turkey, so you can count on me, M. If Jack remains difficult, tell him you'll cut out the Greek Islands; that should help to soothe his nerves."

"Why?" M asked her brother, frowning. "I don't understand."

Lorne held her steady gaze, explaining, "I believe Jack will go along with you providing you promise to remain docked in the harbor in Istanbul, and just go off on day trips around the Turkish coast. There's a lot of port security, and don't forget that ships are much more vulnerable floating around a group of islands. He'll be thinking about all that."

The drinks had arrived; Lorne picked up his glass and toasted them. "Here's to you two lovebirds, and your *honeymoon.*"

"And to you, Lorne," Larry murmured.

M said, "I found this great yacht, Lorne. It's called *Skylark,* and it has six cabins for twelve guests, twelve in crew; it's about one hundred and seventy-five feet, and was built in Bremerhaven. It's very luxurious and has everything we could possibly want to have a wonderful time. Linnet told me that Simon would enjoy it but that he would only want to stay a week. I hope you can be with us for two weeks, Lorne. And do you want to bring your current lady friend?"

He laughed hollowly. "I would if I could, but there is no current lady friend. I don't seem to be able to hang on to any of them these days."

He had tried to sound miserable, but M caught the laughter in his eyes, and she knew he was playacting, which he did for a living as well as for pleasure, or to throw his family off the scent.

Larry said, "How serious is the relationship between Simon and Linnet, M?"

"Yes, do tell us," Lorne interjected. "I'd love to know, and I hope you're going to say it's serious."

"I think it is, from what she said this morning. And I hope so, too, because it would be wonderful for her to have a companion. She's been so lonely since Julian died."

"Don't I know it." Lorne picked up the menu, looked at it, and then eyed his sister. "My Italian's lousy. What can you make out of this?" he asked, putting the menu down.

"Larry, you're the clever one with languages. Tell us what's for lunch," M exclaimed.

He perused it quickly and rattled off, "A wonderful fish cooked in a salt casing, veal scallopini, some kind of shrimp dish, another fish, and lots of different pastas. But let's ask the maître d' for recommendations, don't you think?"

After the headwaiter had told them about what was on the menu and they had ordered fish, and white asparagus to start, Lorne said, "I have a number of friends in Istanbul, as you know, M, since I've been going there for years, and I have one friend in particular who's going to be really helpful if you want to see a few of the special sights."

"Who is that?" M asked, sounding curious.

"Her name is Iffet, and she's actually a professor of archaeology, but she also owns a travel agency. Iffet has great expertise and knowledge. You'll like her, M, she's a lovely woman, very sweet. And a terrific guide. Or she can just hang with us if you want to stay put."

"She sounds great, and I like to have

contacts in foreign countries," Larry said, then went on, "Before I forget, my mother wants us to go to dinner, Lorne, and for you to come along with us."

"How nice of her, and I'd love to. Will Portia be there?"

Larry looked at Lorne alertly. "Odd you should ask that. My mother said I should tell you Portia is going to come. If you are."

"Ha! Ha!" M cried, staring hard at her brother. "Do I smell a romance blooming?"

"No, you don't," Lorne said in a firm voice. "But we've known each other for years and like each other a lot."

"I wasn't suggesting anything improper," M protested.

"Not 'alf," Lorne muttered.

Jack Figg was halfway up Mount Street when he felt the mobile phone in his breast pocket vibrating against his chest. He pulled it out and flipped it open. "Figg here."

"Hello, it's your Wharton friend."

"Hi!" Jack exclaimed. "Good to hear from you. *News?*"

"Affirmative. Riddles are the order of the day. Okay?"

"Mighty fine, Wharton."

672 BARBARA TAYLOR BRADFORD

"You know the company I am one day to inherit?"

"You mean the nature of it?"

"That's right."

"Then, yes, I do."

"That is what our friend has. His own private plaything. For himself. And for others, of course."

"Do you have its name?"

"Oh, yes, and it's all aboveboard. Nothing phony. And *everything* is stashed there."

"*Really.* That's very interesting."

"There's a partner. A new partner. Well, he's been around a couple of years."

"Who is he? Or she? And from whence does he or she hail?"

"I'll give you details later. A couple of days. Suffice it to say that caviar is a favorite."

"I got it."

"I'm making headway with the . . . keys. You know what I mean?"

"I do, yes."

"Okay."

"I'll be waiting." Jack closed his phone down.

✾

On a small side street in Hong Kong, Richie Zhèng did the same. Then he placed the cell phone on the ground and stamped on it, threw the debris in a garbage bin. New phone, now smashed. No trace.

Jack was sitting at his desk in the study of his flat in Kensington when the landline began to shrill. Picking it up, he said, "Hello? Jack Figg here."

"It's Simon. Do you have five minutes to spare, Jack?"

"Hello, Simon, and course I do. What's up?"

"Can I come around? I'm literally five seconds away. I need to talk to you."

Jack laughed. "Sure, come on up to the flat. We can have a drink together. I'm just messing around on my computer."

"That's great. Thanks. See you in a few seconds."

Jack glanced at his computer and was about to turn it off when a name suddenly appeared on the screen. It was grisha lebedev. It was a name he had never seen before, and he was momentarily baffled; then a smile spread across his face when he saw the word caviar come up next to it. He looked at the screen, seeking to identify the sender, and saw another name he'd never heard of. He chuckled quietly to himself. Richie Zhèng, the computer whiz, had obviously sent it through one of his compadres, as Richie called his computer buddies. Jack glanced at the date. It said the ninth of May, just two days since Richie's phone call. Richie had said he'd be back to him in a couple of days and he was.

Suddenly more words came streaming onto the screen. First Jack read BELVEDERE-MACAU PRIVATE BANK. And then there was a message. It said: "I'm twenty-one today. I've got the keys of *all* the doors. Except one. I'm twenty-one and rich."

Jack threw back his head and laughed. Richie was telling him that he had twenty-one codes or passwords or keys, which had to do with all of Ainsley's computers at Belvedere Holdings in Hong Kong, and that he was missing only one. And the word *rich* was a play on his own name.

Peering at the top of the document, he saw that there was a different name for this sender. Another one of Richie's compadres, he had no doubt. Despite the seriousness of it all, there was a twinkle in Jack's eyes as he continued to stare at the screen.

At the sound of the doorbell, Jack rose,

walked to the entrance hall, opened the front door, and welcomed his nephew. As he led Simon into the sitting room, he told him about the messages. "I'm glad to give you good news. We have the name of Ainsley's Russian partner. It's Grisha Lebedev, Grisha being the nickname or pet name, if you like, for Grigori, and we now have the name of the private bank Ainsley owns, although that would have been easy enough to get, I'm sure. He's not keeping the bank a secret. Richie's doing good for us."

"He certainly is," Simon murmured and sat down when Jack waved his hand at him, indicating he should take a chair. "What's the name of the bank, Jack?"

"Belvedere-Macau Private Bank," Jack told him and crossed to a trolley where there were bottles of liquor and an open bottle of white wine in a silver ice bucket. "Wine or a drop of the hard stuff?" Jack asked.

"I wouldn't mind a vodka on the rocks, please," Simon responded and leaned back in the armchair, crossed his legs, relaxing finally after a long day at Harte's.

Once Jack had made the drinks, he joined Simon, gave him his glass. "Down the hatch!" he said.

Simon repeated the toast. "I want to talk to you about Linnet, Jack. I know you might think it somewhat strange that we are very serious when we've only been seeing each other for about a week, but—"

"She told me a little bit, Simon," Jack cut in softly. "And I don't think there's anything strange about it at all. You've known her a very long time. Now, miraculously, you've discovered you're in love."

Simon nodded and gave Jack a quizzical look. "You sound approving."

"I am *very* approving. I love Linnet the most of all the Hartes. You're a lucky chap, I can tell you that. And I'm glad this has happened; she needs a man exactly like you."

"Do you think her parents will be all right about it? What I mean is, well, we do want to make this permanent, Jack."

"I'm sure Paula and Shane will welcome you into the family with huge smiles and loving hearts, Simon. After all, they've known you since you were a child, so that's not a problem. And in any case, Linnet is of age. She's going to do what she wants whatever they think or say."

Jack took a swallow of his gin and tonic,

and continued, "I've known her since she was a baby, and of all the Hartes she is the one most like her great-grandmother Emma Harte. Not only in her appearance but in character and personality. It's uncanny. Sometimes, when she's talking, I think it's Emma, the way she phrases things and in some of her gestures. And she can be tough like Emma. The odd thing is, she never knew her great-grandmother. She's just inherited everything. It's in the genes, I guess."

"I think you're right. M is so very different, wouldn't you say? Not only in her appearance but in her personality," Simon now ventured.

"Yes, she is, but you know, there are moments when M also reminds me of Emma. She's a true Harte woman, I think, with her business smarts, and she can be stubborn and bloody tough, I can assure you of that." Jack eyed Simon for a moment and then murmured, "You think she's more like an O'Neill than a Harte, don't you? But take a look at her mother sometime, Simon, and you'll see M in Paula . . . in the whole . . . cut of the jib."

Simon smiled. "Cut of the jib is not a nice way to describe a beautiful woman, is it?"

"No, it's not, but the words just came out of my mouth! So, you want to talk about M, don't you, old chap, and the yacht trip? That's one of the reasons for this visit, isn't it?"

"It is, yes, Jack."

Jack sighed and sat back in the chair, looked off into the distance. "I guess I'll agree to it. But only if James Cardigan is onboard, as well as the two security men he has looking after M and Larry. And *you.* I want *you* to be there."

"I will be, Jack. I've tried to analyze this whole thing, and I do believe we'll be safe if we stick to the harbors."

"You'd bloody well better stick to them! Or I'll have everybody's guts for garters!"

"Will you come, too?"

"It all depends on what's happening. I hate to be away from the store; on the other hand, Ainsley's not going to hit the store again. He's been there, done that. I believe that's the way he looks at things. But a yacht's an easy target, as you know,

Simon." Jack's voice trailed off; he cleared his throat, then said, "However, not even Ainsley would be dumb enough to try to blow up a yacht in a harbor as filled with police as they are these days. Not to mention the yachts of his friends and colleagues in the world of high finance."

Simon said, "M wants you to know she'll stick to the harbor in Istanbul and skip the Greek Islands, because she knows that the yacht could be vulnerable at sea. So, what's the verdict?"

"I'll give M a ring first thing tomorrow morning. I'll let them do their yacht trip . . . and, in fact, I'll join you for several days."

Simon gave him a big smile. "M will be ecstatic."

Jonathan Ainsley knew that the best thing he had ever done for himself was build this yacht. This beautiful and most elegant yacht: safe, secure, streamlined, swift, and a sailing palace to boot.

Now, standing on the upper deck, staring out at St. Petersburg from the vantage point of the Neva River, he thought about the big party he was going to give toward the end of May. He had been planning it for a long time, just as he had planned the design of his yacht for a long time, and he couldn't wait to welcome his friends on-board. It would be a party to show off his yacht to the world he inhabited these days . . . a world of high society, show business, politics, and billionaires. He himself was a billionaire, and he was at the pinnacle of his career. Of his life. He had become the man he had always wanted to be: successful, rich, and powerful. *Untouchable.*

He leaned against the rail of the yacht, continuing to stare at Hare Island, upon which St. Petersburg had been built by the will of Peter the Great, who founded it on May twenty-seventh in 1703. And what a city of beauty it was, filled with palaces and other buildings so magnificent they boggled the mind.

Now, as the sun set and the lights of the city came on, it looked like the most magical of places, and so it was for him. When he wasn't working at his desk, he enjoyed visiting those palaces, to admire the architecture and the unique art. Most especially he loved the European paintings bought, collected, and transported to Russia by

Catherine the Great, and housed in the Hermitage, that gallery of incomparable beauty, which she had had built for this purpose.

It was there that he would happily spend some of his leisure hours, staring at the paintings by some of the world's most talented painters, filled with admiration for their genius.

To Jonathan Ainsley, St. Petersburg was an extraordinary city, and it offered him many other pleasures, as well as its art and architecture. In particular, women of unusual beauty, who generously catered to his many whims. Just as important, it was the perfect place to meet with his Russian partner, Grisha Lebedev, who rarely traveled and who also enjoyed the luxury of this yacht.

So Jonathan frequently brought the yacht here to do his business with Lebedev, but he was anchored most of the year in Istanbul. That was his favorite city of the two, and even though his yacht was both a home and an office, the center of his working life, he had recently bought one of the loveliest yalis on the Bosporus. This had been expertly renovated and remodeled by the best artisans, under the direction of

Angharad, who had turned it into a unique and most luxurious villa.

*Angharad Hughes.* Although at times she could truly aggravate him, he was glad he had married her. After all, she had brought him back to life by taking him to the clinic in Zurich. And when the time came, she had made sure he had the very best of plastic surgeons. All of them had done a brilliant job in reconstructing his face. If he wasn't the old Jonathan Ainsley, he was still a very handsome man whom women found alluring. All the scars on his face and body had healed perfectly. She was to be commended for this.

Only one thing troubled him, and that was Angharad's inability to give him another child . . . the son and heir he longed for. He did not bother too much with his daughter, Elizabeth. The four-year-old was a poor substitute for the son he needed to inherit the empire he had built single-handedly. Besides, she had red hair and green eyes. His only child, Elizabeth Ainsley, was a daily reminder of Emma Harte, the grandmother he hated with virulence.

The Harte women would soon be destroyed. He would make sure of it. So far his people had managed to bungle things, but his next attack would be successful. Sam had assured him of that, and Sam would keep his promise. Otherwise he would be a goner just like Bart, another failure. Yes, Paula and her hateful brood would soon be dead.

Moving away from the rail, he turned and went down the stairs, holding on to the banister. Jonathan Ainsley was heading for the lounge and bar, admiring everything as he moved slowly through the rooms, pleased when he realized he was barely limping tonight. He had named the yacht the *Janus,* after the Roman god who, in mythology, was the god of portals and beginnings and endings. He had thought it appropriate since this three-hundred-and-eighty-foot yacht was a portal for him, a door to the world, and surely his reinvented life was a new beginning.

Jonathan took immense pride in this yacht, built to his own specifications by Blohm & Voss in Germany. He smiled to himself. The Russian oligarch and billionaire Roman Abramovich, owned the three-hundred-and-seventy-seven-foot yacht *Pelorus,* which had been known as one of the largest privately owned yachts in the world. But Jonathan's *Janus* was larger, and this pleased him.

Angharad looked around as Jonathan walked into the bar. She couldn't help thinking how fantastic he looked tonight. He was her own creation, in a sense, since she had put him back together. Or rather directed everyone to do that. She had given him back his health, his good looks, his very life. And she had presented him with a child. But a girl wasn't good enough for him. Especially a girl with red hair and green eyes, who looked like a miniature replica of Linnet O'Neill, and Emma Harte, and was therefore not very beguiling to him. Quite the opposite. Angharad knew she would give him a son eventually. She had to. There was no alternative.

Even though he messed around with other women the entire time, he still wanted *her* in his bed every night. And yet she did not get pregnant. She was forever disappointed. And so was he. But she managed to hold him captive sexually, and she made him happy in other ways.

Jonathan interrupted Angharad's thoughts when he came to a standstill and said, "You look ravishing, Mrs. Ainsley. Are you available tonight? Much later, of course, after our guests have left?"

She gave him the benefit of a seductive smile and said, "I am indeed. And I have a few new presents for you, my darling. They will amuse you, I have no doubt."

Sliding off the stool, Angharad walked around to the other side of the bar and swiftly mixed him a dry vodka martini, which only she could get *exactly* right. "Here you are, my sweet," she murmured as she slid it toward him across the black marble top.

He thanked her and took hold of her as she came back to the barstool, pulled her close, kissed her on the mouth, and held her away from him. "You look like a long strand of beautiful pure silver in this dress. Divine, Angharad. Is it new?"

"Yes. It's from Chanel. I'm happy you like it."

"I love it on you, it's extremely sexy. Better order another one. I'm literally going to rip it off you later." He brought his face to hers and whispered something in her ear, but so quietly she could hardly hear him. Knowing him as well as she did, she knew what he had said. It was vulgar, but it pleased her. He was obviously hot. There'd be a chance tonight to make a baby.

Lifting his martini glass, Jonathan now said, "Here's to you, my darling. And death to the Hartes."

Angharad burst into laughter. "Death to the Hartes! That's a new one, and a nasty one even for you. Toasting their deaths. Good God!"

"Please don't laugh, Angharad. It *will* happen. I promise you. But if it doesn't, and if I should die before them, you must promise to pick up my sword. You *must* destroy them."

She gaped at him, then smiled lovingly. "You know I'll do anything you want, Jonathan. *Anything.*"

"I do know. That's what I've always loved about you, your willingness to please me. That's why I married you. The reason I stay married to you. I know you'll even commit murder for me."

Angharad cringed inside at these words, knowing he was verging on the psychotic again. She forced a smile, picked up her glass of champagne, touched it to his. "Here's to our rendezvous later. And to the joy of making babies."

He laughed. Then he swiftly turned around at the sound of voices, recognizing the growl of Grisha Lebedev. And as he set eyes on one of the stewards bringing his partner and a woman across the lounge to him, he caught his breath.

Hanging on Grisha's arm was probably the most wondrous-looking woman he had ever seen. She appeared to be eighteen or nineteen, and she was a willowy, gorgeous blonde with an hourglass figure, voluptuous breasts, and endlessly long legs. He had to have her. No matter what the cost. He had to have this woman.

Grisha was kissing Angharad on her cheek, then giving him a bear hug, and all Jonathan could think of was this girl. All he wanted to do was feast his eyes on her.

Suddenly, he was holding her hand, leaning forward, inclining his head. And wanting her. Vaguely he heard her saying hello, heard Grisha exclaiming, "This is Galina. My fiancée."

Angharad, who rarely had her eyes off Jonathan and missed nothing, had witnessed his reaction to the Russian girl, and she was furious. Skillful, as always, she hid her feelings behind a smile and said, "Let's go to the bar, Galina, and you, too, Grisha. We must celebrate your engagement."

Since marrying Jonathan Ainsley, Angharad Hughes had become a clever and charming hostess, and she managed to make the evening work for everyone. Throughout dinner she kept Grisha engaged in conversation and left her husband to monopolize Galina. But she was concerned. Not about the girl and his obvious lust for her; after all, she herself would reap the benefit of that later, in their marital bed. Jonathan would fantasize that he was making love to the Russian beauty and be at his best sexually, and she prayed that she would conceive. What concerned her was his mood.

Angharad knew he was entering one of his psychotic phases, and this genuinely troubled her. Also, he was talking about a party he was giving in Istanbul next weekend, and she had never heard a word about it. What was going on in his head? she wondered. Surreptitiously, she watched him, distracted him constantly, and so prevented him from making a fool of himself in front of Grisha, a valuable business partner. One they could not afford to lose. And he was a proud man who could turn vindictive if aggravated enough; he could easily become a ruthless enemy.

# Forty-four

That was a splendid dinner, Tessa, everything I like," Lorne said, his voice full of affection, his eyes loving as he looked across
the table at his twin. "And I especially enjoyed the *fraises des bois,* which are so
difficult to find. *Anywhere.*"

Tessa looked back at him. Her expression was as warm as his when she said, "I
really had to hunt them down, those elusive little wood strawberries. God knows
why they've become so rare. And I'm glad
you enjoyed dinner."

"And being with you, my darling, and

talking to you. It's not often we get to be alone these days, is it?"

"No, we don't. And I'm so glad you decided to stay for a few days. I always seem to have so much to tell you. Or ask you. Which reminds me, I want to ask you about Simon Baron. How involved is he with Linny?"

"Very. And I for one am awfully happy about it, Tess. She's been so lonely, and you know how stubborn and independent she is. Whenever I've asked her out she's either been going away on business or going to Pennistone Royal, or working. Usually it's working."

Tessa began to laugh, and she shook her head wonderingly. "And just think, *I* used to be like that. The workaholic woman, always at the store, my head bent over a desk, or my feet running along corridors or running through the floors, checking different departments. I must have been quite . . . *awful.*"

"Not awful," Lorne said, "just frightfully ambitious and determined to be the Dauphine, the heir apparent. And you were bossy, stern at times, and very tough. Tough as a bloody old boot, actually."

"Was I that bad?" she asked, rolling her eyes at the ceiling.

"Yes. And thank God I introduced you to my dear friend Jean-Claude Deléon. He took you by surprise, didn't he?"

She smiled beatifically. "He did. He took my heart in one minute in front of the whole of Paris, at his book signing, and he still has it. He will always have it, Lorne. He's the love of my life."

"I'm so happy for you. You've got the best marriage in the world. I don't seem to have much luck these days, with women, I mean."

"You'd better hurry up, my lad, otherwise you might well turn into a crusty old bachelor."

*"Me?"* he exclaimed, giving her a look of mock horror, and then he chuckled. "I'm not yet forty, so I won't be crusty for a long time yet. I think *I've* got a bit of time left to find the right woman. Actually, do you have any girlfriends you could introduce me to?"

"I wish I did. But we digressed, Lorne. What *about* Linny and Simon?"

"They're good. As good as gold, and I think he's the best thing that's happened to her. She's mourned Julian for too long, and in Simon she's found a kindred spirit. I've always liked him myself, and he's a good guy. To borrow one of Linny's favorite phrases, he's true blue."

"And good-looking in a blond, Greek god sort of way. Quite a hunk, I'd say."

"That's true, but he's extremely intelligent, and tough as nails. I mean tough in the sense of strong and masculine, and I think he's tough mentally. If push came to shove, he'd be terrific. Our little sister is going to be in good hands. And let's not forget, *Jack* helped to raise him."

"How's everybody reacting?"

"I don't think they are, not really. It's almost like it's a given. Jack's taking it in his stride, full of geniality about them, and so are Mum and Dad. I might even detect a sense of relief floating around, especially at Pennistone Royal."

"That's marvelous. I'm happy for her, she deserves a life of her own away from the store. That all-demanding store."

"Spoken like a happy woman, a Dauphine no more." Lorne chortled and pushed back his chair, went over and kissed his sister. "Come on, let's have coffee in the library."

"You go ahead. I'll bring it to you," Tessa said, getting up. She waved him out of the dining room, adding, "I think I might have a cognac with my coffee, Lorne. Please do the honors, darling."

"I will," he answered, wandering through the circular entrance hall and into the library. He had always loved Clos-Fleuri, Jean-Claude's charming eighteenth-century house set in a little private park on the edge of the Forest of Fontainebleau. He had visited Jean-Claude here long before he had introduced his twin to the well-known writer, and it was here in the country that he and the Frenchman had developed an enduring friendship.

Walking across to the French doors, Lorne looked out at the gardens, thinking what a truly beautiful night it was: a black velvet sky, filled with sparkling stars and a brilliant full moon. A romantic night, if one had someone to be romantic with. Lorne Fairley had been feeling lonely lately, and he envied his sisters and their newfound beaus. Well, Larry Vaughan was no longer a beau; he was a husband, and he obviously adored M.

Portia Vaughan suddenly crept into his

mind. She was a beautiful woman, and she'd always knocked his socks off with her looks and talent, but she'd never shown any real interest in him. Until now. Was it really *interest*? All she had apparently said to her mother was that she would go to the dinner for M and Larry if he came, too. Well, perhaps it was a start. He did fancy her, always had.

Tessa glided in carrying a tray, and he went to take it from her, then set it down on the iron-and-wood coffee table near the fireplace.

Tessa said, "Do you want a fire? It just needs a match, you know. I think I ought to have started one earlier, the house gets so cold in the evenings, even in summer, and it's still only spring." She shivered. "Of course, who wears chiffony things like this dress on a cool night? Only me, naturally. Well, let's see if the coffee warms me up."

She poured, added cream and a sweetener, and took a cup to her brother. "How about that cognac, sweetie?" she asked, flashing a smile at him.

"Coming right up, Beautiful One. What time is Jean-Claude getting here?" Lorne asked as he went over to an old wooden garden cart used for drinks, picked up a bottle of Napoleon, and poured cognac into two balloons.

"It'll be about eleven-thirty or midnight, I think," Tessa replied. "There was a reception at the Élysées Palace and then a dinner, and it's hard to get away from those sorts of evenings. But Hakim will drive him, and he'll be able to relax on the way out here. Anyway, there's less traffic at this hour." She glanced at her watch. "Goodness, it's already eleven, Lorne. How time flies when you're with your one and only twin."

After drinking a cup of coffee and taking a few sips of cognac, Tessa was still shivering; she stood, went over to Jean-Claude's desk, and picked up a box of matches.

Lorne, who was standing near the fireplace, stepped to one side, and Tessa bent down, struck a match, put it to the paper and chips in the grate. The fire took hold immediately, started to crackle and burn, and flames flew up the chimney.

Then there was a huge explosion in the chimney, and the grate and logs were thrown out into the room. The inside of the chimney began to tumble down.

Tessa and Lorne didn't know what hit them. They were thrown backward by the blast. Lorne hit his head on the edge of the coffee table, and Tessa landed with a crash against the stout legs of a wooden table. They both passed out amidst the burning logs blown out of the exploding grate.

The fire on the carpet burned quickly. Flames instantly spread to the floor-length draperies at the windows, then to the chairs, with their summer fabric slipcovers. Within minutes the room was an inferno.

It was Lorne who came around first, and as he struggled to his feet, he realized his sports jacket was on fire. He wrestled himself out of it, threw it on the floor, ran over to Tessa, saw that the chiffon dress was aflame around her body. Without regard for his hands, he tore off as much of the dress as he could, then taking hold of her feet, he dragged her into the hall. He closed the library door to contain the fire.

Though loath to leave her, he ran down the short corridor to the kitchen. None of the help was in sight, but he shouted, "Fire! Fire!" as he filled a pan with water, ran back to his sister. Lorne threw the water over her face, hair, and shoulders, and ran back to the kitchen for another panful.

He was filling two pans when Gerard, the houseman, appeared, looking frightened as he pulled on a shirt. "Fire!" Lorne shouted at him and ran out of the kitchen. "Get everyone out of this house. And bring the pan of water first," Lorne thought to say as he headed back to Tessa.

He emptied the water on her, dousing the smoldering dress. Then he heard Adele screaming, "Mummy! Mummy! What's happened?" The nine-year-old clattered down the front stairs, followed by the younger children's nanny, Christabel.

"Uncle Lorne, what's happened to Mummy?" Adele cried, then screamed when she saw her mother's inert body and the burned chiffon dress.

"Stop it! Shut up, Adele!" Lorne shouted at her. "She'll be fine. Go back upstairs, get the little ones out of bed. Go on! Go! And you, too, Christabel, don't stand there gaping."

The two of them fled, and Gerard ran to him, shouting, "I've called the police. They come quickly. And ambulance. Here's the water."

"Thanks," Lorne said and poured the water on Tessa once again. And then, kneeling down, he looked at his sister and gulped. Her hair and one side of her face had been badly burned. He took hold of her hand, put his fingers on her wrist, and found a pulse. It was slow but steady. Tessa began to moan, and her eyes fluttered slightly. Then she lay very still. He stifled his fear.

Looking up at Gerard, Lorne said, "Go upstairs, please, make sure Adele is rounding up the twins, and François." Just as he finished his sentence, he saw them all trooping down the stairs, being led by Christabel; behind them came Adele, who was as white as a sheet.

Lorne stood up and shepherded them out through the front door, endeavoring to shield them. "Go and wait for Papa," he said to them, motioning to Christabel, not wishing them to see their mother's burnt clothing and hair, not to mention her face. He realized that her legs were also badly burned.

Adele hesitated, and he said to her in a kinder tone, "You've got to be brave, darling. For your mother's sake. You're the eldest, so please go and look after your little sisters, see to Chloé and Constance."

"Yes, Uncle Lorne, but—"

"No buts. Go on, do as I say, darling."

One of the three-year-old twins escaped from Christabel, came running to him. He saw that it was Chloé, although it was hard sometimes to distinguish between them. "Oh, Maman, poor Maman!" Chloé cried, and before he could stop her, she was kneeling next to Tessa, patting her hand gently. Lorne scooped her up, hugged her to him, and carried her outside. "Now we shall wait for Papa," he murmured, handed her over to Adele, and went back into the house.

In the meantime, Gerard's wife, Solange, had appeared, carrying two fire extinguishers. She and Gerard cautiously opened the door of the small library; together they sprayed foam into the room and did the best they could to blanket the burning carpet and curtains with it. Warning Solange to watch herself, and not to go inside the room, Gerard ran down to the kitchen.

He returned within seconds carrying two large buckets of water, which the two of them threw onto the fire. The couple hurried back to fill the buckets once more, and they made a good job of containing the fire. They had been determined to prevent it from spreading through the house.

When he saw their efforts, Lorne exclaimed, "You're doing great! Keep going. I have to attend to my sister."

Kneeling on the floor next to Tessa, he let his eyes sweep over her, endeavoring to ascertain how badly burned she was. He couldn't tell, although he believed her legs were the worst. The chiffon dress had been ankle length, and it had really been set aflame. He closed his eyes momentarily, then snapped them open as he heard her moan. Her eyes were still closed, and she was inert. There was nothing he could do but wait. He knew better than to move her. That would endanger her life.

Suddenly shivers were running through him and his hands were hurting. He looked down at them and realized for the first time how burned they were. But he had been lucky. . . .

A commotion was erupting outside, and Lorne struggled to his feet, feeling slightly nauseated and dizzy as he made his way to the front door. There were two ambulances coming to a standstill, two fire engines, and three police cars. Behind these vehicles he saw Jean-Claude's vintage Jaguar. The firemen and paramedics went into action immediately.

Taking a few deep breaths to steady himself, Lorne went down the steps to tell Jean-Claude what had happened. It was only at this moment that he realized why he had made everyone go outside the house. At the back of his mind had been the name *Jonathan Ainsley.* He had wanted Clos-Fleuri empty because he was worried there were additional explosives planted in other rooms. He must inform Jean-Claude immediately, explain why he suspected this.

Lorne began to sway just as he reached Jean-Claude, and before he could say a word he passed out. The ambulancemen ran forward with a stretcher.

It was Gerard who told his boss what had happened, but because he knew nothing about a man called Jonathan Ainsley, he did not mention his name. However, Jean-Claude thought of him immediately and experienced a sick feeling. That maniac could have been responsible for the explosion. It also occurred to him that he should have Clos-Fleuri searched at once by the police. But first he must get to his injured wife and his children.

As he ran toward the ancient house, his heart was pounding and fear was spreading through his limbs. He saw Adele, his two little girls, Chloé and Constance, and his four-year-old-son, François, and waved to them. And went on running. To get to his darling Tessa, the light of his life. He prayed to God she was alive.

Gerard, who had returned to the house, was waiting for him in the circular hall with Solange. The paramedics had just entered, but they stood to one side when they recognized him.

Jean-Claude knelt down next to Tessa, murmuring her name, holding her hand, and finally she opened her eyes. She tried to say his name, failed, and closed her eyes again.

Jean-Claude, stricken and shaking, looked up at one of the paramedics, his eyes pleading. His mouth was so dry he could hardly speak. "Is she—"

The paramedic cut him off. "She must go immediately to the burn unit at the American Hospital of Paris," the man said, nodded, and gave Jean-Claude a half-smile. It somehow told him that Tessa would make it.

❁

Jean-Claude insisted everyone, including Gerard and his wife, go back to Paris. He wanted Clos-Fleuri torn apart for bombs. Hakim drove the family; Gerard and Solange followed in his Renault. Jean-Claude knew he must telephone Tessa's parents, but he wanted to be sure his wife was properly installed in the hospital before he made the call. As he sat next to Tessa in the ambulance, he silently prayed with all his heart for his wife to live. And he prayed for her twin brother, Lorne.

❁

The Hartes flew to Paris the following day.

In the early hours of Saturday morning, Paula and Shane O'Neill; their youngest son, Desmond; M and Larry; Linnet and Simon; along with Jack Figg, boarded the private jet owned by O'Neill Hotels International which was waiting at Stansted Airport.

Once they were settled in their seats and the Falcon was airborne, Shane spoke. He said, for the second time, "Tessa is going to be all right. I just want you all to know that. I've had several calls from Jean-Claude, and the doctors in the burn unit are positive. Good news about Lorne. He's much better. He has concussion and his hands are burned, as are his ankles. But Tessa and Lorne are going to live, and they'll have the best care for their burns."

"But what about Tessa's face?" Desmond said, staring at his father. "I thought you said she was badly burned." The twenty-one-year-old, who had always been close to his half sister, stared at his father, obviously distressed.

"She will be as beautiful as ever, Des, honestly. I wouldn't lie to you. Jean-Claude told me they can perform miracles with plastic surgery these days."

M interjected quietly, "This is the work of that bastard Jonathan Ainsley." She glanced at her mother, who was white-faced and strained, and then at Jack. "Don't you both agree?"

Paula could only nod.

Jack said, "Certainly I do. It has his

signature all over it. We're going to take care of him, M. I promise you." He smiled reassuringly at Paula. She nodded, trusting him.

"I just want to get to the hospital," Linnet said, reaching forward and taking hold of Paula's hand. Seeing how worried and nervous her mother was, she added, "Dad's right, Mummy. Tessa will be fine, you'll see. She's a fighter."

"She's a Harte!" M exclaimed. "And we won't let anybody defeat us, least of all that, that—"

"Bastard," her mother interrupted, supplying the appropriate word.

Looking across at M, Shane now asked, "I do hope you canceled that yacht and the cruise, M. You did, didn't you?"

"I left a message on their answer machine, Dad, explaining I would have to reschedule for late September. Or perhaps even cancel. They weren't open when we left the flat this morning. I'll telephone the charter company again once we've seen Tessa at the hospital. Anyway, they've got my deposit, so I'm sure they're not worried."

"Good girl," Shane murmured and gave his youngest daughter an encouraging smile. "You can't expose yourself to any danger. I won't allow it."

Desmond looked at M. "Can I go in with you when they let us see Tessa?"

"Yes, of course, Des. Try not to worry, she *will* be all right."

"Her face," he said again, very softly. "Her very, very beautiful face."

"I know," M murmured and blinked back her tears.

Faraway in St. Petersburg, Jonathan Ainsley stood on the top deck of the *Janus,* looking out to sea, pressing a cell phone to his ear.

"Hello?" he said, knowing exactly who it was. This was the mobile he kept for his chief hatchet man. No one else had the number. This one was reserved for Sam Herbert Samson.

"Boss?" Sam said. "It's me. Calling from gay Paree."

"Do you have good news, Sam?"

"I certainly do. The party went off as planned. The one we had in the library."

"That's very good news. Well done."

Sam clutched the phone tighter, listening to that cultured, aristocratic voice. It had always intimidated him. He was now wondering how to explain the next bit of news. Taking deep breaths, Sam finally jumped in feetfirst. "I still have to check how many are left around, Boss. Unfortunately, I had to leave the party early. I'm going back now. I'll give you a jingle later today."

"Very well, Sam. Do what you have to do. I have the utmost faith in you. After all, I know you are thorough. I know you won't become another Bart and make yourself redundant. Are you staying at your usual place?"

"I sure am, Boss," Sam answered, his throat suddenly dry with nervousness.

"I'm glad to hear it. Call me as soon as you know the final results of the party."

"I will, Boss." Sam closed his phone. The Boss had already cut him off. But that was his way. As he pocketed his phone, he couldn't help worrying about that mention of Bart, long since dead. He hated it when the boss referred to him. Bart had died in mysterious circumstances.

❀

On Tuesday, May fifteenth, Richie Zhèng landed at Heathrow Airport. After he had cleared customs, he took his rolling carry-on bag and hurried outside. He saw the chauffeur at once. He was carrying a sign which had the name Croesus printed on it. He smiled. Jack was creative.

Once he was settled in the backseat, Richie told the driver, "The Grosvenor Hotel, please."

"Yes, sir," the driver responded, sounding as if he knew this already.

It took about an hour to reach the hotel, and Richie went immediately to the front desk, where he registered under the name on his birth certificate and on his legitimate Canadian passport: Richard Thomas Sutton. He used the Canadian passport.

Within seconds he was shown up to his suite, where he unpacked his bag and then freshened up in the bathroom. Returning to the bedroom, he took stock of the room in general, lifted his two laptops out of the carry-on, and slipped them into a double-sided canvas tote. After pocketing the key, he left the room, went down in the elevator. As he crossed the lobby, Richie glanced around, saw nobody he knew, and hurried out to the hotel's courtyard.

Walking at a steady pace, enjoying the fresh air on this sunny spring morning, he headed for Mount Street and Cardigan International.

Jack Figg was waiting for him there. He introduced Richie to James Cardigan, and the three of them sat down in James's private office.

"Did you get everything done in Switzerland?" Jack asked, knowing the answer before Richie spoke. He trusted this young man implicitly. He was brilliant, efficient, and dedicated. And as trustworthy as his grandfather Zhèng Wen Li.

"I did, Jack. It all went smoothly. I also have all the passwords, codes, and Jonathan Ainsley's personal identification number, the security code for his personal computer at the bank."

"So explain again what you're intending to do so that James can understand it as well, Richie."

"With all these codes now in my possession, plus my knowledge about filling out the online forms, I can transfer money anywhere in the world."

"In other words, you are now in control of Ainsley's money," James asserted.

"That's correct. I also control my grandfather's money, the hundred million he invested with Ainsley. Because he gave me all his codes. And I control Grisha Lebedev's investment with Ainsley in his Belvedere-Macau Private Bank."

It was James who, looking startled, asked, "How the hell did you manage to do that?"

"*I* didn't. But as Jack knows, I am currently employing six hackers, the most brilliant in the world, and they hacked Lebedev's computers and got everything we needed."

"Who are they?" James gave Richie a searching glance and went on to probe, "And where are they?"

"I can't tell you who they are, that's confidential, and anyway, you have no need to know. There's one here in England, another in Macau, one in Stockholm, two in Germany, and yet another in Iceland. They're scattered."

"So what's the final plan?" Jack asked and sat back.

"I can explain it, Jack, but I'm going to do it in broad strokes because it becomes very complicated. And you're not all that into computers, are you?"

Jack smiled ruefully. "No, I'm not."

"All right, here goes," Richie said. "At your meetings with my grandfather, you and he agreed that the best way to stop Ainsley was to go after the money. And it was Wen Li who dreamed up the idea of using me as an instrument, in a sense. This idea he put into motion by dangling the carrot in front of Ainsley: one hundred million U.S. dollars as an investment in Ainsley's bank, *providing* I was given a job at Belvedere to learn more about the business of banking before inheriting my own bank from Grandfather."

"I remember every detail," Jack murmured. Looking across at James, he added, "And Ainsley took the carrot. Also, he saw Richie as a future partner, in my opinion. He always grabs the main chance."

"Apparently he had no option. Over the last few years, as he's recovered from his many operations in the clinic, he has been playing silly games with the money, and he's rendered himself vulnerable," Richie confided.

"In what way?" James asked, focusing on Richie.

"He spent a lot of his own money on that ridiculous yacht; competing with Roman Abramovich by making it slightly larger than his was so foolish. He has not, as yet, dipped into my grandfather's money, but he has used some of Lebedev's investment with him. Now, and here's the whole point of the plan, Lebedev is highly suspicious, and he's going to start asking tough questions real soon. Also, he's pissed off at Ainsley, because Ainsley made a play for the new woman in Lebedev's life, a woman called Galina. I see a blowup imminently, and that's why I have to act in the next couple of days."

"I know you have incredible sources," Jack said, giving Richie a reassuring smile. "But would you mind explaining one thing? How do you know about Lebedev's attitude toward Ainsley?"

"I have someone inside Lebedev's trading company, an impeccable source. A man I went to school with."

"In America?" Jack asked.

"No, in Toronto. Trust me, Jack, he is dependable, trustworthy, and on our side."

"I do trust you, Richie. So just give me a brief outline of what's going to happen in the next few days, would you?"

"I am going to start moving money out

of Ainsley's personal account at Belvedere-Macau. *I* will not be doing this directly, one of my hackers will. The money will go into a dummy account in a legitimate bank. However, within forty-eight hours it will be sent to another dummy account, in another bank somewhere else in the world. Each dummy account will be closed after the transfers. When it has been moved three times by six different hackers working for me, the money will end up in one of three accounts in Switzerland."

Jack said, "*Numbered accounts,* I assume."

"That's correct," Richie responded.

"So in essence Ainsley's money will just disappear into thin air," James interjected. "Am I correct?"

"Yes, you are, James," Richie answered. Turning to Jack, he went on. "In Zurich yesterday I opened the three numbered accounts. I used fake Canadian passports, which were bought for me on the black market. Each passport obviously has my photograph in it, to prove my identity, but the names were totally fake. I can never be traced."

Reaching inside his jacket pocket, Richie took out an envelope. "Here are the names of the three banks and numbers of the accounts, Jack. As you agreed with my grandfather when you were in Hong Kong, Ainsley's personal money, which in effect we are moving out of his private bank, will be used for children's charities around the world, to be decided on by you and my grandfather. In other words, when the time is right, you and Wen Li will start to distribute the money to needy children in a discreet and orderly manner through the charities."

"That's right, Richie, and I couldn't have said it better."

"When I transfer Wen Li's original investment, his profit is going to him as well. And Grandfather said he would give me enough to pay the hackers." Richie grinned at Jack. "But mostly they do it because they have to do it. They're *hackers,* and they enjoy the thrill of it all."

James said, "There's one thing I'm curious about, Richie. How did you get a mole into the Lebedev company? And so quickly?"

"I didn't, James. It was a stroke of luck, one of those peculiar coincidences. I remembered, suddenly, when I was talking to one of the hackers, that my old school buddy was working for a Russian oligarch. When I looked him up on my computer, I discovered he was with the Lebedev Group. And what's more, he is leaving this week, because his contract is up. He's heading to Bali for a rest and some fun. So no suspicion can fall on him either."

James smiled, and so did Jack, who then said, "So I wish you luck with all this, Richie. You've done a magnificent job for us. And your grandfather will be very proud, I'm sure."

"I hope so. He loathes and detests Ainsley, blames him for my father's downfall and death. Well, there's nothing like revenge, Jack, nothing at all."

"That's true, and it's best eaten cold," Jack said drily.

"Oh, Jack, one other thing!" Richie exclaimed. "Only you and my grandfather will have the numbers of the numbered accounts. And while I don't want to teach you how to suck eggs, I have to say this: You only need the number of the account to withdraw the money. You don't have to show identification."

"I was vaguely aware of that," Jack replied. "But thanks for reminding me. Well, let's go and have lunch. And by the way, Richie, where are you going from here? Or are you going to start the operation from London?"

"No, I'm not, Jack. I'm going to Istanbul. I have a fantastic hacker there who plans to help me to get started. Also, Istanbul is very convenient for me. It's only four and a half hours by plane from there to Hong Kong, and to my grandfather. Wen Li misses me when I'm away, so I want to get back to him soon."

# Forty-five

Grisha Lebedev, one of the richest and most powerful oligarchs in Russia, stood on the balcony of his vast double suite in the Çirağan Palace Hotel Kempinski in Istanbul. His gaze was directed across the beautiful flower gardens and the beach to the Bosporus and Jonathan Ainsley's yacht, the *Janus,* anchored there.

For the last few hours, on this beautiful Saturday morning in May, he had been cursing the Englishman under his breath, calling him every name he could think of in every language he knew.

Lebedev, a tall, good-looking man in his

late forties, was smart enough to know that his investment with Ainsley, which had gone missing, could never be recouped. Trouble was brewing for the Belvedere-Macau Private Bank, and his gut instinct told him the bank was going down. The owner of that bank, with whom he had invested a great deal of his oil money, had been criminally negligent. Lebedev removed the word *negligent.* Ainsley was a criminal, a cheap crook, and he, Grigori Lebedev, was going to have his revenge.

He swung around at the sound of the door opening, and a faint smile crossed his face as Galina came into the room. "Did you find what you wanted?" he asked and knew that she had by the huge smile on her face and the shopping bags in her hand. Chanel, Louis Vuitton, Escada, and God knows what else she was carrying, but he didn't care. She could have anything she wanted.

"I did, Grisha, I did. I found a seductive dress."

"I want to see it on you," he murmured, walking across the room, taking hold of her, kissing her on the mouth, filling with desire for her. She dropped the bags and gave herself up to him, kissing him back, leading him to the bedroom, and pulling him in the direction of the bed.

Letting go of her for only a moment, to close the blinds, Grisha pulled down the bedcover and began to unbutton his shirt.

Galina, laughing delightedly, pulled off her tight-fitting Leonard dress, took off her bra and panties, and walked toward him in her perilously high heels. "How do I look, darling?"

He was already stretched out on the bed, and he began to laugh with her, his sky blue eyes sparkling. "Good enough to eat," he answered and waved her forward.

It took her a split second to join him on the bed, and as he rolled over and began to kiss her breasts, she murmured, "I never thought when I took this job that I'd have such a big bonus."

Lifting his head, staring into her incredibly beautiful face, he asked in a tight voice, "What bonus?"

"Oh, Grisha, don't play silly with me," she answered, her eyes full of happiness. "*You.* You're the big bonus. Being in bed with you all the time, making love, that's the bonus. And I thought I was just going to be one of your bodyguards."

"Yes, that's true, that's your job. So guard my body." As he spoke he pulled her on top of him and muttered, "Take it, do it, take my body, my little bodyguard."

Galina kissed him, wanting to stop the chatter, needing to get down to the business of conquering this powerful man through her beauty, her techniques, and her sexual expertise. And within minutes she had him moaning with pleasure under her. Suddenly, he turned them both over and began to seriously make love the way she liked, bringing them both to a climax swiftly.

As he fell against her, he said, "It's never been so fast with anyone. Jesus, Galina, what do you do to me? The way you make me feel has never happened to me before. You're such a sensual woman, and I can't get enough of you. You're *my* woman, aren't you?"

"That's right, I am. I will not let another woman have you. Ever. Say this is forever, Grisha. Say it, tell me you love me, tell me you're mine."

"I am," he said. "I'm yours and I love you. And this body is yours." As he was saying the words, merely wanting to please her, he realized he meant them. And what he was about to ask her to do was suddenly unpalatable to him. He lifted himself off her and sat up against the pillows, surprising her. After a moment he said slowly, "When you came to work for me, it was as one of my bodyguards, and you knew you might have to kill someone in order to save me, didn't you?"

Startled by the seriousness of his voice, she could only nod. Finally she said, "Yes, I did, Grisha, and I will protect you. With my gun, and with my body if I have to. I would stand in front of you and take the bullet."

"Good. Now listen carefully. Earlier I said I wanted you to go and see Ainsley and seduce him so that you could extract information from him. But all that's now changed."

"You don't want me to go to his yali?"

"Yes, I do want you to go to his villa. But I don't want you to look too enticing, Galina. And I certainly don't want you getting into his bed. You are mine, you belong to me, and I love you. And I am going to marry you. But you must do this one thing first."

"I will do anything, Grisha," she said, filled with ecstasy by his words, kneeling next to him. She touched his lean and handsome face, the face she had loved since she'd first seen him.

"He's stolen a lot of my money. *Our* money, Galina. I'll never get it back from him. He's a crook, and his bank is going down within days. I discovered that this morning. And so I must have satisfaction."

"What do you want me to do, my sweetheart?"

He stared into her honey-colored, almost golden eyes, reached out and touched the exquisite face, marveling at this nineteen-year-old girl, who was so bowled over by him it took his breath away. And then he said in a low voice, "I want you to set him up and take him out."

❖

Jonathan Ainsley could not believe his luck.

When Galina had telephoned him at noon, he had been taken completely by surprise. Though he had given her his mobile number the last time he saw her before leaving St. Petersburg, he had not really expected her to call him. She was with Lebedev all the time. Jonathan had also been taken aback when she said she was in Istanbul for the weekend with Grisha and wanted to see him. Alone.

The only thing that had troubled him was her insistence that they meet here at the villa. She had said it was better, because being on the yacht, where Angharad was ensconced, made her extremely nervous. She did not want to run into his wife, she had explained. He had eventually seen the sense of that and had agreed to the rendezvous here. But not in the villa itself. He had told her to come to the small side jetty, around the corner from the main house, and said that she should take the path to the summerhouse near the rose gardens. She had agreed to this and had whispered a few suggestive things before saying she would see him at six.

Having extracted himself from Angharad with some lies about meeting one of his partners from Hong Kong, Jonathan had come to the yali, where he had put on a casual shirt and cotton pants.

Now, as he stood in the living room of

the summerhouse, staring out the window which faced the sea, he saw Galina walking up through the garden. He smiled to himself. Finally he was going to take possession of this exquisite young woman. He wondered if she was thinking about him.

Galina was not. She was thinking about the man she loved with all her heart, the only man who had ever treated her with kindness, given her a sense of dignity. *Grisha Lebedev.* Physically abused at age eight, sexually molested at ten, raped consistently at twelve, thirteen, and fourteen, she had known only the brutality of men.

Because she was turning into the most beautiful woman and was therefore even more irresistible, her three elder sisters had found the money to have her trained in the arts of self-defense. She soon became a crack shot on the range, got a black belt in karate, was the best swordsman in the fencing class. She could run long distances with ease, leap in and out of moving vehicles, and she was so physically adept she had once toyed with the idea of being a stuntwoman in movies. But then she had seen Grigori Lebedev at a public function when she was seventeen and fallen in love. At eighteen she had managed to get a job as one of his body-guards. Being close to him had given her life a purpose.

He had treated her with respect and in a businesslike fashion. He had slept with her only because she seduced *him.* On a trip to London six months ago, Grisha had become morose and sad, had finally admitted to her that he was lonely, that he still mourned his fiancée, who had died in a car crash in Moscow three years ago. Galina had used her wiles to entice him into her bed, and he had never left it or her. He was her world.

The idea of fraternizing with Jonathan Ainsley after a morning in bed with the man she adored was enormously repulsive to her. But she must grit her teeth and flirt with him, then do what she had been trained to do.

Ainsley opened the door as Galina reached the top of the path, a smile on his face. He glanced at his watch. "Just six p.m., you're right on time, Galina."

"I'm always punctual," she responded, then said, "Good evening, Jonathan."

"Good evening, Galina," he responded

politely and opened the door wide, ushered her into the summerhouse.

She looked around the sitting room, decorated in white and cream, checking everything; she noted the silver bucket holding the bottle of champagne sitting on the coffee table, made a mental note of the landline, his cell on the coffee table. Nothing unusual here. Through an open door she could see the bedroom.

Turning to him, Galina asked, "Is there a bathroom I could use, Jonny? I can call you Jonny, can't I? It's much more *intimate.*"

He beamed at her. "I like the idea of being intimate with *you.* . . . We *are* going to be *intimate* tonight, aren't we?"

"Oh, yes," she breathed in her sexiest voice, then went on. "Do you have some music? I love music, it's so romantic. Why don't you put something on, and open the champagne? There *is* a bathroom, isn't there?"

"Yes, my dear, it's over there." He indicated a door on the left side of the living room.

"I'll only be a moment," she murmured and glided across the carpet. She turned, looked at the sofa, and mentally measured the distance between it and the coffee table. Once inside the bathroom, Galina took the revolver out of her trouser pocket, clicked off the safety catch, and put it back in the pocket. She was careful not to touch anything as she peered in the mirror, waiting until she heard the music. A moment after Celine Dion began to sing, Galina heard the clatter of the ice in the bucket.

Using a tissue, she opened the door carefully, wiped the knob on the outside, then stuffed the tissue in her other pocket and quietly left the bathroom. Creeping across the floor, she stationed herself near the white sofa, immediately behind Jonathan. He was fiddling with the metal top of the champagne bottle, and he had not heard her approach. Celine's voice filled the room.

Taking out the gun, Galina aimed it at the back of his head and fired. She hit her target with accuracy.

There was a strangled cry, and Jonathan Ainsley slumped forward onto the coffee table. Galina walked over, stared down at him, and knew he had died instantly. To be absolutely certain, she shot him again in the side of the head, pocketed the gun, and left the yali on silent feet. Following her training, she again used the tissue when she opened the door and then closed it from the outside.

Without glancing back, she walked calmly down the path through the garden, went along the jetty and into the arms of Lebedev, who was waiting for her. Without a word, he helped her into the speedboat. One of his other bodyguards took her hand as she stepped into the Chris-Craft.

Lebedev followed her and nodded to Boris, who went back to the wheel, turned on the ignition, and sped away down the Bosporus, heading for the Çirağan Palace Hotel Kempinski.

Lebedev had one arm around Galina, holding her close to him. Finally, he spoke. "You followed my instructions?"

"I did. He's dead. Two shots to the head."

"Where's the gun, Galina?"

She gave it to him.

"Do you have the tissues?"

"Yes. Here they are."

He wiped the gun clean of prints and then threw it overboard. Looking at her, realizing he hadn't needed to wipe the gun, he gave her a wry smile and shrugged. "Training," he muttered.

She nodded, reminding herself that, like Putin, he had been with the KGB for years before going into the oil business.

"Everything is packed," he now said. "After we pick up the luggage, we're heading to the airport. My plane is waiting . . . the G-IV. We're going back to Moscow tonight. I've arranged for us to be married tomorrow, and the next day, Monday, we leave for New York."

Startled but happy, she gazed at him adoringly. "New York? Why New York?" she asked.

"You told me you wanted to go there on your honeymoon, Galina. You aimed to kill. I aim to please." Lebedev took her in his arms and kissed her. Against her cheek, he whispered, "You're safe now. You'll always be safe, you're with me."

At the other side of Istanbul, in a comfortable flat not far from the Grand Bazaar, Patrick Dalton, one of Jack Figg's operatives, was fast asleep. It was his wife, Fatima, who answered the ringing phone.

"Hello," she whispered, not wanting to awaken Patrick.

"Ima, it's me, Ismet," her brother said. "Put Patrick on the phone. It's urgent."

She knew better than to argue with her brother and did as he said, shaking Patrick, then handing him the cell. "It's Ismet. He says it's urgent."

Patrick took the phone and mumbled hello, then asked, "What's up, Ismet?"

"There's been a murder. It's that Englishman. The one you spoke to me about yesterday."

Sitting bolt upright, Patrick exclaimed, "Jonathan Ainsley? He's dead?" His surprise echoed down the phone.

"He is. Shot in the head. You'd better come down to headquarters. Immediately. I'll give you the information. Foreign press are going to be on it before you can say . . ." Ismet, an inspector with the Istanbul police, paused, then went on. "What's that stupid English expression you're always using?"

"Before you can say Jack Robinson," Patrick answered with a dry laugh. "See you in half an hour." He clicked off the cell, and jumping out of bed, he said to Ima, "Go back to sleep, it's only four o'clock in the morning. I'm going to headquarters. The man Jack was interested in, the one with that humongous yacht anchored on the Bosporus, is dead. Apparently murdered."

Ima simply gaped at him in astonishment.

❖

Jack Figg always slept with half an ear listening, and when his phone began to ring on Sunday morning, he reached for it automatically, glancing at his electric clock. It was five in the morning. The time surprised him, and when he said, "Hello?" he sounded snappish.

"Jack, it's Pat Dalton. Sorry to call this early, but I've got some extraordinary news."

"It better be at this hour," Jack answered.

"Jonathan Ainsley's dead."

*"What?"* Jack was out of bed in an instant, moving across the room to the small desk, his mobile pressed to his ear. Sitting down at the desk, he said, "Are you absolutely sure about this, Pat? I was told *that* five years ago, only to discover it wasn't true. Much to my disappointment and aggravation of late."

"You can believe it this time. I've seen

the body. He was shot in the head twice. From behind and then from the side. His brains were blown out, not to mince words."

"And you have *seen* the body?" Jack pressed. He was taut inside, anxious and also wary.

"Yes. At the morgue in Istanbul. If you recall, my brother-in-law, Ismet, is an inspector with the Istanbul police. He phoned at four o'clock in the morning to tell me. Oddly enough, I'd had lunch with him yesterday, and I asked him to let me know if he ever heard anything peculiar about Ainsley. Whatever it was, I needed to know. As I told you, Ainsley's yacht suddenly showed up about a week ago, parked on the Bosporus. Ismet was still on duty last night when the body was discovered—"

"Where was that?" Jack interrupted.

"At his yali on the shores of the Bosporus. Ismet immediately went out there with some of his officers. Ainsley's body was slumped over the coffee table in the living room. Blood everywhere, apparently. The coroner said death was instant, and that it occurred around six-fifteen last night."

"Who found the body?"

"His wife, Angharad Ainsley. She became

alarmed when he hadn't returned for dinner by nine, so she went on one of the tenders over to the villa, taking the chief steward with her."

"I presume your brother-in-law interviewed her?"

"Extensively. Ismet said she's not a suspect, since she was on the yacht all day and all evening, and obviously she was seen by the various staff members that entire time."

"It sounds to me like a contract killing. An assassination."

"I tend to agree, Jack," Patrick said. "No evidence at all, and no fingerprints. It was a professional job."

"You're right. And he'll never be caught. What about staff at the villa? What did they know?"

"Just a housekeeper there, and a gardener. Neither saw anything; in fact, they didn't even know Ainsley was coming until the last minute. Apparently he went in to say hello to the housekeeper; he said he had a meeting in the summerhouse, that's a small house on the property. He made it clear he didn't want to be disturbed."

"Did the wife know *why* he had gone ashore?"

"Yes, she said he went to meet one of his partners from Hong Kong. That's all she knew. And that's all I know."

"I see. Stay in close touch with me, Pat. I'll be on my mobile all day. And thanks for calling me so promptly." There was a pause, then Jack finished. "He got what was coming to him."

# Forty-six

At eleven o'clock that morning, Jack Figg sat in the living room of Linnet's house with Larry Vaughan, Simon Baron, and James Cardigan. M and Linnet were in the kitchen making coffee.

Jack had called them all together to tell them what had happened the night before in Istanbul. Paula, Shane, and Desmond were still in Paris, needing and wanting to be there for Tessa and Lorne. And they were both doing well, much to everyone's relief. Jack had phoned Paula and Shane to give them the news, and the rest of the

family also now knew that Jonathan Ainsley was dead.

"By the way, James, I want to thank you
for your help, you've been invaluable,"
Jack said, genuinely meaning this. "I'd like
to add that I phoned Richie on his cell earlier, expecting to find him in Istanbul, but
he'd already gone back to Hong Kong. I
reached him there, and I also spoke to Wen
Li. They were both startled by the news of
Jonathan Ainsley's death. But there was
great relief all around, even though they
hadn't anticipated an assassination. Like
us, they just wanted to render him penniless."

James nodded, and looking across at
Simon, he said, "And *you* have had a load
lifted off your shoulders, haven't you?"

"And how! Watching somebody's back
is always bloody tough, but when it's somebody you love, it's even harder," Simon replied.

M and Linnet came in with the coffee.

Larry said, "M and I haven't really been
able to take it all in, Jack. It's quite a shock."

"I know. It came as a big surprise," Jack
replied.

After taking a sip of the coffee, Jack told them everything else he knew, in precise detail, knowing nothing less would do, stopping the flow of his story to answer questions. These were mostly posed by M, and occasionally by James.

Finally, Jack finished. "And so you can be damn sure that Ainsley is dead. Patrick saw the body in the morgue."

"I always told you we should get a hit man," M said, staring hard at Jack. "And I was right, wasn't I? Because obviously somebody else did."

"You *were* right," Jack conceded, giving her a little salute. "From the details, or should I say from the lack of evidence, it does sound like an assassination to me."

"And Angharad had nothing to do with it?" Linnet asked, her head to one side, giving Jack a curious look.

Before he could answer, M said, "She *might* have a hand in it! I mean, she's as bad as he was. Maybe she has a lover whom she persuaded to bump him off."

Linnet looked at Jack. "What do you think about *that* scenario?"

"It's clever, but it doesn't quite fly for me," he answered. "I believe that Ainsley was killed because of money, by someone in business with him."

M said, "I don't want to move away from Ainsley just yet, Jack, but there's something I don't quite understand. You told Linnet and me that your old friend Wen Li was helping you, and us, as was his grandson. *But why?* I mean, why would they do that?"

"Here's the story," Jack said. "And I'll try to give it to you in simple terms. Many years ago, Zhèng Wen Li acquired a mistress. He had a wife, but she had been left paralyzed when she fell down a flight of stairs, and he was still young, needed female companionship. Later, his mistress became pregnant, had the child, but sadly, she died just after the birth. Wen Li gave his son to his favorite cousin, another banker who was childless. His name was Chiu Wan Chin. He was wealthy, and brought up the child like his own son. Wen Li was happy because his child was within the family and he could see him all the time. He was the favorite uncle, in fact."

Linnet exclaimed, "Jack, I know that name, Chiu! But why?"

"You probably heard it from your mother,"

Jack answered. "Just listen for a few more minutes and you'll understand everything. Wen Li always took an interest in his son. But he became disenchanted with him just after his adopted father, Chiu Wan Chin, died. That was in the 1980s. By this time Wen Li's illegitimate son was a grown man. He had taken over his adopted father's bank, and he was a partner of Jonathan Ainsley."

"After Mummy threw Ainsley out of the family!" Linnet said, nodding, remembering everything now.

"That's correct. As it turned out, Tony Chiu, Wen Li's biological son, was crooked. He was a drug dealer, a money launderer in the Golden Triangle, and thanks to Paula he was sent to jail in Hong Kong. However, Jonathan Ainsley managed to evade conviction. And Tony Chiu took the fall." Settling himself more comfortably in the chair, Jack continued.

"Jonathan Ainsley was married to a beautiful Englishwoman whom he met in Hong Kong, Arabella Sutton. When she became pregnant, he was overjoyed. But the son and heir turned out to be a Chinese baby, or rather Eurasian. Tony Chiu was the biological father. And Richie Zhèng, as we know him, is the child of Tony Chiu and Arabella Sutton."

"What a story," Linnet exclaimed, staring at Jack. "Mummy never told me any of that."

"She didn't know, Linny. I only learned about it when I saw Wen Li in Hong Kong recently. When he found out Jonathan was still alive, his rage knew no bounds. You see, Wen Li blamed Jonathan for Tony's downfall. He believed Ainsley had corrupted his son. Also, he felt Tony had been made the fall guy, because Ainsley was never put in jail, and he considered Ainsley as guilty as Tony."

M said, "But why wasn't Ainsley punished, too, Jack? I mean, if he was in cahoots with Tony Chiu, he should have gone to jail as well."

"Yes, that's right, but he somehow managed to evade conviction. Tony contacted Zhèng Wen Li when he was in jail, informed him that he had known for some years that Zhèng was his biological father. Apparently Chiu Wan Chin had told Tony the truth on his deathbed."

"I bet Tony wanted Wen Li to know he

had a grandson floating around out there," M said in a knowing voice. "And most probably Wen Li was angry about Ainsley's treatment of Arabella and the baby."

"You're right," Jack said. "The problem was, Tony didn't know where Arabella Sutton was."

"So how did Richie Zhèng appear on the horizon?" M asked, her curiosity aroused.

"He didn't suddenly appear. Just before he died of cancer in jail, Tony unexpectedly received a letter from Arabella Sutton, telling him she had gone to Toronto with a man called Christopher Swanson and had subsequently married him. And that's how Wen Li found his grandson. They met several times, took a liking to each other. When Richie was ten, his mother died. Wen Li went to Toronto to get him because his stepfather was also dead by then. So Richard Thomas Sutton became Richie Zhèng when he was ten years old and went to live in Hong Kong with his biological grandfather."

"Voilà," M said, staring at Jack. "And why would Richie be on our side in our fight with Ainsley?"

"Because he still blames Ainsley for his

mother's ill health, their hard life during his early years. Thrown out by Ainsley, divorced by him, she had quite a struggle when Richie was a little boy. She might even have resorted to prostitution to help them survive. Richie has never forgotten any of that."

M nodded and asked Jack, "I understand why Richie would hate Ainsley, and I'm glad we've had his help."

"Yes. We needed to keep track of Ainsley, know what he was up to. We were hoping it was something illegal that we could report to the police: fraud, embezzlement, money laundering—"

"But Ainsley was killed last night," M cut in, eyeing Jack carefully. "And now we don't need to 'shop him,' do we, Jack? The drama is all over, isn't it?"

Looking across at her, Jack answered, "You're absolutely right, M. *Ainsley is dead.* He surely can't rise from his coffin a second time—"

"Or can he?" M interrupted, adopting a deep, overly melodramatic voice.

She sounded so comical everyone laughed, relieving the tension in the room. Jack exclaimed, "Well, to hell with this coffee! Why don't we crack open a bottle of champagne?"

"Make it pink," M said and jumped up, rushed over to her sister. Hugging her tightly, then sweeping her around the room in a jig, she paused dramatically. "Linnet, you and Simon should get engaged. Right now. Wouldn't that be wonderful?"

"I'm all for it," Simon said, looking across at Linnet, smiling hugely. "Come on, darling, say yes in front of all these witnesses."

"I think it would be perfectly wonderful to get engaged to you now, Simon. Absolutely, positively I say *yes.*"

The champagne was opened and served, everyone toasted the newly engaged couple, and M invited them all to Sunday lunch at the Dorchester Grill. They all accepted, and she went off to the den to make the reservation. The others moved around the sitting room, sipping their champagne and chatting. Their relief was enormous. Knowing they no longer had any need to look over their shoulders seemed to make them giddy.

At one moment, James drew Jack to one side and said, sotto voce, "Did Richie mention anything more about the plan?"

Jack looked James right in the eye, gave a slight nod. "Of course. He put it into action on Friday. The first thing he had the hackers do was transfer his grandfather's investment back to him. So the hundred million was moved to Hong Kong."

"Just one other question. When would someone have known peculiar things were happening?"

"Hard to tell. Richie purposely set everything into motion late on Friday and over the weekend. However, somebody constantly watching their computer very closely might have noticed oddities in the early hours of Saturday morning," Jack said.

"Somebody like a suspicious Russian?"

"Could be," Jack answered quietly. "And he might have sent an assassin on a mission."

Turning slightly, Jack focused his eyes on Linnet and M, the two of them in a huddle near the fireplace. They were laughing, and his heart lifted when he saw how relaxed and happy they were. For them it was over at last, and their fear had evaporated.

As if they realized his eyes were on them, they stared across at him and gave him huge, very loving smiles. He smiled back. These two young women were like the daughters he had never had, and he was so thankful he had kept them safe; that was all that mattered to him.

Giving his full attention to James, still standing by his side, Jack said, "We must never talk about this again. *Understood?*"

"Understood," James answered.

At this moment M walked over to join the two men, followed by Linnet. Jack noticed at once that M had that expression which signaled she had questions on her mind.

Before she even opened her mouth, Jack said, with a knowing look, "I'll answer them all, M, if I possibly can."

She grinned at him, nodded. "Just out of curiosity, now that Ainsley's dead, what happens to his private bank? Who takes over and runs it?"

When he didn't answer her, M shrugged and said, "Well, I guess you don't know. It struck us that Angharad might move in there. She's an ambitious woman and usually on the lookout for the main chance."

"I agree with your assessment of her character," Jack said finally. "But in this instance she won't be making any moves.

At least not in the direction of the Belvedere-Macau Private Bank."

"Why not?" Linnet asked, eyeing him carefully. She had noticed an odd look on Jack's face, was sure he knew more than he was saying.

After a split second, he replied, "There is no Belvedere-Macau Private Bank. Not anymore. It's defunct."

"How can that be?" M asked, her voice rising slightly. Staring at Jack, she went on. "He had other investors, didn't he, as well as Richie's grandfather? And also partners?"

"Yes, he did. They are all cursing Ainsley right now, I'm certain of that. And if he weren't already dead, they'd be out for his blood, I can assure you. The bank doesn't exist anymore because all the money has disappeared without a trace. There isn't one single penny left in it."

"But where has it gone?" Linnet asked incredulously. "How can so much money just disappear?"

"Hackers!" M exclaimed, sounding positive. "The money has been shifted electronically, hasn't it? And over the past few days. Of course that's it!"

Jack smiled slightly.

"It's Richie Zhèng and Wen Li. They've done it, haven't they? You just said they were all surprised Ainsley was found murdered, that all they'd wanted was to render him penniless. And they tried to do exactly that . . . they rendered him, and the bank, absolutely penniless by employing hackers." She couldn't keep the triumphant look off her face, and she gave Jack a wicked smile.

"Right again, M. It was a most beautiful plan hatched by Wen Li and Richie, with a few suggestions from me and also from James. As you are aware, Richie is a whiz at the computer, and he knows hackers all over the world. A system was set up and put in motion this past Friday. No one noticed the movement of huge amounts of money because it was the weekend, and the transfers moved very quickly through different companies in three legitimate banks, then each company's account was closed after the money had been moved on."

M's dark eyes locked on Jack's, and they exchanged pointed looks. Then she said, "Brilliant! Absolutely brilliant! But where *is* the money now? There were hundreds of millions of dollars in Belvedere-Macau, according to you."

"It all ended up in a Swiss bank," he told her, his voice low.

"In a numbered account?" Linnet queried, an auburn brow lifting eloquently.

"There was nowhere else to put it," Jack explained.

"Is the money going to be returned to the investors?" Linnet stared hard at Jack, her green eyes narrowing.

"No it's not. They're all crooks and criminals just like Ainsley . . . ill-gotten gains. They won't see a penny."

"So what will happen to the money?" M shook her head. "It can't just sit in a Swiss bank, can it?"

"It could. Nothing could possibly happen to it. But in a few days, part of it will go to a new charity called SAFE, founded by several anonymous donors who intend to use it to good purpose. They plan to support and nurture the underprivileged children who are at terrible risk . . . in every country. Within months large amounts of money will be sent to different legitimate charities which care for children. The charity SAFE will be monitored by Wen Li," Jack finished and then added, "with my help."

"Oh, how wonderful," Linnet interjected, a radiant smile crossing her face.

"Yes, it is," Jack agreed.

"All that 'bad' money being used to do good, what a wonderfully ironic twist," M said, looking at Jack, then James, before turning to her sister. She continued. "I can't think of anything more fitting than that . . . keeping children safe. And what a perfect name to choose. It's very meaningful, wouldn't you say?"

# Forty-seven

It was wonderful to be back here at Pennistone Royal, walking through the gardens she had always loved so much. Memories of her childhood came flooding back. They were centered on these gardens, the creation of her mother, for she had come with her own little trowel to help out, to dig a hole, plant a bulb, and be her mother's only assistant.

On certain days, in the very late summer and early fall, when the weather was suddenly stupendous, her mother would take hold of her hand and say, "Come on, little

Em, let's go and enjoy this Indian summer day." That's what they had done, and she had been so proud to be the one chosen.

Now on this sunny morning, as she strolled along the paths, M lifted her head and glanced up. She caught her breath. It was August, the month when the heather bloomed in full, and the moorland was like an undulating sea of intense purple against the far horizon, at the edge of the pale blue sky.

Moving on toward the famous Rhododendron Walk, designed, built, and planted by her mother for Emma Harte many years ago, M now thought about her husband; she was happy that he had fallen in love with this lovely old house and the grounds. It was a very special place to her, and it gave her pleasure that Larry also saw its intrinsic beauty inside and out here, and appreciated how unique it was. A moment later, she heard his voice. He was calling her name, and as she looked toward the house, she saw him hurrying down the path, waving to her.

She waved back, stood and waited, and when he finally came to a stop, she said, "Close your eyes and turn around."

"Why?" he asked, looking at her, smiling hugely.

"Just do it, please."

"Okay." He closed his eyes, turned around, and asked, "So when can I open them?"

"Now. Open your eyes *now* and you'll have a big surprise."

"I'll be looking at something special, is that it?"

"Yes. A spectacular sea."

"We're on a *beach*? Very well." Larry opened his eyes, and a little gasp escaped. "The moors! The heather! You're right, it *is* a spectacular sight. A purple sea. How extraordinary. But why didn't I notice yesterday when we came for a walk?" he asked, sounding astonished.

"Because we were on the other side of the house, and this view is partially blocked. I'd half forgotten about the August heather myself and was just as surprised as you when I looked up and saw the purple moors. Grandy's Moors, that's what we call them, because she loved them so much. She grew up on them, but not here at Pennistone Royal. Some distance away, in Fairley, a moorland village."

Larry nodded. "You've mentioned Fairley before. But one thing you've not told me is when your great-grandmother bought this magnificent house."

"It was in 1933, and it was apparently in quite a sorry state when she found it. But she fell in love with it, restored it, and furnished the house herself. And my mother never changes it, she just replaces fabrics and restores things when that's needed. She keeps it exactly the same. And most especially the upstairs parlor, where we had drinks last night."

"A beautiful room. And so is the house. What I like about it is that it's grand without being pretentious, and it's very comfortable."

"I'm glad you feel that way, because I love it here. It's my childhood home, and Mummy and Daddy want us to come whenever we can. You will, won't you? When we're in London and can spare the time?"

"Of course I will. Wherever thou goest, I go, my love. Anyway, try and keep me away. I love it here, and as you know, I've never been to Yorkshire before. I think it's perfectly suited to me, just as you are, my Yorkshire girl."

They began to walk toward the Rhododendron Walk, then all the way to the top
of the hill and down it again, and then they
headed toward Pennistone Royal village.
A wide path led to the village, and this was
flanked on both sides by woods filled with
filtered sunlight.

"Let's go through there!" Larry suddenly
exclaimed, taking hold of her hand and
leading her to the woods on the right side
of the path.

Instantly, M froze. Without realizing it,
she had taken them toward the spot where
she had been accosted by the two men in
the van in March of last year. All she wanted
to do was get away. She exclaimed in a
harsh tone, "Come on, Larry. I don't want
to go through there! In fact, I want to go
back to the house. Now!"

She pulled him away from the woods,
and he stared at her, somewhat startled.
"Whatever's the matter? You've gone very
white, M."

"Nothing's *wrong.* I'm just tired all of a
sudden, and I want to go back to the
house. It's getting late anyway. Mummy
hates us to be tardy for lunch, not to mention Margaret, who can throw a fit at the

drop of a hat. She worries about the food spoiling."

"But I did want to have a look at the village, M," Larry replied. "Be a sport. Let's go on through the woods. I can see a path and a clearing, and you did say the village was at the other side."

"I don't want to go in there!" M cried, and she stared at Larry, tried to tug him away. When he didn't budge, she let go of his hand and stood glaring at him. Everything came rushing back, and she clearly recalled that day when the man called Bart had raped her not a stone's throw from here. She burst into tears and stepped away.

Larry rushed over to her at once, put his arms around her, and held her close to him. "What is it, darling? Why are you so upset? Tell me, M, *please.* There's nothing you can't tell me, you know, after all you've been through with me. Does this place hold a bad memory for you? Why are you suddenly so afraid and upset?"

She looked up at him and saw the kindness reflected in his crystalline blue eyes; she clutched him, leaned against his body, and the tears flowed.

Larry held her tightly, said not one word, and endeavored to soothe her. And finally, after taking a few deep breaths, she began to speak. And she told him everything: how she had been stopped by two men in a van and raped by one of them in the clearing in the woods. And explained that she had managed to escape, had found Gypo nearby and galloped away, hell for leather, to Pennistone Royal and safety. All of the facts were laid bare for him, and after twenty minutes of nonstop talking, she stopped.

"And that's the way it was." Those were her last words before she took a tissue from her trouser pocket and wiped her streaming eyes.

Larry waited until she was more composed, and then he took her hand in his and together they walked slowly back to the house. He knew her well, understood her completely, and when he sensed she was calmer, he said quietly, in a low and loving voice, "You should have told me, darling. I think it would have helped you to unburden yourself, and I would have understood. I promise you I would."

"I realize that now, but last year, when

we met in New York, it was all too fresh. And there's something else. I had buried it deep inside. I called it the Bad Thing, and I wouldn't let it come out. And I coped. Somehow you helped me, Larry, your love and kindness were healing for me."

"I'm glad of that . . ." He hesitated for a moment before asking, "Is that why you were so apprehensive the first night we met, when I took you to Le Refuge? Outside, when I kissed you, and you pulled away?"

M nodded. "It was, yes, and then the next day I realized I might frighten you off, so I invented the story about the rough boyfriend. Because I didn't want you to know about . . . the rape."

"I understand. But I'm here now, and I always will be. You're safe with me, M. And when you feel up to it, maybe you should go and speak to a professional. . . . It might be helpful."

"Yes, it might. I'll think about it." She turned to look at him, held his attention. "Listen, Larry, only Linnet knows, and Jack. Please don't speak of it to them, will you, though? And no one else either. This is our secret."

"Don't worry," he said, putting one arm around her and drawing her closer to his side. "All I want to do is look after you, and love you, my darling wife."

Paula stood at a window in the upstairs parlor, Pennistone Royal, staring out across the Moors, Grandy's Moors, which she had loved in all the seasons of the year. She herself had inherited that love of this implacable northern landscape and had frequently wandered across those undulating hills, as Emma had done throughout her long life.

They tempted her this afternoon. But she did not have time to go today. The purple heather gave them new summer life under a pale blue sky. Not a single cloud marked that cerulean arc, and it was beautiful.

She looked at her watch. It was almost four, and in a short while everyone would join her for afternoon tea. It was a family tradition started almost seventy-four years ago, when Emma had bought Pennistone Royal and made it her family home.

Paula smiled to herself. There had been so many changes in her life over the years. But this had never changed, tea at four in the upstairs parlor. It was one thing in her life which had remained a constant. And this pleased her.

Lingering for a moment longer at the window, Paula thought of Jack. He had done so much for them over these many years. And it was Jack who had finally freed them of her evil cousin, if somewhat indirectly. Always her enemy. He was dead at last and could no longer harm them, and for that she was glad. They were lucky that he had been the only bad apple in the entire family.

Walking toward the fireplace, Paula stood and looked up at the painting of Emma Harte, which she had recently brought here from the Stone Hall. It had been executed when Emma was in her forties, looking beautiful in a white gown and Paul McGill's famous emeralds. You knew, Grandy, she thought. You knew what Jonathan was. And Paula recalled with clarity the day the twins had been christened at Fairley church. And on that day her grandmother had warned her not to trust her cousin Jonathan. How right she had been. But all that was over. Her daughters were safe.

A small sigh escaped her. . . . Life was

such a fragile possession, one that could be so easily broken. But they were all whole. Even Tessa was recovering well from the burns on her face and legs, becoming slowly beautiful again after skin grafts, plastic surgery, and the best care available.

Lorne was as handsome as he had always been. The burns on his hands had quickly healed, and he had thrown off the damages of the fire and was full of laughter, jokes, and quips, enjoying life to the fullest. She was relieved the twins were doing so well, and particularly happy that Tessa's face would one day be perfect again.

Paula's eyes swept around the room. The upstairs parlor had looked the same since Emma first decorated it with mellow antiques and floral fabrics, so colorful against the pale yellow walls. Paula had found the Savonnerie carpet, which Emma had originally used on the dark polished wood floor, and brought it up from the storage room. Its pastel tones highlighted the dark wood, and the bleached-oak fireplace drew everyone because of Emma's portrait hanging above it. Across the room, the famous Turner landscape Emma had cherished took pride of place, and it was Paula's favorite. On the end wall Paula had hung the portrait of her grandfather, Paul McGill.

Paula had kept the room exactly the same because she knew it *was* perfect. As she moved toward the fireplace, she nodded, pleased with the flowers Linnet had arranged in several vases and placed around the room, echoing the summer gardens.

*Linnet.* It filled Paula with great joy to know that her middle daughter was happy again, that she and Simon had so fortunately discovered their love for each other. They were engaged and were going to be married quietly in a small ceremony at Pennistone Royal church this coming Christmas.

"We've made it safely, Grandy darling. Our Harte luck has held," Paula said, as she stared at the portrait.

At this moment the door flew open, and M came in first, said, "That's a sign of old age, Mummy! Talking to yourself."

"I'm not talking to myself," Paula answered. "I'm talking to your great-grandmother."

"I often do that," Linnet interjected, sounding quite serious. "Especially at the store when I can't make things work out the way I want. I keep asking her how she ever did it."

Tessa, still limping slightly, joined in the laughter as she came in after Linnet. Watching her carefully, Paula realized that the limp was another reminder of the ordeal she had been through. Her face was still tight in places, but it was healing, and her wonderful silver-gilt hair had grown back in three months, framed her face in a halo of light and hid the scars on one side. Thank God her looks hadn't been ruined, Paula thought, knowing Tessa would have been devastated if she had been disfigured.

A minute later Margaret, their bossy but beloved housekeeper, came rushing in pushing a large tea trolley, exclaiming, "I don't know, Paula, there's so many here for tea we should have had it in the dining room."

"No, we shouldn't!" Paula shot back swiftly and a little sharply but giving her a warm smile. "Tea at four in the upstairs parlor is a Harte tradition."

"And one that must never be broken," M announced with firmness and went and sat next to her mother. She took hold of Paula's hand and squeezed it. "It's lovely to be home," she said, looking into her mother's extraordinary violet eyes. "I've missed you and Daddy and Pennistone Royal. And my lovely Gypo."

"I'm overjoyed you're home at last, Emsie. And I want you to know yet again how proud I am of you, the way you went off and did your own thing and made a success all by yourself. It's the fulfillment of your dream."

Tessa sat next to M and said warmly, "I'm proud of you, too. And of you, Linnet, darling. You've both outdone yourselves in every way. And I thank you for the love you've given me, and for coming to see me in Paris so often. You're the best sisters in the world."

Linnet's green eyes swept over M and Tessa and her mother as well. Then she looked up at the portrait of Emma Harte, the woman she so resembled in every way, and she addressed the painting. "What do you think of us, Grandy? Aren't you happy we're all just like you, albeit in different ways?"

It was Paula who answered. "She couldn't have done it better, that I know. Grandy used to tell me that the secret of life was to endure. And this you all have surely done. . . . You have endured and triumphed like the true Harte women you are."

# Epilogue

September
2007

M sat at the small dressing table in their bedroom at the Beekman Place apartment, putting the finishing touches to her makeup. There, that's it, she thought, staring at her face. Half an Audrey, that was her look for tonight.

She smiled to herself, sat back in the chair, her gaze shifting to the view from the window . . . the East River and Long Island City beyond. It was a lovely September evening; she was happy to be back here for a few months with Larry before returning to Paris in December to prepare for the new spring collections, to be shown next January.

Her thoughts suddenly shifted to the meeting she'd had yesterday with Dr. Melissa Glendenning, a psychiatrist who specialized in treating rape victims. M had liked her immediately and made an appointment for another session next week. She had promised Larry to seek counseling once they were in New York, and she was glad she had finally taken that step. So was he.

"Are you ready, darling?" he asked from the doorway, startling her, and she swung her head to look up at him. "Yes, give me five minutes." As she spoke she went to the clothes closet, took out her favorite black dress. Showing it to him, she said with a smile, "I thought I'd wear this, Larry. I was wearing it the night I met you and Geo ran into James again. A lucky dress, wouldn't you say?"

"It is. But come on, love, hurry up, we're running late."

"Zip me, please," she murmured, swiftly took off her cotton robe, stepped into the dress, and turned her back to him. Once he had zipped it, she put on large pearl earrings, picked up a small black purse and a cashmere stole, and ran out of the bedroom after him.

He was waiting in the front hall, looking more handsome than ever, she decided, the blue shirt he was wearing emphasizing the blueness of his eyes. Smiling at her, he nodded his approval.

Outside on Beekman Place, the car and bodyguards were waiting. Larry bundled her in and told Craig the address of the art gallery in Chelsea, then exclaimed, "We are going to be late. What a nuisance, and we've been waiting for this event for many months."

M moved closer to him on the seat and slipped her arm through his. "Don't worry so much, it's all right. It *is* an art show, after all, so we don't have to be there on the dot."

Turning to her, he gave her a small smile. "Why is it you always manage to make me feel better?"

"I don't know, actually, but I'm glad I do." She drew even closer to him and said quietly, "Are you sure you're not upset we finally had to cancel the yacht and our cruise on the Bosporous?"

"Not at all."

"But we haven't had our honeymoon," M protested.

"Being married to you is a permanent honeymoon, M, my darling girl," Larry answered, grinning at her. "And we can always take a cruise next year, you know."

She smiled at him and squeezed his hand, leaned back against the seat. They didn't speak much after that, lost as they were in their own thoughts.

The moment they arrived at the Gresham Art Gallery in Chelsea the flashbulbs began to pop; the photographers swarmed around them when they stepped out of the car. Stuart escorted them into the gallery and stayed with them as he always did. They were the "in" couple, adored by the world and the press, and there was always a potential risk to their safety. Larry called it the price of extreme fame.

The minute they entered the gallery the noise stopped, and everyone stared at them. Suddenly there was Geo, smiling and waving, hurrying forward to greet them, followed by James, with Dax in tow. They all hugged one another, and M took hold of

Geo's arm and said, "Sorry we're late. So much traffic. And I hope my favorite painting hasn't been sold."

"No, it hasn't," Geo replied. "Come and see it. It looks much better now that it's framed."

"It was fantastic without a frame," M shot back, happy for Geo, whom she knew was about to become very famous.

They trooped to where M's favorite painting was hanging, followed by some of the other guests. Larry stopped a waiter, and they all took glasses of champagne. After they had clinked their glasses, Larry said, "Congratulations, Geo. The show's going to be a huge success!"

Geo simply smiled, linked her arm through M's, and murmured, "I hope Larry's right."

"Of course he is," M reassured her. She turned to Dax and continued, "You've got one movie under your belt, so what's next for you, Dax?"

"Another movie." He grinned at the two women he cared so much about and exclaimed, "We made it, M, didn't we? And now it's Geo's turn. She's about to become the new star in the art world."

"She certainly is," M answered, then shifted the direction of her gaze.

Larry was staring at her. Their eyes met and held, and they began to walk toward each other. And suddenly, M knew that *he* was all she wanted. Nothing else mattered. Not really. He was her life, just as she was his, and they would always be together. *Forever.*